PRAISE FOR CH

"*Chick Magnet* has one of the best epilogues I've ever read, and it's a perfect demonstration of why writers keep going back to small-town settings. Because underneath all the cupcakes and cruel memories, there is one great promise at the heart of a small-town romance: there's always a first time for second chances."

—*New York Times*

"Barry is insightful when she hints at the painful social shifts initiated by the pandemic, infectiously cheerful while describing Nic's interactions with her clucking comrades, and especially evocative when she tackles Will's internal struggles . . . A comforting small-town romance, with chickens."

—*Kirkus Reviews*

"Barry handles both characters with care and delivers a powerful message about seeking help for mental illness even as she infuses the story with ample comic relief. Pet-loving romance fans should flock to this one."

—*Publishers Weekly*

"One of the chief pleasures of being a romance reader is getting to watch Emma Barry's complex, honorable characters forging themselves into stronger, happier versions of themselves. *Chick Magnet* is Emma Barry at the peak of her powers: hilarious and humane, it will restore your faith in the power of love."

—Jenny Holiday, *USA Today* bestselling author

"Intoxicating and deeply romantic, *Chick Magnet* delivers a riveting opposites-attract, slow-burn-with-the-hot-guy-next-door small-town romance. I fell in love with Will Lund from the first grumpy meeting."

—Zoe York, *USA Today* and *New York Times* bestselling author

PRAISE FOR *FUNNY GUY*

"This ingenious friends-to-lovers romance . . . [is] a fresh take on a favorite trope that perfectly marries humor and heartache."

—*Publishers Weekly* (starred review)

"It's a tug-of-war that would be hard for a less adept writer to pull off, but Barry's work has always thrived on this kind of interplay. She seems to be feeling her way to a new kind of structure here, one that's organic and messy but still generates a vital catharsis."

—*New York Times*

"With *Funny Guy*, Barry achieves that rare specialness found in the best romances: writing main characters who you come to love like they are people you know, for all their frustrating flaws and foibles. Sam and Bree have crackling chemistry together and a deep, abiding love for each other (another tough balance to strike, and Barry manages it beautifully), and I rooted for them to find themselves and to find their way together. A layered, lovely love story infused with sharp wit and soft humanity."

—Kate Clayborn, author of *Love Lettering*

"Sharply drawn characters and moments of sweet, aching vulnerability. *Funny Guy* is the friends-to-lovers romance of my dreams."

—Mia Hopkins, author of the Eastside Brewery series

PRAISE FOR *BAD REPUTATION*

"Barry has continued to get better and better with every romance she writes, which makes us all the more excited for her latest."

—*Paste*

"*Bad Reputation* by Emma Barry is for every reader who begs for a worthy, deliciously enamoring slow burn . . . There's much to appreciate here, from the lush prose to the impeccable characterization and the delightful romance. Readers are in for an unmistakable treat."

—Marvelous Geeks Media

"Original, brilliant, impressively memorable, and a fun read from start to finish, *Bad Reputation* . . . [is] the stuff of which Hallmark Channel movies are made."

—Midwest Book Review

"With *Bad Reputation*, Emma Barry has woven a delicate treasure of intimacy and sweetness, all wrapped up with the sexiest (him)bo. Stories about growing from past mistakes don't always give characters so much grace, but Barry's tender handling of this Hollywood tale makes it impossible not to root for Maggie and Cole completely."

—Ali Rosen, author of *Alternate Endings*

"Barry always manages to perfectly capture such tenderness between characters, in a way that hits you right in the feels. Immersive in both the contemporary worlds she creates and the exquisite depth of her characters . . . *Bad Reputation* is a deep and delicious treat."

—Charlotte Stein, author of *When Grumpy Met Sunshine*

BOLD MOVES

OTHER BOOKS BY EMMA BARRY

Stand-Alone Novels

Bad Reputation

Funny Guy

Chick Magnet

Political Persuasions Series

The One You Want

The One You Need

The One You Hate

The One You Crave

BOLD MOVES

A novel

Emma Barry

This is a work of fiction. Names, characters, organizations, places, events, and incidents are either products of the author's imagination or are used fictitiously. Otherwise, any resemblance to actual persons, living or dead, is purely coincidental.

Published by Montlake, Seattle

www.apub.com

ISBN-13: 9781662520853 (paperback)
ISBN-13: 9781662520860 (digital)

Cover design by Caroline Teagle Johnson
Cover image: © RobinOlimb, © sanchesnet1 / Getty;
© Chipmunk131 / Shutterstock

Printed in the United States of America

For H, who taught me how to play chess and of whom I am so proud, and for Jane Austen, from whom all second-chance romances flow

PART I

OPENING MOVES

Chapter 1

The doorman wasn't impressed. "You gotta understand, lots of guys show up here looking for Scarlett. She's one of those femmes fatales."

Jaime Croft was familiar with Scarlett Arbuthnot's power. Seventeen years ago, back in their hometown of Musgrove, Virginia, she'd felled Jaime with a look. It had been like something out of a rom-com she would've mocked. But unlike in the movies, when she'd had him in her thrall, she'd ground his heart to bits.

Look, heartbreak was bad enough, but most of the time, you could lick your wounds and forget. Forgetting hadn't been an option here.

Scarlett was a grand master, and while they didn't exactly cover chess on ESPN, she played the game the way other people fought for heavyweight titles or chased Oscars. She walked red carpets; she gave blockbuster interviews; she even posed for tasteful nudes in *Vogue*. That last one . . . it had been plain old *cruel* to remind Jaime of the glorious curves he wasn't allowed to touch anymore.

The doorman's smirk suggested he'd seen those pictures too.

"I realize this looks sketchy," Jaime said, voicing the obvious. "But I promise I'm an old friend of Scarlett's." Friends revealed all their deepest secrets to each other, discovered how to give someone else an orgasm, and broke each other's hearts, right?

They'd wrecked each other in the *friendliest* way.

"Could you call up and tell her James Croft is here? We can let her decide if she wants to see me."

"Nope."

Jaime had . . . absolutely no comeback. An Upper East Side doorman had upended his brilliant plan.

Granted, the odds had been long here, but it wasn't every day Videon told a showrunner that thanks to the surprising success of his supposed-to-be-obscure limited series, he could make whatever project he wanted next.

And what Jaime wanted was to adapt *Queen's Kiss*, Scarlett's memoir.

Not simply because she'd written it. No, he wanted to prove he had range. This wouldn't be another gritty docudrama about drugs and lies in a small town. It would let Jaime show folks he could handle a big budget and classy drama too.

Besides, he could envision exactly how good her book would be on screen. The fearless working-class protagonist taking on the snobs of the chess world, making a fuss about sexism in the game and popularizing it in the process, and doing it all on her own terms. With the right writers, producers, and director, *Queen's Kiss* was going to be amazing, and his was exactly the team for the gig.

"You tried her agent?" In New York, doormen probably knew all the ins and outs of the entertainment industry.

"Yeah."

Her agent had been clear: Scarlett wasn't interested in selling the rights. Not now and not ever. Undeterred, Jaime had gotten on a plane . . . only to run into the force field that was her doorman.

"It sounds like you have your answer then, pal."

Jaime's career would've gone nowhere if he'd settled for the first answer—or even the tenth. When Dad had been arrested, it would've been easy to give up. To stop writing, to stop messing around with cameras. It would've been easy to sink into the pain of what his father had done and the loss when Scarlett had decided she didn't want to stick around for the fallout.

But after a few weeks of hiding out with his mom and baby sister, Jaime had crawled out of the hole. He'd gotten a job, managed to get through school, and generally kept on keeping on. It wasn't perseverance as much as goddamn stubbornness, but until this moment, that desire to be in control and to act like he was had served Jaime well.

Once again, Scarlett was the nut he couldn't crack, which was poetic, if depressing.

"Guess I thought I might be able to make a good case in person. Could I leave her a message?" He was a writer, after all.

The doorman sucked on his teeth, considering. At last, he said, "Have it your way."

Jaime fished a crumpled bagel receipt and a pen out of his pocket and tried to put into words his reasons for coming. He was tempted to go with the truth: *I loved what you wrote in* Queen's Kiss. *You can trust me with it.*

Ha. Scarlett hadn't ever trusted Jaime with herself. For all that he'd tried to break through her shell, to get her to see they could be a team, she'd never needed him. She'd never needed *anyone*. That independent streak had served her well—look at what she'd achieved. The only thing Scarlett and Jaime could share now was the adaptation of her book. She ought to have enough confidence in him for that.

All of that would've been more than any written message could possibly convey, so Jaime simply jotted down his name and cell number. When that seemed too scrawny, he added, *Please call me.*

He stopped himself from underlining the *please*. Scarlett would understand he was begging. She'd always understood everything about him, especially the parts he most wanted to conceal from everyone else. In the end, he hadn't been able to hide from her, and for a while, she'd made him feel as if he didn't need to.

Jaime pushed the receipt across the desk, and the doorman gave him a pitying look.

As with so much of his history with Scarlett, Jaime should've known this was hopeless. He should've stayed in LA and kept pushing for a meeting through her agent and publisher. But when he turned to go, Jaime caught a break—or a blow to the solar plexus.

Just inside the doorway stood a familiar figure.

"Jaime Croft, is that you?"

"Hi." He'd thought he was ready to see her again. He'd been wrong.

Scarlett wore a peacock green wrap dress, faded navy Chuck Taylors, and a white motorcycle jacket—because black would've been obvious, and Scarlett was never predictable.

What she was, what she'd always been, was extremely beautiful.

A pause.

Then she asked, "It's been, what, fifteen years?"

In that instant, Jaime almost blurted out something stupid, like *Seventeen years—but who's counting? And you, you look exactly the same.*

That wouldn't be quite true, though. Scarlett had grown up, but the ways she'd come into herself had made her even more stunning. She still wore fire-engine-red lipstick, but now it didn't seem like a put-on. Her hair was the same rose gold shade, the one that always seemed to catch all the light in a place until she was the only one in color. That was the thing about Scarlett—she was so much herself that everyone else wilted in comparison.

She was a bird of paradise in a world of faded crabgrass.

Scarlett pushed her sunglasses on top of her head, which made her hair frame her face perfectly. It was probably too much to ask for a few strands to be out of place. Or for her to be the least bit tripped up by Jaime's surprise appearance.

Well, he'd always suspected he'd been in deeper than she'd been. Having that confirmed was a shot of phantom limb pain, years after the amputation.

They stared at each other for an ice age.

He finally said, "It's been a while."

"What are you doing here?"

Her question was perfectly neutral. Scarlett had always been difficult to read, which was probably why she was such a great chess player. Her ability to slam that shield in place made Jaime feel like a mess, since his own feelings refused to be hidden. Maybe if they'd had more time together, he could've learned the trick of it.

"To see how you've been."

"That's a lotta ground to cover." For an instant, her bottom lip caught between her teeth. Maybe she was trying to keep a smile in.

He could hope, anyhow.

"Hmm. How have I been, taking into account all the scandals?"

"And the bestselling book and the women's championship and the international celebrity," he added.

Scarlett gave a half smile. She'd picked up on the fact that he'd been following her career. "Pretty damn good. You?"

"Less good."

She almost winced, or maybe he saw it because he wanted her to. She'd been remarkably cool-eyed at the time, much more focused on what came next. Meanwhile, Jaime had been slack-jawed, trying to come to terms with how his father's criminality had swallowed his world.

"How bad was it?" There wasn't any doubt about what *it* she meant.

Scarlett's mom had left town shortly after her daughter, and they hadn't been from Musgrove in the first place, so Scarlett probably hadn't gotten the full play-by-play.

For all that Dad's arrest and incarceration had dominated the second half of Jaime's life, Jaime frequently had to remind himself how small the fallout had been. It only felt as if everyone on earth knew the sordid details, when in reality, anything anyone outside of Musgrove knew was because of Jaime's work. He was the one who'd hung their dirty laundry up on Main Street.

"It sucked." Like a bruise cycling from purple to yellow, the initial shock had melted into mortification. How hadn't Jaime and his mother *known*? The humiliation, the shame, the hurt: those first days were a splatter painting of shitty emotions.

Those emotions were smaller now, but they were still there. They'd probably always be there. When your father—the person you had looked up to more than anyone else on earth—was convicted of trafficking prescription opioids; when every day you had to see the families of the folks whose lives he'd ruined; when you dug deep, trying to understand what drugs with names he could barely pronounce had done to your community, it was fitting to feel bad.

"I'm sorry. I thought about you . . . a lot." Scarlett didn't seem to want to admit that. "I wondered how you were."

"My mom's house still has the same phone number." After leaving him, Scarlett had never used it.

Something flashed across her face, so fast Jaime would've thought he'd imagined it if he hadn't been watching her so closely.

Except he was, so he knew the truth: she'd thought about calling him. Which maybe meant he had a shot here.

"So you came to New York to play catch-up?"

"Not quite. I wanted to ask you for something."

"You okay here?" the doorman asked Scarlett.

Jaime startled. He had clean forgotten that they had an audience for this reunion.

"It's okay, Francis," Scarlett replied. "Jaime and I go *way* back."

That they did.

Scarlett crossed the lobby, taking her time about it too. That was fine with Jaime since it gave him more of an opportunity to appreciate the roll of her hips and the way the light played over her hair and her skin. So many things about the last two decades didn't make sense to Jaime, but he had no trouble grasping why and how he'd fallen for Scarlett.

She was good looking, sure, but she was also like some twisting modern sculpture in a museum. Something that looked different from every angle, turning in on itself and confusing all your expectations about what a piece of art ought to be. Scarlett was messy and controlled, fresh and familiar, empathetic and ruthless all at once. If things had been different, Jaime would've spent a lifetime trying to untangle the double-knotted shoelaces of her.

But things weren't different. So he'd have to settle for the next best thing: putting her story on Videon.

Scarlett stopped inches from him. The last time they'd been in the same room, the last time she'd been this close, she'd been telling him goodbye.

"Your book. I'd like to adapt it for Videon. I'm here with . . . well, pretty much a blank check from them. All you have to do is say yes."

Maybe because Jaime wasn't as controlled as Scarlett, he could sometimes feel the mood in a room shift with the inhabitants' emotions. It was like when music was playing down the street, and you couldn't quite hear it but the beat still made your gut twitch.

Right now, Scarlett was trying to pretend she wasn't, but he knew some part of her was *curious*. "I saw *The Devouring Sun*." She gave a little shrug. "It was pretty good."

Pretty good? It had won a pack of Independent Spirit Awards. Jaime had been a finalist for *Time* magazine's Person of the Year and had been interviewed by seemingly every news outlet in the country. Except *pretty good* were the same words she'd used to describe herself, and her own life had been . . . incandescent.

"I was hoping we could talk about it." Jaime knew he sounded overly eager, but he'd flown across the country for this. There was no use in pretending he had any chill when it came to this project. "Maybe we could grab a coffee—now, if you have time, or tomorrow. But I'd like to pitch my vision to you."

Jaime had an entire presentation worked out. It'd be a miracle if he could remember a word of it, though. His eyes needed a few more minutes to adjust to seeing her again.

"Hmm."

Scarlett gave Jaime a long perusal, from the tips of his shoes up his jeans to his jacket, until finally, she met his gaze. Today, her eyes read the same saturated green as her dress, but he'd seen them gray and blue, depending on the weather and her clothes. When she'd wanted him to, which hadn't been often, he'd seen everything there: pleasure, pain, wonder.

The thing about teenage love affairs is that you didn't know how to hold your emotions back. You weren't smart enough to keep each other at arm's length.

At least that was what Jaime had told himself in the last two decades. The scars that he still carried from Scarlett under his skin, those were part of first love. Anyone would feel them. Hell, he'd heard Taylor Swift's lyrics. Lots of people *did* feel them.

But now, breathing the same air as Scarlett and with her gaze spearing him, it was difficult to believe that what he'd felt had been some universal thing. She'd always made him feel like a butterfly pinned by a collector. He hadn't minded that before, but today, he might as well have been undressed.

You're a smart, accomplished professional in your thirties. You only think *that she's the most beautiful woman on earth and that you'll never get over her.*

"What do you say?" he asked, his voice low and husky. "Will you hear me out?"

"Better not."

The rejection was so firm, so sudden, that Jaime was amazed he managed to remain upright as he walked out of her lobby.

Chapter 2

Scarlett stopped on the landing between the second and third floors, breathing hard. Jaime Croft in her lobby. Freaking Jaime freaking Croft in her freaking lobby. She hadn't been expecting *that* when she'd gone for a walk, hoping to enjoy the autumn sunshine and find a double espresso and a bagel. Not her ex—and definitely not her ex wanting to option her book.

Violet, her agent, hadn't mentioned Jaime had offered for *Queen's Kiss*, but why would she? Scarlett had been pretty darn clear that she wasn't interested in seeing her life dramatized like an episode of *I Survived a Crime*. One time through the real version had been enough, thank you very much.

You free? Scarlett texted Violet.

Violet might've followed Scarlett's instructions, but Scarlett was going to need every detail.

She hadn't written *Queen's Kiss* to crow about her success . . . or at least not *only* to crow. It had mostly been a primal scream about everything she hated and loved about chess. About the things she'd gotten right and the things she'd gotten really, really wrong.

Critics—the dingbats—had praised the book for being one big middle finger to the establishment, but they'd missed all the places where she'd talked about her own doubts and criticized herself. At best, it was a pair of coy middle fingers, to the establishment and to herself.

The thing no one had understood about Scarlett was, for all that she would call you out at your own funeral and wear a bright-red dress while doing it, she didn't leave herself out of her tirades.

Well, Jaime had understood that. Scarlett had tried to hide her feelings from him, like she did with everyone else. But despite her best efforts, Scarlett had always had the sense he had seen her down to her bones. It had made her feel like a trapped wolf—snarling to hide her fear.

But his hold on her had also been an anchor. When they'd met, she could've broken bad. Whatever the odds that she would become a chess grand master and an international celebrity, it had been much more likely that she would've ended up on a reality show about wayward teens. Those had been the glory days of *16 and Pregnant*, after all. Getting tangled up with Jaime had been the escape pod from the life she might have led.

Her phone rang in her hand. Scarlett suspected Violet was never more than twenty-four inches away from a device. She was basically part robot.

"What's up?" Violet said when Scarlett answered.

"Quick question: Did you turn down an offer for *Queen's Kiss* from Jaime Croft?"

"I'd have to check, but if he asked, I would've declined. You were pretty clear. You said something like 'Not even over my dead body.'"

Yeah, that sounded familiar. If anything, Violet was downplaying Scarlett's forcefulness.

"Why do you ask?"

"Oh, Jaime and I grew up together."

Which didn't come close to capturing the problem here. Scarlett ought to let this go, the way she'd done so much of the past. Nothing good could come from picking at this particular scab.

But since Jaime would never know she'd asked Violet to see his email, the only feelings she was risking were her own. And she tended not to be very kind where those were concerned.

"Want me to search my archive?"

"Yeah. Sorry. I'm . . . curious." And stupid. Mostly stupid.

"Give me a minute."

From the moment Scarlett had waltzed into Tokyo a few weeks after her high school graduation and won a match against the runner-up from the previous world championship match, the bozos at the Panel de Ajedrez International—everyone called chess's governing body PAWN, even though the acronym didn't quite work—had cast her in the role of the brilliant drama queen who didn't give a fig for anyone's feelings. They all said she was fearless and confident. This could be a compliment. Usually it was a curse.

Sometimes, Scarlett wished she were beautiful and terrible rather than a redneck who faked her way through self-doubts every day of her life.

But Jaime had always seemed to see more of the truth than anyone else, hadn't he? From that first moment she'd walked into their English class and had almost swallowed her own tongue when they'd locked eyes, it felt as if he'd seen *her*.

Teen movies had prepared Scarlett for those royals of American high schools, the kids who'd come into their bodies and their good looks while the rest of their classmates were still gawky or short or shy. The ones with their parents' platinum cards, who had the right cars and the right clothes and the right ambitions.

But of all of them, Jaime Croft had come into himself the most. Like, *whoa*.

The first time Scarlett saw him, Jaime had been sitting in the front row, those long, long legs of his sprawled out in front of him. Scarlett had had to step over his foot to present her new-student schedule to the teacher, and when she'd shot him a dirty look over her shoulder—just to let him know that she was prepared to hate him on principle—something had passed between them.

Clean and white hot as lightning. Smelling of ozone. Making the hairs on her arms stand straight up. Even now, Scarlett could still feel the shock of it.

She didn't believe in love at first sight. Who the heck could? But she couldn't deny the burning chemistry she felt between them.

So she'd done what anyone would've done—avoided him and told everyone that she didn't like athletes or rich kids, and she especially didn't like Jaime Croft.

But then they'd been paired to peer-review each other's "My Plans for the Future" essays, and she'd stupidly blurted out her dreams to him. Jaime was the prince from a fairy tale, the one who had never heard *no* or that his family couldn't afford it. What was the harm in saying *I want to be the chess world champion* to a prince?

It was like wishing the sandcastle you'd built at the beach wouldn't crumble—harmless and hopeless at the same time.

Except Jaime had told her that she would do it. He'd said it instantly. Confidently. Without hesitation or doubt. Then he'd asked when her next meet was, and Scarlett had thrown out that she'd been invited to the junior national championship game. She'd been trying to brag (who wouldn't?), except he'd asked where it was.

Jaime had been *interested*. The bastard.

Scarlett had explained that she was going to have to turn down the invite because the school didn't have a team. And of course her mother, who was more of a mother in name only, couldn't cover the cost.

That sucks, Jaime had said.

The next day, he told her he'd mentioned the situation to one of the football team's boosters, some golf buddy of his dad's. That guy was happy to make a donation to the school for a chess team as long as Scarlett competed on it.

This school could use a national champion, he'd said, as if it were that easy—and for someone who was rich, she guessed it must be.

But what the hell did she care, if the offer came with a bus ticket and a hotel room?

The entire thing had been more intoxicating than the whiskey Jaime and Scarlett had nicked from his parents later on. Across time and space and all the freaking water that had flowed under the bridge in the last decade and a half, Jaime's confidence in Scarlett still made her head spin.

She'd made a wish, and Jaime had made it come true. How the hell was she supposed to resist him after that?

So she'd clean forgotten to be jaded. To know her place in the world. To take care of all the soft parts of herself, extra-especially her heart. For the first time in her life, Scarlett had stopped being a maverick and let someone in.

What had followed had been like a plane crash, scattering wreckage over half a dozen lives. Even now, Jaime didn't get the full scope of it, because Scarlett hadn't explained. If he hated her now, when all he thought she'd done was leave him behind to go get famous, imagine how much more he'd loathe her if he knew the truth.

Scarlett was reckless, but she wasn't *that* reckless.

"Here it is," Violet said. "Yup, he'd like to option it for Videon."

"Would you have passed this proposal along if I hadn't told you not to?" Scarlett asked.

"It's my job to field offers, and this is a good one. Croft is legit. I loved *The Devouring Sun*, and this seems to have Videon's seal of approval, so it isn't going to get stuck in development limbo. It's going to get made, and probably pretty quickly. That's what I would've told you." She paused. "Wait, are you considering it?"

"No. Maybe."

If Scarlett were going to be honest with Violet, from the moment Jaime had said he wanted it, she'd been kinda, sorta . . . intrigued. She'd seen *The Devouring Sun* too—more than once—because who wouldn't watch their ex's much-buzzed-about streaming docudrama?

The first time, she'd expected it to suck, and then she'd put it on a second time because it hadn't. She'd watched it a third time because she'd been feeling homesick, and there were the Appalachian Mountains, the scent of which she'd never been able to wash off. And then maybe she'd watched it a fourth time because hearing Jaime's voice still could set off a boil in her gut. For reasons Scarlett didn't want to poke at, no one else had ever been able to make her simmer like that.

She'd drawn the line at watching it five times, though. That would've been too far.

Of course she'd watched the Emmys, though. Scarlett didn't know crap about Hollywood, but everyone including her enjoyed judging the clothes. That was just human nature, and Scarlett's nature was even more human than most people's.

When Jaime had lost, she'd been crushed for him. But everyone thought he *should've* won, and that was almost as good, maybe even better, because he'd been brimming with artistic credibility. Obviously Videon had believed in him enough to let him pursue the next project he wanted, and it just so happened to be her book.

So for all the crap that had happened to him and his family, Jaime Croft hadn't been devastated. He'd stayed in Musgrove, sure, but he'd helped out his family and gone to school and become a director anyhow. Then he'd competed for some awards, and he'd kept his hair.

That he'd succeeded despite everything made sense. Under Jaime's golden-boy exterior, he had a good soul. That was why she hadn't been able to resist him, in the end. Why he was the poisoned apple that she'd just had to wolf down.

If she were going to give anyone the rights to *Queen's Kiss*, she'd give them to Jaime. He'd do right by her. He was the only person who would.

She still wasn't going to let him have it, though.

"I like the sound of *maybe*." Violet had always thought Scarlett's position on this was daffy.

"It's closer to a warm no," Scarlett warned.

But Violet could smell blood in the water. "You want me to send this proposal to you?"

Scarlett ought to decline. Stop this right here. But before the good sense of that could make it through her brain, she said, "Sure, what's the harm in taking a look?"

"No harm at all." A few keys clicked over the line. "Okay, sent."

"I'll call you back." Just to close the loop on this, to assure Violet that Scarlett had returned to her senses. She'd write Jaime a note, thanking him for coming to New York but explaining that she couldn't possibly agree to the adaptation.

Scarlett started up the stairs, feeling better, feeling balanced. Now that she and Jaime had seen each other, if it ever happened again—at a party in Hollywood or at South by Southwest or any of the other places she'd worried she might stumble into him—she didn't have to be nervous.

Hey, remember me? I left my virginity in your bed and broke your heart. That was bananas. *So how have things been?*

They could just skip that part now and stuff those feelings under the bed, only taking them out for ten minutes of booze-fueled what-ifs on New Year's Eve, like normal people. Thank God.

And now that the initial meeting was out of the way, Scarlett didn't have an objection to seeing him again. It might even be nice—as long as they could skip reminiscing. No good would come from *that.*

Scarlett unlocked the door to her apartment and tossed her purse on the nearest armchair. Imagine if she'd led Jaime up here. Imagine if she'd let herself hear his entire pitch. Imagine if she'd tried to explain why she'd left Musgrove and what had preceded that decision.

Imagine.

That would've been ridiculous.

Jaime looked good, though. That wasn't ridiculous. His hair, still dark and full, was shorter now. It didn't fall in a tousled mess over his forehead, making him look as if they'd just played hooky and ended up in the back seat of his car behind the water tower. Again.

There were deeper lines on his face too. Clearly the man still liked to spend a lot of time outside, and he didn't have any more time for sunscreen now than he had in high school, but it was working for him. It was so unfair how society let men "weather" like that, age like fine bourbon in a cask, while screaming at women who didn't have at least five steps to their nighttime skin care routine.

That was yet another example of the sexist double standards she faced every day as a female grand master.

It was probably rude that Scarlett hadn't heard Jaime out. It would have been . . . neighborly. And once upon a time, they'd been awfully neighborly to each other.

The memories had her temperature beginning to climb. In the round mirror behind the couch, she watched her cheeks pinken. She and Jaime had never lacked for chemistry. Everything else, sure, but not that.

Yet there wouldn't have been any point in hearing him out. If she weren't going to give him the rights, it would've been cruel to lead him on. Surely Jaime thought she had been, even though she'd tried hard not to be.

Which left her . . . where?

If she wasn't going to tease him and she wanted to see him again, she could let him adapt the book.

It would be fun, wouldn't it, to watch him do it? To get to say to an entirely new group of people—the ones who hadn't yet read *Queen's Kiss*—what she thought about chess. To say that it didn't have to be stuffy and elitist, that it was actually one of the most accessible games in the world, one that anyone could play and get good at without coaches or fancy equipment or any of that nonsense. That if you were willing to do the work, even a hick and a loner like Scarlett, coming from nothing, coming from nowhere, could become a grand master. And that women ought to be able to play with the boys if they wanted to—and she wanted to.

Jaime probably had a real good plan for adapting her book too. Maybe he'd made some mood boards. She did love a good mood board. Maybe he'd gone so far as to think about casting. She'd pay a lot of money—and she could afford it now—to see who he thought might be up for playing her.

"Ha." The thought was so amusing she actually laughed out loud.

No one would want to play her. Scarlett was *living* herself, and she didn't want to, some days.

Look, she'd seen him again, and she'd done it without exploding. She'd be even better the next time she saw him. Even more in control, even more lashed down—or at least as lashed down as she ever got.

And she could set the rules. When Scarlett had first said she didn't want to sell the option, Violet tried to convince her to reconsider. "You could insist on cowriting the script," she'd said. "You wrote every word of that damn book on your own, and it's a bestseller. They're not going to deny you. And you could force them to make you a producer. That way nothing ends up on that screen that you don't like."

Of course, Scarlett would also demand to be on the set and to teach the cast chess—because if there was one thing she didn't have patience for, it was bad chess scenes in movies. Because if they were doing this, they were going to do it right.

Because she wanted to do this.

Scarlett's mouth dropped open. "Holy heck."

It turned out that Jaime didn't have to convince her. He just had to present himself, and she supplied the rest.

"This is stupid," she told her reflection.

But the good sense of those words didn't matter. Once she'd decided something, the only way out was through.

With shaking hands, she dialed Violet. "Okay, I'm in. But I have some conditions."

Chapter 3

Jaime hadn't anticipated flaming out so spectacularly. Even the Hindenburg had flown for a while before going kaboom. Jaime hadn't even made it three minutes.

A zeppelin had outperformed him.

He flopped face down on the bed in his hotel room, the rayon comforter scratching his cheek. How was he going to tell Nate Pace, his coproducer and cinematographer, that he'd failed? *She'll hear me out. I got this.* He'd said those exact words only a few hours ago.

Jaime had been confident because Scarlett considering and accepting his proposal made sense for both of them. He had the right vision to adapt her book, and it would benefit them both.

Except she hadn't had the slightest interest in his offer, dammit.

Before Dad had gone to jail, Jaime had been amiable but aimless. Afterward, he'd had to make a choice: step up or lose everything. Jaime chose the former, rebuilding himself as a tower of strength and will. Support his mom and sister and hold their family together through the storm? No problem. Commute to college while working full time, and graduate? Totally doable. Make a docudrama about his dad's crimes on a shoestring budget and win a truckload of awards? Nailed it.

Through it all, Jaime had learned that he *liked* to be in charge. He was good at managing details and people, which was why filmmaking suited him.

But that was useless here. Scarlett and Jaime were two massive storm systems, clashing together and spinning off tornadoes. He couldn't overpower her, and he definitely didn't dazzle her. The only surprising part was why he'd thought he could.

In his pocket, his phone buzzed. Nate.

Jaime flopped onto his back and answered. "Hey, what's up?"

"So I'm *dying* to hear how it went," Nate said, talking over him.

There wasn't any point in being coy. "Not well."

"She didn't like the presentation?" Nate—who totally believed Jaime was a force of nature—was shocked.

"She didn't hear the presentation. Rejected it out of hand."

Nate whistled. "Dude, I can't remember the last time you whiffed."

Because Jaime usually got what he wanted. "I may have overestimated how much my history with Scarlett could help." He hadn't told Nate the full story; he hadn't told anyone the full story. It had been easier to simply say *We went to high school together.*

Truth be told, when he'd found out Scarlett had written a book, he'd been terrified that he was going to find a no-holds-barred account of their relationship in it. Even now, he had no idea if he ought to feel comforted or insulted that he wasn't in there.

Did we mean nothing? But it had been a high school relationship. It wasn't as if they were soul mates.

"Look, it isn't your fault. She clearly doesn't want to sell the option. We've tried everything at this point, and we've run out of road. That's just the way it is sometimes. No big deal."

It felt like a pretty big deal.

"It's the one I wanted." The other projects Nate had pitched to Jaime didn't come close to getting his blood up the way Scarlett's memoir had.

Jaime's phone sounded, and he glanced at the screen. It was a message from Larry Gomez at Videon, with the subject line Good News re: QUEEN'S KISS.

"Um, do you see Larry's email?"

Jaime was already pulling it up. Arbuthnot accepted the terms! Congrats on landing her book. We knew you'd get it, the message began.

Nate was shouting into the phone, "Was this a joke? You asshole, it *was* a joke. Goddamn it. You really had me going there. You sold the fuck out of that. I should've known. I should have *known*. You always seal the deal."

"Ha," Jaime said, without any humor. A sandstorm raged in his head. This couldn't be right. It couldn't. It had to be some kind of mistake.

But there it was, undeniable in the pixels on his screen: Scarlett's agent had called Videon to say she was glad someone had finally made the right offer to Scarlett and to lay out their terms.

Wait, their *terms*?

"I can live with most of these," Nate was saying. "I mean, whatever it takes to get her on board, right? We always knew she was going to want some stuff. Beyond money, that is."

The money stuff was all on Videon. Jaime couldn't care less where that was concerned—even if it was an eye-popping amount. Jaime had seen her apartment building, so he knew Scarlett had bills to pay.

"The coproducer credit, we anticipated that. Her serving as the chess consultant on set, I mean, we would've wanted that anyhow. Our worry would've been getting her to agree to it. The cowriting thing, though, that one gives me pause. We think she wrote this book"—meaning that she hadn't used a ghostwriter—"but we aren't sure. And even if she could write a memoir, that doesn't mean she can write for television."

Up to now, Jaime hadn't used a writer's room. He'd worked in a couple of them on friends' projects, just to get a sense of how they worked—Christ on a cracker, he had Hollywood friends like Zoya Delgado now! Those writer's rooms had been fine. Historical romances like *Waverley* weren't exactly his cup of tea, but he'd learned more about the business, and that was priceless.

The idea of writing his own project with someone else was another matter, though. It made him want to crawl out of his skin—and if the person in question were Scarlett . . . holy shit.

Jaime had breathed the same air as her for three minutes in her lobby, and his brain had rebooted. He'd become the human version of the blue screen of death. Would he be able to function alongside Scarlett on set?

Well, there would be dozens of people around during filming, and he would have a job to do. If he worked himself up to it in small doses, Jaime might be able to inoculate himself, like building up tolerance to a poison.

But first, they would have to write the scripts, and writing wasn't like filming. It was private and painful, and it took a *long* time. Jaime couldn't handle weeks or months of alone time with Scarlett. He couldn't. He'd vaporize.

"Yeah, I'm not sure about it either."

"Then why did you say yes?"

Yup, Larry had forwarded Violet Kemp's email to Jaime and Nate, and there it was: Scarlett was especially glad that Mr. Croft agreed to co-write the first-pass scripts together. She wants to maintain editorial control over her own story, and she *only* agreed to the deal because Mr. Croft is giving that to her.

Scarlett had clearly made the calculation she would be better off saying that Jaime had given her everything she wanted. Which was . . . ballsy and very much like her. It was Scarlett's latest bold move in a lifetime of brash play.

She knew Jaime wasn't going to risk scuttling the deal by saying that they hadn't agreed to shit, even if they hadn't, because he'd showed up on her doorstep and begged. She knew exactly how invested he was in this story, and so she had all the power.

Jaime was in awe of how her mind worked.

"I didn't think I had a choice," he said to Nate.

"You probably should've run that past me—and Videon—first."

"That's a fair critique."

"You wanna try and renegotiate it?" Nate asked. "We could get Craig Gillespie"—a lawyer they worked with sometimes—"to call this Violet person up. He can play hardball when he wants to."

Jaime knew Scarlett, though, and she wasn't going to budge. She would only do this if she could be involved in every step of the process. And since *Queen's Kiss* was the only project he wanted, he was going to have to pay the piper and figure out how to write the damn thing with his ex.

"No, don't call Craig. Scarlett was clear about this." At least in her agent's email.

"Divas," Nate said with a knowing sigh. "Let's hope she can write, then. Or if she can't, that she's content sitting there and watching you do it."

Ha. Scarlett had never been passive a day in her life.

"I don't really blame her," Jaime admitted. "It is her memoir, after all."

"True. It's not as if you would've handed *The Devouring Sun* over to someone else."

"Definitely not. Scarlett and I . . . we'll find a way to work together."

Jaime had no idea what that might look like. One thing was for sure, he was going to have to quit lusting after her. Especially since she'd seemed to be totally unaffected by him.

Which was good. Detached professionalism was the only way they were going to get through a year and a half or more of a *lot* of togetherness.

"I hope she likes moody."

"Hey, I'm not moody."

"You absolutely are. But you make up for it by being exceptionally talented."

Jaime snorted.

The shock of Scarlett's Molotov cocktail was fading, and Jaime was starting to crawl out from underneath the furniture. He'd gotten the project that he'd wanted. He was going to prove to everyone he wasn't a one-hit wonder and he could make work that wasn't based on his own life. He blew out a long sigh of relief.

"I'm really pumped," Nate said. "When do you think she'll want to start working?"

"No idea. She didn't mention her schedule." In the version of this where Scarlett had listened to his proposal and agreed to grant him the option like someone who wasn't cosplaying as a feral cat, Jaime had been hoping to get started before the holidays. Getting a workable version of the scripts was the necessary precondition to everything else: scouting locations, planning the shoot, casting, and all the rest. The sooner they could hammer those out—and if he and Scarlett were involved, there would be hammering—the better.

"I'll write Larry back as soon as we get off this call, with a few dates," Jaime told Nate.

Scarlett would probably want to work here in New York. Jaime stood up and crossed to the window. Pushing the curtains apart, he looked down at the street, an asphalt ribbon at the bottom of the dizzying canyon of buildings. He enjoyed the city for short stretches here and there, but he couldn't imagine having to be here for a substantial length of time. He'd miss his regular visits to see Dad, and he'd have to find someone to cover his support group for friends and family of incarcerated persons. New York would be like LA for Jaime. Parachuting in for work now and again was fine, but no place that wasn't Musgrove would ever feel like home.

Then, like a shot, it struck him.

"The one thing we agreed on, though, that's *not* in Violet's email was where we were going to work."

"Oh?"

"Yeah, she wants to write it in Musgrove." If Scarlett could play this move, he could too.

"You invited her to the cabin?"

"Yup. She sounded *very* excited to get back home for a bit."

As far as Jaime knew, Scarlett had never been back to Musgrove, not even for a vacation. But the only way Jaime was going to be able to get through this was to do it in a place where he felt comfortable, not a place he simply endured.

Musgrove might have been where he'd experienced the worst moments of his life, but it had also been where he had lived through them and where he had found himself. There wasn't anywhere else where he'd be able to write these scripts.

"Okay, sounds great," Nate said. "I'm just relieved we got it."

And Jaime was just sorry he was going to miss Scarlett's reaction to him claiming home field advantage.

Chapter 4

Two Months Later

"Shit fire and save matches." Scarlett climbed out of her rental car. Her flip-flops sank into the gravel driveway and her sunglasses slid down her nose as she took in Jaime's place.

She'd laughed her butt off when Violet had called to ask if she'd actually agreed to spend eight weeks in Musgrove writing with Jaime. In making her play to get what she wanted, Scarlett hadn't expected him to return the favor.

Well, Jaime had always given as good as he got. She'd tried to decline his offer to stay at his house, but after Violet's assistant had sent Scarlett every single Airbnb listing and hotel room in a twenty-mile radius of his place, Scarlett had relented. There really wasn't anything else that would've worked.

Except she hadn't known she was saying yes to . . . this. To two stories that were more modernist than log cabin, with lots of mirrored glass. Off the back, there was what appeared to be a massive porch, and then the hillside tripped and fell into the valley, where pines and rocks poured out as far as the eye could see.

"It's nothing fancy," he'd said of a house that could've been the set of an A24 movie.

Nothing fancy—ha. Jaime had never had a sense of proportion. When you grew up as one of the richest kids in town, it came naturally, she supposed.

Scarlett wiped her hands on her jeans. She felt truly nasty and not at all herself. During the drive from Richmond, she'd unfortunately discovered that the rental car's AC couldn't handle the unseasonably warm Virginia December day. She might as well have been an ant cooked under a magnifying glass.

A glance in the side mirror revealed that she was as flushed as she felt. She ought to have stopped at a Motel 6 for an hour-long shower, some fresh clothes, and a thick coat of makeup, because she couldn't face Jaime without lipstick. Could not.

So of course the front door to the glam cabin opened right then, and Jaime strolled out, looking better than it was fair for him to. His white Oxford appeared to have just been pressed—the preppy jackass.

"You made it," he called.

Unfortunately. "Hard to get lost in your own hometown."

Scarlett hadn't seen Jaime since that day in her lobby, and her eyes were eating up the sight of him. *Down, girl. You'll get plenty of chances to stare.*

She was scheduled to be here for eight weeks. Just shy of sixty days. Scarlett glanced back at his house. On second thought, maybe it wasn't massive enough.

"Yeah, Musgrove hasn't changed much."

A total lie. Musgrove may have looked the same, probably because it had already been run down even when she'd lived here—Main Street was still dotted with closed storefronts—but the old Blockbuster had become a rehab halfway house, and there was a methadone clinic next to the Piggly Wiggly. That was new.

"The water tower didn't used to be blue."

Jaime's brows shot up, probably because they'd spent too many afternoons up behind the water tower, with her hand wrapped around his—

"Bags. Do you need help with your bags?" he coughed out, probably because he was flooded with the same memories she was.

"Nope," she said sweetly. "I'm a big girl."

While Scarlett would've preferred a full set of armor, or at least a fresh application of deodorant, messing with Jaime did make her feel more in charge. Pretending to be a brat in order to show everyone that she was the boss was kind of Scarlett's thing. And sometimes, the person who most needed to be reminded that she wasn't powerless was Scarlett herself.

That was what she had to remember: she was in the driver's seat here. Jaime needed *her*, or at least he needed her book.

She popped the trunk open, hefted her backpack over her shoulder, and then claimed two large suitcases.

"What about . . . ?" He gestured to the third.

"I'll come back for it." She closed the trunk with a snap as he started to reach for her last piece of luggage.

Jaime might still be every inch the southern gentleman, but Scarlett wouldn't—she couldn't—indulge that crap. They had a job to do.

"Lead the way."

He didn't budge. "My mom would kill me if she knew I let you carry your own bags."

No, his mother would kill *Scarlett* if she knew exactly why Scarlett had left town.

"I've carried my own bags literally around the darn world. Show me to my room."

A long pause. Then, "Fine."

"This is some place," she said as she trailed him toward the house. "Did you buy it from the Cullen family?" It certainly resembled the home of a certain group of sparkly vampires.

"That explains the baseball diamond."

She wouldn't be surprised if this place boasted one, actually.

With a pained sigh, he reached for the front door handle. "Moderate your expectations."

"I don't do moderate."

But inside, she could see why he'd said it. This gorgeous building was mostly empty. The front room would obviously be stunning at some point. But for the moment, there was no furniture. No rugs. No art. And definitely no broody teens with fangs.

"It isn't all like this," Jaime promised. "I've just been busy, and well, I may have run out of money once they finished the structure. Damn thing went over budget."

Scarlett opened her mouth to tell him that she'd practiced chess on a pile of boxes in her living room the entire time she'd been in her apartment—but then she remembered that she wanted to keep things impersonal. "It has four walls and a roof that doesn't leak, right? What are you apologizing for?" she demanded. "Besides, the view makes up for it."

Even his front yard was gosh darn picturesque. The driveway snaked around, hiding the house from the main road. With the curtain of trees, they might as well have been deep in the forest and miles from civilization. But then again, Musgrove had always felt like its own world.

"I guess it does. The bedrooms are this way." He led her down a hallway and pushed a door open. "This one is yours."

At least he'd gotten some furniture for this room: a bed with what appeared to be a brand-new headboard in some kind of glowing burled wood that matched the house perfectly, and it was piled high with crisp white linens. Scarlett was going to have to scrub the sweat and dirt from her face before she dove in there.

"The bathroom next door is all yours. I have a suite at the end of the hall."

The perks of being the owner.

"This is really nice," Scarlett said, because it was. And because Jaime was clearly so mortified by the emptiness of the house, and his embarrassment would probably undermine their work. "Thank you for letting me stay here. I need to get cleaned up, but when did you want to get started?"

His eyes crinkled, even if he didn't quite smile. "Oh, I figured we could wait until tomorrow. Say nine a.m.?" He'd mentioned in an email about logistics that he liked to keep pretty normal hours and was more of a morning person.

Scarlett's inner night owl protested in advance. "Um, okay. Where's the nearest Starbucks?" She hadn't seen one since Charlottesville.

"Unless you want to drive to Kellysville, you'll have to hit the Royal Farms. And you don't want to do that."

"So where do you get caffeine?"

She must have sounded as desperate as she felt, because Jaime did offer her a knee-meltingly gentle grin then. "I realize you probably won't believe me after seeing the living room, but my kitchen is reasonably well stocked. I have a coffeepot. Also, I intend to feed you. We can expense all of this to Videon. There's a budget—a pretty nice one—for the show."

"Hmm, we'll see about that." The folks at Videon hadn't met Scarlett yet, and they didn't know that she didn't do cheap. Having not had enough for the first eighteen years of her life, Scarlett vowed to always spend whatever she had for the rest of it.

If they were making her life story, they weren't going to make a cheap version of it, that was for sure.

"I'll get out of your hair, but holler if you need anything."

After a long shower—Jaime hadn't skimped on the plumbing—Scarlett changed into fresh clothes and sank into the chair by the window. She pulled up the group chat she shared with Kit Callahan and Martina Vega.

Kit had been protesting PAWN long before Scarlett. PAWN had ruled that Kit and other nonbinary and trans players were free to compete in the open division, but they were banned from the women's league—which was absolute bullpucky, particularly because the open division was in no meaningful way *open*.

Besides Scarlett, Judit Polgár was the only woman who'd gotten an invitation to compete in the open division of the Candidates

Tournament—the tournament to determine who got to challenge the reigning world champion—and that had been twenty-five years ago. Scarlett didn't know how anyone could look at that fact and not know that the system was utterly busted.

In the wake of Scarlett's okay performance in the open division at Candidates (she'd won three matches, drawn five, and lost six), she had refused to defend the women's world championship she'd won eight years ago. That period of her career was over. When Scarlett had dropped out, Martina and several other high-profile players had also refused to compete in the women's league. Things had to change. Now.

It had felt strange, going from fighting on her own—her default position—to fighting *with* others. But it had also been . . . nice.

At least until PAWN had retaliated, the squirrely bastards.

PAWN introduced some screwy new measures to combat ranking inflation and deflation—and what do you know, with those controls, Scarlett's Elo rating fell below 2740. As a result, she failed to get a second invite to Candidates.

Oh, but she'd been pissed. Pissed enough to write *Queen's Kiss* and go scorched earth on them, and Martina and Kit had been especially supportive. They'd asked for updates on the adaptation, so she sent them a quick text: Arrived!

How is it? Martina immediately responded.

Pretty luxe for a cabin in the woods. Even if it was sparsely furnished. I'll survive.

Somewhere in the house, there was a thump. Jaime was walking around—which was fair. It was his place. In an email, he'd insisted that she wouldn't even know he was there . . . but it turned out she totally knew.

Now that they'd reconnected, Scarlett was fairly certain she'd feel him vibrating on the dark side of the moon.

I can't believe you're going out of town for two whole months, Kit added. You need to get ready for Stavanger.

Scarlett was trying to qualify for Candidates again, and that path ran through the open division of the Norway Chess tournament. She had to play *very* well in Stavanger. Like, winning-the-whole-thing well. If she couldn't manage it, she was going to have to make some tricky decisions about whether she would be happy throwing bombs from the outside of the chess world for the rest of her life.

Endorsements, teaching, and now the show: Scarlett could eat on those things. But she knew if she didn't manage to get into the open-division chess world championship someday, she would always wonder if she could've become the first woman to take it. Trying and not getting it was one thing, but if she never got into the room where the championship was decided, it would haunt her forever. And if she failed, it might send the message that PAWN was right and that women could only compete in a lesser, protected league.

I'm prepping. Scarlett was. Sort of. And we'll go into beast mode when I get back.

Kit and Martina were Scarlett's favorite training partners, and she was happy to pay them for their support and expertise. Where else was she going to find two other grand masters who could put up with her and who loathed PAWN as much as she did?

Changing the subject, I for one am glad that you finally found a producer you like, Martina wrote.

Jaime wasn't only a producer, but Scarlett had to bite the correction back. Violet was thrilled.

You should be thrilled! Everyone wants to see their life on screen.

Maybe? I might be getting overexposed. Everyone probably wants a break from me.

They can't get enough of you, and you know it. And the news will have everyone buzzing about how you'll do in Stavanger.

Great. I'll be walking around with a target on my chest. Scarlett had sincerely considered getting a dress made with an actual bull's-eye on it, but that would probably violate some obscure rule about not distracting your opponent.

Once upon a time, Scarlett wouldn't have cared. She would've relished getting censored and then holding a press conference to bitch about it. Now, she was wearier.

Not wanting to admit that—it was more personal than she tended to get with Kit and Martina—she just wrote, *But it'll be worth it when I run the table.*

Jaime had assured her they would be done in two months, and then she'd be able to start preparing for the tournament for real. The stakes were scary high, but these were the moments Scarlett lived for. There was nothing like playing when something was actually on the line.

It was a good thing Scarlett had never tried gambling. She would've gotten hooked in a heartbeat.

More soon! she texted, though she didn't know why she wrote that. Kit and Martina didn't need updates on every second of her life. No one cared about Scarlett that much.

Without the shield of the group chat, she didn't have any reason to stay in her room. Scarlett took a few seconds to talk herself up, and then she slipped out into the hallway. She wove through the open living room and then down a hallway, both of which were empty—of people, of furniture, of decorations of any kind. The house truly was a shell, as if it were waiting for someone to discover it and fill it up.

At last, she found Jaime. The kitchen occupied the back of the house, so it had a truly stunning view over the porch and down into the valley.

"Feeling better?" he asked.

She was suddenly aware of her wet hair. Scarlett must look like a drowned cat—but it didn't matter. She wasn't here to impress the man. "Yup. Just thirsty."

"Glasses are in here." He got one from a cabinet. "Ice is in the freezer." He filled the cup up to the brim with ice cubes—which was exactly how she liked it. How she'd always liked it. "And use this tap for filtered water."

She almost fell on the glass and gulped half of it down. "Thanks. You on well water out here?" It didn't taste like it.

"The city. They extended the pipe." He winced and added quickly, "Not just for me. There are more houses out this way."

He addressed her as if she were a local. When people asked for her hometown, Scarlett said Musgrove, but the words always stung a bit, like poking at a bruise because the ache was satisfying in the sickest way.

In Musgrove, you were a local because your grandparents had grown up here. Because your ancestors figured in local legends and were planted in the cemetery by the police station. Because you remembered before they'd built the new firehouse and back when Spottswood Road used to be called the Mill Road.

But Scarlett didn't remember. Her mom had moved to Musgrove from Kellysville to get away from a man, a common event, and they'd only stayed two years. Sure, Scarlett had graduated from Musgrove's high school, but saying she was from here had also been easier than explaining she'd lived in twelve apartments in eight cities before she'd left home because her mom went through jobs and dudes the way other parents went through Kleenex. It was way easier than admitting that they'd been evicted twice and that she still had nightmares about being homeless sometimes.

Scarlett didn't have a claim on Musgrove, not in the way Jaime's family did.

Folks here might even cling to the Crofts harder because his dad's arrest was part of the town's legend now. For all that Dr. Croft had hurt people here—killed people here—the people of Georgina County protected their own. And Scarlett was nothing to them.

She sipped her water. "I know that we're not starting until tomorrow, but do we need some ground rules for working?"

"Such as?"

"No talking about the past." To start. She was also going to suggest they eat their meals separately, try to avoid each other outside their writing time.

He started to smile, but he looked out the window until he was able to school his expression into something boring. She hated boring.

"Scarlett, we're supposed to be writing your life story. How can we do that without talking about the past?"

"I mean *our* past."

Up until now, neither of them had acknowledged that they'd had a past. It was as if they'd only sat in a few classes together and nothing else.

Jaime looked back at her and worked his jaw. "I don't know."

He was rejecting her very reasonable suggestion?

"What good could come from it?" Scarlett sounded more desperate than she intended to, but she meant the question in the most literal way. Talking about the past wouldn't end well.

"We might both get some clarity."

"Clarity is overrated." It was much better for things to stay confusing and vaguely muddy and overrated, like a Christopher Nolan movie.

"Don't you think it might come up? I mean, you mention the water tower and we both get ideas."

Okay, he had her there. She'd set herself up for that charge. "I'm sorry about that. I was . . . stirring stuff. But I'll stop doing that."

"Writing stirs stuff, Scarlett. It just does. There's no two ways about it. You wanted to help write this thing. You insisted on it. In fact, you told a lie—"

"Which you knew was a lie. You could've called me out." Scarlett hadn't been trying to deceive him, not in the classic sense. It was a gambit, which was a different category of thing.

He must not be pissed about it, though, because he huffed out a laugh. "So it was okay because it was a tactic?"

"Jaime, I play chess. Everything is a tactic."

"Scarlett, I make movies. I understand."

Oh, but he didn't. "I'm just saying—"

"And I'm disagreeing. We won't be able to avoid the past."

When she'd arranged things so that she could write the show, she'd thought she'd won. Now she was worried that he'd lured her into hanging her bishop. "I know that you don't believe me, but I don't like drama."

"You love it."

"I like it when I can be above it. When it's the sea and I'm sailing over it, sure." But with Jaime, she'd never been able to exist separate from the angst. Everything with him was too personal, too deeply felt. "I want this show to be good."

"I do too."

It was imperative that Scarlett convince him about this. She clenched her hands into fists until her nails burrowed into her palms. "I just want us to be able to work together . . ." *And not chew each other up again.* "The last time got messy."

"There was a time when I didn't like mess either. But now, I know that there's no avoiding it. Life is messy."

Somewhere in the house, a door opened and a voice called, "Jaime!"

"In here, Ev!"

Of course, it must be Evelyn Jean—Jaime's baby sister. In Scarlett's memory, she was a precocious preschooler, all blond curls and blue eyes, and always, always wearing a tulle ballerina skirt over her clothing.

But the young woman who strolled into his kitchen with a bag of groceries balanced on her hip was definitely not that.

Gone was the blond. Evelyn had dyed her locks jet black and had them cut into a sharp bob. A sleeve of tattooed roses climbed up one of her arms, and her earlobes boasted multiple piercings of the black-and-chrome variety.

Holy snakes, Jaime's sister was a baby goth.

"Evelyn?" Scarlett accepted the hug Evelyn offered her, feeling suddenly very old and very square.

Generally, Scarlett was the one walking into a room wearing "edgy" fashions. But then again, in the chess world, Scarlett often lowered the average age of the rooms she walked into by a good ten years.

"You look incredible," Scarlett said, meaning it. "I almost didn't recognize you without the tutu, though."

"Ha, don't remind me. Mom wishes I'd go back to those." Evelyn shot her brother a wry look. Jaime's mother had basically been a mascot for Talbots, and so it wasn't hard to imagine how she must feel about her daughter's style one-eighty. "Jaime said you were coming, and I almost didn't believe him. It's been too long."

"It's been . . . a while." And it had been very much on purpose.

"I loved your book. You are such a badass."

An amusing thought, since the last time Scarlett had seen Evelyn, the girl couldn't read.

Ev couldn't remember Scarlett, not really. For starters, Scarlett had refused to be Jaime's girlfriend. *Girlfriend*—ha, that was one title she wasn't interested in. Scarlett was a team of one, thank you very much.

Gasping hookups against the back wall of the gym were fine and dandy, but Scarlett didn't need a date for homecoming because she wouldn't be caught dead at homecoming. This had been a point of some debate between Scarlett and Jaime, but she'd flat-out said no when he'd begged her to make things between them official.

But despite Scarlett's best efforts to float by, as free and uninvolved as a bird in the landscape it flies over, she'd touched the entire Croft family—and she needed to remember that. Scarlett sometimes tried to pretend that what she'd done before she'd skipped town had been solely about her and Jaime. That wasn't true. It had involved a lot of other people. A lot of other innocent people.

Scarlett had specifically not written about the Crofts in *Queen's Kiss*, and she'd only mentioned Musgrove in passing. She couldn't offer them much, but she could try not to make things worse. And getting tangled up with Scarlett's own messy reputation tended to do that to folks.

Wanting to change the subject, Scarlett asked Evelyn, "What are you up to?"

"Finishing art school in Richmond."

"She paints murals," Jaime explained.

"My thesis project is about revising abandoned buildings with art, and well, there are a lot of them around here." Which was a nice way of saying that Musgrove looked bombed out. It was a place that just kept getting sadder and sadder, but somehow more stubbornly proud about its sadness.

"That sounds incredible," Scarlett said.

"If you have time, I'll take you to see some of my work."

Because Evelyn was old enough to drive now—ha. Scarlett was a crone.

Evelyn's gaze shifted back and forth between Scarlett and her brother, assessing, and Scarlett was suddenly worried how he'd explained this scenario. They might not have officially been together, but not putting a label on things in high school had had the opposite effect than they'd intended: it had only increased interest in them.

He's just using you, a cheerleader had once said to Scarlett in the bathroom.

No, I'm using him, she'd replied—which had shut the girl up and might also have been true.

But Jaime had still dragged Scarlett to his house for dinner as a member of his study group or, when he'd really wanted to be a pill, as his "friend."

Friend, she'd mocked when he'd had her pinned underneath him later.

Yeah, right.

When it came to his family and not high school gossips, Jaime's father had adored Scarlett, his mother had loathed her, and his baby sister had followed her around like a puppy. In different ways, Scarlett had betrayed them all.

It was hard to remember how Scarlett had talked herself into giving Jaime the rights to *Queen's Kiss*. It hadn't occurred to her that she'd signed up to return to the scene of the crime, where she'd come face to face with some of her victims.

Her stomach pricking with all kinds of unwanted emotions, she tried to remember that Jaime was still a spoiled golden boy. Disdain for the type had her curling her lip in two seconds. It was better than Pepto for unwanted guilt.

"I'd love to see your work," she said to Evelyn. Then she added, tartly, "Do you always pick up Jaime's groceries?"

Evelyn laughed. "Nah. I took some requests during my latest Costco run. I always stop there on my way home."

Scarlett shot Jaime a look thick with disdain and drawled, "Some things never change."

The implication wasn't fair. It wasn't Jaime's fault he looked like a prince of privilege, and he'd proved himself a thousand times over after his dad's fall from grace.

But the brown paper bag Ev had brought stirred something else in Scarlett. She didn't have Jaime's family and their pedigree. She didn't have a loving sister or a stable mother. She didn't have the support of a community or the kind of long history that bought her grace anywhere. No one brought her groceries.

Scarlett only had herself and her smart mouth, and so she had to wield both like weapons. If she didn't, she might fall into the trap of imagining that she was defenseless.

She gave Evelyn a pat on the shoulder. "It was good to see you again. But I'm going to grab a nap."

Then Scarlett made a tactical retreat to her bedroom, where things made sense.

Chapter 5

A few hours later than Jaime had wanted to start, Scarlett reclined on a couch in his den, looking like an empress. The only thing messing up the picture was the mug of coffee dangling from her hand. Regal folks probably didn't need caffeine.

For so long, Jaime had only seen the celebrity version of Scarlett Arbuthnot, and he'd only caught glimpses of that on TV and social media. She showed up at every tournament looking impossibly glamorous, putting her femininity on display as if to say *If you want to make it an issue, fine. Here I am dressed like a pinup girl.* Her image was a finely honed thing—and it was a mask.

In contrast, the woman across from him was *real.* Her hair was still styled and her lipstick was still perfect, but this was Scarlett, not Scarlett™. That Jaime was privileged enough to peek behind the construction threatened to turn him into a marshmallow.

He had to resist the urge, though, because he needed to keep some distance here. They had a job to do.

Her lips twitched. She knew Jaime was watching her. After a few beats, she sent him a sidelong glance. "Will this get less weird?"

"Less like the first day of class?" Because things between Jaime and Scarlett could never be less weird.

"Yup." Scarlett splayed a hand on the coffee table between them and leaned toward him. In a low voice, she said, "Tell me"—in that moment, he would've told her anything—"how *do* you write a television show?"

"Well, shit, Scarlett, I was hoping you knew."

She laughed that big laugh of hers, the one that always seemed to find all the little drafty corners of his soul and plug them up. After a minute, she flopped back onto the couch and gestured with her mug at the yellow legal pads he'd hopefully piled in between them. A lipstick kiss stained the rim of the mug, which was endearing as hell.

"I'm serious—I don't know what I'm doing."

He wanted to ask why she'd finagled her way into this, then, but he swallowed the words down. It would only lead to a fight, and he needed to set the right tone for their first day since he was basically in charge here.

"The first thing we ought to do is to figure out how we want to break the book down. Like, what are the necessary chunks, and how do we want to structure the episodes?"

"How did you do that for *The Devouring Sun*?"

It was difficult to even remember. "I didn't know what the hell I was doing when I started. I didn't even realize it was going to be a docudrama. I didn't think it was going to be anything. It started as a journal, and became . . ." Jaime trailed off.

Across from him, Scarlett watched him steadily. There wasn't a hint of prompting or pressure from her.

He'd watched footage of her matches on YouTube, and one of the things that impressed him the most about her play was how contained she was, and how patient. High-stakes tournament chess matches could take *hours*—hours to do what the very same players might accomplish in a few minutes in a blitz match.

Whatever else chess was, it was a mindfuck. And Scarlett was obviously extremely good at that side of it. When she wanted to, Scarlett could wait as long as it took for someone to make their move.

She waited for Jaime to be ready, as still as a statue. As if time had ceased to matter.

Finally, he said, "I wanted to—make amends. Dad hurt a lot of people." Even now, years into it, Jaime doubted that he'd taken the full measure of the destruction. He'd probably never catalog it all.

Scarlett didn't say anything, just kept watching him.

"At first, I was just writing about what I knew had happened, and speculating about what I thought *might* have happened." Since he was saying it out loud, and saying it to someone who actually understood versus an entertainment reporter who didn't know or care about Musgrove at all, the words began to come out in a big rush. "Then I started interviewing people, at least the people who would talk to me, and those who were still alive." Not to mention those who weren't in prison themselves, though Jaime had visited folks in prison, too, as long as they were willing to talk to him. "The more people I talked to, the more I just kept writing. At some point, I looked up and I had hundreds of pages of notes, and I had to decide what the hell to do with it."

With *Queen's Kiss*, he knew exactly what the final product would look like. So much of this was already defined for them. *The Devouring Sun* had been totally different.

That kind of absolute freedom frankly scared the piss out of Jaime. He didn't know if he would ever be brave enough to write something like that again. He'd take the guarantees and certainties of what he and Scarlett were up to here over the amorphous possibilities of that any day.

Scarlett's mouth twisted into a grin. "And so you invented a new form?"

"No. Plenty of films blend fiction and nonfiction. *The Act of Killing*, *Nomadland*, *Four Daughters*. I didn't invent crap." Jaime was always quick to point out the filmmakers whose work he'd built on. Just because *The Devouring Sun* was the first film of this kind some people had seen didn't make it the first one.

"Modesty doesn't suit you."

"Then it's good I'm not being modest."

Scarlett's answering smile indicated she liked that. Scarlett had always reveled in a good back-and-forth. No one he'd known before or since was a better sparring partner than she was. All Jaime's subsequent relationships had been . . . safer. Gentler. But without that tug-of-war, he'd felt as if he were playing at love on easy mode.

Her eyes went nova bright as she said, "You know what we should do? We should watch it."

"Um, do we have to?" Jaime hated watching himself on screen—and hearing his own recorded voice was basically nails on a chalkboard.

Scarlett got to her feet and began hunting around the coffee table for the TV remote. "It'll be fun. You can do, like, a live commentary track. I promise I'll be very impressed."

The look she shot him over her shoulder nearly singed him. He swallowed, hard.

Tossing herself back on her couch, she said, "Resistance is futile, Jaime."

With her, it always was.

She turned on the television and navigated to Videon. Then she pulled up the first episode of *The Devouring Sun* and hit Play. "Here we go."

"Hooray." Jaime didn't try to keep the sarcasm out of his voice.

He'd taken the first shot on his phone, and it showed. The colors were flat, sterile. Jaime was in his father's truck—which was still sitting in the garage at his mom's house, across town—driving down Main Street. The brick facades flashed by on screen, and then Jaime came to a stop at a red light. No one was coming the other direction.

A critic had said that was a metaphor, but Jaime knew he hadn't been that thoughtful.

On the TV, Jaime began speaking. His voice sounded thin and reedy. "My father's family goes way back in Musgrove, Virginia. The town was founded when the railroad was built to connect with a mine in 1882. A Croft was the second mayor of the town. Crofts have sat on the city council and the school board. My dad always took great pride in that history, and he often said that the reason he came back to town after medical school to become a general practitioner was to keep it up. So it was more than a little surprising when he was arrested the week after my high school graduation. He eventually pled guilty to more than eight hundred counts of illegally distributing controlled substances, for which he received a sentence of forty-one years. He lives in the Federal Correctional Institution in Petersburg, and he'll probably be there for the rest of his life."

The streetlight turned green, but before the truck rolled forward, there was a cut to the actors who played his parents, in the actual kitchen of his parents' actual house. Then to the faces of half a dozen people Jaime would interview in the show: a judge, an addiction counselor, several of Dad's "patients," a woman whose husband had died of an oxy overdose.

The speed of the cuts kept accelerating, until the montage felt like a whirlwind. Jaime had no idea how many times he'd reworked this sequence. How many different songs he'd tried under it before he'd chosen this jarring banjo piece.

When they'd acquired the film for distribution, Videon had warned Jaime that this moment—two minutes into a streaming program—was the most important juncture. This was the place where you either kept your audience or they flipped to something else. He'd had to nail this bit.

Jaime had realized then that whatever dreams he had about making art or self-expression or justice, those goals didn't matter for shit if no one stuck around to see the film. It was all well and good to want to say something, but it'd just be a tree hitting the forest floor unless somebody saw it. He wanted them to see it.

Maybe caring about having an audience made him a sellout, but if so, Jaime could live with it.

The title card flashed on the screen, the words stark against the black background. Before it faded, Nettie Gill's voice came on. "Sure, I know Dr. Croft. Everyone knows Dr. Croft."

Scarlett probably knew Nettie. She'd been a teller at the bank, at least until her life had fallen apart, all thanks to Jaime's father.

Off-screen, Jaime's recorded voice said, "What do they know him for, Nettie?"

"He's one of the only doctors in town."

"Is that it?"

She swallowed. "He'll give you whatever you want. If you make it worth his while."

Across from him, Scarlett was watching, rapt. She lifted the remote and paused. Nettie froze midgrimace. How appropriate.

When Scarlett looked at Jaime, the only thing that made the moment bearable was that there wasn't a whiff of pity in her expression. "Why did you decide to start the show this way?"

Jaime had to detach himself from the sick mess of emotions in his gut. Even after years of therapy, the guilt and revulsion that he still felt when he thought about what his dad had done, and Jaime's family's blindness to it, was unbearable.

He drew several sharp breaths before the nausea passed and he could find the words to answer Scarlett's question. "To hook people. And I figured that a son investigating his dad's crimes would be pretty darn hooky." *You can't look away*: that was what all the reviewers had said.

"So you began with your dad's guilt?"

"He did it. That was never a question." Once Jaime had gotten over the shock of it, he'd never once thought that Dad might be innocent. "I wanted to know what caused him to do it."

"Your real question was why?" This seemed to surprise her.

"Yup."

It sounded so cut and dried, but it certainly hadn't felt—and didn't feel—that way. Even now, the things he'd recorded in *The Devouring Sun* made Jaime itchy. Actually, corporally itchy. As if he could've taken a Lava bar into the shower and removed enough of his skin to feel clean again.

The answer that Jaime had uncovered, essentially that his dad had done it because of a mix of greed and hubris, had been so depressing. He'd done it for money? For fucking *money*? How gross.

Many people didn't get that the name of the show was a reference to Icarus.

"We're getting off track," Jaime said. "We need to get back to *Queen's Kiss* and how we want to structure the episodes."

"Hmm." Scarlett tapped the remote on the couch, pondering. "I dunno that I understand my own book well enough to break it down like that, and I wrote it."

"I've got some rough notes, but it may take us a while to wrap our heads around the structure. You know what occurs to me, though: we've both written memoirs."

They'd worked in different mediums, and they'd had different goals. Scarlett had wanted to create institutional change, that was clear. For all that *The Devouring Sun* intersected with questions about the law and policy, Jaime hadn't been trying to say anything about those things. His focus was much smaller, much more personal than that. He'd written the show for himself first, and anything else had come later.

That was why Jaime had wanted *Queen's Kiss* to be his next project, why anything else would've seemed like settling. Because in adapting Scarlett's book with her, he might have his only other shot to answer something large and abstract he hadn't nailed in *The Devouring Sun*: How did you know what had really happened?

"When I was writing *The Devouring Sun*, it was hard for me to know how to tell the truth. To know what the truth even was."

"Well," Scarlett said, "I sure as heck don't know."

"I guess we'll have to figure it out together."

She lifted the remote. "Can you take more of this?"

"I can stand it if you can."

That could be the motto for them working together, really.

When the first episode of *The Devouring Sun* had finished, Scarlett turned the TV off. Jaime was trying to act tough, but he was clearly struggling to watch it, and she didn't want to torture the man. She'd put him through enough.

"Well," Jaime said before trailing off. He was sprawled out on the couch across from hers, his gray Henley riding up to expose several inches of his taut belly, which Scarlett was studiously ignoring.

Most of the time.

It was a cosmic joke that Jaime could've passed for the best-looking guy on the ninth green but had ended up as a writer. Some wires had gotten crossed somewhere along the way, and only a mean and meddling deity could explain it.

Even still, Scarlett could give the guy an out. "I didn't know you worked on *Waverley*." Violet had told her that when they'd been signing the contract. Her agent had been awfully curious who had finally managed to get Scarlett to fork over the rights to her precious book.

Talking about his career—and not his previous film—clearly settled Jaime down. "Zoya Delgado and I met at an incubator for showrunners, and we became friends. Scottish historical romance isn't my normal stuff, but thanks to Zoya, I got to know some execs at Videon, and in the end, that paid off."

Scarlett wanted to ask how much of the steamy stuff he'd written—*Waverley* was awfully sexy—but she knew that she needed to play things closer to the vest. They had a job to do here. She had to stop juggling knives around him, or eventually she was going to drop one and sever a toe.

Jaime scrubbed his hands over his eyes, which pulled his shirt up farther. He'd grown up, that was for sure. Back when she'd been fingering those abs, he'd been as hairless as the statue of David over in Italy. Now, he was all man, with the dusting of dark hair to show for it.

It *really* worked for her.

But she didn't have the time, not to mention the emotional capacity, for it to work for her. They needed to write this show so she could get out of Musgrove and back to her real life.

"So how did you approach *Waverley*?"

"Zoya already had things pretty much worked out," Jaime admitted. "We were just refining her vision. And don't start—I see that taunting smile."

"It was more heckling." *Taunting* was meaner than she wanted to be. Mostly, she just wanted to tease him some.

Tease him in the absolutely most platonic way.

"If I'd been as directive as Zoya, you would've fought me," he said flatly.

"Of course."

"Plus this isn't my story. Tell me this: Why did you write the book?"

"Spite. I had this big blowup with PAWN when they said I hadn't qualified for the last Candidates Tournament, but really, they were punishing me for making a stink about how they run things. My fight with them goes back to my very first tournament, way back in Tokyo."

The tournament she'd left him to play in. The tournament she'd opened a credit card to pay for, maxing it out and risking everything—if she hadn't won enough prize money to pay it off.

That sat between them for a long minute.

"They kept insisting that the restricted league is for women's own good. That without it, no woman could even play at the international level. So I realized that the only way to force their hand was to go public."

"I'm surprised you didn't just announce that they'd agreed you qualified."

"Ha. Well, unlike you, they would've called my bluff."

"How did you know I wouldn't?" Jaime asked.

"I didn't. It was a calculated risk."

"Do you approach everything as if it's chess?"

"When that'll help. Look, chess is about memorization and psychology. There are a finite number of moves on the board. There are only twenty possible openings, for crying out loud. Things get more complicated after that, of course, but if you're willing to study, anyone can become a decent player."

"But not a great one."

Scarlett didn't know what it meant to be a great chess player. Some of the winningest players were also some of the all-time biggest jerkwads. Scarlett was no picnic, but she also wasn't Bobby freaking Fischer.

She shrugged. "Computers have the market cornered on studying. If all we care about is winning, humans should get out of the chess game. I'm not knocking hard work, but I don't want to feel like a machine, you know?" Scarlett knew she was too mercurial, too earthy for that. "My strength as a player comes from my unpredictability."

"The psychology is why you've always refused to play computers." Jaime wasn't asking it as a question. He already knew that was the answer.

"Yup. I like chess because of the human element. I wouldn't want to play against a machine for the same reason I wouldn't want to fuck one." Scarlett rarely cursed outright. She didn't want to give ammunition to people who expected a girl who'd lived in a trailer park to be low class. But since Jaime had heard worse from her before, she chose the most vulgar word possible to bait him.

Only it didn't work quite as well as she hoped, because he didn't get flustered. He just shot those fathoms-deep brown eyes of his to her and said, "Oh, same."

His pronouncement revved her libido out of hibernation as surely as one of those old-fashioned alarm clocks, the ones with the bells on top that could wake the dead. Which made sense: her sex drive had basically been on life support. All Jaime had to do was reference sex and it sat bolt upright.

This is what you've been waiting for: he's the real deal.

The air between Jaime and Scarlett pulsed with heat, so tactile and real that she was almost worried about the coffee table between them bursting into flames.

Yup, they still had it. They would probably always have it. Their attraction was like plastic. It couldn't be destroyed, and it would never degrade. Except there was nothing synthetic about it.

After a moment of letting the heat wash through her body, Scarlett pushed it aside. She had to. It was the third rail of this project, and she wasn't going to touch it.

Tease him about it, sure. Think about it, definitely. But that was where it stopped.

She shook her head, sending a message to herself . . . and maybe also to him. "The point is, I don't accept cheap substitutes." Not anymore, and not ever again.

Jaime scrubbed a hand over his face. "Okay, so we want to put that in the show. The *feeling* of playing in a high-stakes match."

"Maybe not even a high-stakes match, because some of my most memorable games were back when I knew you." While the stuff that had come later had been wonderful, there was something about those early years that had been electric. Maybe it was not knowing if she would reach her goals. Maybe it was not being jaded. Maybe it was everything feeling so flipping fresh. Whatever the reason, when she pictured her wins, it was often those first ones, not the later, bigger ones.

This seemed to amuse him. "You're saying you played matches when you were, like, fifteen that you still think about as much as matches against the world champion?"

"Absolutely."

"That's—good." Suddenly, Jaime sounded very far away. He sat up, which sadly made his shirt fall over his torso.

Goodbye, happy trail.

Jaime began tapping around on the coffee table for his notebook and a pen. He'd gotten some basic yellow legal pads for her, but he still used a black Moleskine notebook with graph paper inside and a Uni-ball Vision pen. He'd mocked her once for not knowing how to pronounce Moleskine, and she'd gotten him back by—

"What if every episode starts in medias res?"

"Yeah, can you translate that for us peasants?"

Jaime shot a glare at her. "You're a genius who's memorized tens of thousands of chess moves and game diagrams."

"But I don't know what in medias res means because I didn't go to college."

"I started at Blue Ridge Community College, and my dad's a felon. Don't go acting like I'm some elitist."

"Some of us are born in the palace, some in the fields."

He rolled his eyes. "In medias res means 'in the middle of things.' So we start in the middle of a game, and it's really immersive. Hyper-close-ups. We see the sweat on your lip, your smeared mascara."

"I wear waterproof for that exact reason."

Now, when Jaime's eyes swept over her, it felt impersonal. He was in director mode now. He wasn't even seeing Scarlett, the woman. He was seeing the show they were going to make.

"Then right as you reach for a piece—"

"Your chess ignorance is abominable."

"—we jump back in time. Weeks, months, we can massage that. But we see you prepping for the match. Or fighting with PAWN. Or whatever else is happening in your life at that time. But the end of the episode catches up with the match we saw at the start. It's like a loop."

Oh, she got it now. "So I have to pick my ten biggest or most important games?"

"Yes. And each one frames an episode."

"I like that." She *really* liked it.

Jaime hadn't heard her, though. He was already working, his hand flying over the page. "Make a list of games," he instructed her, not looking up from his notebook. "Ones that you think might make for a juicy episode—when you were learning, or fighting against something, or when your opponent was especially interesting."

"Ones where I looked super hot?"

"Sure."

But he was so absorbed in his work, he didn't look up. Or maybe he was smarter than she was, determined not to fall into the danger zone again.

"Okay."

And so she got to work.

Chapter 6

Jaime cursed as some of the onions he was sautéing spilled over the edge of the pan, splattering across the cooktop. He was absentminded after a good first day. He and Scarlett hadn't put a single damn word on paper that would be filmed, sure, but they'd made some major decisions.

Across the house, a door opened. Bare feet padded down the hallway, then the front door opened. Was Scarlett . . . leaving?

Jaime turned the heat off and slipped out of the kitchen. In the entryway, Scarlett was collecting an order from a delivery driver.

The guy was getting an eyeful since the strap of her Barbie-pink tank top was falling off one of her shoulders, revealing a glorious expanse of cleavage and sports bra. Paired with skintight leggings it was . . . quite a look. Quite a good look.

With a whoosh, Jaime released a long breath. When they'd knocked off an hour ago, he'd invited her to eat with him, but she'd only said, *We'll see.*

Jaime could've accepted her rejection and retreated. But he leaned against the wall, crossing one leg over the other and effectively blocking her path back to her bedroom. He could at least make her feel guilty about ditching him.

Scarlett gave the driver a wave with her free hand before closing the front door, then jumped when she saw Jaime, almost dropping the white paper take-out bag in the process. "Hot damn."

"You get enough for two?"

She rolled her eyes. "Please, you don't want to eat with me. We've been together all day."

"I wouldn't've offered if I didn't." When Nate and Jaime were writing together, they tended to work more or less around the clock. Jaime had decided that it was his job to make sure they stayed reasonably healthy and took some breaks, and he'd made it Nate's job to track their progress and manage the to-do list.

Jaime needed to figure out how he and Scarlett were going to divide the writing, but he had no idea why dinner couldn't be part of the bargain.

"We don't have to do this."

Setting aside that he wanted to be with her, there were logistic reasons why he'd offered to cook for her. "Do you know how to work the raccoon lock on the trash can?"

"You have a raccoon lock on your trash can?"

"It's the country." He wasn't going to mention the bears. That would make her bolt for sure. "Come eat in the kitchen at the very least." Eating in her room would be like having room service—and everyone knew that sucked. "Then I can show you how the trash works."

For a few seconds, he wasn't sure she was going to agree. Scarlett sometimes seemed almost feral, as if she didn't know how to be with other people. But then she swished off toward the kitchen.

One thing was certain: Scarlett never walked anyplace. Even just crossing the house was an event when she did it.

But now Jaime faced the problem of how long it had been since he'd seen her in the flesh wearing so conspicuously little. So much between them had changed, but the one thing that hadn't, which at this point he might have to admit would *never* change, was how attracted he was to her.

Inside his heart, Scarlett had punched out a cookie-cutter hole that only she could fill. Everyone else he'd tried to fit there hadn't been right. Only Scarlett could stanch that wound.

"Plates?" she asked, blissfully unaware of how he was lusting over her.

"Here. And silverware's in that drawer."

He turned back to the fried rice he was making, grateful that cooking gave him something to do other than feel addlepated.

"There's some beer and wine in the fridge," he offered over his shoulder.

"Nah, I'm still not fully rehydrated from my trip here. I never drink enough water when I'm traveling."

Jaime dumped a bowl of brown rice into the pan where the veggies had been cooking. "How do you feel about our first day?"

"Well, we didn't actually write anything."

He snorted. "You expected us to?"

"At the very least, I thought we'd litter the floor with crumpled-up pieces of paper."

"You've been watching too many movies. You regretting signing up for this?"

That made her roll her eyes. "I might be nervous, Jaime Croft, but I'm not having doubts."

She popped open her take-out container. Of course it was a pulled-pork sandwich from County Grill. That had always been her favorite place in town. Jaime should've thought to suggest it for dinner for both of them last night. Maybe then he could've established a routine where they ate together.

He dumped the sauce into the pan, then transferred a good portion of the fried rice to a bowl and topped it with cilantro and green onions.

Scarlett applauded. "You *can* cook."

"You don't have to sound so surprised."

"Back when I knew you, you couldn't boil water."

"That was seventeen years ago." Once Mom had gotten a job and he'd had to start taking care of Ev on the days when Mom had the late shift, he'd had to learn life skills real quick.

"I'm impressed."

Jaime grabbed a beer from the fridge and sat at the table with his dinner. "You mean that a privileged prick like me isn't a total idiot?"

"I never thought you were an idiot."

That was an answer and a half.

"If your opinion of me was so low, why did you date me?" He threw it out like a lure, half hoping she'd bite and half hoping she'd swim past it.

She surprised the stuffing out of him when she swallowed it whole. "I didn't date you."

"I'm pretty sure the stuff we got up to is what you do with the people you're dating."

"Or the people you're fucking."

He almost choked on his fried rice. She was attempting to rile him. It worked.

After a long sip from his beer, he had himself put back together. "The two sometimes go together."

"Uh-huh."

"But as long as we're on the subject—"

"We aren't."

"You could've fooled me." He had her here, and they both knew it. "So let's clear the air."

"I thought we said no talking about the past."

She had said that—but she'd also started them down this path. He was getting the distinct impression that Ms. Arbuthnot didn't have a clear sense of what she wanted here, which suited Jaime fine. He still hadn't gotten his head on straight since she'd surprised him in the lobby of her building and ripped the rug clean out from underneath him.

"But we haven't really written anything yet. Come on, Scarlett, are you chicken?"

She blinked slowly. Just like when she'd emerged from her car—messy and beautiful—she wasn't wearing a lick of makeup. Her mouth looked so naked like this, without that coat of bright-red armor. She looked so young without it, so like the girl he'd worshipped.

"What do you want to know?" she asked softly.

"Was there any way we could've worked out?"

He wanted to know what she thought about that—and he really, really did not want to know what she thought about that. Because if the answer was yes, if Scarlett said that if he'd gone with her to Tokyo, everything could've been different . . . well, that was the kind of regret that might fester and give him sepsis.

Even if Jaime knew there were no guarantees in life. Even if there was no way to be sure what might have happened in some multiverse world where he'd been a totally different person who could've abandoned his family in their greatest hour of fucking need. Even with all that, he would have a lot of trouble moving on if she thought there had been as much as a sliver of a chance.

But then she gave the answer that he wanted even less than yes.

"Nah. We were doomed from the start." Scarlett shook her pretty head. "From that very first moment in English, we were gasoline and a match. We should've stayed away from each other."

Wanting to wash down the arguments that were rising in his throat, Jaime drained his beer and grunted. He sounded petulant and stubborn and pissed off, which wasn't far from the truth.

Even if he could go back, knowing how it was going to end, knowing how many years it was going to take to pick himself up off the dirt, Jaime would've signed up to relive it all over again. That was how good it had been.

Scarlett shot those green eyes of hers at him. She knew he was barely restraining himself from arguing with her.

"You think I'm wrong?" she asked.

Jaime honestly didn't know. He didn't like the idea that there had been no chance for them, and he hated the idea that they could've made it. "I don't mean to be starry eyed, but we couldn't have stayed away from each other."

He and Scarlett had had the kind of chemistry people wrote songs and movies about. The kind that made Neanderthals paint on cave walls and medieval fiefdoms start wars. Teenagers just weren't equipped not to give in to that kind of temptation. No one was.

It would have been good *not* to have the accident, sure, but he and Scarlett had been eighteen-wheelers facing off down on a single-lane road. Their crash had been unavoidable.

Even now, he watched her swallow in response to his words. Watched the small movements of the muscles of her jaw, watched her throat work, watched her draw in a deep breath, and watched her chest swell as a result, and every memory was there, as fresh as the day he'd formed them. Scarlett under him: her stomach's soft skin pressing into his, her warmth pouring into his hands, her breath roaring in his ears.

It was the kind of recollection he hadn't taken out often, worried it might fade if he handled it too much. And it was good to keep some things as vivid as when they'd happened.

Scarlett was desire, and she was tenderness, and she was intimacy. The kinds he hadn't known before or since and might not know ever again. Scarlett was what an art professor he'd taken a class from had called sui generis. One of a kind.

No, even knowing that he couldn't keep her, he still would've wanted to have her.

"Was it worth it?" she asked.

Ah, so they both had things they couldn't help but wonder about. That was a relief.

"Yup. Was it worth it for you?"

She pulled her feet up to the edge of the chair and wrapped her arms around her knees. There was something youthful in that pose. It made this night feel timeless. As if it could've been in the past or the future or any point in between.

"I'm not good at romance," she said after a long pause. "At forming connections. I'm a total maverick."

Which was absolute bullshit. "You had plenty of friends back then. Emery what's-her-name, and that Finn guy."

"They were more lunch buddies than true friends—and I haven't talked to them in seventeen years."

"Because you left without a backward glance."

He didn't blame her exactly. Musgrove had not been friendly to Scarlett back then. For all that the town prided itself on being friendly, it wasn't always *welcoming*, and Scarlett had been an outsider.

"In the chess world," Scarlett said, "I am . . . not popular. I have a little circle of chess outcasts I occasionally chat with—but if I didn't go back to New York, if I gave up playing, I bet we'd lose touch too."

"You don't know that," he said reflexively. But Jaime had to remind himself he didn't know her anymore. Still, he wanted to go to battle over her self-perception. She ought to understand that people cared about her. Otherwise, her life might feel lonely, and it didn't need to. "You have this warped notion of how people respond to you, and you use that to justify whatever you were going to do already."

It was like knowing the answer before you did the experiment. No, it was even worse. Scarlett was shaping the experiment to confirm her hypothesis. Pushing her thumb on the scale until it registered the number she wanted. It took a will of iron to make the world the way you wanted it to be, but it also wasn't very honest.

Across the table from Jaime, anger smoldered in Scarlett's eyes. "Because I know myself. I know I have to take care of myself because no one will do it for me."

"Maybe because you won't let us."

At that, Scarlett snapped to her feet and began scooping up her trash. "I told you earlier, I don't want to rehash the past."

"Okay. After tonight, I won't ask." He would try not to, anyhow. "But I have to know: How serious were you about asking me to come to Japan? If I had said yes, would you have been disappointed?"

Those days were such a smear of emotions, Jaime didn't trust his own memories. What had been real, and what had he added after the fact? He had no idea. But he didn't like how simple Scarlett seemed to be trying to make things—and how pessimistic she was that it ever could've gone down any other way.

Scarlett was facing toward the window with her back to him, and he could see her face reflected in the glass. Against the inky night, she glowed like a candle.

"I don't know," her reflection told him.

"Yes you do. You *always* know." Because she was always in control. Always acting deliberately.

He trusted her recollection more than he did his own. He was the emotional one, the impulsive one. Everyone would look at them and think he was predictable, professional. He was the filmmaker controlling every detail, planning everything in advance, and she the mercurial chess champion, the one who sparked like a live wire, sometimes dazzling her opponents and sometimes detonating like a percussion shell.

But they both knew the truth: when Scarlett blew, she meant to, while Jaime acted on impulse that most people wrongly understood to be deliberate.

"If I answer," she asked, "you'll let it go?"

"Yes."

He had to. This had to be the only moment when they exhumed the dead. His heart wouldn't be able to take it otherwise.

Slowly, very slowly, she turned.

He wasn't going to get used to seeing her again, that much he knew now. She was still going to take his breath away every time. The cream of her skin. The arch of her brows. The declaration of her nose. The pout of her mouth. No other face was ever going to mess him up like this. Snare him this tight. This was *the* face of his life. Always had been, always would be.

"I meant it, Jaime. But I was a kid, and it was a mistake. If you think I did a number on you when I left—it would've been even worse later on."

And there it was.

At least at the time, she'd thought they had a chance. At least at the time, she'd wanted him.

His head was a squall: all winds and rains and everything upside down.

"Thank you for . . . answering," he managed. "I've always wondered."

"Stop wondering. Stop thinking about it. Those days, they're over. When I'm playing in a match, I have to let each move go as soon as I've made it. Once I release the piece, there isn't right, there isn't wrong. I can only play the board that I have now, not the one I might have had if I made different choices."

"No regrets?"

"No regrets."

But he didn't believe she lived that motto. Not for an instant. Scarlett analyzed every move later; of that he was sure. How else would she improve?

It wasn't his job to pry or accuse her of lying, though. He'd asked a question, and she had answered. That had to be good enough.

"Well, I have some regrets," he said at last. "And one of them will be that I didn't believe you when you invited me. I couldn't have gone, regardless, but . . . I'll always wish I did."

Jaime wasn't as good as Scarlett at keeping emotions off his face or from influencing his decision-making. He was always going to be softer, always going to be more open. And that was why he would always be fascinated by her. She was everything he wasn't. Everything he would always want.

"You didn't, though. So let it go. I know that we're going to write about the past, but we have to start pretending it happened to other people. Otherwise we'll get burned again."

Then she was gone.

Chapter 7

Scarlett didn't want to be the type of person who always assumed everyone was staring at her. How cringe. But when everyone in the Kellysville Harris Teeter was blatantly gawking at Scarlett and Jaime, she didn't have to pretend to be modest anymore, did she? She never should've agreed to eat her meals with Jaime. Then she never would've come with him on this errand.

"I don't want to alarm you," Scarlett said to Jaime under her breath, "but we seem to have become zoo animals."

An older white man had parked his cart next to a stack of apple boxes. He'd crossed his arms one over the other on the handle and was chewing a piece of gum and baldly watching them.

This was worse than *The Metamorphosis*. At least Gregor Samsa had woken up in his own bed.

For his part, Jaime was unperturbed by the attention. He was calmly sifting through a bin of romaine lettuce, trying to find the best one. "If they are, it's because of that *Vogue* spread."

At that, Scarlett's attention snapped back to Jaime, from the nosy man. "Oh, so you saw the *Vogue* spread?"

"It's seared on my retinas, woman."

Scarlett knew she was a pretty girl, and she had cleavage for days. Why all the Victoria's Secret models hadn't been plus size, she would never know. It was easier to flaunt it if you had it, and Scarlett had it.

Except posing for those pictures was one thing. Knowing Jaime had seen them . . . that was another.

Wanting to focus on his awkward feelings and not hers, Scarlett drawled, "It's the one with the giant pawn that really stuck with you, isn't it?"

The image had been in black and white, with Scarlett sprawled out behind a seven-foot model of a pawn, wearing approximately $10.6 million in borrowed Harry Winston jewels—and only Harry Winston jewels. The pawn had kept it on this side of porn, but if it slipped over the line, well, it was *classy* porn.

Jaime began coughing violently.

"It was all lighting and Photoshop," she assured him.

Jaime moved from the lettuce to a bin full of melons. From how closely he was inspecting them and from how tightly his hands were clenched, Scarlett could be forgiven if it seemed as though he was determinedly *not* looking at her—but that was probably wishful thinking.

"It wasn't all lighting," he finally got out.

If Jaime had been anyone else, she would have started joking that he thought she was cute . . . but that would've been too far and too much and too mean. And Scarlett was trying so hard not to be mean.

She was also trying darn hard not to think about how he'd obviously spent a lot of time with her nearly naked high-fashion spread.

Changing the subject, Scarlett gestured at the produce section. "What can I grab?"

She wasn't used to full-size grocery stores. The aisles of her local bodega were so comfortably snug. This was a lot of space for untrusting eyes. The nosy man had finally moved on, but that woman over there by the pickles, the one glaring at Scarlett, she might have been their gym teacher. Just looking at her evoked the pulsing refrains of *Jock Jams*.

Scarlett offered her a jaunty wave and a smile. In response, the maybe gym teacher only glared harder.

"I'd forgotten how friendly Musgrove is," Scarlett muttered.

Jaime glanced up, and after a jolt—seriously, that woman could give anyone the creeps—he made his own half wave. "They're real good at the welcome wagon here."

For an instant, Scarlett thought he might throw an arm over her shoulders as a gesture of support . . . and Scarlett almost wanted him to.

Instead, Jaime said, "How about you get some baby carrots?"

"If you keep eating those by the handful, the bottoms of your feet are going to turn orange," she warned.

"That's a risk I'm willing to take."

When Scarlett returned to the cart, Jaime was loading it up with apples and oranges and potatoes. But then, someone even scarier than the gym teacher walked into the grocery store.

Jaime's mom was wearing a pink sweater set and khakis, and she still had the Dooney & Bourke purse and the gold tennis bracelet and the serene smile. The picture of the perfect suburban wife, except for the fact that her husband lived at FCI Petersburg now.

"Your mother is approaching us," Scarlett muttered under her breath.

"That she is," Jaime said cheerfully. "Hey, Mom!"

"Jaime." She accepted a hug from her son. Over his impressive shoulders, she locked eyes with Scarlett. "And Scarlett Arbuthnot. Back in Musgrove."

Scarlett would've expected—and would've deserved—a frosty glare, but Mrs. Croft always had had an impressive poker face. Her look was carefully, beautifully neutral. Being able to summon that expression was probably a requirement for joining the Junior League.

"Mrs. Croft. It's—" Scarlett let her voice drop out there for a minute. She had no idea how to characterize this moment. It certainly wasn't *nice*, but *surreal* or *painfully odd* weren't polite. "—to see you."

Jaime's mom almost snorted, picking up on exactly what Scarlett had done and why. One thing was for sure: the woman had never been stupid. For all that Jaime thought his mother hadn't known that her son was sleeping with a girl from the wrong side of the tracks, Scarlett had been certain Mrs. Croft had seen right through his attempts to hide things.

Scarlett respected the heck out of her shrewdness, even as she bristled at being the object of Mrs. Croft's skepticism. Maybe if things were different, she and Mrs. Croft could've been friends.

And then surely the area's pigs would've taken to the skies and migrated to Saint Lucia for the winter.

"How long are you back for?" Mrs. Croft asked.

"Two months," Scarlett said. "Just enough time to write the scripts." *And then I'll leave again, for good this time. Promise.*

"The writing's going well," Jaime lied. "Scarlett's a natural."

Oh, he might be risking hell for that one. Scarlett had no idea what she was doing, other than distracting Jaime.

"That doesn't surprise me at all. Scarlett has many gifts," Mrs. Croft said tactfully. "Congratulations on the women's world championship. I was sorry to hear you lost the title two years later."

"Actually, I refused to defend it." Scarlett sounded defensive, but honestly, she hadn't lost her title, in the sense that no one had taken it from her. Not playing was quite different from not winning. "It was a protest to get PAWN to eliminate the gender division in chess."

"Won't that hurt the women's game?"

"Not necessarily. There are different ways they could handle things." They could divide the leagues by Elo ratings rather than by gender. Something like over and under 2700, for example.

But Scarlett found that older women were more likely to believe that a gendered division in sports was a good thing. The argument that it wasn't—let alone that having two binary categories might not make space for everyone who wanted to play—didn't always go over well.

Scarlett had tried to understand it a hundred times, but the women who'd seen Billie Jean King win the Battle of the Sexes before triumphantly returning to the women's game often couldn't understand Scarlett's goals. They thought she had been trying to prove she was as good as the men, when really, Scarlett wanted to obliterate those false divisions in the first place.

"I see." Mrs. Croft turned her attention back to her son. "Maisie mentioned that you found a replacement T-ball coach for them."

"Well, I knew I couldn't do the spring season, so it only seemed fair that I find someone else."

"You coach *T-ball*?" Scarlett asked. She really ought to be trying to cut this conversation short, but she wasn't prepared to let that fly by without comment.

"It's something of a family tradition," Jaime said as he shared a long look with his mother.

"Well, Maisie's real grateful." Her gaze moved over her son. "You look thin. I should bring you a lasagna."

You, because she would clearly only be bringing a lasagna to Jaime. Or maybe she just didn't think Scarlett looked thin.

"I can handle making one, if it comes down to it," Jaime said gently.

Scarlett knew he could. He'd cooked for her since she'd arrived—that one night of DoorDash aside—and it had been a nice change of pace. Scarlett had done most of the cooking for her mom and herself when she'd been young, but that had mostly meant hot dogs and coleslaw. When it came to lasagna, the Arbuthnot way was to buy a Stouffer's, take it out of the box, and pop it into the oven, which, by the way, worked fine. You still had a lasagna at the end.

"Hmm." That was clearly Mrs. Croft's version of *bless your heart*, and she brandished it the way other people did a seven iron. She ought to have shouted *Fore!* first.

In some other reality, Mrs. Croft and Scarlett could've been very good friends. In this iteration of the multiverse, though, Scarlett had wrecked Mrs. Croft's life.

Mrs. Croft turned back to Scarlett. "Well, I wish you . . . luck."

"Thanks." But Scarlett did her best not to rely on luck. It was a fickle gremlin.

The next day, the early afternoon sun had the wooden floor of Jaime's den glowing red like a moon from *Star Wars*. Scarlett opened her mouth to say something about it to Jaime, but she swallowed the observation when she realized he was working. Of course she would be the one who was pretending to work while he was actually getting stuff done.

It was her sixth day in Musgrove, and Scarlett wasn't feeling any better at this screenwriting stuff. She had difficulty working with other people around. She liked people fine, even if they made her feel like an alien who'd never fully acclimated to human ways. But it was hard to lose herself in studying or writing if she had an audience.

Playing a game of chess was the rare exception to that rule, but despite being public, she was still constantly choosing which parts to show to the world and which to keep private.

From that first international tournament, Scarlett had cultivated a facade she could put on in public. If she flashed a sexy smile now and again, rolled her hips when she walked, and set her shoulders at a coy angle, everyone seemed to fall at her feet. The act kept people off balance and dizzy around her, and that allowed Scarlett to be in control. But damn if it wasn't a lot of work to maintain.

Jaime didn't have a persona. He could just be *himself.* Maybe that was why he was able to get lost in his work and act as if he were in the room alone.

"How's it going?" he asked, looking up at last.

Scarlett set her hand over the yellow legal pad, which she'd filled with scribbles. "Okay."

His eyes crinkled. "You didn't get jack, did you?"

She hated that she could be so transparent to him. "Nope."

"Let's take a walk."

"Excuse me?"

He stood up and rolled his shoulders. "We've been at this for, like, three hours, and we need a break. I am going to get some fresh air. If I stay inside too long, my brain gets stale."

Back in New York, she went for long walks every day, but the air in Central Park West was not notably *fresh*. "Does hiking help?"

"It does for me. Nate goes for long showers. Zoya Delgado likes meditation. You have to find your thing."

Scarlett's thing was usually forcing herself through every permutation, grinding herself through it until she figured it out or snapped. That didn't sound too good, now that she put it together like that. "Hmm."

Jaime stretched, and several of his joints cracked. "Come with me. You need an infusion of vitamin D more than anyone I've ever known."

That didn't seem to be a double entendre—which was a crying shame.

"Well, I'll try anything once," she said.

Ten minutes later, Scarlett found herself scrambling up a rock and regretting her willingness to give this a whirl.

"A new thought is coming to me," she huffed out.

Jaime wasn't even winded. Before they'd left, he'd put on an Avett Brothers ball cap and sunglasses—and it was unfair how good he looked.

"For the first episode?"

"For kicking your butt."

"You're smiling, though. It can't be all bad."

That was just because out here, it smelled like pines and it was good not to be sitting on that couch in his den. But admitting that would only make Jaime more smug, and he was already approaching dangerous levels of it.

"Next time, we're breaking up the monotony of not writing with a game of chess." At least she was good at chess.

Jaime started down the trail—which wasn't even a real graded trail as much as a break in the trees and ferns. It had probably been foraged by deer or bigfoot or something. "I still don't understand how the horses move, by the way," he called to her over his shoulder.

That was an old, old joke of his, one that Scarlett had corrected and explained more times than she could count. Whether Jaime had forgotten or whether he was teasing her, she didn't know.

"At this point, you should just double down on your ignorance. Think how amused all the TV critics would be if you told them that you can't set up a chess board."

She'd tried to teach him to play many times, but it had never worked out because she'd always ended up flat on her back on the board—and not at all sorry that the pieces were scattered all over the floor.

The man had other talents than chess, that was for sure.

"We'll put it in the press packet that I can't tell a bishop from a rook. That's why I have you."

Scarlett let that one whoosh past her, but there was one thing she was curious about: "Why did you want to option my book if you don't care about chess?"

If she had more self-confidence, maybe she'd take it for granted that *Queen's Kiss* was innately interesting, but for all that she was supposed to be the most conceited person on the planet, Scarlett didn't. She knew why *she* was fascinated by chess, but when you were that chess weirdo who could frequently tell you were boring everyone around you by ruminating on the history of castling, you could either delude yourself or admit you were an acquired taste.

"Like I said the other day, I think we're both really interested in the truth."

Scarlett didn't want to go down any paths with him that were marked *Honesty*. If only he knew all the stuff she was keeping from him . . .

"I don't think 'truth' is something I discuss in *Queen's Kiss*."

He stopped for a second and considered their path. After a second, he pointed and took off again. "If you want to change chess—and clearly you do—you must buy your version of things, at least compared to PAWN's version. That seems like an argument about accuracy."

No one could trust PAWN's version. Their version was exclusionary—and also it sucked.

"And look, beyond that," Jaime went on, "chess is a metaphor. I don't have to understand the intricacies of the game to know that."

"The intricacies? My dude, you don't know the basics."

"Fair enough. But I care about you." After a beat he added, "As a protagonist."

Not wanting to hint that she felt overwhelmed by what he'd unknowingly said, Scarlett replied in her most obnoxious tone, "So true. I am very interesting."

But Jaime didn't take the bait. He stopped and turned to watch her. When he spoke again, he was completely serious. "Your voice is very powerful, Scarlett. On screen, your story is going to be electric. That's why I wanted the book."

Scarlett wanted to touch her neck, to twist her hair between her fingers, to look away, to make another joke. The last few days, she'd found herself in conversations like this, ones that were too personal, too revealing. She'd finagled herself into this so she could help adapt her memoir. Not to bare her soul with her ex.

"So is it chess itself that drives you, or is it the winning?"

That . . . was unexpected. It was the kind of question Scarlett should want Jaime to ask. It wasn't about their past. It wasn't too personal and therefore dangerous. It was related to the entire reason they were here, and it would help him write the show better.

But his question disappointed her for being safe. For being on topic.

God, she was a mess.

Scarlett looked deep into the trees. A few yellow and brown leaves were still clinging on here and there, but mostly, the forest was a thicket of bare, twisted branches, stark against the pines. "I'm not sure I can separate the two. I loved chess, and I wanted to not be poor. At first, chess took me out of where I was. It was cheap to play. It wasn't like riding lessons or even tennis." Things that other kids did but she could never dream about. Heck, even horse toys had been too expensive for her to dream about. Her mom had found one of those Breyer models at the Salvation Army once, and for all that the hooves and mane were chipped, Scarlett had loved the heck out of it.

She wiped her eyes. The walk had made them watery. Scarlett hoped Jaime hadn't noticed.

"I could get all the chess books I could read at the library." The libraries in the towns where she and her mom had lived hadn't bought many new books since the 1990s, but they often had shelf after shelf of ancient chess-strategy books. Ones that treated the Soviet Union as a clear and present danger, sure, but the basics were the same. "And even I could afford to get a chess board at a secondhand store."

Thank God the first set she'd bought for fifty cents hadn't been missing any pieces. They were hollow plastic and weighed so little that they'd move around if you sneezed. But that hadn't mattered, not in the least.

"Then I started winning tournaments, and the prize money was enough to buy some luxuries." In high school, she'd purchased all her own clothes, and she'd been able to contribute to the grocery money. That admission was too bald, too embarrassing, to make out loud, though. The shame wouldn't have only tainted Scarlett; it would've splashed over her mom too.

Alma might not have been much of a parent, or much of an employee. But she'd loved Scarlett, and she'd done the best she'd known how to, to feed and care for them both. If, in maturity and competence, she was more like a little sister to Scarlett than a mother, well, that was just how it went sometimes.

The smile Scarlett was able to summon at the memories wasn't faked. All of this—it felt like a win. It had been a win. "As I got better, this world spread out in front of me: eating in actual restaurants, getting to travel overseas, having my picture in magazines, receiving free designer dresses, becoming a celebrity. The works! And I had to seize that with both hands. I know that you think . . ."

Actually, Scarlett had no idea what Jaime thought. Based on his questions earlier this week, it was something he pondered frequently and was still broken up over, but she hadn't been able to indulge in the same what-ifs. She wasn't being a brat, even. She simply hadn't had the same choices he had.

"But I had to take it. I never considered not leaving."

Jaime hadn't asked about that directly today, but she knew what he'd asked today was connected to what he'd asked her the other night.

And he needed to understand it. They both did.

In leaving Musgrove, Scarlett had saved herself. She'd saved her mom. And whatever it had cost her, it had been worth it.

"I understand," he said gently. "I just wish I could've gone with you."

That calm resignation and acceptance pissed her off more than if he had argued with her. But since Scarlett didn't want to contemplate *why* she was mad at him, she said, "Time for us to get back to that fancy house of yours."

Chapter 8

"So you wish they *hadn't* green-lit your series. Is that what you're saying?" Zoya Delgado, Jaime's friend and another showrunner for Videon, didn't bother to keep the incredulity out of her voice.

Jaime wouldn't have, either, if the situation had been reversed. He lifted the phone from his ear to bop his head against one of the kitchen cabinets a few times. Yup, he made no damn sense. "I'm floundering. I feel like I don't know what I'm doing."

He and Scarlett had been working for a week now, and they still didn't have a single usable page written. They were going to have trouble hitting their deadline if they didn't crack this egg soon.

Instead of doing his damn job, Jaime had found himself fixating on the past . . . and lusting in the present. It was dumb and unprofessional, and he needed to stop doing it.

"Of course you know what you're doing. You do realize that thousands of other people would do serious crimes to be where you are?" Zoya asked, stating the obvious.

"Yup." Once upon a time, Jaime would've been one of them.

"You said to me, several months ago, 'This is the only project I want next.' You told me your only backup plan was to get into hemp farming."

"Hey, that wasn't a half-bad idea." Jaime had spent an entire sleepless night researching hemp cultivation on the internet. It wasn't clear whether it was a con or a high-growth industry where he could get in on the bottom floor.

"It was an *entirely* bad idea. But I didn't call you to hear about how hemp is the cash crop of the future."

"It is, though."

"Get over your existential crisis, Croft. You're a pro. You got this. Now that the pep talk is over, here's the real reason I called: I found the perfect girl for you."

Jaime almost said *I don't want a girl* before he realized Zoya wasn't offering to set him up on a date with someone: she'd found him an actress.

And despite the fact he still didn't have anything close to a finished script, something inside him—some small ambitious scrap—sat up. "For *Queen's Kiss*?"

"Yup. We're auditioning for season four of *Waverley*, and she wasn't right for us, but she's got the exact energy for Scarlett—and she's from North Carolina, so her accent is perfect."

"She couldn't handle the brogue?"

"I wouldn't let an American affect a brogue on set—I'd get raked across the coals by the Scots more than I already do." *Waverley* was a hit everywhere except Scotland, where Zoya had been accused of turning their history into soft-core porn.

Oh well. Everyone was a critic.

"Anyhow, her name is Clara Hess. She's a vivacious strawberry blonde with a southern accent who you can't help but root for. And she's super smart. I'd have no problem believing that this woman could be a chess grand master. If you don't get her on contract stat, I swear to God I will write something else for her just so that I can use her."

He knew Zoya would do it too.

"Can you send her agent's info to Nate?"

"Yes. But you need to get her to do a reading in the next few weeks or someone else will snap her up."

"I appreciate the heads-up." This was good on several levels. Jaime needed a deadline. Nothing got words flowing like the promise of contract or production consequences.

"Of course. Why isn't Nate there, keeping you on task?"

"He's busy."

Which . . . wasn't entirely true. Jaime had asked Nate not to come.

Jaime's producing partner was the rare person he could stand during the writing process. Nate was funny, self-sufficient, good at everything, and an excellent sounding board. That was why they'd been working together since they'd met in college.

But this time, Jaime couldn't have been clearer if he'd hired a skywriter: he wanted to be alone with Scarlett. He wasn't going to parse why he felt so strongly about that. It was locked behind a door labeled *Here Be Monsters*.

"Busy with what?" There was a teasing note in Zoya's tone—an entire teasing symphony, in fact. The woman had been writing and directing romances for too long.

Jaime had successfully hidden his history with Scarlett from Nate and Videon, but he probably hadn't managed to keep the glow out of his voice enough to fool Zoya. The woman was like a bloodhound when she got a whiff of romantic potential—potential generally, but romantic potential *specifically*.

Her ability to see who would be good with whom was why she was so good at casting. If she said Clara Hess was the real deal to play Scarlett, then she was. But Zoya's prognostication was a problem for Jaime because he'd rather keep his pointless pining for Scarlett to himself.

"Nate's mentoring some film students from USC." Which was true, though it wasn't the real reason he hadn't come to Virginia. "Anyhow, thanks again for the tip about Clara."

"Anytime. And you'll crack the scripts. I know you will."

Jaime sent a quick text to Nate—I'm going to get you some pages by Monday so you can schedule a reading for an actress Zoya found—and he found himself feeling better. Zoya was one of the hardest working and most talented people he knew. If she had confidence that Jaime would figure it out . . . well, then he'd probably manage to do it.

A glance at the clock confirmed that it was nearly nine—his prearranged breakfast time with Scarlett. The thump of bare feet in the hallway followed a second later.

"Morning, sunshine," Jaime said as Scarlett stumbled into the kitchen.

Over the first week of working together, she'd abandoned more of her polished facade. Today, she had on what he now knew were her favorite plaid pajama bottoms, topped with a torn *Achtung Baby* sweatshirt, and not so much as a lick of makeup. She hadn't bothered with her contacts yet, and she was blinking behind her thick-framed glasses. It made her look so young that his heart double pumped for a few beats.

Like a time traveler whose machine had glitched, Jaime was stuck in two moments. His emotions were those of a naive seventeen-year-old who had no idea why he shouldn't sink into his crush on her, and the rest of him was a jaded thirty-three-year-old who realized that was fucking stupid.

Somehow, he had to get all of himself into the present and toughen the heck up. Then the words would be bound to start flowing.

Jaime pushed a mug across the counter toward her. She accepted it with an incoherent "Gah" that he understood as thanks. In the last few days, as they'd lurched toward something like a routine, he'd learned she started the morning bleary eyed and silent until he poured approximately one and a half pots of coffee into her.

He could almost watch Scarlett come back to herself, milligram by milligram, as she consumed caffeine. It was a relief, honestly. The quiet, vulnerable version of Scarlett freaked him out. Made him feel protective. He much preferred the version of herself that she turned into midmorning, the one who was utterly willing to sink her claws into Jaime if he stepped so much as a toe out of line. The self-aware, strategizing genius who could outthink anyone around her—that was the woman he wanted to write with and about.

He picked up the bowl of oatmeal he'd abandoned when Zoya had called him, and for a few minutes, Jaime chewed and Scarlett sipped in peace. It was easy in moments like this to pretend there was some version of them that could be friends, if nothing else, but then he would remember that she had a world championship to win. That she'd only agreed to let him adapt her book in order to stick it to PAWN. That once the show filmed, he'd never see her again.

Which was sufficiently sobering to get him back, all in one piece, to this moment.

When he'd finished his breakfast, rinsed his dishes, and put them in the dishwasher, he leaned against the counter and watched his writing partner. Her eyes were a tiny bit more focused now, which soothed Jaime.

"Were you talking to someone?" she asked.

"Zoya Delgado. She wanted to pass along a tip about an actress." When Scarlett didn't respond to that, he asked, "You sleep okay?" That seemed a safe enough question to broach. He would've asked Nate the same thing if he'd been here.

Scarlett drained her cup and pushed it toward him. "Still adjusting to the quiet."

Jaime filled her cup again. She took her coffee black, which made him feel like a wimp since he doctored his with loads of cream and sugar. "You'll probably get used to the country again about the time we wrap up."

Scarlett smiled into her coffee cup, and Jaime would've been jealous, but of course, he'd put the brew in there. So it was kind of *his* smile.

"Maybe. Are we going to get some words down today?" she asked.

Dear Lord, he hoped so.

"I wanted to run something by you. What if we make the protagonist of the show . . . not you?"

Scarlett huffed out a laugh. "Um, isn't it an adaptation of my memoir? How could the protagonist be not me?"

"She could be thinly fictionalized. It'd give you a little privacy."

And it might unstick Jaime. Ever since Scarlett arrived in Musgrove, he'd become obsessed with what was real and not real, and it was getting in the way of writing. If they washed her stories with a rinse of fiction, he might be able to stop autopsying the past—hers and theirs.

"You were complaining the other day that everyone sees the book as confessional—"

"They just mean it was written by a woman."

"—and if the show isn't about you, then they'll stop saying that."

Scarlett considered this for several long seconds. "Maybe it also lets us reset."

"Not get hung up on what's true or not?" Both with the show . . . and with them.

"Yup."

Jaime could only hope this was what they needed. "Get some breakfast, and then we'll start. We need some pages by next week so we can test this actress."

Uncharacteristically docile, Scarlett accepted a bowl of fruit and some yogurt from Jaime. He'd convinced her it probably wasn't a good idea to have all that coffee on an empty stomach. But despite all the crap he'd spewed about nutrition, he knew his motives were entirely selfish. They were getting off to a slow start here, and Jaime needed them healthy and rested if they were going to meet their deadline. Anything less would make him a piss-poor leader.

After they'd worked all day, stopping only for lunch, Jaime glanced up from his laptop. Scarlett had sent him a batch of pages, and now she was doodling on a whiteboard that he'd picked up from Ev's house yesterday.

"Is that a middle finger?"

"It seemed classier than writing *Aldo Rivera, go fuck yourself*."

"I still cannot get over the fact that you said that to the president of PAWN."

"If you aren't willing to say it to someone's face, it'd be rude to write it down." She gave Jaime a guileless look, as if to say *Duh*. "He told me the fact there are only forty living women grand masters, compared to seventeen hundred men, proves women can't compete with men. He's lucky I *only* told him to go fuck himself."

"Why didn't you try to charm him?" Scarlett was plenty good at pouring honey over her voice and manners when she wanted to, certainly.

"He didn't deserve it. You can't corral the women in their own tournament and then complain we face less competition. That's not fair, and it's not logical—and he wants me to buy that men are better at impartiality and logic. If he believes women can't compete, let us try it. If he's right, we're just going to lose. But the men don't want us to, so PAWN had to invent a convoluted fairy tale to justify being dumbasses instead. I knew I wasn't going to be able to sweet-talk someone like that into the real championship game."

"But telling him to fuck off didn't get you into it either."

"Sure, but nothing I could've done would've. And being a brat got me and my argument into every paper in the world."

Every moment of Scarlett's life was like that, Jaime had realized. She was better than anyone he'd ever known at analyzing her situation, seeing what the rules and the variables were, and figuring out what she needed to do *now* in order to get what she wanted several moves down the road. It was how she approached chess, but it was also how she lived her life.

It was mesmerizing as heck, but he also got the sense it was exhausting. How many balls did Scarlett have in the air at this moment, how did she keep track of them, and did she ever drop one?

"How *are* you going to get into the open-division championship game?" he asked.

Her eyes went to the window, as if she were watching something approach from a distance. Something glimmering and rare and worth waiting for. "You'll see."

And Jaime was . . . breathless.

All Scarlett had to do was flash that confidence of hers and he lost his mind. It was science. With that expression on her face, he'd be damned if she weren't the most beautiful woman in the world.

Which was the kind of thought he only ought to have in the context of writing Emily, the fictional veil they'd invented for Scarlett. He needed to channel all those feelings into writing *Emily*.

Maybe tomorrow he'd manage it.

"I'm certain I will. Let's knock it off for the day," he said lightly, getting to his feet.

"You sure?" She trailed him into the kitchen.

"Yup. I'm making burgers."

"I can cook, you know."

Back when they'd been in high school, she'd basically made every meal she and her mom had eaten, though those had been mostly sandwiches, and Lean Cuisines when they were on BOGO special. She'd been especially good at getting the skin of hot dogs crispy. He'd honestly never met anyone who cooked a better hot dog in his life.

These days, he got the sense that she mainly survived because of New York's army of delivery drivers. But since she'd told him she frequently studied twelve hours a day to prepare for a tournament, he could understand. If the delivery options were any good here, he'd probably use them more too—at least when Videon was on the hook for the bills.

"You can make the salad," he told her.

"Promise to not say anything about excessive ranch?"

"My only point was that the lettuce isn't a garnish."

From the smolder in her eyes, Jaime had the sense that if they'd been in the living room, Scarlett would've tapped the middle finger she'd drawn on the whiteboard. "Can it, Croft. I make an exemplary salad."

"Yes, ma'am." Everything she did was exemplary.

In the kitchen, he turned on the tiny TV he'd rescued from his mom's garage. It had literal bunny ears on it, and the picture was kind of fuzzy. He always left it tuned to channel eight, and he only put it on for one hour every day: the one boasting *Wheel of Fortune* and *Jeopardy!*

"I hate these freaking clues," Scarlett said, getting the salad bowl out of the cabinet. She'd begun navigating his kitchen as confidently as if she lived there. "They never make any sense, and they make me feel like an idiot."

Jaime was certain that Scarlett was the smartest person he'd ever known. She certainly had the best memory and the most discipline. But all he said was "*A glamping adventure* isn't the first thing you think of when someone says *Event*?"

"Sadly, no."

As he headed to the fridge to grab the ground beef he'd thawed overnight, Jaime picked up the copy of *Consumer Reports* off the counter. He'd been reading it this morning before Zoya had called. "Here, I dog-eared a page for you."

Scarlett took the magazine from him and read aloud. "Best cell phones for battery life?"

"You mentioned yours kept dying in the middle of the afternoon."

"And you thought this was your problem?"

"No." But Jaime had thought he could help. This was something of a reflex of his, but, well, it was a *good* reflex—just like how he kept tabs on Ms. Winifred, an old "patient" of Dad's who'd just gotten out of rehab for the third time, and on Mr. Jefferies, whose wife had died in November after all their kids had moved away. When you saw that someone needed help, you stepped up. That was the way you kept a community together.

Scarlett flicked her eyes up to him, an amused smile curling on her mouth. "Why the hell do you even get *Consumer Reports*? Does it come standard issue with your AARP card?"

"Habit, I guess."

But two seconds later, when the actual reason hit Scarlett, she didn't try to hide her shock. "It's your dad's subscription, isn't it?"

Moments of emotional realness from Scarlett, the times when she didn't affect a glamorous facade or her "Aww, shucks, me, mister?" mask, still went through Jaime like a shot.

Which was why he gave her the truth. "Yup."

"Does your mom renew it for your birthday every year?" Scarlett had gotten ahold of herself, and the question was light and teasing.

"You joke, but it's helpful."

"Do you clip out articles and mail them to your mom and sister?"

He texted them photos—which Scarlett would probably howl over, so he said nothing.

"An incriminating silence, Mr. Croft." Scarlett picked up a cucumber and set it on the cutting board. But rather than slicing it or continuing to tease Jaime, her tone went serious. "What other duties did you inherit?"

What *hadn't* he inherited? "Mowing their lawn. Doing their taxes. That kind of thing."

"You were just a kid."

Scarlett's statement opened a trapdoor inside Jaime, and a softness he shouldn't feel leaked out. The more time that they spent together, the more it happened. But those tender feelings multiplying in him were like spider crickets, the kind that never stayed in the basement.

Jaime's voice was rough when he said, "Someone needed to take charge, so I did." His mom had always seemed so capable to him that it had chilled Jaime to the bone when he'd realized she'd just let his dad manage so many things that went to the core of her life. Of all their lives.

He'd been so worried he would mess something up at first, but eventually, he'd realized that almost all adults worried they might be messing up pretty much every moment of every day. You just learned to accept the existential fear at some point—and that was the definition of adulthood.

On the day of Dad's arrest, Jaime had been thrust into it sooner than most folks were, that was all. In the end, he discovered he liked dealing with that stuff. It made him feel competent, helpful. It wasn't as if he worried Mom wouldn't love him if he didn't take care of things, but he suspected that his helpfulness didn't hurt.

"You did good, Jaime," Scarlett said, her voice soft and even.

His vision was suddenly blurry, and it took a lot to keep the sob that rose in his throat inside. He hadn't even realized he'd wanted those words, and wanted them from *her*, until she gave them to him.

"Well, I didn't have much choice." It had been like being swept off a boat in a storm. He'd had to paddle for his life.

"You want a beer?" Scarlett asked, as he said, "This calls for a beer."

Yup. He was going to have several, in fact.

She pulled the fridge open and handed him a bottle before grabbing one for herself. "To Jaime," she said, after he'd opened them. "Who turned out to be something of a badass."

"And to Scarlett, who always was one."

The smile she gave him while she drank was dangerous.

The coziness of cooking and watching *Wheel of Fortune* and shooting the shit together might feel right, but these evenings with her were more treacherous than taking a stroll on the railroad tracks. Jaime had barely survived their first encounter. He shouldn't be courting danger a second time—and yet here he was, wining and dining it.

Worse still, some part of him had wanted these nights, with all their seductive peril. When he'd cornered her into writing the show here, *this* was what he'd been angling for.

Because underneath it all, he wasn't very bright.

Chapter 9

Three weeks after returning to Virginia, Scarlett made a catastrophic error: she asked Jaime where he bought the sourdough bread he kept using for sandwiches. She wasn't normally someone who cared about that kind of thing—she sure as heck couldn't tell the difference between a shiraz and a merlot—but it was such good bread that it scrambled her judgment.

"The farmers' market." Jaime's reverent tone had matched the way someone else might say *El Dorado* or *Bloomingdale's clearance shoe sale*.

"Musgrove has one of those?" Back when Scarlett had lived here, there'd been farm stands, but the town hadn't had anything bougie enough to qualify as a market.

"You have to come with me to the next one," he'd insisted.

Despite her intention to put him off, when Saturday morning rolled around, Scarlett allowed herself to be dragged along.

This kept happening. She'd draw a chalk line on the sidewalk and Jaime would skip right on over it as easily as if they were playing hop-scotch. But the worst part was that rather than enforcing the boundary and telling the man to stay on his own damn side, Scarlett would find herself asking *Well, what's the harm?*

The harm was when he grabbed a stack of canvas bags out of his trunk and she said, "Of course you're a PBS donor."

Sweet sardines, she was flirting with him about his reusable bags.

"Oh, it's worse than that—I'm a sustaining member. Those Ken Burns documentaries won't finance themselves." Jaime waggled his brows.

That made parts of Scarlett want to waggle along. She was in a mound of trouble here, and she had no one to blame for it but herself.

But Jaime, who was blissfully unaware of how much grief he was causing her insides, was just pointing to the surprisingly large market. "You wanna start with the baker, or you wanna browse the vegetables?"

Before Scarlett could answer this scintillating query, someone shouted, "Scarlett Arbuthnot, is that you?"

There, at a stand whose sign declared **Bleat Dry Skin, Try Goat Milk Soap!**, a woman was waving at her.

"Emery Cartwright?" Scarlett called back.

Emery had eaten lunch with Scarlett almost every day in high school. She'd helpfully joined Scarlett in hating Jaime when she'd been trying to do that . . . and then had tactfully not mentioned the previous hating after things had changed between Jaime and her. Emery and a sweet, nerdy guy named Finn Lamott, who'd been *way* into *Star Trek*, had been the closest things to friends Scarlett had had back then, and Scarlett had repaid them by not keeping in touch when she'd skipped town.

Oh boy. Emery probably loathed her.

Jaime tipped his head at Scarlett to ask if she wanted to go over there and say hi—but it was entirely too late to run now. She had to face the music.

Scarlett's feet felt heavy as they crossed over to the soap stand. Emery's hair was much longer than it used to be, but she had the same amused gleam in her eye and clearly the same fondness for plaid.

Even more odd was that, when Scarlett got to the stand, Emery wasn't scowling. Indeed, if they hadn't had a folding plastic table between them, Scarlett had the distinct impression that Emery might hug her.

"It's Emery Matthews now." Scarlett's former lunch buddy beamed and held out her left hand. A medium-size diamond sparkled on the fourth finger. "I didn't know you were back in town."

"Yeah," Scarlett said carefully. "Jaime and I are working on some scripts for—"

"*Oh my gosh*, are you adapting *Queen's Kiss*?" Emery squealed at Jaime.

"I am." He gave a modest shrug.

Then Emery did the darndest thing: she started jumping up and down. "I am so excited! It's going to be amazing!"

"You . . . read it?" Scarlett asked, shocked.

"Of course I did! Everyone did!"

That couldn't be right. Scarlett thought no one here beyond Jaime and Evelyn had followed her career. She'd always assumed it would've only made sense to folks here if she'd gone to Nashville. That they might've put up signs declaring the town *Home of the Musgrove High Muskrats and Country Superstar Scarlett Arbuthnot.*

Scarlett *wasn't* sad about the lack of recognition or anything. She didn't want it. And besides, she and Musgrove had always tiptoed past each other, the same way a guard dog and a cantankerous cat kept their distance from each other by mutual agreement.

Except Emery's delight was too genuine to be fake.

"We read it in our book club," Emery was saying. "We would've asked you to be a guest speaker, but we figured you were too busy."

For maybe the first time in her life, Scarlett had no idea what to say. She was still adjusting to the fact that not everyone in Musgrove loathed her—and that, despite Scarlett never giving them a reason to, some of them might have been cheering her on.

"That's . . . flattering," she finally managed.

"Will you come and sign our books?" Emery demanded. "We meet on Tuesdays at the county library. Jaime knows where it is."

"Sure." What else could Scarlett say except that?

Emery was still beaming at Scarlett as if she couldn't believe she was real. And for all that Scarlett was used to being famous, it was uncanny to be treated as if she was by someone she'd known when she was a kid. There was something doubly disorienting about it.

Thank God Jaime never treated Scarlett like that.

"How are things going?" Emery asked Jaime.

"Pretty well. We're screen-testing an actress to play the lead next week."

"Anyone whose name I know?" Emery was almost levitating now.

"No, she's a newbie, but we have high hopes."

"Well, she'll have to be a goddess to play our Scarlett."

Our Scarlett? She wasn't *anyone's*, and she didn't want to be—did she?

Wanting to change the subject, Scarlett interjected, "Didn't you leave for college?"

Back in high school, Emery had been almost as excited to get out of town as Scarlett had been, which was saying a lot. That had actually been the basis for their camaraderie: neither of them had thought Musgrove was nearly as cool as most of the people here did.

Emery nodded. "I did. But after a few years in Richmond, Ben and I wanted a slower change of pace. I'd gotten into soapmaking, and I needed room for some goats." She gestured at the tarp hanging behind her, where she'd tacked up a dozen pictures of different goats.

In her defense, they were extremely cute.

"And nowhere else except Musgrove really felt like home," Emery added.

"Oh, oh—yeah," Scarlett said for lack of a better response. *Home* was one of those words that almost seemed to come from a language Scarlett wasn't fluent in. In the vaguest sense, she knew what other people meant by it, but it was an empty concept to her.

She owned an apartment in New York, but she didn't have any emotional attachment to the place, beyond her pride that she'd earned enough to buy it.

Scarlett cast a glance around the parking lot off Main Street where the farmers' market was being held. She remembered walking through it next to Jaime during the Christmas Stroll one year, carefully not holding his hand but holding his full attention in a way that mattered so much more to her.

The truth was, Scarlett had a zillion memories like that here. For better or for worse, she had an emotional connection to Musgrove. It could never be neutral for her.

Whether that was what Emery meant by *home*, or what Jaime meant by it, she had no idea.

Luckily, Emery was too buzzed on reconnecting to pick up on this. Scarlett could only hope she was masking the turmoil inside her well enough to also hide it from Jaime.

After a few more minutes of pleasantries, Scarlett bought a hundred dollars' worth of goat-milk soap from Emery—she didn't know what else to do—before she and Jaime waved goodbye. Then they picked up several loaves of incredible bread, a jar of honey, and a case of local hard cider.

"It's much less sweet than that crap they make in Albemarle County," Jaime assured her, which wasn't something Scarlett would ever have worried about.

Jaime greeted pretty much everyone at the market, including several people whom, he explained, he knew from a support group he ran for families of incarcerated folks. And as they were leaving, they ran into Evelyn, who convinced them to have lunch with her at the deli across the street, a meal that ended up stretching out over an hour.

Through it all, Scarlett couldn't shake the feeling that it would be entirely too easy to spend a lot of Saturday mornings like this.

The realization made her so itchy even Emery's goat-milk soap probably couldn't cure it.

◆ ◆ ◆

Several hours later, after they'd finished their trip to the farmers' market and lunch with Ev, there was no escaping Jaime's den and their writing.

Scarlett was beginning to hate this room, with its demands and expectations. She was used to being competent—more than competent. She was used to being the best.

She was also used to thinking of Musgrove as a crap place she'd escaped from, a place where no one cared about her. But seeing Emery messed up that story. The entire morning, with its sunshine and its six varieties of local honey, with the way Ev had made her laugh and the approving gleam in Jaime's eyes when he'd watched her, had been disorienting.

Scarlett felt like a shaken-up snow globe. Uncomfortable emotions were billowing around her insides, and she wanted to pound her fists on the glass dome and get out. To go back to her real life, where she was alone and in charge.

"I don't think the climax of episode two is working." Jaime liked to pace when he read, or at least when he read the *final* final draft, not to be confused with the final draft or the polished draft or the almost final draft or any of the others that had come before the *final* final.

The fall of his feet on the wooden floor had started to set Scarlett's teeth on edge. The slightly syncopated bum-*bum*-bum of his gait. The ruthless way he always found whatever they were getting wrong and dragged it back in front of them, making them hash through it until they'd improved it to his satisfaction.

"It's *totally* acceptable, dude," Scarlett huffed. "We need to move on to episode three."

"But episode three grows out of episode two. We can't move on, not until we get this one right."

It was as if he thought this were a chess match and they were blundering. Scarlett had assumed the best part of writing was that they weren't locked in. That they could keep revising, at least until the moment they shot the thing. It wasn't as if they were stuck with a move the instant they touched a piece.

They needed to get this written—the sooner, the better. Then Scarlett could leave this cursed place and get back to her real life—not the fake version they were writing. She was getting too comfortable here, and it was endangering everything she'd built for herself.

"Someone's being anal," Scarlett said, faux sweetly.

"And someone's being lazy," Jaime replied, amused.

No, she was being tetchy, probably because Scarlett could feel herself going soft. Which was happening because being in Musgrove and with Jaime was nice, and if there was anything Scarlett despised, it was niceness. Wheat Thins were nice, and everyone knew those were the worst crackers. Bland. Brittle. *Unsatisfactory.*

The problem was that when she'd agree to come here, she hadn't realized, in the years since she'd known him, Jaime had become an adult. A list-making, responsible adult.

Scarlett normally barreled through life with at least one gaping wound, whether it was a doctor's visit she couldn't seem to schedule or a bare pantry she couldn't seem to fill. Once, she'd gone through not one but two different tournaments with a hole in the sole of her favorite chocolate-suede boots before throwing them away. She still hadn't filled that slot in her wardrobe. The point was, Scarlett tended to wait until something became so loathsome to her that it was a matter of dealing with it or expiring, and even then, she gave considerable thought to expiring.

Jaime would never put up with that. Not for himself, and not for the people around him. Every day, Scarlett discovered another area in which Jaime had realized what she needed and made sure she had it. He'd stocked the medicine cabinet in the guest bathroom and then refilled it when she'd run out of toothpaste. He'd offered to include her dry cleaning with his. He'd made sure every meal included fresh fruits and vegetables. His wholesomeness made her want to go on a ten-day bender, and it made her never want to leave. At the same time.

"Do we need to knock off early?" he teased.

Which would entail retreating to his kitchen, cooking and watching freaking game shows, and laughing like an old married couple. Or a frisky middle-aged married couple.

At first, the scene had nauseated her. Now, and more concerningly, the nausea had faded.

She found herself *liking* it.

It would take so very little for Scarlett to sink into the fantasy of this situation, but she'd poisoned the well. For all that Emery had been glad to see her today, Scarlett knew that there were people here who despised her—or who should despise her.

Even now, with Jaime giving her that sly, familiar grin, she was tempted to say that yes, they ought to stop early. She wanted to let him feed her. She longed to pretend for one more night that they were back in time, back before she'd inexorably wrecked this.

But the impossibility of that fantasy was probably why, with her next words, she broke the pleasant present, as surely as a cat pushing a glass off a shelf while it looked you dead in the eye.

"No. I think I should go back to New York."

If Scarlett had slapped Jaime, he couldn't have been more surprised. *"What?"*

"We've gotten a good start here, and I don't really know what I'm doing anyhow. You can finish the rest without me." If it wasn't *why* she wanted to leave, her reasoning was true enough. This time, Scarlett was determined not to lie to him when she lit out of town.

Jaime was still processing what she'd said. "Excuse me, what?"

"I really should start getting ready for Norway Chess. I only insisted on cowriting to make sure you were going to do a decent job, and you are."

If anything, Scarlett trusted Jaime more now than she ever had. He cared about writing this in a way that was compelling, entertaining, and accurate. He'd be fine without her. He'd be *better* without her.

He popped his jaw, but he didn't say anything.

"We've talked through every scene," she said. "You have everything you need. I'm just getting in your way. I'm just someone else for you to take care of."

She couldn't have predicted it when they were kids, but Jaime had grown into one of the most conscientious people she'd ever known. Scarlett was dead selfish compared to him, and dead clueless too. She couldn't so much as keep a houseplant alive, and he'd managed to support his father in prison, help his mom keep her house, and raise his sister—all while putting himself through school and building a career as an indie filmmaker and making a difference to the people of Musgrove in a dozen ways.

If Scarlett did manage to become the first woman to win the world chess championship—the actual world championship—it would be a toss-up if that accomplishment could sit next to Jaime's on the shelf and not feel shabby in comparison.

"Why are you saying these things?" he finally got out.

"Because it's true. And I'm . . . bored."

"That is a lie."

Sakes alive, she hadn't meant to tell that one, but she'd panicked. "So what if it is? Why do you care?" He ought to be cheering. He ought to be delighted to cut her deadweight.

"Because if you're going to run away again, I deserve an explanation this time."

Oh no, he had not just said that. They'd managed to go several days without talking about their past; this was no time to bring it in to spoil things, like a specter at the feast or a colony of termites in your walls. "Don't make this about us."

"*Of course* it's about us." Because Jaime thought—and repulsively, he was right—that their romantic past was the subtext for everything that was going down here.

Unable to take the intensity of his brown gaze anymore, Scarlett moved away from him. She crossed to the window where, outside, everything was breezy sunshine, with the boughs of the pine trees swaying gently and the soft blue peaks of the mountains in the distance.

The way she was disappearing into the comfort of this vacation from her real life was terrifying. Left to her own devices, Scarlett might forget to pick up mouthwash every now and again, but she'd never been able to rely on other people before. She'd never had the luxury. Forgetting that now would be dead stupid.

She had to climb out of this sinkhole, even if she had to scratch them both up in the process. "Fine. Other than your mom and sister, do people in Musgrove know what you're working on?" Emery had certainly seemed surprised by the news.

He blinked rapidly. He hadn't been expecting that. "No, but I—"

"Which is exactly like before. I never cared that you treated me like a dirty secret back then, but—"

"I *never* treated you like a dirty secret."

She'd known that accusation would fire him up. That was why she'd said it. When in doubt, poison the well: that was how Scarlett's mother always managed things.

And while Scarlett generally tried to handle things differently than Alma, it was the right play for this moment. Underneath it all, Jaime had as much of a temper as Scarlett did. It shouldn't be too hard to get him pissed at her and to throw her out, and that would be better for both of them.

"Sure, Jan." Scarlett hefted as much disdain as she could manage onto her words. "Which is why you took me to prom and gave me your ring and held my hand on the quad."

"You never wanted those things!"

Scarlett hadn't . . . and she very much had. But it would've been embarrassing to ask for them, would've been embarrassing to reveal how deep she'd been in things. Drowning in her feelings for him had made her basic, like one of those Stepford kids from school who were convinced that it was never going to get any better than senior year of high school because, for many of them, it was going to be all downhill after that.

She hated that she wanted to wear the pretty dress, that she wanted the attention of the popular boy, that she wanted everyone to know that he was *hers*. Wanting someone in this dopey way made you vulnerable, and Scarlett didn't want to be vulnerable *or* dopey. She wanted to be mean and strong, and away from this place and the scary things it made her crave.

"Of course I did," she admitted. Because she no longer wanted that stupid stuff. "I never asked for those things because you didn't want to give them to me."

"Scarlett, *everyone* knew how I felt about you."

"No, everyone knew that we were fucking." She hoped choosing that word would help Jaime understand she was serious here. "Those are not the same. If we're going to do this, then we ought to do it on the level."

Scarlett and Jaime had been the talk of the school; he was right about that. But everyone had assumed things were what they'd seemed like: the town's golden boy slumming it with a girl from the wrong side of the tracks. That assumption had been right enough, in the end. If the trope version flattened some things out, it wasn't a total lie.

"Okay, fine. Let's do this on the level." He spit that out as if it were battery acid. "You run away the second things get hard."

"What? I work my butt *off.* I'm not lazy."

"You work hard, that's true. But the second things get complicated emotionally, the second you lose control, you're out of there. You didn't want to stick around, you didn't want to stick with me, through what was going to go down with my father."

Oh boy. "I will not talk about that time with you. I won't do it."

"Okay, then let's talk about what you've done since and how you sabotage yourself all the time. You aren't wrong about PAWN, but you undermine the case you're trying to make when you pose naked in *Vogue*—"

"Don't you dare slut-shame me, Jaime Croft."

"I'm not, swear to God. I highly support you posing naked in every goddamn fashion magazine on earth. But you embarrassed PAWN when you rubbed your celebrity in their faces, which makes it less likely that you'll get what you want. It's why you wrote your book! Becoming the center of attention puts you back in the driver's seat."

She wanted to heave the couch at him, and if he didn't knock it off, she was going to get mad enough to Hulk out and do it.

"You ass," she spit. She didn't say *you liar*, because Jaime wasn't lying. Running away wasn't something Scarlett was going to apologize for. Hiding was good. It was safe. It made sense. But he was being an ass.

"You said to do it on the level, and that's how I feel."

"And *I* feel like you're punishing me because you've never gotten over me."

"I've never tried to hide that."

Oof.

How could he *do* that, stand there with all his feelings hanging out there like that—his real feelings, not some dramatic mask version of them he'd slapped over himself? She'd get hives if she tried it.

But the rainbow spill of things his words had set off in her gut had her reverting to the thing she did best: she left.

Chapter 10

Every visit Jaime made to FCI Petersburg, the prison where Dad was incarcerated, went the same way: arrive early to allow for the crowds at security. Leave his belt and cell phone in the car. Wonder again at how many locked doors he had to go through and how cold the place was.

Then Jaime would wait at a cafeteria table, trying not to think about how the scene felt like a middle school lunchroom but sadder. About how everyone sitting around the room was trying so hard to look hopeful, but not managing it. About all the kids—the kids were the worst part.

The first time he'd gone to see his father at the Georgina County lockup, he'd been a kid too. But at eighteen, Jaime had been old enough to know what was happening, and *why* it was happening. The toothless baby perched on its mom's hip across from Jaime, the one who was smiling at him so hard, almost *willing* him to smile back—that baby didn't have the slightest clue. All it knew was that this place was dark and it echoed and no one here smiled.

So Jaime managed to crack a grin, and the baby broke into a wide peal of laughter, a sound that couldn't have been more out of place. A rainbow in hell would've been more likely.

Kids made sense to Jaime. Unlike, say, Scarlett.

Jaime had gotten into his car this morning unsure of whether he'd still find her when he got back home. Scarlett was spooked, that much was certain. But by what, Jaime couldn't begin to say.

For all that they'd been working together for three weeks now, he had no idea what made her tick. He'd gotten a handle on the character they were writing, but the fictional Emily wasn't the real Scarlett. For one thing, Emily did what he told her to.

The weirdest part was that as Scarlett had hollered at him yesterday, Jaime had the strongest sense that she didn't know what she'd been doing either. She'd been trying to provoke him, and he'd fallen straight into her trap. *Why* she'd wanted him to, though, he had no idea.

Before Jaime could figure it out, Dad sat down on the bench across from him.

Dad hadn't appeared in *The Devouring Sun* until episode seven. *Your dad is the shark in* Jaws, Nate had joked once, and that wasn't wrong. Except rather than being terrifying, Jaime thought his father had seemed smaller, sadder, on screen. Great harm can be done by the most ordinary people for the most mundane reasons: that was what Jaime had been trying to say in the show.

In real life, he also came across as diminished. They didn't wear orange here, so Dad had on what looked like beige scrubs with a long-sleeved blue T-shirt underneath. For a dizzying second, Jaime could almost pretend they weren't sitting in a prison. That the last seventeen years hadn't passed.

Dad had been everything back then, the sun at the center of the Croft family universe—and a good-sized star in the town of Musgrove. He'd coached all of Jaime's sports teams, which meant that every kid knew him. When the Croft family went to dinner, he would've treated at least one family member of every person in the restaurant. He was a fixture on the links at the Georgina Country Club and a member of the Masonic lodge.

Everyone knew him. Everyone *liked* him. And it was only later that Jaime realized how those facts had made everything else possible. That maybe Dad had cultivated all those relationships in order to cover up whatever else he'd been up to.

The gravity of the entire system changed in an instant when Dad had been arrested. It was a wonder they hadn't all crashed into each other, but that was why Jaime had had to step up. Jaime plugging the hole had been the only way to maintain the order of things.

"James! It's good to see you."

Dad was the only person who called Jaime *James*. He thought the nickname made his son sound like a kid. But Dad wasn't around anymore to correct folks, so his son had become Jaime to everyone—except in this place. It was like a Bizarro World prison nickname.

"How have you been, Dad?"

"I can't complain."

That was what he'd always said. They might as well have been golfing or fishing on Ricky Southerland's boat. *Can't complain* about prison—ha.

These visits still made Jaime *ache*. While he had gotten better at being a kid to an inmate over the years—he ran a family support group, in point of fact—after his fight with Scarlett, he was feeling as fragile as a molting chicken, all puffy and exposed and embarrassed. All he had left in the tank was chitchat.

"They feeding you okay?"

"Fine, it's fine. Mom and Ev were busy?"

"Yup. They send their regrets, but they'll be here next week."

As long as Dad had enough visiting points, his family could come by on Fridays, the weekends, and federal holidays. Mom tried to make it to Petersburg at least twice a month. This was one of only a handful of visiting days Jaime had made that Mom had ever missed.

She'd set the tone from the first one: they were all going to go, as much as they could. They were going to stay a family through this. As shocking and embarrassing as it was, the real embarrassment would be for them to fall apart, and she wasn't going to let them.

Dad nodded and folded his hands together on the tabletop. "So you working on something new?" He was obviously not going to let Jaime ask an hour's worth of questions about what Dad had gotten up to in the yard and how his work in the prison laundry was going before sneaking off.

One of them had accepted the permanency of this situation—and it wasn't Jaime.

"Yeah, I'm doing a series about . . . chess."

"Chess? Like the kind played by that girl, Scarlett what's-her-name?"

"Exactly like that. It's an adaptation of her memoir. Scarlett's in Musgrove, working on it with me."

Dad's brows arched.

Yesterday, Scarlett hadn't been wrong, exactly. Jaime *had* kept their teenage relationship a secret, but he'd taken his cues from her. She'd ignored Jaime at school and made other plans the night of prom. In his defense, high school labels were insufficient for whatever he and Scarlett had shared. They hadn't "gone steady"—this hadn't been *Grease*. It had been a heady mix of lust and potential that kept shape-shifting before Jaime could define it.

For all that Scarlett had never let him know her, Jaime had always believed down to the quick of his fingernails that they were meant to be. Meant to be *something*, at any rate. Something permanent and life altering.

That was why he'd insisted on introducing her to his family, despite her protests. Dad had always liked Scarlett, had always teased her and shot Jaime looks like *This girl is a hoot.* Mom had not, but she would've come around.

No, Jaime's discretion hadn't come out of a desire to hide Scarlett. It had been far more complicated than that. But even still, Dad had always peppered Jaime with questions about whether Scarlett was really just his friend, whether he was sharing the full truth.

Which was goddamn ironic, when it came down to it.

"Sounds interesting," Dad said at last.

"It's going to be great. Very different from *The Devouring Sun.*" Which was the goal. The success of Jaime's first project worried him a bit. What if people thought he could only make gritty, low-budget autobiographical stuff? He was determined to do something different, to show people he had range. If he and Scarlett ever managed to finish writing the thing, he was confident *Queen's Kiss* would help him do just that.

"Well, that's good," Dad said. "You were ready to start something new."

Jaime wasn't quite sure what they were talking about now: the show, or whatever Dad assumed it meant in terms of Jaime and Scarlett's relationship.

"Yeah, it's coming along." Or it would be, if Scarlett would tell him what the hell was going on and if they could work through it together.

"So what are you reading?" Dad asked.

"A new oral history of D-day."

"Oh, is it good?"

It was fine, but Jaime hadn't picked it up to enjoy it. He'd picked it up so he could tell Dad about it.

Dad's incarceration had shrunk their relationship down to the size of a pen cap, but if a pen cap was what he got, then Jaime was going to hold on to it tight. Because his dad might be a felon who'd fucked up in any number of ways, but he was also the only father Jaime would ever get.

You didn't get to pick your family any more than you got to pick where you were born. All you could pick was how you related to them.

Jaime's dad was more flawed than most, but that only meant Jaime had to be better to balance the scales. That obligation had defined the last seventeen years of his life. Making amends for Dad's transgressions was Jaime's core philosophy.

"I'll see you in a few weeks, James," Dad said when Jaime finally got up to go half an hour later.

His dad gave him a hug, the kind that starts grabby and then goes self-conscious and embarrassed. Visitors were only allowed to touch inmates briefly at the beginning and end of visits, and Dad often only went for the closing hug. As if he wanted to ration those moments and make them even more precious than they already were.

Jaime wrapped his arms fast around his dad's back. "I love you." As always, Jaime's words were a promise that, despite everything, he still wanted his father in his life.

"Love you." And Dad's response was an apology for everything.

Maybe there were crimes so great you never finished making up for them. Maybe what Dad had done fit the bill.

Jaime had tortured himself with those kinds of thoughts at first, and the only thing that had ended the spiral was the realization it wasn't Jaime's job to decide. He wasn't the judge here, wasn't the jury. He was the son. And so his job was to hold his family together and to tell his dad's story. As a warning, as a witness, and as a way of paying restitution.

Jaime knew he'd made his own mistakes in not realizing what his father had been up to, not being able to stop all that harm. That was exactly why he always strove to be competent and in control. He never wanted to miss anything that important ever again. He had no excuse for being ignorant now.

As Jaime drove home, he turned his thoughts to Scarlett and the odds that she would still be there. And whether he wanted her to be.

His thoughts chased each other like squirrels for hours. It was only once he'd pulled into the driveway and saw her rental car—sitting exactly where it had been when he'd left—that he realized if she'd gone, he would've been crushed.

There were no two ways about it. This was going to end with his heart in pieces. All he could try to do was to delay the pain as long as possible.

◆ ◆ ◆

Scarlett researched flights and started packing her bag. But she hadn't done any laundry in a few days, and thanks to Jaime's fondness of long midday walks—hikes, more like it—most of her bras and panties were gross.

Most of the options had been night flights out of Dulles, and a glance at the clock revealed she had time for a load of laundry. That was just her being practical. No one wanted to carry a bunch of dirty underwear back up the East Coast.

But also, laundry would take a good ninety minutes, which would keep her from doing anything impulsive. Scarlett wasn't going to do a Cinderella dash away from Jaime's place, leaving a pile of lace and satin panties behind.

The thought did make her chuckle, though.

While the washer was going, Scarlett spent an embarrassing amount of time standing in the living room staring at the spot where, until a few hours earlier, Jaime's car had been parked. He'd left without a word, but then again, she was the one who'd flounced off last night. And she'd stayed holed up in her room this morning, not creeping out to the kitchen with its sweet, sweet supply of caffeine until she'd heard him go.

Wherever Jaime had headed off to—the grocery store, his mom's house, a strip club—he really ought to be back by now.

Scarlett hadn't meant what she'd said. Well, she didn't know if she meant it. She meant it, and she didn't mean it. It was the Schrödinger's cat of emotions.

There ought to be someone you could call to determine such things, like an Am-I-the-Asshole hotline.

Or a friend.

This was what people asked their friends, wasn't it? Dammit, she really ought to have made some of those along the way. She'd simply never imagined she would need someone to tell her if she'd been too much of a jerk or not enough of a jerk.

Scarlett picked up her phone and opened her group chat with Martina and Kit. This question was more personal than weighing the merits of the Benko Gambit, but Scarlett really needed a ruling here, preferably from someone whose opinions she respected.

Feeling foolish, Scarlett dialed Kit. Talking it out would be awful, but Scarlett couldn't bring herself to write it down. Seeing the words would make her feel like an even bigger ass.

Kit answered on the second ring. They were an early riser. They'd probably already been for a long morning walk and played ten or fifteen games of blitz chess online.

"How are things going?" Kit said by way of a greeting. "Did you get the care package?"

Scarlett had never in her life received a care package, so when a box had arrived filled with bagels and a cardigan, she'd felt dizzy and confused.

At the very least, Virginians were apparently under the false impression that bagels were dense bread. Scarlett could live without real bagels, of course, but life was certainly better *with* real bagels.

"I did, thank you. I'm sending you some goat-milk soap in exchange." Scarlett had enough of the stuff to bathe an army.

"Sweet," Kit replied. "I saw the sweater at Beacon's Closet, and I knew you had to have it. It looked like something a writer would wear."

If there was one thing Scarlett was good at besides chess, it was dressing for impact. Once she'd had enough money to go shopping without too much stress, she'd realized that fashion was an entire other way to communicate with people. It remained *astonishing* to her that so many of the men in chess wore the same old interchangeable outfits. Did they not understand the right tie, the right accessory, could communicate volumes?

Oh well. Once again they proved how small minded they were.

Despite the fact the sweater Kit had sent looked as if a cat might've attacked it at some point, it had been soft and warm. In fact . . .

Scarlett dug the cardi out of the pile waiting for her to pack into her suitcase and held the phone against her ear with her shoulder as she struggled into the sweater.

"You prepping for Norway Chess?" Kit asked.

Scarlett ought to be. "No. But I need some advice . . . the personal kind. I need to know what to do."

Criminy, this was awkward.

"Sure, fire away." Kit didn't seem put out in the least.

"You would do that?"

"Of course. We're friends."

They were? Well, hot damn.

Scarlett opened her mouth to say *I picked a fight, and I want you to tell me that it's okay to come back to New York rather than apologizing.* But even more, she wanted Kit to arrive at that conclusion on their own. So Scarlett had to start at the beginning.

"The thing is, Jaime and I have . . . a complicated past."

"As in?"

"We may have dated." Scarlett had rejected that word with Jaime, but it was the simplest thing she could say to Kit to convey what had happened.

"Did he take you to prom? Was there a mortifying corsage incident?" Kit teased. They thought this was *hilarious*—which, if the situation were reversed, Scarlett probably would too.

"No. We were more like each other's . . . dirty secret."

"Nice. But that was decades ago. Why is it complicated now? Unless it was a much bigger deal than *dating*."

"It wasn't a big deal." What a lie. Scarlett had to stop doing that. "But, I mean, maybe it felt like a massive, world-ending deal at the time. If you've ever met a teenager, you know *Romeo and Juliet* is realistic."

"You two decimated a town—is that what you're saying?"

"Pretty much." Scarlett squeezed her eyes closed until she saw spots. "Does this surprise you?"

"Not at all. I've never seen you in a relationship"—no one had—"but you never do things small."

No, Scarlett didn't. "Yeah, that's me. I just—Kit, I wrecked this man, and then I skipped off to play chess without a backward glance."

"A tale as old as time."

Scarlett had to laugh. This whole baring-your-soul-to-friends thing, it wasn't half bad.

"And after you split him like kindling, you granted him the rights to your book and are staying in his house. Am I missing anything?" Kit asked.

So many things. Jaime's confession that he wasn't over her. What Scarlett had done directly before leaving Musgrove seventeen years ago.

But Scarlett tacked on only the most important bit: "Last night, I may have picked a fight with him and said I was going back to New York."

"Why?"

Scarlett was tempted to pitch forward onto the bed and howl. "I don't . . . I don't really know."

"At times like these, my therapist often asks, 'Don't know, or don't want to say?'"

"Your therapist sounds awful."

"Tell me about it."

Scarlett twisted a lock of hair between her fingers. "I don't want to say."

Kit was wisely silent for a long time. A long, long time.

Then in a tiny voice, Scarlett admitted the truth. "I wanted him to throw me out. Because being here with him, it's really nice."

But it wasn't only the routine or even being with Jaime. It was seeing Evelyn regularly and running into Emery and finding out that a local book club had read *Queen's Kiss*. Even Mrs. Croft hadn't been mean to her, come to think of it.

For all that Scarlett had thought she hated Musgrove, the reality of the place wasn't half bad.

"So, I guess, my question is whether I should leave or not."

Rather than answering that, Kit lobbed another question. "Do you still like him?"

The words should've sounded impossibly silly, but everything about this situation had pitched Scarlett back into the headspace of being a teenager, so actually, Kit's question was perfect.

Did Scarlett like Jaime? Did she feel anything as tame as *like* where he was concerned?

When too long passed before Scarlett answered, Kit threw out a few more ideas. "Or maybe you despise him. Or maybe you do this with everyone."

It was the last one. It had to be the last one. "Are you suggesting that I'm difficult?"

"I'm not suggesting anything. I'm flat-out saying it: you're really difficult." It helped that when Kit said it, it sounded like a compliment.

Scarlett wanted to believe she was difficult in the way chess was difficult. She was worth studying, worth investing your time in, because she wasn't easy to figure out and to master, like checkers, or a game of simple chance, like Candy Land.

No, she was freaking *chess*: the game that taught you philosophy and analysis and tactics and strategy and history. The game of kings, and the one that peasants could challenge them at.

Or maybe Scarlett was a problem that could be solved by a computer and was now hopelessly outmoded.

"Fair."

"You said you need to know what to do?"

"Yeah. So my main options are staying or going," Scarlett helpfully summarized.

"What's the case for going?"

"I don't have to apologize, for one. And I'm not good at this. I don't know what I'm doing here." Other than dipping her toes into water she had no intention of diving into.

"And why would you stay?"

"It's my book. If I'm here, I have more editorial control." Certainly that was what Violet would say. Not to mention Scarlett was contractually obligated to help write these scripts. Jaime probably wouldn't make a stink, but he would be entitled to if he wanted.

But Scarlett didn't give a hoot about contracts. Instead, some part of her worried that Jaime was right and leaving would be cowardly.

"And it would be . . . mature to stick it out."

Jaime had accused her of running away when things got hard, which wasn't untrue. Scarlett ran toward hard things, sometimes. She'd memorized literally thousands of chess diagrams. During a match, she sometimes imagined dozens of scenarios before making a play. Even now, rather than quitting the sport, she was trying to fix it.

But other times, she didn't have enough fight in her. Or she worried that fighting and losing was a higher price than she was willing to pay.

Seventeen years ago, when she'd gone to Tokyo, she'd been chasing a dream, sure. But she also hadn't wanted to tell Jaime what she'd done. Hadn't wanted to see the light dim in his eyes when he'd looked at her.

"Those are solid reasons. But what's the big one?" Kit seemed to have sensed what Scarlett wasn't saying.

The work they were doing was challenging; it was also rewarding. But the truth was that Scarlett liked eating with Jaime every night, and she'd even come around on those godforsaken time-outs in nature.

It was more than the routine he'd imposed, though. It was the way she and Jaime knew each other and how, because of all that history, they seemed to be growing together. Scarlett felt as if she were stretching for the first time in a long while. All through her muscles she could feel the sweet ache that could only be satisfied by *more*. The wound and the cure, both at once.

"He's nice to me, he takes care of me, and I like it."

"That *asshole*," Kit said, with faux intensity.

"Kit, I'm serious."

They chuckled. "I know you are, but it doesn't sound like you need advice. It sounds like you know exactly what you want to do."

"Arg." Scarlett bashed her head into the pillow several times. "I was hoping you were going to talk me out of it."

"Then you need to make a better case for leaving. You know I only respond to facts."

Scarlett wished *she* were that way, but it was well documented that her emotions, when they flared, got her in trouble. When she analyzed her blunders, the matches she should've won and had bungled instead, it almost always came down to moments when she'd let her heart and her gut run the show.

Her entire life, Scarlett had been at war with herself. The battle lines were between the rational part of her that had mastered the Pirc Defense and the volcanic push-pull of her feelings. This was just the latest skirmish.

"You aren't worried that if I give in now and stay, I might stay forever?" Scarlett asked.

"Nope. Because I know you aren't going to run away to a small town and become a trad wife and bake bread every day for forever."

If Kit had eaten the sourdough bread with honey butter Jaime got at the farmers' market, they would mock less. "No, it's not about the place—"

It's about him.

The realization hit Scarlett like a dead satellite, falling out of its orbit and smacking into the earth.

"Oh shit," she said.

"Shit," Kit agreed.

And there it was: the core truth of this that Scarlett hadn't wanted to see, but which was as undeniable as the sunset streaking out over the mountain behind her. She was every bit as drawn to Jaime as she ever had been. Musgrove felt right because it had Jaime in it.

That was why she'd talked herself into giving him the rights, and how she'd finagled herself into writing the scripts with him. This had been inevitable from the moment he'd shown up in her lobby.

She realized that last night, when he'd said he hadn't gotten over her, she'd wanted to bolt because she'd never gotten over him either.

"So what are you going to do about it?" Kit asked.

Well, that was as tricky as knowing what to do when you faced a critical decision in a match. With chess, she would evaluate her opponent's position, try to understand what he was aiming for, and consider all the ways she could counter—but how did you counter when it was your heart, and not your king, that was in jeopardy?

"I dunno. I mean, I said I was going to go back to New York." Running away had always been a solid gambit.

"And so you think you have to leave now?"

"I did sort of block myself in."

"No you didn't. Just don't leave. Pretend that conversation never happened, and it will be like that time when you lost in Reykjavík and you acted like it never happened rather than unpacking it with us."

Oof, that had been a hard one. "That loss still pisses me off so much."

"Babe, everyone knows that."

"It completely undermined my argument for the open league, and I don't think to this day that I've regained the ground I lost, and I—"

"I really do understand."

Kit had been fighting PAWN for longer than Scarlett had. So few people understood chess at the level they both did *and* understood what buttheads the folks who made up PAWN were. Scarlett was incredibly grateful to have Kit as a sounding board.

"Right. Wow, I feel bad about dumping on you like this."

"Emotional dumping can be your signature move," Kit told her.

"And here, I always thought that was the Queen's Kiss," Scarlett deadpanned.

The Queen's Kiss was one of the most devastating forms of checkmate. It was when you landed your queen squarely in front of your opponent's king, but they couldn't take it—because if they did, then their king would immediately be taken by another piece of yours. It was an absolute power play, and Scarlett adored delivering it.

Kit snorted. "Nah, it's being simultaneously messy and brilliant."

"I just feel guilty about getting my emotional bile all over your hands."

"Martina and I love you, even with all your drama. *Especially* with all your drama. In other words, we are soaked—totally soaked—in the same emotional bile."

That made . . . a lot of sense. Even if all of this was unfamiliar, it was nice.

Once Scarlett figured out what the heck was going on with Jaime, she was going to have to digest the fact that Kit and Martina were apparently her friends. Which meant that she was going to have to learn how to be a friend back.

Apparently, it involved care packages and listening. She could probably do that.

"We should all shower more."

"That's really just a recipe for a better life. Have you ever had a disappointing shower?"

"Tons." But those had been back in Scarlett's childhood, before she'd known that the water didn't have to come out like a lukewarm tinkle.

It was the little things, really. Once you knew good water pressure, you'd do anything not to go back. That alone was enough to drive Scarlett toward chess dominance.

"Forget showers—you have bigger fish to fry."

"Such as the fact that I like this man?"

"Yup. And I doubt running away is going to take care of that one."

Scarlett knew this to be true. If she hadn't gotten over Jaime in seventeen years, she wasn't going to get over Jaime. Some scars you carried for life.

"I really should leave," she said softly.

"But you won't," Kit replied, because they truly knew Scarlett.

Because Scarlett and Kit truly were friends.

"Thanks, Kit."

"Anytime."

So Scarlett put her clothing away in the small dresser, zipped up her suitcases, and returned them to the closet, which felt, ridiculously, more final than making up her mind to stay had been.

It should have been scary, but it wasn't. Now she just had to get right with it.

Scarlett left her room for the kitchen, and by the time Jaime returned, she'd put together a tuna noodle casserole and slid it into the oven.

It was her turn to feed him for a change.

"So I see you're not in New York," he said, by way of greeting.

Scarlett couldn't bring herself to make eye contact with him. She was worried that he would see something—everything—in her gaze.

"You see right," she admitted, training her attention out the window.

"Are you staying?" he asked.

I shouldn't—because I've realized how vulnerable I am here. But even if she were brave enough to say those words, and she wasn't, they wouldn't be true. And he cared about truth.

She'd admitted how far into this she was today, but if she were willing to examine herself more, she was certain she would've figured out the same thing on the very day he'd walked into her lobby.

For a supposedly smart woman, Scarlett could be really stupid sometimes.

"I am," she answered him. And then on a deep breath, she turned her eyes to him. "I'm sorry for melting down yesterday."

Now that she'd let herself admit that she hadn't gotten over Jaime, that she was still as attracted to him now as she'd been in high school, her eyes were devouring the sight of him. The scruff on his chin. The curl of his hair. The shape of his hands, set on his hips.

Speaking of hips, his jeans—worn down by work, not by a tailor—were perfectly molded to them. Lucky jeans.

"You wanna talk about what prompted it?"

"Nope." Not now, and probably not ever. Going down that path would only hurt them both.

"Okay," he said, accepting this.

Scarlett needed to come up with a new plan of attack to match the new circumstances in which they found themselves. But for the first time in memory, she had nothing—which scared the ever-loving crap out of her.

Chapter 11

The next few weeks were like running a marathon, if Jaime were doing it barefoot and on eggshells.

Scarlett had refused to explain what had motivated her meltdown, but that was fine. Jaime didn't need her to explain. He just needed them to get the work done.

And they were. The words were finally flowing, and more than half the episodes were written. As long as they avoided any more snags, they were going to meet their deadline. The actress Zoya had recommended had turned out to be great, and they'd gotten her on contract, so Nate and Videon were thrilled.

But underneath all those accomplishments, Jaime felt like a *mess*. In the heat of his argument with Scarlett, Jaime had blurted out that he wasn't over her. God, what a mistake.

Not *what a lie*—it wasn't a lie.

Saying it, though, had been dumb.

All Jaime could do was pretend it wasn't true. He didn't have room in his life for those feelings, and he ought to be trying to smother them with a pillow.

But they were so freaking present. Hunger that cracked his chest in two when Scarlett would laugh. Pride that made him smile like a loon when she liked a line he'd written. Lust that blazed in his veins when she stumbled into the kitchen in her pajamas.

Or bent over something.

Or sighed deeply.

"Okay," she said, looking up from her laptop, "now we just have to write the blocking for the chess match."

"We can leave it vague," he protested. Jaime was feeling too vulnerable to withstand Scarlett in full chess-genius mode. "You can handle that on set—"

"No, we can't." Scarlett's eyes, Jaime would've sworn, sparkled. It was as if the Perseids were falling in there, and he wouldn't put it past her to arrange that somehow. "You're always saying that if it's dramatically significant, we have to spell it out in the script."

This was what he got for explaining his philosophy to her. "But—"

"We've also been at this for six weeks, and you still don't understand chess."

Unwilling to watch her pretty, mocking face any longer, Jaime scrubbed his eyes with the palms of his hands. "Damn it, I don't have to. That's your job."

"I never took you for a coward."

If Jaime weren't a coward, he'd tell Scarlett why he couldn't look straight at her anymore. Why, for the last few weeks, he'd cut their after-dinner conversation shorter every night. Why he felt as if there wasn't enough oxygen in the air these days.

It was pure self-preservation. All too soon, she was going to leave him again. He needed to put up some walls around his heart if he was going to survive it.

"I'm just efficient," he replied with an impressive amount of coolness. That was the note he needed to hit with her more often. "We don't both need to be good at everything."

"You ought to be at least *proficient* at this," she insisted. "Maybe we're not writing things in the most dramatic possible way because there are elements that you don't get."

He dropped his hands. "It's too late for me to understand this game."

"It's never too late, Jaime Croft."

For chess, or for something else?

See, this was exactly what had his teeth on edge. It was one thing to crave Scarlett the way he did, so sharply he could almost taste the longing. But it became another thing when she looked right at him and said something like *that*. Something so provocative that it was all he could do not to step over the coffee table and kiss the words straight off her lips.

He could ask her what she meant. Or he could try to snag the piece of cheese she'd used to set the trap.

Because she was right and he was a chicken, he did the latter.

"*Fine*," he gritted out.

"Really?" Scarlett jumped to her feet, which did amazing things to her figure, and dashed across the room to get her chess board.

So far, she had written every single line in the script that had to do with the mechanics of chess. She'd explained it all to him, walking through the moves on this board, but mostly, Jaime had watched her lips move. Basked in the half smirk she didn't bother to hide while she explained the trap she was luring some imagined opponent into, the brilliant joke she was about to play on them.

He hadn't understood any of it, but he'd *felt* it. Felt her pride and her intelligence and her wit. And they'd just been more fuel on the fire of how much he wanted her.

Scarlett set the board down carefully on the coffee table before grabbing a throw pillow off her couch and dropping it onto the floor. She sat down, crisscross-applesauce style, and began setting up the board.

Jaime muttered curses under his breath while he watched her. This was going to go so badly for him, but it was making her happy, so he would endure it.

When she was done, she gave each of the knights a twist so the white ones faced each other, and the same with the black.

"That's not necessary," she explained, "but I think it looks cool."

Which he'd remembered from when they'd been kids. That was pretty much the only thing he remembered, and it was a thing about *her*, not a thing about chess.

"Sit." Scarlett pointed to the bit of floor directly across from her, and he slid down to take his designated place.

"So, um, I think I remember how all the pieces move."

"How about you tell me, just to refresh." Yeah, unlike Nate, Scarlett wasn't going to fall for his bullshit.

Jaime quickly ran through how the pawns, bishops, and knights could move. He got to the rooks, which had always been his favorites. Their linearity was comforting. "And last but certainly not least, the queen can do anything."

"Queens are powerful like that." Scarlett shrugged, accepting that she was a queen, at least when it came to this. "It seems that I was wrong. You do know the first thing about chess."

Jaime wanted to pound on his chest. He wanted to crawl around the table and pin Scarlett to the floor until his yearning receded.

But none of that would fit with his new detached affect, so instead, he just shrugged. "I do what I can."

"Here's the thing, though: you're thinking about it all wrong."

"You don't start with how the pieces move?" That seemed like a necessary precondition to everything else to him.

"Not if you want to get good. No, you have to learn to see the board."

"I see the board fine." Jaime double-checked just to make sure, and yup, there it was, as clear as day: a chess board.

Scarlett rolled her eyes. "Have it your way—you're a master at the rules of the game. But if you only think about how the pieces move and not what you're trying to create, you'll never improve."

"My goal isn't to win a world championship. I just want to make a television show."

"One that hinges on the drama in Emily's matches, right? Don't you think you need to learn to analyze the board for that?"

"That's what my on-set chess expert is for."

Somehow, he was going to have to make those four months on set enough to last a lifetime. Maybe he could find a way to snip up the way she made him feel and sew it together into a quilt, one he could huddle under when she left and the nights were cold again.

"And your on-set chess expert thinks it would be even better if you were both bringing something to the table."

He was going to bring plenty to the table, including an understanding of the mechanics of filming the damn thing. "You plan to weigh in on camera angles?"

"You bet I do."

Scarlett meant it too. She was ineffably competent. A few weeks into filming, and she'd probably be as good at it as he was. She was going to step in Jaime's world and adore it. All the different kinds of people on the crew, the careful way they gathered shots, like building up paint on a canvas. The sheer power of watching actors work in person. It was going to be a joy to see.

The thought warmed Jaime through. "Okay, fine. Tell me how to *see* the board."

Scarlett gave one of the black knights another twirl. Jaime loved the rapid, elegant way her fingers moved. The way she touched the pieces was almost indecent.

"I'm not saying that you need to, like, memorize the algebraic notation and work up to blindfolded chess or anything—"

"You can play chess blindfolded?"

"I used to play several blindfolded games a day, just for kicks."

The thought was unexpectedly erotic. Jaime had a zillion other questions, but out of a sense of self-preservation, he swallowed them.

"You have to make moves in order to do something. To serve some kind of strategic goal. My game really improved once I began to work backward," she said. "What kind of an endgame did I want to play? And so what did I need to do in the opening or in the middlegame to achieve that? But that's too complicated for a beginner."

"Thanks," he said dryly.

"So let's go with this. For now, imagine that there are only pawns on the board. It's an old thought experiment of Seirawan's, but it's legit.

Pawns are *so* crucial for helping you get to the board you want to have. So the first thing you need to do is to think about your pawns. What do you need to move and when and where to open up the board the way you want while also keeping your power pieces protected."

Explaining this lit her up. It was scary how easy it would be to pretend that they were still kids. That this brightness of Scarlett's came from youth and naivety, that it wasn't affected by a world-wise woman. He couldn't afford to forget what he'd learned and what it had cost him—even if he wanted to.

"Pawns only. Got it."

"Then analyze your knights and bishops. Try to avoid losing them early. And if you do sacrifice one, get something good for it."

In *Queen's Kiss*, one of the most gripping games Scarlett described had her blundering early on and surrendering a bishop, only to battle back and win. That was the game where her creativity and tenacity had become legendary.

In contrast, Jaime tended to see a move and jump before he checked all the risks. Even now, when he ought to know better, there was a certain arrogance to the way he crashed into things. He tended to believe he was doing the right things for the right reasons, and it emboldened him. Showing up in Scarlett's lobby to beg for the rights to her book was fairly on brand for him.

But that had worked out pretty well, in the end.

"You can be white." Scarlett said this as if she was doing him a favor—which she was. White always went first. "And"—she cast a quick glance at Jaime from under her lashes—"let's make it interesting."

"How? You won't defeat me in four moves? You'll toy with me for a while first?" Much as a cat might choose to get its rocks off with a mouse before devouring it.

"Sure, that too. But I was going to say if you can take one of my major pieces, I'll take my top off."

The breath left Jaime's lungs in a great whoosh—like patrons running from a movie theater after someone had pulled the fire alarm.

"You'll . . . what?" he managed to say.

"Jesus, I was joking," Scarlett insisted. "But based on your expression, it's clearly the perfect bribe. Take one of my nonpawns, and I'll disrobe. What do you say?"

Her expression was coy. Which was to be expected. Scarlett's expressions were always coy. But underneath, he thought he saw something else. Something more honest. More vulnerable.

Scarlett wanted to see that Jaime still wanted her.

Which . . . that couldn't be it. Jaime unmistakably did want her. He'd already said as much to her, and clearly he always would feel that way. He'd only been pretending not to want her the last few weeks—which should have put him in line with her feelings on the subject.

Unless it didn't. *Unless she wanted him too.*

Scarlett couldn't. She didn't. Which was why he sputtered out, "But everyone with a *Vogue* subscription has seen that."

For a second, Scarlett seemed almost stunned by Jaime's feint, and he almost immediately confessed that he was playing, that he would give up his right thumb to see her topless.

But as quickly as her expression fell, Scarlett tugged it back into place. "Except they haven't seen one of my regular cotton bras. That was La Perla."

If she'd custom-made that line just for Jaime, it couldn't have fit better. Jaime would take the everyday cotton over the swanky couture lingerie, for sure. The bra she'd chosen for herself. The one she wore for comfort and not simply for some silly fantasy.

Scarlett really wanted this from him . . . and well, as much as this might hurt, letting her see that he still wanted her would only be admitting what was *true*. He was the one who kept going on and on about honesty. Who kept insisting that both Jaime and Scarlett's work meditated on truth.

"Well," he said slowly, "who could resist that?"

Triumph turned up the corners of her mouth. "Let's go, then."

Jaime reached for one of his pawns—in a script, Scarlett would insist they write *the queen's pawn*—and pushed it forward two squares. "It can do that, right? On the first move?"

"Yup." Scarlett moved one of her knights forward, vaulting over her own line of pawns in the process—which she'd more or less told him she was going to do. Her eyes shot up to his. "Your move."

Jaime was so jittery inside, thinking was almost impossible. Strategy? Ha. He couldn't have recited the alphabet.

That she'd offered this meant that Scarlett might still want him. Might.

Acting on it would be a catastrophically bad idea. Chewing tinfoil was probably wiser than Jaime and Scarlett getting tangled up in each other again. But the possibility for it was there, twisting the fabric of space-time around them as surely as a black hole would.

Maybe they could. Maybe they both wanted to. Holy shit.

Jaime reached for a piece, if only to do *something*, then he stopped himself. He needed to make the right move here, or at least not make a silly move.

Pretend there are just pawns. See the whole board. Consider what attacks you could make, and what attacks she could make.

Jaime didn't have to take Scarlett's king. The goal of this game wasn't to win in the traditional sense. It was to take a piece of hers that wasn't a pawn.

Right now, that lone knight of hers was the only power piece she'd put in play, and he couldn't reach that.

Think about how to open the board.

He needed to get more of his pawns out there in order to give himself more options. He advanced another one.

Scarlett moved a pawn. He played a knight. She advanced a bishop.

After a few more moves, she took one of his pawns. "First blood."

"Is that good or bad?" he asked.

"It means I'm more aggressive than I should be."

Scarlett could be as aggressive as she wanted where Jaime was concerned. If she'd tell him what exactly she was up to with this stunt, for example, he'd be over the moon.

Jaime advanced a pawn to protect another one of his, proud that he'd seen the play she'd been about to make.

"Good."

He felt her compliment in parts of his body that had been hibernating, but he couldn't give those parts free rein here. Not until he knew what she was up to.

They continued to trade moves. She took another pawn of his. He took a pawn of hers.

"So close," she said of the attack he'd been planning that she'd interrupted.

"I'm highly motivated."

"I can tell."

Scarlett castled, transplanting her rook with her king—the only way you could move two pieces at the same time. It still made no fucking sense to him, but he could understand how hiding the king back in the corner like that would be an advantage.

Then suddenly, Jaime could see it. He could take her bishop with his queen.

It was a senseless move in terms of winning the game. It wouldn't put him into a strategic position, but it was a perfectly logical move if his goal was to take one of her power pieces—and at the moment, that was one of the primary goals in his life. It went *reduce his carbon footprint*, *take one of Scarlett's power pieces in this game*, and *do his part to achieve world peace*. In that order.

When Jaime glanced at her, feeling high, feeling drunk, feeling reckless, Scarlett returned his gaze. But her frosty confidence was as thin as pond ice after the thaw had begun.

She saw what he'd seen.

"That's been there for, like, two moves," she told him.

And she hadn't blocked it.

"I'm a little slow."

"You gonna take it?"

"Hell yes. I may never get another shot like this."

His fingers steady but his pulse a percussive mess, Jaime took her bishop. He set her piece to the side of the board with a thunk.

"Well done." Scarlett's voice betrayed no emotion. Her eyes were another story. Even she couldn't hide their luminosity.

She was pleased. She'd wanted this as much as he had, and that sent him clear over the edge.

"I guess you aren't hopeless at chess after all," she drawled.

"I guess not." Jaime swallowed.

Scarlett rolled onto her knees, and he wanted to say that she didn't have to. That it was silly. That he didn't need a bribe and she didn't have to take her shirt off—and why the hell had they even made this bet in the first place? They weren't teenagers.

But then she was tugging the hem of her shirt up, and the words melted in his mouth.

He'd seen the *Vogue* spread. No, he'd *studied* the *Vogue* spread as if it were the Dead Sea Scrolls and he was a scholar of ancient languages who alone could crack the code. But a photo of her skin and her actual skin—that of her stomach, soft and pale as moonlight—were not the same. Not remotely the same.

Without a hint of shame, Scarlett tugged her shirt up and over her head. She sent it sailing through the air. It landed next to Jaime with a soft thud.

His brain stalled. There were suddenly too many stimuli to make sense of. He couldn't tear his eyes from the swell of her cleavage. From the many inches of velvety skin. From her flushed lips and her wide eyes.

Jaime's attention riveted to her had Scarlett breathing deep, and his own labored inhales matched hers. Goddamn—just goddamn.

He sucked in another breath, and there was the scent of her perfume or lotion, vanilla and something spicy. Something he couldn't have named on pain of death—but what a way to go.

Every cell in Jaime's body was suddenly heavier. Staying upright was damn near impossible. How had he survived seeing her naked?

And how had he survived *not* seeing it?

"You glad we played?" she asked, settling back on her cushion.

"Yup." He couldn't have gotten any more words out.

She draped her arms along the couch behind her, relishing his appraisal. The appraisal he'd tried so hard to hide from her but which was undeniable.

Jesus, she was perfect.

"You want to finish this game?"

He shook his head. There was no point.

"Too bad. I have checkmate in two."

No, she already had Jaime in check, and there was nowhere for him to hide.

Chapter 12

Evelyn materialized the morning after the strip-chess incident, looking as if she'd gotten lost on her way to a rave. "Hey, y'all," she called out as she waltzed into the den.

Scarlett had barricaded herself behind a pile of notebooks and her chess board. Jaime was pointedly *not* on his couch across from her. Instead, he was typing furiously on his laptop at a folding card table across the room.

Ev took in the nonstandard setup and then quirked a brow at Scarlett, as if to say *What's up with this?*

Scarlett could only shrug. It wasn't as if she could explain how and why she'd pissed in the punch bowl.

Ev turned to her brother. "Mom wanted me to let you know that the guy showed up to clean the gutter yesterday."

"Good." Jaime offered this without glancing up from his computer. "I didn't want to have to fire him and find someone else."

Because that was yet another thing he was taking care of for some-one else.

"And"—Evelyn turned to Scarlett—"I'd said I wanted to take you to see my art. I know you two are mostly done, so if you're free today, I thought we could—"

"Yes!" Scarlett nearly yelled, cutting off the end of Ev's question. Scarlett had never needed to get out of the house for some air more in her life. "Let me grab a sweater."

Jaime shot his sister a look. "I think she's trying to get away from me."

Of course Scarlett wanted to bolt. Jaime's house had become . . . stifling.

It was Scarlett's fault, naturally. She'd baited the man and then taken off her clothes in front of him. If she'd planted herself in his bed wearing a whipped-cream bikini, she couldn't have been more shameless.

She'd never really seen the point in shame, but she was paying the price for that now. Over the last few weeks, Jaime had attempted to erect a wall in between them. He'd pulled back from her the smallest bit, but she'd felt the withdrawal sharply—and she'd resented it.

She'd wanted to know if he still wanted her. Now she knew he did.

And what the heck was she going to do about it?

Yeah, Scarlett hadn't the slightest idea. So it was safer to run away until she'd figured it out. At least in real life, unlike in tournament chess, she didn't have to seal her next move in an envelope before taking a break for the night.

"This seems a little normie for you," Scarlett teased as she climbed into Evelyn's Honda Civic after grabbing a sweater and her purse. The car was black, sure, but otherwise it gave suburban-commuter vibes that didn't remotely fit with Ev's neo-goth look.

It was ten o'clock in the morning, and the girl already had on approximately as much smoky eye shadow as Natalie Portman in *Black Swan*.

"It was Mom's."

Yeah, Scarlett could've guessed that.

Evelyn drove them along Musgrove's main street, past the parking lot where she and Jaime had attended the farmers' market the past three Saturdays. He'd even taken her to Emery's last book club meeting, which she'd discovered he sometimes attended. The entire thing had been kinda lovely.

But rather than turning into the residential neighborhoods, Evelyn turned toward the country. They drove past several scrubby farms and dozens of electrical poles overgrown with kudzu before arriving at an abandoned switch house near the railroad tracks. It was one of those structures that could've been built any time between the end of the Civil War and the 1970s, the kind that littered the back roads of the South.

Predictably, the switch house was covered with graffiti, and something about it—perhaps it was the partially collapsed roof over a window that made the structure look as if it were winking in farewell—made Scarlett sad.

Evelyn parked on a spot where the long grass and weeds covering the yard had been tamped down. She took off her seat belt and twisted to grab a bag from the back seat.

"Are we trespassing?" Scarlett asked, as she followed Ev out of the car. They clambered over the broken-down fence surrounding the building.

"That a problem for you?" Ev's expression was mischievous.

"Nope." Scarlett had never been one for following the rules—or at least not the rules that didn't make sense to her. The rules in chess, those made sense. The game wouldn't work without them. Weird social systems, though, about who you should talk to and when you could wear white shoes and what you were allowed to do: those were an entirely other thing.

Though maybe Scarlett was beginning to find some respect for ones such as *Don't undress in front of your ex unless you know what the heck you're hoping to do about it.*

But that wasn't a reasonable thing to ponder in front of Jaime's baby sister.

"So my thesis is about finding abandoned buildings like this one," Evelyn explained. "Places that are magnets for tagging." The plaster walls of the switch house were indeed covered in spray-painted names and initials, sexual comments, and profanity.

"I'm sure there are plenty to choose from around here."

"Yup. Then I do things like this." Ev led Scarlett around the house to the side that faced the tracks. There, she had painted a massive mural with a distinctive art deco–social realism vibe. The figures were highly stylized, a diverse mix of men and women, Black and white and Latine and Indigenous people. They were working in fields and mines, caring for children and teaching, voting and working in stores. It was a vision of what life could be here that was rooted in the past but not nostalgic for it. As if Musgrove were peopled exclusively by diverse superheroes.

Looking at the mural, Scarlett wanted to stand up straighter. To be *better*. That was probably because of the colors, which reflected the landscape. The entire image, actually, seemed as if it belonged here. As if it had grown onto the building rather than being grafted on it.

"Holy crap, Ev," Scarlett breathed. "You're like the Diego Rivera of Appalachia."

But Evelyn, much like her brother, had trouble taking a compliment. "Not really."

Unfortunately, the graffiti artists who'd covered the rest of the switch house hadn't left Evelyn's work alone. Here and there, they'd begun covering Evelyn's piece with names and cusswords.

Scarlett pointed to a note about the size of someone's package. "You gonna paint over that?" Surely it would be possible to cover it up and restore the image to how it had looked when Evelyn had finished it.

"Nope. I'm going to document it." Ev pulled a hulking Nikon and a fancy lens out of her bag.

"Nice camera," Scarlett said, because it clearly was.

"Thanks. It was a Christmas present from Jaime a few years ago." She set about photographing the scrawls that were marring her own work of art.

"This doesn't . . . make you mad?" Scarlett asked.

"No way. I don't own this building any more than they do. I'm trespassing as much as they are. Mine may look more 'artistic,' but it's graffiti too."

All of this went to show that Scarlett had never understood art. Sometimes, if she had time off at a tournament, she tried to class herself up. She'd been to the Louvre, the Rijksmuseum, and the Prado, but underneath it all, she was still a hick who didn't understand why Thomas Kinkade wasn't considered quality.

But what really mattered here, she guessed, was that Evelyn was happy. Scarlett didn't have to understand this project. Ev did, and that was what mattered.

"Can I ask you something?" Scarlett said when Evelyn had finished taking her pictures.

"Of course."

"Are you okay?"

Scarlett meant—well, she meant a lot of things by the question. But if she spelled them out, it would feel as if she were prying or forcing the girl to reveal things she might not want to reveal. So Scarlett could only load the word *okay* with as much meaning as possible and then wait for Evelyn to pick out what she wanted to share.

Luckily, Evelyn was smart, and so she went right for the heart of it. "You mean with my daddy in prison?"

"Yeah." What had happened to the Crofts would've broken the average family. A below-average family such as Scarlett's would have shattered entirely.

Evelyn stowed her camera and considered this. "I'm not glad that it happened, but we're healthier *because* it happened."

"You're *healthier*?" Scarlett echoed stupidly.

Evelyn gave a tight nod. "I spent a lot of time thinking *what if*, not because I wanted to undo it but because I legitimately wondered what it would've been like if he hadn't been arrested. And unless I could rewind the tape and go back to before it began and convince him not to do it, well, then I guess Jaime, Mom, and I ended up better for it. We all got help. I've been in therapy for as long as I can remember. And my mother—I mean, can you imagine her darkening a psychologist's office without this to process?"

"Nope."

"If Dad hadn't been arrested, we would be like some dark domestic HBO drama. We'd all be lying to each other and trying to pretend that we didn't see what we all clearly saw. It would've been deeply fucked up. As it is, we have to talk to each other, and we have to be honest. There's no hiding and there's no false pride. I wish it hadn't happened mostly because I wish he hadn't hurt people. But for myself, I would choose this over whatever other version of my life I might've had."

Whatever Scarlett had been expecting Evelyn to say, it wasn't that. The words made a lot of sense, but it wasn't the outcome that Scarlett or anyone else would've predicted when Dr. Croft had been arrested. It would've seemed more likely the family would've entered the witness protection program and melted away, hoping that nobody ever recognized them or connected them with these events.

But that obviously hadn't been how Jaime had played it. And she suspected that if Evelyn took her to see more of her murals, Scarlett would find some of them probably commented directly on Evelyn's dad too.

Jaime and Evelyn Croft were so much braver than Scarlett would've been in the same situation.

Though . . . maybe they hadn't processed it in the same way. Scarlett wondered if Jaime—who'd had a very different relationship with his father than his baby sister had—would also see the upside in his father's arrest.

Jaime had lost an entire version of himself. He'd deferred college, lost friendships, and been humiliated by it in ways that Evelyn hadn't been. For her, this had been all she'd ever known. Maybe it was easier for her to see the upside in ways Jaime or Mrs. Croft might not be able to.

Carefully but—she hoped—warmly, Scarlett said, "I'm so glad it didn't ruin your life." She'd limit her comments here to Evelyn herself rather than including her mother and brother in them.

"I wouldn't've let it." Evelyn seemed so certain about that, so certain that she was a force of nature, sturdier than the winds that had come rushing toward her seventeen years ago. She'd proved that she was, though, hadn't she? The entire Croft family had.

Scarlett knew people looked at her and thought she was "strong." At some level, she probably was. It took discipline to memorize thousands of chess moves and diagrams. To hold it together during high-stakes matches and to fight back after you'd blundered.

But no matter how much Scarlett won, no matter how much she tried to prove she wasn't the little girl trying to convince another manager not to evict her mother after they hadn't paid the rent, she didn't always believe it. She usually didn't believe it.

Scarlett envied Evelyn's certainty.

Evelyn began walking back to her car, with Scarlett trailing behind her. When Ev reached it and stowed her bag, she shot Scarlett a look. "Can I ask you something now?"

From the expression on Evelyn's face, Scarlett was certain she should say no. This—whatever it was—was going to hurt. But after Evelyn's bald admission, what exactly was Scarlett supposed to do here? Lie?

"Sure." Scarlett braced herself.

"When I walked into Jaime's house—well, let's just say that there are mad scientists' labs with less chemistry going on in them than there was in his den."

Yikes. Also . . . true.

"I'm not hearing a question here," Scarlett said, in order to hedge.

But she had absolutely no problem identifying what Evelyn was asking without asking: *Are you sleeping with my brother?*

No—but I want to.

Evelyn watched Scarlett steadily for a few beats, and Scarlett worried for a second that she might be as transparent to the little sister as she was to the big brother.

Finally, Evelyn said, "I just hope you're being more honest with him than you're being with me."

That was certainly a negative. "You Crofts, you're obsessed with honesty."

"You can understand why."

Yes, Scarlett could.

◆ ◆ ◆

An hour later, after some truly excellent barbeque sandwiches, Evelyn dropped Scarlett off at Jaime's. It was nice that they got to see each other frequently. She wasn't surprised by how connected Jaime was to the town and to his family, but Scarlett could see the appeal of all that now, in ways she never had as a teenager.

Not ready to face Jaime, Scarlett went to hide in her room. The entire trip had stirred things up in her, like leaves whipping through the breeze in October, so she dug her phone out of her pocket and dialed her mother.

Alma answered on the fourth ring. "Hey, darlin'."

"Hey . . . Mom." Scarlett didn't call her mother by her first name, but she'd thought of her that way ever since she'd been eleven because that was when Scarlett had gotten into the habit of filling out all the school paperwork, not to mention all their leases and Alma's job applications and any official form for the government. People always marveled at how good Scarlett's handwriting was, and she knew it was because she'd had to learn to write as a passable adult before she'd been in middle school.

"How the hell are you?" her mother asked.

"I'm good." In an absolute sense, that was true. Scarlett was well fed and well rested. Her bank account was full. She wasn't in any mortal danger.

She was simply in a whirlwind of emotions, without any break in sight. She had to figure out what to do about the stuff she'd realized about Jaime, and she had to do it in a way that didn't break either of them. And she didn't tend to be any good at delicate operations of that sort unless they took place on a chess board.

"You in New York?" Alma asked.

"No, Musgrove." Scarlett had explained that she would be there for two months, two months that were more than halfway through, but she wasn't surprised Alma hadn't remembered.

"How's that pit?" Her mother didn't bother to keep the scorn out of her voice.

Every place they left was a pit. It was the Emerald City when they were on the way there, but as soon as that lie had revealed itself to be, you know, a lie, then it would be downgraded to a pit. That was the way of things with Alma.

"It's more or less the same." The changes that had happened in town wouldn't be interesting to her mother, and besides, Scarlett wasn't certain how to say *It feels sadder* without sounding as if she were judging—and for once, she really didn't want to do that.

"And how's Jaime Croft?" Of course Alma remembered him perfectly well.

Scarlett had always refused to discuss her love life with her mother. One thing that was certainly true of Alma was that she was never without male companionship. She didn't really do "alone," which had ironically meant she was well suited to motherhood.

She'd treated Scarlett as an equal from the age of five on up. Maybe before that, even, but Scarlett couldn't remember before kindergarten. If, sometimes, Scarlett would've wanted Alma to wield some authority or to have advice to offer her daughter, well, that was just tough cookies. Scarlett had the kind of mother who'd paint your nails and make you a margarita. She did not have the kind of mother who'd help you study for the SATs—not that Scarlett had ever taken them.

In the years since she'd grown up, Scarlett had taken the measure of the mothers and fathers she'd encountered, and she'd realized that whatever quibbles she might have with Alma's style, she certainly hadn't done Scarlett any harm. And that was more than she could say for many of the parents she'd met.

"He's . . . I actually think he's well."

Scarlett had spent half her life assuming Jaime and Evelyn were broken. But after spending these weeks with Jaime and after what Evelyn had said today, Scarlett marveled at how they'd come out the other side emotionally grounded and all grown up. That was just *bizarre.* One of them ought to have become a jerk just for fairness or something.

"Well, whatever people say, I guess the apple does fall away from the tree, because his father—"

"We don't need to rehash that." For all that Scarlett didn't like what Dr. Croft had done, she didn't feel the need to crow over the man's fate. It was sad enough on its own.

"Jaime did! I saw his show *The Hungry Sun*."

"*Devouring*," Scarlett corrected, though the idea of the sun chowing down was pretty amusing.

"Whatever. I saw it, and I don't mind saying that that boy can fill out a pair of jeans. But you always did go for the cute ones."

These days, Scarlett went for the ones who asked the least of her. The ones who didn't mind that she didn't do strings, that she wasn't looking for a commitment. When she was preparing for a tournament, Scarlett did chess fourteen hours a day: studying diagrams of old games, spending hours playing blitz games at the Marshall Chess Club, then nights on a burner account on CheckMate.com, hoping no one would recognize her style of play.

No, the only men Scarlett could have in her life were those who wouldn't comment on how, frankly, unhealthy it all was.

That was why she and Jaime could never have a future.

Or at least that was *one* of the reasons. If he saw how she was when she wasn't here, he'd say that she was wearing herself thin, that she didn't sleep enough or walk enough or get enough potassium.

"He's adapting my book," she said instead.

"Oh good. Then I'll finally read it."

What Alma meant was that she'd finally *watch* it. She'd started listening to the audiobook when it had come out, but then she'd lost her phone in Daytona, or at least that was what she'd told Scarlett. It might've hurt except Scarlett had never expected Alma to even bother.

Long ago, Scarlett had realized that she could either take Alma as she was, or she could spend a lifetime being pissed that she wasn't someone else. For once, Scarlett had chosen the mature path, and it had saved her a lot of grief.

"I hope you'll enjoy it." And Scarlett meant that.

In the background, someone said something about dinner.

"Is that Jaxson?" Scarlett asked.

"No," Alma replied, "it's Sean."

Jaxson was probably long gone—and that was what Scarlett got for not talking to her mother more frequently. It was probably quite a story; stories about Alma's love life tended to be.

"Just a second, Sean, I have to wrap up talking to Scarlett." Then, to her daughter she said, "Do you need anything, sweetie?"

That was the thing: if Scarlett had needed something, Alma would've tried to get it for her. At least if it were a cute bathing suit cover-up or tickets to an MMA fight or bail money in Atlantic City. Underneath it all, and in the ways she was capable, Alma loved Scarlett. That knowledge had soothed whatever bumps there had been along the way. Her mother truly loved her.

"Nope, I just wanted to hear your voice."

"It was good to hear from you too! You call me back real soon."

"I will."

After she hung up, Scarlett stared out the window at Jaime's front yard for a long time. The pines were swaying in the breeze, sending patterns of light and shadow over a tooth of bedrock that tore through the earth. Scarlett had read an article in an airplane magazine once about how the Appalachian Mountains were more than a billion years old. Older than the Rockies. Older than the Grand Canyon. So old it made her dizzy to contemplate.

The little dramas and paper cuts that made up Scarlett's life—what would they look like to something that ancient?

Meaningless, presumably. Everything Scarlett did for good or for ill was a sneeze to the mountains. Less than a sneeze: a heartbeat.

When she'd been young, Scarlett hadn't worried about trying to do good. She'd only wanted to *survive*. Later on, when her closet and belly were full, she'd wanted to thrive, including fighting for other people.

To do that, she'd made some dubious choices, hoping the ends justified whatever little harm she might have caused along the way. However, Evelyn's pronouncement that she was better off now than she would've been if her father hadn't been arrested twisted things around. Specifically, it made Scarlett think that her most suspect choices, the ones that had caused her the most grief, might not have been bad at all.

Which changed *everything*.

Feeling twitchy, she finally got up and found Jaime. He was still in the den, but he'd pushed his computer to the side and was staring out the window. The view from here was of the back porch and the valley spilling out before them.

"Sorry I didn't get back sooner." In truth, Scarlett was sorry about so many things. But this was the best she could offer him.

"No problem."

"I couldn't face work today." *I couldn't face* you *today.*

"You've earned a break," he said without judgment. "And Ev's right, we're almost done."

Very soon, Scarlett would head back to New York. She needed to start preparing for Norway Chess in earnest, especially since she'd be taking another break in order to be on set when *Queen's Kiss* filmed. But the last few weeks . . . they'd mixed her up about what mattered, about what was real.

"I want to say something."

Her tone must have given away that it was serious, because Jaime finally turned toward her. He was smiling, but it didn't touch his eyes.

When he said, "Oh boy," the joke was forced, not genuine.

"I think sometimes, the last few weeks, you've wanted answers from me. About why we broke up. About whether we could've made it. Was there some other multiverse in which things didn't end up the way they did between us." That was what she'd thought he'd been asking, anyhow.

He just watched her, steadily, patiently. Not contradicting her summary of what they'd talked about sometimes, when they were feeling brave or stupid, or both.

"And maybe I've wanted answers too," she said. "Maybe that's why I refused to give the rights to *Queen's Kiss* to anyone but you. Because I thought if I let you have my book, I could learn how you've been. Whether your life had been . . . destroyed when your dad went to prison. And today with Evelyn, I finally found the answer I was looking for: no."

Or at least she hoped he saw things the way Evelyn did.

"You could've just asked me that," Jaime said. "I could've told you I wasn't."

Thank God. "But I needed to *see* it. I needed to . . . believe it."

"And you do now?"

"Yup. And so, because I'm confident about that, I think I can finally offer you what you want."

He seemed to find this possibility amusing. Or intriguing. "And that is?"

"It wasn't a tragedy that we broke up. It wasn't because of what happened with your dad. It was just that we were young, and we wanted different things. I loved chess—I do love chess. And playing has given me so many things I never would've gotten any other way. I've been around the world. Do you really think that would've happened for me if I had stayed here and worked at the Waffle House? Honestly, can you imagine me working at a restaurant?" Or even worse, an office—yikes.

"Nope." His smile was bittersweet.

"*The one who got away* is a seductive idea, but it isn't real. Leaving you made all my dreams possible. And I know now that even if your dad hadn't been arrested, you wouldn't have come with me. You would've gone to Tech, and you would've grown in different ways too." *And you would've met women who aren't as difficult as I am.* "And so we still would've broken up. We still would've . . . hurt each other." It just would've been in a different moment and in a different way.

Jaime buried one of his hands in his hair, as if he needed to hold his head into place while she knocked his world off kilter. "You know, staying didn't ruin my life either. It just changed it. Obviously I didn't stop writing just because I didn't go to college right away. I didn't stop filming stuff. My path was messy, but I still got to make movies in the end. I wish it had been easier sometimes, and I really wish so many people didn't need to get hurt, but I still got where I wanted to go."

"Yup. Maybe it's been comforting over the years for us to dwell on the coulda, shoulda, woulda. But it's like thinking, on vacation, that you ought to move to the beach. If you really did it, you'd still have to make money somehow, and you'd still have to scrub the floors of your cabana. And you aren't ever getting away from laundry—it'll follow you into the grave! No, you don't want to move to the beach—you want to be on vacation all the time. Pining for the one who got away is actually pining for . . ."

In Jaime's case, it was probably pining for *someone*. Jaime clearly would do well with a family. He was built for it. He'd be good at being a husband, being a father. He could be the true paragon his father had pretended to be.

In Scarlett's case, it was probably pining for a time when her life had been simpler. For when she wasn't an object of fascination for the entire chess world. Or for those days with Jaime before everything had changed and she'd realized her potential and her power.

". . . for the past," she finished weakly. "You're a pawn, so you can't go backward. You just have to keep advancing. So that's my answer, Jaime Croft. Breaking up wasn't what either of us wanted, but it was our only play."

Jaime sat with Scarlett's speech for a long time.

"Thanks," he finally said. "For telling me that."

She hoped he felt grateful and that, at some point, when she gave him the rest of the truth, he'd stay grateful. For now, untangling this piece of it—articulating it, reckoning with it—left Scarlett feeling as if she'd just gotten over pneumonia. It was going to take a good long while to get back to fighting weight here.

Scarlett got to her feet. "I think I'm going to take a nap."

But as she was leaving the room, she thought she heard Jaime say under his breath, "Answers aren't the only things I want from you."

Chapter 13

The days slipped past each other like grains of sand through the narrow waist of an hourglass. The words did too. Page by page, week by week, Jaime and Scarlett had toiled away, and they were close to finishing the scripts for *Queen's Kiss*.

They had worked together well, at least once Jaime had adjusted himself to the reality of being madly attracted to his cowriter.

"How much longer do you think we have?" Scarlett asked as she gathered the dishes from the table after dinner one night.

Early on, she would've asked that question eagerly. Now, it was careful, as if she were worried about how he was going to answer.

In the moments when he'd thought he understood her the best, he'd wanted to believe it was because she wanted him just as much and she'd needed the cover of knowing she wasn't alone in her neediness. But he'd never been certain if that was a delusion or not.

You just want her to be worried.

Jaime was loading the dishwasher and trying to come up with more work for them to do—and failing at the second thing. They were on the cusp of finishing, and unfortunately, he'd set up too many redundancies for Scarlett to believe they'd had a catastrophic file failure.

Damn cloud storage.

"Three days. Maybe four."

"I ought to start looking at flights." Scarlett's tone was strained.

Or maybe Jaime *hoped* it was strained. He'd gone from admitting he wanted her back to trying to pretend he didn't. After her declaration that *the one who got away* was a mirage and they needed to move on, he'd been reduced to looking for a crumb of possibility in everything she said, searching for some tiny sign that maybe she was finding it as hard to take her advice as he was.

"What are you going to do when you get back to New York?" he asked, trying to sound casual, without any hint of his inner panic.

"Start studying for Stavanger."

Before Jaime consciously formed the words, an answer was in his head: *You could study for the tournament in Musgrove.* Jaime still had a lot of work to do to take their first-pass scripts and turn them into a plan for shooting the series. There would be loads of preproduction meetings, casting sessions, location scouting—she ought to weigh in on all that as a producer on the show.

But Jaime couldn't think of how to word a pitch so it wouldn't sound ridiculously needy. And realistically, it all boiled down to the fact that he didn't want Scarlett to leave him. If he said anything other than *Don't go, I like having you here*, even if only inside his head, it would be a self-serving lie, and they'd spent enough time lying to each other for a lifetime.

"You looking forward to competing again?" he asked instead.

"I guess. Right now, the prospect feels . . . exhausting. But at the end of the day, I am really competitive. Once I get in the groove of preparing, the desire to win will carry me."

That much he believed.

"Good luck." But his words were as hollow as a drum. Jaime did wish her luck, but the house was going to feel damn empty without her. Everything was going to be so drab when she got into her rental car and left Musgrove in the dust again.

When the final dish was stowed in the dishwasher, Scarlett and Jaime navigated the now familiar mild awkwardness of saying good night to each other. The first few weeks, he'd talked her into watching movies with him, but when you turned off the television, you were left sitting there in the dark together. Sitting, in a moment when, in the past, they would've found a way to fill the time. A very sexy way.

Now, Jaime had to fill the space with his heated imaginings, which were a sucky substitute.

"I'm going to bed," Scarlett said a little too sharply, right as he said, "I think I'll sit outside for a bit."

Well, that took care of that. With any luck, it would be freezing out, and Jaime would be able to put his libido into a state of semihibernation. But when Jaime settled himself on the porch, where it was brisk but not cold enough to settle himself down, with only the stars and a beer to keep him company, the loneliness didn't last.

Approximately seven minutes after he'd sunk into one of the Adirondack chairs, Scarlett's voice came from the door leading from the kitchen to the porch. "Jaime?"

She hadn't turned on the overhead lights, but the LED displays for the stove and the microwave had her hair sparkling in spots.

"Out here."

Her bare feet were soft on the deck as she crossed over to him.

"Where's your sweater?" As she got closer, he could see that she hadn't put on that soft-looking lumpy cardigan she'd worn almost every morning while they'd written.

"I'll only be a minute. I just wanted to ask you something. I was thinking—wait, what was that?" She twisted away from him, her arms crossing over her chest.

That made sense. His reflex was to protect her magnificent cleavage first too.

"An owl."

Scarlett turned back to him, her eyes wide and incredulous. "Honestly?"

"Yeah, there are great horned owls around here. I see them flying sometimes."

They were massive, with bodies nearly as long as a toddler's. Jaime had almost pissed himself the first time one had swooped overhead when he'd been out here, but if he said that, it would be a steroid for her fears.

He changed the subject back. "What did you want to ask me?" That came out soft. Everything with Scarlett and Jaime was soft now. It was as if they'd stripped off their prickles along with their armor after she'd threatened to go back to New York. She'd said they ought to give up on the fantasy of the past, but maybe—and here was delusional Jaime again—that meant there was the reality of the present. The reality of two bruised, mature people finding their way back to each other.

They'd certainly figured out how to be themselves again. Their grown-up selves, sure, but they were no longer posturing the way they'd been when Scarlett had first arrived in Musgrove. And maybe they weren't mad anymore. Or at least Jaime wasn't mad.

Maybe, maybe, maybe: it was the refrain of a hundred pop songs, an idea that got repeated because there was nothing more tantalizing than the idea that something could be.

Or in Scarlett and Jaime's case, that something could be again.

"I can't remember." Scarlett had turned around, away from him, and she was still scanning the trees for the source of the noise. As if she could protect herself if she just knew where the owl was.

Jaime set his beer on the arm of the chair and stood up. "Should I get you some night vision goggles?"

"Do you have some?"

Before he could answer, the owl hooted again, and Scarlett backed straight into Jaime's chest. Her hair rubbed against his cheek, smelling like herbs and spices, with vanilla as the creamy background.

Christ, he'd missed the scent.

Jaime wrapped an arm over her neck, keeping her close. Comforting herself and himself at the same time. "There's nothing to be scared of."

"It's a giant predatory *bird*. What's not to be scared of?"

The pounding in Jaime's ribs, maybe, which he'd spent weeks trying to stop. Trying to ignore. But his feelings weren't going away, and it would be easier to disregard a tornado. Some things were so large, so real, that you couldn't deny them. This was one of them.

"Come on, killer," he said, towing Scarlett toward the house.

She matched her strides to his, and the brush of her ass against his pelvis was obnoxiously arousing.

Why did this woman have to be his match in every way?

And why, once he'd managed to get the door open and the two of them through it, did she have to turn and throw her arms around his neck and nestle into his chest? Why did that have to split him open, letting all the tenderness he had for her spill out as surely as his guts would if she sliced him from hip to hip?

"Scarlett." It was a warning and a promise and a question. Two syllables that contained everything.

Since the day she'd challenged him to that match of strip chess, they'd been on a collision course with this moment. When the reasons why they shouldn't fall into each other's arms grew too loud to ignore. When the present and the past blurred into one stream of wanting.

When Scarlett raised her head and pressed her mouth to his, it was everything he'd been hoping she'd do, and everything he'd been terrified she never would.

Her lips were . . . so soft. Too soft, really, for how smart and sharp her mouth could be. Too soft for the force with which she was pressing into him. How could something that supple be that strong?

Witchcraft. It was the only explanation.

The potency of their first kiss after so long told him she hadn't kissed him by accident, instead matching his own surging certainty. This wasn't a glancing brush, or a thank-God-we-survived-the-killer-owl buss. No, this kiss was a riptide, yanking Jaime out of his kitchen, a place of rules and rationality and good decisions, and tossing him into a churning sea.

He was so goddamn grateful that she'd done it, but oh Lord, this was going to hurt. He could still summon a lick of how it had felt when she'd left before. His heart ached at the memory—and the premonition of what would inevitably happen again.

Except before Jaime got his nose bloodied and his heart shattered a second time, it was going to be wonderful. After so long, after so much, he needed some wonderful. Whatever the cost, he was going to seize this while it was on offer.

Jaime made a needy noise in the back of his throat, midway between a moan and a growl, and he grabbed Scarlett's ass and pulled her into him, hip to hip, with no space or light between them. That was better.

Not *enough*, but it was better.

Jaime kissed her back with everything he had in him. All the longing, all the wanting. And Scarlett matched him. The woman kissed like she did everything: twice as enthusiastically as anyone else. A grappling tumble of a kiss that turned Jaime inside out.

After a minute, Scarlett's chin popped up, unsealing their mouths. "Stop."

He did. Instantly.

Breathing hard, she pushed her hair behind her right ear. "Did you decide to adapt my book knowing this was going to happen? Wanting this to happen?"

With the blood throbbing in his dick, in his stomach, Jaime had no idea how to answer, or even what an answer was. "I don't know. Maybe. Yes."

That felt right—yes. The answer was yes. Yes, when he'd gone to New York, some part of him had hoped this would happen.

"I've wanted you back for . . . for seventeen years," he admitted. "I wanted you back from the moment you walked away from me. I didn't plan this." He couldn't've. "But I wanted it."

What he didn't say was that sometimes, Jaime would wake up in the middle of the night, aching for her. Even after this long, even after falling—legitimately falling—for other people, it had always been Scarlett.

She probably could sense that. But Jaime wasn't going to give her that admission unless she pushed for it. He wanted to at least pretend that he had some dignity here, even if he very, very much did not.

"Okay." Scarlett accepted this—and then, for what felt like an hour, they stood there watching each other. Finally, she set her hands on his shoulders. "Okay." Then she was kissing him again.

There was so much they ought to say to each other first. So much they ought to figure out. But all Jaime could do was to trail his lips over her jawline and to pull her earlobe in between his teeth. Such a tiny scrap of skin, but from experience, he knew that it had a direct link to the nerves of all her sensitive places.

Sure enough, she gasped—and that sound had a direct link to the nerves on all *his* sensitive places.

"You always sound so surprised," he muttered around her earlobe.

"Because it's always a surprise." *It* being how strong the wanting was between them, and *always* because even if they spent a lifetime doing this, neither of them would ever get used to it.

"Let me see if the other side works."

Scarlett tried not to react. Jaime could feel her steeling herself, could sense her biting her bottom lip. But when his canine tooth grazed the shell of her ear, her resistance crumbled.

"Jaime."

Her breathy shock was the ultimate turn-on. His mind was . . . blown. The only thing that had stopped him from ripping their clothing off and *burying* himself in her was a desire to hear that sound more. The faster this went, the less of that he'd get.

Jaime dropped to his knees, which brought his face between her glorious, glorious breasts. Even through her thin tank top, he could smell her skin, which he swore smelled different from the skin anywhere else on her body. More . . . delicate. More enticing.

Her hands tangled in his hair, and Scarlett had no shame about directing Jaime's attentions exactly where she wanted them. Since it was exactly where he wanted them, this suited everyone.

He bit her through her shirt, and there was that gasp again. As if she'd never gotten used to pleasure. As if the fact of it shocked her every time.

Jaime pushed his hand under her shirt, over the soft skin of her belly and around to her back. Thank God her sports bra had a clasp. He fumbled with the hooks for a second, but he managed to free her and then to shove all of it, shirt and bra, out of the way.

When his mouth found her breasts, he was rewarded with a long, keening "Oh God, oh God, oh God."

The first time they'd done this, she'd started to beg.

What do you need? he'd asked. He would've burned down the world to give it to her.

Not sure was all that she'd been able to make out. *But please.*

He'd figured out what she'd needed eventually, and it turned out that seventeen years later, she needed the same thing.

"Here?" He pressed her clit through her pajama pants.

"Yes."

Making her come again was like riding a bike: hard-won knowledge that had never left him. Where she wanted to be touched, how much pressure she needed, where she wanted his mouth on her, none of it had changed.

The answering roar in his body was the same too.

When her orgasm hit her, Scarlett laughed. Actually laughed. The kind of gurgling giggle that comes up from your diaphragm and out of your throat. The kind that made Jaime feel like he'd done something heroic. The kind of accomplishment Homer would write an epic poem about. And the truth was, Jaime had made Scarlett Arbuthnot come, and that *was* epic. For whatever reason, she'd decided to kiss him again, and he'd proved he was worthy by making her come.

That was pretty damn impressive.

He rolled to his knees, kissing up her body in the process. Saying hello to the inside of her elbow. The sweep of her collarbone. The freckle on her temple.

But when he locked eyes with her, she threw out a dare. "Do you have condoms?"

She was going to hate him. "No."

"You really didn't plan this." She was more amused than angry. "And you haven't had anyone here?" She was asking if he'd slept with anyone since moving into the house. Well, that was the simplest thing she was asking, anyhow.

"Nope." The last woman Jaime had dated had been when he'd been in LA working on *Waverley*. In Musgrove, there weren't many single women Jaime's age. If he hit a bar and tried to pick someone up, it would've gotten back to his mom—the ultimate form of birth control.

"We don't, that is—we could get a hotel, pick up some condoms, and—"

"A hotel?" Jaime huffed out a laugh.

"Because you might not want the memories here."

That was thoughtful. But the horses had already bolted from the barn. "Scarlett, our first time was in my childhood bedroom in the house my mom still owns. You weren't worried about memories then."

"Yeah, well, how did that work out for you?"

"Touché." The truth was Jaime and Scarlett had already made an inconvenient number of memories in this house too. For all that they hadn't been touching in the last two months, she was in every room. Whatever she was trying to spare him here, it was too late. "Maybe I want the memories."

"Do you?" She made a sound as if he couldn't, but that if somehow he did, it would make her world.

"I want you." Jaime kissed her again, kissed her until they were gasping. Until she was moving against him in ways that were incendiary. "I want to have you in every room in the house. In my bed. In the guest bed. On the couch. Over the kitchen table. I want the memories to haunt every room in the house when you're gone."

"Because you know I'll be gone?"

While it slayed him, he did. She'd been totally clear about that.

But he needed her to understand that he wasn't the same man who'd stood in her lobby and begged for the rights to her book. He'd grown over these months together, and he'd let go of some of the pain of the past. She'd helped him do that.

If they were going to do this, she needed to understand he was different. "I'd never want to tie you down. If this is just for tonight—I still want it. I still want you."

"I'm a bull in a china shop, Jaime. I don't want to get rung up for breaking you again."

"You won't. Cross my heart."

"Then let me see the owner's suite."

He took her hand, and their fingers rolling together, tight as a zipper, was every bit as intimate as anything else they'd done.

Jaime towed her through the dark house and into his bedroom. He skipped the overhead light and went for the lamp by the bed instead. It cast a golden circle of light over the bed and the floor.

Scarlett stood on the edge of it, with only her toes fully illuminated. Her nails were painted bubble-gum pink, and his chest squeezed at the sight.

"You getting cold feet?" He hoped that came out as the joke he'd intended it to be and not anything more desperate.

"Nah, just thinking about what a huge deal it was to see your bed that first time."

Technically, Jaime hadn't been allowed to have girls in his room back then. But he hadn't cared much for technicalities where she was concerned. Whatever risk of discovery they'd taken, it had been worth it.

Jaime sprawled out onto his bed, hoping he looked enticing. "How does this one compare?"

"It's even better." She was staring at him, not at the bed.

This was so heavy. But the very weight of it made everything hit harder.

"Take your clothes off," she said.

Jaime's fingers were clumsy as he reached for the hem of his T-shirt. He dropped it onto the floor on the far side of the bed—though it was tempting to follow her lead from the other day and send it sailing toward her. Then he unbuttoned his jeans and shucked them and his boxers off.

When he flopped back down, totally naked, Scarlett edged into the light. She was so utterly, outrageously beautiful.

"I'm no longer eighteen," she said, as if she were apologizing for something.

But Jaime had never seen—and never expected to see—anyone he found as beautiful as he did her. She was his perfection.

"What do you know, neither am I."

"But one of us hikes every day, and the other one pays her bills by playing chess and endorsing stuff."

"And posing naked in fashion magazines."

"That's haunted you, hasn't it?"

"Come here and let me show you how much."

She took another step closer.

"Are you . . . nervous?" he asked. The idea of Scarlett being nervous about anything almost spooked him.

"I wish we'd already done it."

"Here's the thing: we have."

"No, *now*. Then I could enjoy the second round. Not be so in my head."

"I'm fond of your head." He reached out and wrapped his fingers around her wrist. Her heartbeat was going like the percussion line during the crescendo for the *1812 Overture*.

Jaime lifted her wrist to his mouth and drew a deep breath. Her scent—that was the stuff. It soothed something in him that had been aching for seventeen years. He ran his teeth along the sinews of her forearm, and she gasped.

Whatever else was true, that was how they were together. Fire and a match.

Against her skin, he whispered, "Honey, take off your pants."

Before, she'd wanted him to beg. The way he'd wanted her, the way he would've done anything to have her, it got her going like nothing else.

An elegant pause. Then she pulled away from him, and in a great rush, she pulled off her clothing. Jaime swallowed. Dear Lord, he'd missed her.

For a second, her eyes were on the floor and her cheeks were flushed, but when she raised her gaze to his—well, it was good he was lying down.

"You have never been more beautiful," he said, meaning it.

Then Scarlett was on the bed, straddling him. The world's softest body hovering above his was almost too much, and he almost lost it right there. The ticklish brush of her hair against his cheek. The intoxicating taste of her mouth on his. The aching firmness of her hand on his cock. Any one of those sensations was enough to push him over the edge.

First, though, he had to take care of her.

Jaime palmed her ass and pressed a fingertip into her folds. She was the warm and wet center of the world.

Scarlett came up for air. "Oh God."

"Yes?" he asked, slipping another millimeter into her heat.

"Yes," she whispered.

Jaime slid two fingers into her, knuckle deep. He'd dreamed about this, precisely this, so many times. The way her breath went ragged. The way her lashes fluttered close. The way she collapsed into herself when he thrust into her, as if she were trying to hold on to the sensation. As if what he made her feel was the most precious phenomenon on earth.

"Fuck," she gasped—and the pace she set with her hand on him, the one that he knew she wanted him to match, was just this side of punishing. Together, they were the hairline fracture between pleasure and pain, and so much more intense for that. A skosh too far or not far enough, and they'd break.

"There," she said insistently, and what she meant was the way he gripped her and the way his heart exploded and the way the light made her jawline glow.

Jaime couldn't have lasted a millisecond longer. Not with the heaving of her breasts over him, and the relentless cadence of her panting, and the way she was clenched onto his fingers.

Her orgasm felt endless, while his was a single spasm, but her long exhale afterward, as she collapsed on him, was entirely the same as his.

"I missed that," she muttered.

I missed you. But he'd promised her he wouldn't ask for too much, so he kept the words inside. This had been about sex—and nothing else. He had to remember that. As difficult as it was, he couldn't lose sight of the limitations here.

"Come on," he said, pushing up on his elbows. "Let me show you the tub."

"Oh my God, you have jets in here?" she said, when he'd drawn a bath.

"It's my house. I had to keep the good stuff for myself." Like, say, having Scarlett back in his bed.

When he'd added several capfuls of bubbles, they slid into the tub together, her back pressed into his chest and her perfectly rounded backside nestled between his thighs.

"What are you thinking?" she whispered as he held her.

"I need to get some condoms."

She laughed—which was what he'd been going for—but his joke didn't begin to cover a fraction of what was in his head.

Mostly Jaime was hoping that the pain, when it came, wouldn't bury him.

Chapter 14

If there was one bad habit Scarlett didn't practice, it was sneaking out of a lover's hotel room or apartment the morning after a tumble in the sheets. She wasn't a thief escaping from the scene of a crime. No, Scarlett liked sex. A lot. When she invited herself into someone's bed, it was very much on purpose. Why act mortified by the hungry creature she'd been, when she wasn't?

But all those other times and all those other men hadn't been Jaime Croft. They extra-especially hadn't been Jaime Croft seventeen years after the first time.

No, this was the sequel to the most devastating relationship of her life, and so if she could've snuck out and gotten away with it, she would've been tempted to do a runner.

With everyone else, Scarlett was on the attack, but with Jaime, she was on defense. And as every chess player will tell you, defensive play is infinitely harder. If an attack fails, you make another attack. But there's no room for error when you're trying to keep your king safe.

So rather than rising from his bed—his! bed!—a groggy mess like normal, the morning after she'd slept with Jaime, Scarlett woke up fully and utterly alert. She entered the kitchen showered and dressed, her hair styled and her makeup in place, with enough adrenaline zinging through her that she could've taken a pass on her coffee.

But she almost started vibrating when she saw what was sitting next to the coffee mug she'd been using every morning.

A box of condoms.

She couldn't tear her eyes from the box. It was a value pack of thirty-six. If she left in five days . . . that was an extremely hopeful number.

But an exciting one.

"Morning." Jaime's voice was scratchy in the best way, and so Scarlett couldn't help it. Her eyes darted to him and immediately regretted it. His gaze was pure fire. Just distilled heat and sex and longing, and every inch of her started to smolder.

She opened her mouth to ask how he'd slept, then she remembered *where* she'd slept, and she half swallowed her own tongue.

The morning after was a flipping minefield when the person you'd boned was your ex.

She was going to have to remember that for the future. *Make dubious sexual decisions with anyone else—but not with the one guy whose heart you broke.*

Jaime filled her mug. It took forever. If he had grown the coffee beans, harvested them, roasted them, and ground them, it couldn't have taken longer. Then with deliberate carefulness, he set the carafe in the machine and began stalking toward her.

Right, the morning after wasn't some hurdle they were going to leap over before never seeing each other again. It was the opening move in the next stage of their game.

A stage she feared and desperately, desperately wanted.

Scarlett drew a harsh breath that burned all the way down her throat. The look on his face was—wow. All of her came to sharp, aching attention as she took a step back and collided with the counter. At least it kept her standing.

Jaime set one hand on the counter to her left. She almost darted right. Then he placed his other hand there, blocking her escape.

"You're trapped," he whispered.

But Scarlett had already known that. For better or for worse, she was caught.

"What are you going to do with me?" If Scarlett could've had some cool dignity here, that would've been awesome. Instead, she sounded like a phone sex operator: ridiculously, comically turned on.

Which she *was*, but she didn't want him to know that.

"This." With dizzying slowness, Jaime pressed his mouth to hers. When he kissed her like this, where the only point of contact between them was their mouths, Scarlett almost lost her mind. The touch was so *delicate* it made her feel precious and cared for and special. His mouth became her only link to the world of emotions and pleasure she was desperate to get to.

It hadn't been like this with anyone else. Kissing and sex were pleasant and pleasurable, but it had been all too easy for some part of her to still be imagining all the ways to get out of a difficult position in the last match she'd lost or what she was going to have for dinner.

When Jaime kissed Scarlett, there wasn't room for anything else. Not even all the reasons this was a terrible idea.

With a moan, Scarlett surged forward, needing to touch him, and obligingly, he pressed her against the counter. Every inch of him was hard, and he worked himself against her until she was making needy, begging noises. This was so not enough.

He moved one of his hands to the base of her throat, and he lifted his mouth from hers. Her pulse fluttered against his fingers like a hummingbird's wings against the air.

"How do you feel about counter sex?" she asked, trying to make the question light. Instead, it was painfully sincere.

"I like it fine"—his smile was amused—"but first, we're going to polish that scene in the radio station."

"I can't work like this." Scarlett wasn't even being coy. Quite simply, her brain needed her to find release, otherwise, the only things she was going to be able to write were *harder* and *faster* and *more*.

"That bad?"

She could tell him. Or she could show him. Trying to look cool, she unbuttoned her jeans and slid the zipper down. Jaime's eyes went wider. His dark-brown irises were nearly swallowed by his pupils.

Then she slipped her fingers around his wrist and drew his hand down her body. They breathed as one while his touch, guided by her, passed over her T-shirt between her breasts. Down over the slope of her stomach. Over the bare skin of her lower abdomen.

By the time she pressed his fingers under the waist of her panties, she was panting. Her nails dug into his wrist while he continued his exploration.

She'd been trying to get her way here with this gambit, but when he pinched her clit—actually pinched—Scarlett made a half cry.

"Shhh." He was spreading wetness from her entrance over her clit. "I can take the edge off."

"I need you. Please. Please." There wasn't much dignity in it, but now that she'd seen the condoms, satisfaction was going to come one way, if it came at all.

Jaime pressed two fingertips into her and worked the heel of his hand against her.

She tilted her hips, trying to increase the contact. "More."

"My greedy, greedy baby."

He had no idea.

For several seconds, Scarlett wasn't certain which way this was going to go. If she was going to get off, but not in the way she wanted to, or if he was going to respond to her appeals and offer what she really wanted.

Given that her eyes were rolling back in her head and that she was already, *already*, so close, the first one didn't seem like such a bad compromise.

But then Jaime's hand was gone, and he was turning her around and pushing her jeans and panties down to her knees. Her hands slapped onto the counter with grateful percussive whacks, and he was ripping the box open. Strips of condoms poured onto the counter, and Jaime was pulling his own pants down and cursing.

Then, after what seemed like an eon but could've been only thirty seconds, he was guiding himself into her and she was crying. She was actually crying. Which felt like too much and felt too silly and felt just right. After so long to have him again was . . . overwhelming.

One of Jaime's hands crushed around her hip, and the other wiped the tears from her cheek. "Baby." He thrust into her, and she raised her ass, needing to take him deeper. *"Baby."*

All the air left Scarlett's body. Jaime filled her up entirely. Every inch, every cavity was all him.

"Is this what you need?" he asked, and the question was so loaded.

"Yes." Whatever he thought he'd asked, that was the answer. *Yes*, she needed him to take her. *Yes*, she needed him to see her tears. *Yes*, she needed him to watch over her.

Yes and yes and yes and yes.

"The way you feel right now," he rasped into her ear, "like you'll explode if I don't fuck you?"

"Uh-huh." She couldn't manage anything more verbal than that. How was he putting together complex sentences?

"That's how you make me feel every goddamn day. Every. Single. Day."

It couldn't be true. To feel this much hunger every day, to not be satisfied for literally decades—surely that would consume a person.

But then again, the smell of his skin in her nose and the taste of him on her tongue were sensations she'd been chasing for years without knowing it. It was only when they reappeared in her life that she'd been able to name the thing she'd wanted.

Jaime.

He touched her then, exactly where she needed it, exactly how she needed it, and Scarlett couldn't help herself. She moaned his name, and with that, she fell over the edge.

Later, when they'd cleaned up, and she'd had her coffee, and they'd launched into a regular work day—albeit with less eye contact than normal—it was those words, not the orgasm, that she kept contemplating.

This thing between them was elemental. Undeniable. Except once upon a time, Scarlett had very much denied it. How and what she'd done in that moment were exactly why she couldn't, absolutely couldn't, have him again.

Right now, she wanted to. Oh, how she wanted to.

But the truth would come out eventually. It always did.

◆ ◆ ◆

When he'd been kissing Scarlett and leading her to his bed, Jaime had known he was tossing sticks of dynamite into the air here, and he couldn't juggle.

He hadn't deluded himself about the likely outcome of this: they were going to destroy each other again. He couldn't con himself into denying that the smart money would be on them flaming out. He ought to be treating this as a sweet coda to whatever trip down memory lane they'd indulged in the last two months and nothing more.

But when one day of them sleeping together became two, and when that became three. When Scarlett lost her scaredy-cat look and became bratty and confident again. When she began to brazenly demand what she wanted from him, in the bedroom and outside it. When their identity as lovers began to merge with their identity as friends and writing partners, Jaime began to indulge in some daydreams.

Or what he hoped weren't daydreams.

Puffy, needy, naked little hopes that could maybe turn into full-fledged prospects, if only Jaime could shelter them from reality for a little longer. Keep them watered and fed. Give them room to grow.

This time, it could work. The words were on his tongue every time he moved inside her. Every time she caught his eyes in the kitchen and looked away because whatever she saw on his face was too much.

Them together forever wasn't some absurd sci-fi thought, like a functional Congress or a natural deodorant that worked as advertised. It could happen.

It could totally happen.

Take Monday morning of their last week together. A few assertive rays of light pushed in around the edges of Jaime's blinds, growing brighter and brighter until, at last, Scarlett stirred on his chest.

"Arg."

That meant she wanted him to make the sun stop shining.

"Sorry, I can't manage that." Though he was willing to try for her.

Jaime pressed his lips to the place where her forehead became a messy tangle of strawberry blond curls and inhaled the scent of her skin, mixed with what was left of her shampoo and the sweat they'd worked up last night. It was an intimate smell. An imperfect one. And it hooked him more cleanly than whatever designer perfume she put on every morning.

"We have to get up," he whispered.

"Don't wanna."

They hadn't actually spent a night together before, back when they had first been together. Sometimes, when her mom was out for the night, they'd set a timer and doze in Scarlett's bed for a few hours, and even that had felt deliciously illicit.

But now that he had her next to him for several nights in a row, Jaime knew that as much as he liked having sex with Scarlett, the simple pleasures of this—holding her in his arms, becoming fluent in the language of grunts and mumbles she spoke in before fully waking up—was a zillion times more cozy.

This was what he wanted, now and forever.

"You sure?" he asked.

"Uh-huh."

Then he set about showing her some of the benefits of being awake.

In the shower afterward, it hit him that Scarlett satisfied an appetite in him that no one else ever had. It wasn't only a first-love thing. It wasn't just him idolizing a ghost. They fit each other like a custom lock and key. They'd filed each other down until they were each other's perfect match. No one else could open Jaime up. No one else was enough for her.

She'd been right when she'd said that their breakup wasn't a tragedy but a result of where they'd been at and what they'd wanted. But now, they were at a different place, and they wanted different things.

Maybe. Maybe this time, things could be different.

God, it was a dangerous notion. But with Scarlett in his home, Jaime had grown used to dangerous notions.

A few hours later, after they'd had coffee and breakfast and started working, Scarlett looked up from her computer. Her smirk was a stroke to his groin. "You aren't formatting those pages, are you?"

"Nope."

Her eyes shifted back to her work, but he knew she was imagining them picking up where they'd left off earlier. "Stop it. You said not until after lunch."

"Morning taskmaster Jaime sounds mean."

"You made me promise." She pointed to the whiteboard where, at his instruction, she'd written *I will not have sex with Jaime until after noon* and signed and dated the pledge.

He hoped Evelyn didn't make a surprise appearance. That would be a hell of a thing to explain to his little sister.

"And besides," Scarlett said in a singsong voice, "the sooner we get done for the day, the sooner we can go back to bed."

That was logical. "I'm going to hold you to that."

"And I'm going to hold onto—"

"Don't finish that sentence until after noon," he warned.

Her answering laugh was low and throaty—and it really didn't aid the cause of getting some work done now.

But as Jaime finally, reluctantly began formatting the damn pages they'd written yesterday, something like calmness settled into his gut along with all the arousal.

He and Scarlett were in their thirties now. They were established and mature. Most importantly, he and Scarlett suited each other like peanut butter and jelly. They could get work done, alongside each other if not together. And their chemistry was the stuff of legend.

It wasn't delusional to see that, to know it, and to hope that before she left for New York, he might be able to convince Scarlett their story didn't have to have the same ending.

They lived in a world of multiverses, right? They just had to find their way into a universe where, this time, things were different.

Chapter 15

They finished the last script for *Queen's Kiss* on a Friday, but Scarlett put off leaving Musgrove until Monday. She made some excuse about that being an even sixty days for her rental car, but Scarlett and Jaime both knew she was lying.

The truth was she wanted one last long weekend with him, and she didn't want to have to admit that out loud. Jaime accepted her lie gracefully, and she was grateful he pretended.

See, they were perfect for each other.

Except . . . she was kinda beginning to worry they *were* actually perfect for each other. Or at the very least, that no one else would ever be as good for her as Jaime was. He just took such good care of her. He made her laugh like no one else, and he challenged her like no one else, and he made her come like no one else. What exactly was she holding out for, if not that?

Oh, right. Someone whose heart she hadn't pulverized.

That was the long and short of it. Every time Jaime hinted Scarlett could stay as long as she wanted. Every time she began to think maybe Musgrove wasn't the worst place on earth and it would be nice to continue seeing Evelyn regularly. Every time he made some mention of something they'd do together in the future and then shot her a look, as if to say *Go on, contradict me*, Scarlett began to wonder if she could pull this off. Could she tell him what had gone down seventeen years ago, and was there even the slightest hope he might see her side of the story?

There was only one sure way to find out. She had to tell him what she'd done.

Ever the coward, Scarlett waited until the last possible moment. Jaime sent the final scripts to his contact at Videon, and Scarlett had said goodbye to Evelyn. She'd even packed her bags and stowed them in her rental car.

But as they stood there in his vestibule, eyeing each other as if waiting for the other to say it, Jaime was the one who took the plunge.

"I'm glad you came."

"I am too." Whatever came next, however Jaime responded to what she was about to say, Scarlett would be glad for these months in his house. She would be glad for the nights in his bed.

"I've been thinking about the last time you left. Specifically your idea that our breakup was just a problem of timing."

"You're adding that *just*. Timing is everything." The line would be more convincing if Scarlett didn't sound as tense as she felt.

She'd wanted to have this conversation. She would've initiated this conversation if he hadn't. But the icy finger of premonition—the one that sometimes came to Scarlett while she was playing a match—poked her in the belly button. This would be the moment she would want to reset the board to, if everything went spectacularly wrong.

She and Jaime were on the knife's edge here, and it was beginning to slice into the soles of her shoes.

"Scarlett." Jaime's expression wasn't playful or sexy. It was stone-cold deadly serious. He was about to put his heart on the line here. "You had to know this was coming."

Yup. She didn't answer him.

"The last few days . . . they've been amazing. And while I said I would be okay with it if a short fling was all it was, and I would be, I keep wondering why this has to be the end. What would be wrong with trying to give this, to give *us*, a go in the real world?"

What, indeed.

Scarlett licked her lips. She wasn't a God-fearing person, but she did believe in karma. She could only hope that she'd banked enough of it to make this next move pay off.

Please. Please please please.

"You're not wrong. But there is context that you don't have, and you should. So before I answer you," she said, "I have to tell you about something I did before I left town last time."

Scarlett took a moment to memorize his face. His empty house and the way the trees in his front yard swayed in the sunshine and the breeze. The way she'd felt here.

Then she began telling him what she should've a long time ago. "When we moved here, it was to get away from a boyfriend of Alma's. Alma has . . . flaws. But the one thing she won't put up with is drugs." In all honesty, her mother couldn't care less about pot or mushrooms. But pills and anything involving a pipe or needles were a serious no-go for her. "He worked at a lumberyard, and he'd hurt his back. The doctor gave him a prescription for oxy."

Jaime went still. Very still.

"I'll spare you the details, but it was the first time I'd seen . . . a lot of things." The first time she'd stumbled across someone who had OD'd, for starters. The first time she'd seen someone promise to get clean before relapsing. The first time she'd realized all those antidrug campaigns were actually important, under the cringe.

It had been an ugly slap to the face, and she'd never truly recovered from it.

"For all that I was never really innocent, it was like finally giving up on Santa or something. I became aware of some stuff, up to that point, I hadn't known about. And when Alma couldn't take it anymore, she dumped him, and we moved here, to Musgrove."

"You never told me that."

"Well, it wasn't very pretty." It wouldn't have made for good conversation over chicken salad and sweet tea at the country club.

"Did he show up again or something?" Jaime pressed.

God, how Scarlett wished that had been it. "No. But watching that play out clued me in to some things I really wish it hadn't. Taught me lessons it would've been better not to learn. After that, Alma was more careful about who she dated and became friends with. Like, if somebody came into her orbit and Alma got a whiff of something druggie, she'd eject them." Her mom hadn't done much to keep Scarlett safe, but she'd been amazing with that. "I think she knew the area was swimming in illegal stuff back then. But sometimes, before she'd realize someone was into bad stuff, I'd meet them. And a few times, when they found out that I knew *you*—I'd get static about your last name." That was the simplest way to put it. If you hadn't been bitten by this particular radioactive spider, there would be no way to explain the spine tingles their responses had set off in her.

"And?" Even after everything, Jaime was still unbitten.

"About the fourth time it happened, I knew that your dad was their dealer."

The pause that followed was endless. This was where Scarlett had expected the explosion, and it hadn't come.

Maybe she was going to be able to thread this needle. Maybe he would understand.

At last, Jaime sighed. "Yeah, well, the cat's out of the bag on that one." There was a slight edge to his voice. Even now, even after all the work he'd done, Jaime was understandably still a little bitter about it.

"Jaime, I'm the one who let the cat out of the bag."

He almost laughed. "What?"

Scarlett had come to the edge of the cliff, the moment where she had to tell him the truth after all this time. He'd either accept it, or he'd hate her. But she couldn't put off telling him what she'd done for a single second longer.

Shaking her hands out, wanting to dry her clammy palms, she spit out, "I called the crime tip line and left a message about your dad. He was arrested two weeks later."

The words hung between them for a good twenty-five seconds. Scarlett's heart counted the beats, the low, deep breaths that didn't quite fill her lungs fluttering over them.

Across from her, Jaime's response was only . . . silence.

Scarlett had been expecting Jaime to react like she would've. At this point, he would've had to peel her off the ceiling.

Instead, he was blinking. His cheeks had colored and his inhales were harsh, but he wasn't yelling.

She'd take not yelling.

"I'd seen what oxy could do. Since this was happening to people I knew, to a community I knew, I had to *act*. You were . . . more protected than I was. I was fairly certain your dad wasn't dumb enough to sell to people in your social circle. But mine, or my mother's, was fair game." Which was its own kind of awful math, but Scarlett didn't want to get into that. "Because he wasn't dealing to people you knew, you weren't going to see what I was. You weren't going to put the pieces together, not for a long time."

His family's ignorance wouldn't have lasted forever. That, Scarlett knew for sure. Their peace had been temporary, and someone would've eventually ripped it away from them.

After a few more beats, Jaime finally responded. "What the fuck?"

Well, at least Scarlett knew that he'd heard her. She'd been worried for a second that he'd shut down.

"I know you're mad," she said needlessly. He deserved to be mad, at least about the fact that she hadn't told him sooner. It had been a mighty big secret to keep. "But when you have time to process this, you'll realize—"

"What the actual fuck?" he repeated. "You called the cops on my father?"

"It was the anonymous tip line." It was a pathetically technical defense. Scarlett didn't doubt she had done the right thing. Not for an instant. But she knew how it looked, and more importantly, she knew how hearing this must feel.

Except the sympathy she had for Jaime was playing tug-of-war with the sympathy she had for herself. It hadn't been easy to put his father's crimes together at eighteen. It hadn't been easy to feel like she was the only one with this information. It hadn't been easy to know what to do about it.

She didn't blame Jaime for being pissed at her, but after he was done being pissed, she would appreciate it if he could see what it had looked like from her side of the tracks.

"I was a kid who'd realized that this so-called pillar of my community was a fucking ghoul. What would you have done?" she snapped.

Jaime's jaw worked. Yeah, he didn't have a smart comeback for that, did he?

"From what I understand, he did it to make a few bucks. Do you know how obnoxious that is? I have actually gone to bed hungry, Jaime. My mom and I spent nights in our car. And there was your dad, with his big house and his boat and his perfect family, selling some pills on the side just to get more stuff."

"That's not . . . I mean, obviously it was sick. He was sick, and—"

"He *did* the thing I reported. It was a harmful thing. This wasn't about the grass being too long or some nonsense. Don't make it sound as if I'm a dictator on the HOA board reporting people for leaving their trash cans out on the street. People actually, literally died because your dad sold them drugs. You do realize that, right?"

That was a low blow. The second Scarlett said it, she wished she could take the words back. Jaime had never pretended his father wasn't guilty, and the bulk of his artistic work had been about making amends.

"Of course I do," Jaime gritted out.

Scarlett pushed her hair back from her face before taking and releasing a long breath. "I know this is a lot to get used to, and I regret how surprising this must be."

Well, that was some formal PTA-style bullpucky. God, Scarlett despised herself right now.

"Are you sorry?" The question was like an anvil crashing onto the floor between them.

Scarlett was shocked shattered boards weren't flying everywhere, like in an old cartoon.

But she wasn't sorry she had done it, only that his knowing she'd done it was rearranging his world. "I am not."

Jaime pulled back, his expression furious. "What I want to know is *why* you did this. You always have an angle, so what was the angle?"

Wow. Scarlett ought to walk away. They should call a break and finish this conversation when they weren't both so wound up. But the fact that she was wound up was why Scarlett couldn't make herself do that. Her reasons had been *good*, and if he could just see that, maybe he could understand.

"I did it for you." Which was true. It was one of the many reasons she'd done it, but it had been an important one.

He flinched. "Like hell you did."

"You would've put it together sooner or later, just like I did. You would've put it together, and then you would've been faced with the same choice I was: what to do about it. I made that call so that you wouldn't have to."

"So it was a *favor*?"

It had been a sacrifice, actually. She'd given up a power piece, and she'd gotten nothing but a broken heart in return. But Jaime couldn't see that, not now and maybe not ever.

"It was a lot more than that."

"Bullshit."

Scarlett wanted to sob. She wasn't much of a crier. A foot stomper, yes, but not a crier. She only shed tears during moments of immense emotional turmoil.

This conversation qualified, but she wasn't going to do it now. Not in front of Jaime.

"Why didn't you tell me? Involve me in this decision?"

"I wasn't sure if you'd believe me."

"You could've convinced me. Why didn't you even try?"

When she'd watched *The Devouring Sun*, she'd realized he had accepted his father's guilt. But back then, when he and his dad had been so close, it hadn't been hard to imagine that Jaime would've rejected the accusation out of hand. "This seemed . . . cleaner. More humane."

"It was cleaner for *you* maybe, but we were together, Scarlett."

"We were kids."

"Don't do that—don't downplay it. Our relationship was real. It wasn't teenage bullshit. You admitted when you invited me to Tokyo, you meant it. Making a decision like this entirely by yourself—that's not something you do to someone you care about."

How the hell would I know? Scarlett wanted to shout. Alma never consulted Scarlett or anyone else before she decided to move to Wheeling or she quit her job or she dyed her hair orange. From early on, Scarlett had learned it was easier to act than to talk things through with anyone.

So of course she hadn't taken this discovery to Jaime. It wasn't a large box she needed him to heave up to the attic. Whatever he said about it now, it would've been messy. Things had been easier because Scarlett had handled it—and kept it to herself.

"You ought to have told me," Jaime was saying, "and together we could've—"

Scarlett held up her hand. This was beginning to stink like three-day-old garbage in August. She had to get out of here before the stench got all over her hands, all over *them*. Besides, she had some crying to do.

"I'm going to run. I have a flight to catch."

Before this conversation, she'd hoped the earthquake she was going to unleash might not crack the foundation of whatever they'd been messing with the last few days. But no relationship was that strong. That wasn't how human hearts worked. And even if they had given things a go, it probably wouldn't have lasted. They might as well end things here, and end things honestly. It was what he'd said he wanted from her.

Scarlett's success in chess had come because she took bigger risks than other people. If you wanted to play for real and you had started from nothing, you had to. Jaime had started with everything, or near enough to everything. He couldn't understand what all this had cost her.

Maybe that was the real problem, the real reason they'd broken up earlier and why they were breaking up now. He saw the wagers she'd made for him as pennies, when she knew they were gold.

After a long minute, he wrenched the front door open, indicating that Scarlett should leave. "Go. It's what you're good at."

And there it was.

So, with her head held high and her chin wobbling, Scarlett Arbuthnot left Musgrove, Virginia, heartbroken for the second time in twenty years.

After Scarlett left, Jaime flipped the dead bolt on the front door with a muttered "Fuck." His heart was going so fast, the beats came on top of each other, with no spaces in between. His lungs couldn't keep up with the pace, and his throat and eyes were burning.

If Scarlett had slapped him with a two-by-four, she couldn't have surprised or hurt him more. He might not ever catch his breath again.

In telling him this *story*, Scarlett had ripped the tablecloth clean out from under the dishes. But she'd done more than that. She'd gone and toppled the table, too, and then she'd kept digging, destroying the subfloor, the foundation of the house. Wrecking all the assumptions he'd built this new version of his life on.

Dad had been the one responsible for his own downfall. He'd acted alone, and so he alone bore the weight of it. That was the story Jaime had been telling himself from day one.

What Scarlett had said was a rogue wave, tearing up the beach and eating up every sandcastle along the way. Now, Jaime had to find a way to live with a new truth: Dad had fucked up, and he'd made all the bad choices. But Scarlett had been the one to tell the cops.

Scarlett. The girl Jaime had loved. The one person he could imagine building a life with.

And she'd done it without telling him. They'd talked every day back then, fallen asleep on the phone together every night, and she hadn't so much as hinted that she had some life-changing information he might be interested in. If she'd been a spy, she couldn't have pulled this off more smoothly.

The cold-eyed betrayal of it—that's what was going to linger.

Why the fuck had she told him about it *now*? She'd gotten away with it scot-free. Why blurt it out decades later?

For good measure, Jaime engaged the security chain on the door. He hadn't even thought he needed a security chain—he effectively lived in the middle of nowhere. Who was going to rob him? But the builder had insisted it was a standard feature, and now, Jaime was glad for it.

He'd given Scarlett a key at one point, and he couldn't remember if she'd returned it to him. In the tumble of the last few days, when they'd started sleeping together again and when he'd been thinking that they were building a new life together—as if he could build a life with the woman who'd torched his family—getting his key back hadn't seemed important.

If anything, ten minutes ago he would've been begging her to keep it, thinking her using a key to his house meant she saw a life here. A life with him.

Jaime slammed a fist against the door. If there had been five other locks there, he would've used them all. He might even brick himself inside, reverse "Cask of Amontillado" style.

It wouldn't have helped, though. All the masonry in the world wasn't enough to keep out the story Scarlett had relayed: she had called the cops on Dad and hadn't shared any of it with Jaime. However she tried to justify it, whatever objections she might have to those terms, that was the outcome of what she'd done.

Jaime dug his phone out of his pocket, intending to call Evelyn. But after a few wobbly steps, he dropped his phone on a side table in the den instead.

Dad had ruined their lives. Jaime knew that. He did.

But.

But.

But for the love of fuck, did Scarlett have to report his father without telling Jaime? Without asking if that was what he wanted?

Scarlett would always be a maverick. Whatever choices she made, she would always make them for herself. He knew that now.

All Jaime could do was fall through an endless, shitty void.

He scrubbed a hand over his face. It was good she'd left. Never mind that ten minutes ago, he desperately didn't want her to leave. He'd never wanted her to leave. Now, he was thrilled that she had. If she were still here, he'd be hollering.

No, he shouldn't call Evelyn. Not until Jaime had managed to shed his rage. Fury was unpredictable. Destructive.

He'd been so mad at his father in those early days after his arrest, and he'd quickly realized that he needed to get a handle on it and amalgamize it into something productive, because if he didn't, it would eat him alive. He'd chosen taking care of his family and fishing what remained of his dreams out of the trash.

He could make the same choice now. As hard as it was and as pissed as he was, he didn't have to give in to those feelings.

Healing was supposed to mean you recognized those harmful feelings for what they were, and with time, you didn't feel them so much. Jaime had had, like, a *lot* of therapy. He needed to put all those coping strategies he'd supposedly mastered to work here.

What would mature Jaime do?

He'd go for a long, long hike, and when he got back, he'd be too tired to rage himself into ulcerative colitis.

That was the best he could do, at least for the moment.

Jaime filled several water bottles. Then he put them into a pack before grabbing his sunglasses, hat, and boots, and heading out.

A brisk ten-mile loop later, he arrived home as the sun was dipping below the horizon. His legs ached. His abs ached. His heart—it still ached.

It was always going to ache.

Jaime knew it the way he knew that water flowed downhill and he'd have a tax bill to pay on April 15. If you put them in the same room, Scarlett and Jaime were always going to want to be together. But Scarlett was a feral cat who didn't want to be domesticated. She would never be someone who could bring a partner all the way inside, and Jaime would always be a person who needed that. They weren't good for each other.

Jaime took a cold, long shower, fixedly *not* looking at the tub where he'd soaked with Scarlett. No, he stood under the icy water until he was uncomfortably numb, and then, and only then, did he emerge.

Once he'd dressed, he found his phone. No text from Scarlett—which was exactly how he'd wanted it.

But there was a text from Nate. Videon loves the scripts. Let's talk tomorrow re: preproduction calendar. I'm feeling October. Do you think we'll be ready to film in nine months?

The last time Scarlett left, Jaime had mourned her—or who he'd thought she was. But she'd been out of sight, if never out of mind.

This time, they still had months and months of work to do together. All he could do was grit his teeth and get through them.

PART II

THE MIDDLEGAME

Chapter 16

Nine Months Later

Scarlett might've been born in a trailer park, but by the tender age of thirty-four, she'd played chess in dozens of countries. She'd been to dinner receptions at Versailles and the White House. She'd hit the *New York Times* bestseller list. But she'd never before faced her ex after telling him that his dad was in jail because of her.

Oh well, she couldn't cry over spilled milk. She had to grab the darn rag off the counter and get cleaning—in the right outfit.

The dress she'd gotten for today was pink, not red, because everyone always expected someone named Scarlett to wear red, and she loathed giving people what they wanted. That was probably why she'd punched Jaime Croft in the guts a second time.

Except how did she explain the fact that her own guts smarted too?

Well, Scarlett was a puzzle. Everyone knew it. Maybe if she arrived in the studio outside of Vancouver for rehearsal and explained it in so many words to Jaime—*me breaking your heart a second time was both* ironic *and* on brand—then he might understand.

But all hope of that evaporated as she strolled into the rehearsal space and Jaime looked up from the script he'd been pointing to. He hadn't cut his hair in a while, and a curl fell over his brow. He'd forgotten to shave, too, which worked for him better than it should've.

Dressed as if for a hike, in a gray fleece pullover and worn jeans, Jaime's entire appearance was vigorous and *hot.*

He was excited about what he was saying to the man standing next to him, but the second Jaime's eyes found Scarlett's, his face went—well, she had seen diamonds that were softer. His mouth dropped into an implacable line. His cheeks went white. The hand he'd been gesturing with clenched.

In the nine months since Scarlett had driven away from Jaime's cabin, they hadn't said a word directly and solely to each other. Someone else had been copied on every email they'd exchanged, and his messages were so formal, so removed, that she'd started calling him *Mr. Croft.*

He'd retaliated by calling her *Ms. Arbuthnot*—a low blow.

After the two months they'd spent together writing this show. After she'd let him in as much as she'd let anyone in. After she'd told him the truth, seeing that *Ms.* had made her want to cry.

It was pathetic. She was pathetic. But seeing his icy regard made her head hurt and her chest hurt and the spaces between her toes hurt.

She had to keep moving forward. He clearly had.

Scarlett mustered as much spunk as she had left in her store—it wasn't much—and strolled over to him. "Mr. Croft, how nice to see you again."

In some alternative reality, they were playing out another version of this moment. In that version, Jaime had listened, had tried to see what she'd done in good faith. He'd reached out after a few weeks of adjusting to it, and they'd talked. She hadn't wasted her study hours for Stavanger fretting about him.

In that world, she hadn't played mechanically but boringly in Norway because her heart had splintered into shards that were ripping her open from the inside out.

But Scarlett had to live in *this* world. The one where she was sad and lost and loathed, knowing that she'd earned all those labels.

She was an Olivia Rodrigo song personified. The only thing she could do now was make sure that she was one of the shouty ones and not one of the sobby ones.

A few seconds passed, and Jaime didn't reply. He just stared at her, breathing hard.

Look, they had *months* of togetherness ahead of them. Rehearsing and shooting *Queen's Kiss* was going to take longer than writing the thing had. If he kept this up, all of Jaime's cells were going to evaporate. He needed to pace himself. Detesting her was a marathon, not a sprint.

With a shrug, she turned to the man Jaime had been speaking to, a slim white guy with a scruffy brown goatee, and said, "Hey, I'm Scarlett."

"Our queen." The man had obviously known who she was before she'd said it. He offered a hand. "Nate Pace, producer, codirector, and jack-of-all-trades."

Oh, so this was Jaime's partner in filmmaking. She'd pictured Nate as older and more harried. "I've heard so much about you." Back when, you know, Jaime had been talking to her.

"Good things?" From someone else, those words might have been flirtatious, but they carried no heat here.

One thing was for sure, that week with Jaime had burned out every one of Scarlett's sexual circuits. She hadn't been able to so much as look at a man without feeling revulsion since she'd left Virginia. At some point, she was going to become kind of pissed about that. It was one thing to dump her. It was quite another to ruin her libido.

But wanting to piss Jaime off, Scarlett gave Nate a smile that would've melted most men and many women. In her sweetest voice, she said, "Yup. And we both know that Jaime always tells the truth. Whether he likes hearing it, well, that's something else entirely."

Yeah, whoever had said the truth will set you free was a liar.

Out of the corner of her eye, she saw Jaime open his mouth—and then snap it shut.

Scarlett turned toward him with a pouty smile. She might be playing coy, but she wasn't wrong. He'd asked for truth; it wasn't her fault if he didn't enjoy receiving it. And so, while he might turn into a pillar of fire at the sight of her, she wasn't going to back down. She hadn't done anything wrong. She wasn't going to act as if she had.

Nate's attention was shifting back and forth between Scarlett and Jaime as if it were a tennis ball bouncing off two brick walls. "The first all-hands production meeting is tomorrow. But I can find a PA to grab you a Tim Hortons or give you a tour if—"

"No, I'm here to meet with Clara Hess." And to show off her new dress and her don't-give-a-crap attitude to Jaime.

She just had to summon the don't-give-a-crap part.

"Right." Nate snapped his fingers. "I can show you where she's hanging out."

"That'd be great. See you again soon, Mr. Croft."

Once again, Jaime didn't say a word. Maybe someone else needed to have a few circuits replaced too.

Scarlett turned on a heel and left the room with Nate.

When the door had closed behind them, the producer gave her a sideways smile. "So you're the woman who broke my boy. Twice."

Scarlett caught the toe of her shoe on the floor and had to slam a hand on the wall to steady herself. The only thing that had made this bearable was her assumption that no one on set would know what had happened beyond Scarlett and Jaime.

Nate was smiling, but it wasn't sharp or mean.

Here was the thing, though: Scarlett was the Wicked Witch of the chess world. What precisely had people expected from her if not this? Shattering a few hearts before breakfast was like some people's morning yoga routine—and wouldn't you know it, Scarlett was crap at stretching.

"Is this common knowledge?" Scarlett asked Nate, as she righted herself and began to glide down the hall again.

"Oh, no," he assured her. "Everyone else just thinks Jaime is naturally grumpy. I'm the only one who guessed who kicked the stuffing out of him."

Scarlett was tempted to point out the experience hadn't exactly been easy for her either. A truer way to put it was that she and Jaime had broken each other, when they'd been kids and again now. But she didn't know Nate. She didn't owe him an explanation.

So she only gave an imperious look. "Yeah, and?"

For a second, Nate didn't seem to know how to take that. Then he threw back his head and laughed. "I can see how it happened."

"Buddy, you can't see bupkis."

Nate only laughed harder. "You two deserve each other."

At this point, Jaime didn't seem to think Scarlett deserved anything, and even if she rejected that conclusion, she did at least understand how he'd gotten there.

"Well, as much fun as this has been, I do actually have an appointment with Clara. So where is rehearsal room A?"

"It's at the end of this hall." Nate pointed. "The one with the blue sign. And, Scarlett? I might be Team Jaime, but I'm rooting for you too."

Pffft. Scarlett was tempted to flip him the bird as she walked away. What the last few months had proved was that Scarlett didn't need anyone to root for her, except for maybe Kit and Martina. But Scarlett could get through life with a very small team. She didn't need to do any recruiting.

Scarlett marched down to rehearsal room A and flung the door open—and came face to back with her doppelgänger.

Okay, so Clara Hess didn't look *exactly* like her. But her hair was the exact same shade as Scarlett's. When she turned toward the door, her green eyes were lively. And the shape of her mouth—Christ, this girl was the younger, movie-star-pretty version of Scarlett.

The actress was Hollywood's idea of plus size, which was to say you couldn't see her clavicle where her shirt dipped low on her chest. She was what you might get if you put Scarlett through one of those filters on TikTok and a cartoonified version came out.

"It's uncanny, right? My agent can't stop talking about it," the girl said.

The shock must have been evident on Scarlett's face. She reminded herself that staring was rude—and Jaime's job—and extended her hand. "I'm Scarlett Arbuthnot."

"Clara Hess." Her shake was soft, all of her was soft, and certainly no one thought Scarlett was soft—extra-especially not Jaime—so that was another point of difference between them.

The actress stepped back and gave Scarlett a wry smile. "You know, it's usually the talent who can't walk across the set without heads turning. But you're going to be, like, the main attraction here. I really ought to thank you."

"Happy to take the pressure off."

Scarlett took a seat at the small table in the room and pulled a travel chess set out of her bag. When in doubt, set up a chess board. The routine of it always settled her.

"I'm also here to help you learn chess."

She twisted the black knights so they were facing each other, then shot a glance at Clara. The girl was watching Scarlett, rapt. If Scarlett had been performing a magic trick, she couldn't have commanded Clara's attention more thoroughly.

"They told me you don't play," Scarlett said.

"Not yet."

When Clara's team had reached out to ask if the actress ought to get a book or something, Scarlett had said no. She'd rather teach her from the start than have her learn something wrong or badly.

Starting from nothing was better than starting from crap.

"I haven't touched a board or opened a chess book," Clara said, "but I've been watching your matches nonstop on YouTube for months."

Many of those had been edited into cheesecake shots of Scarlett's cleavage. They weren't exactly a way to learn about the game. It was more a window into how some of the men in chess objectified the women who had the audacity to play in their sandbox.

"Jeez, if you're going to do that, maybe I should make a playlist of the okay ones."

"Don't worry, I know the internet can always be counted on to internet. You are always so gorgeous, though. You have to know that." Clara sat down across from Scarlett. "I'm sorry, I'm babbling. I'm feeling a little starstruck. It's really *you*."

Scarlett had to laugh. "I'm pretty sure that's supposed to be my line."

"No one knows who the heck I am."

"They will, though."

"You sound like my agent."

"Why did you want to take this job?"

Scarlett had no choice about being herself. Clara had signed up for this, and while there was a paycheck, it might not cover the emotional damage. As far as Jaime was concerned, Scarlett was basically quicksand. Wasn't Clara worried about sinking in it?

"It's a great part. You are—you are amazing."

On her best day, Scarlett was a manipulative pill. On her worst—well, she would have to ask Jaime . . . if he ever started talking to her again.

"I am kind of crap, actually. But luckily for both of us, I'm good at chess."

Clara reached out and touched the white queen lightly. "And I have to figure out how to make people think I am."

"Eh, that's easy. It's just about attitude. And if Jaime hired you for this, it's because he thinks you have it."

Jaime might loathe Scarlett, but he was darn good at his job. If he thought Clara was right for this part, she was right for this part.

"All the moves are written out for you," Scarlett told Clara. "It's all choreographed, so it's not like you have to learn how to play if you don't want to. But you have to convince people that you're coming up with the plays spontaneously."

Scarlett quickly ran through the names of the squares and the abbreviations for the pieces, since that was how she'd written the notation in the script.

"I know how the pieces move," Clara said proudly. "I had a crush on a guy on my high school chess team—it's why I read the script. And I set up an account online after I read for the part, but the computer kept kicking my ass."

"Don't play the computer," Scarlett said. "The way it plays . . . I don't like it. The human element is what makes the game. How different is it when you're running lines on your own versus working with a great scene partner?"

"Point taken."

"I'll play with you as much as you want."

"But you're, like, a pro."

"I'll go easy on you." Whatever Jaime might think, Scarlett was capable of that. "Let's play now."

Clara reached for the white pawn sitting ahead of the queen and moved it ahead one space.

"You can move a pawn two squares the first time you move it, and you should. You want to take control of the middle of the board."

Oops. Scarlett couldn't help but coach.

Scarlett moved, and then Clara bit her lip and laughed. "I don't . . . I never know what to *do*. I can react, but I don't have any strategy."

"Capture my king."

"But—how?"

Scarlett couldn't rewind her thoughts and get back to the time when she hadn't had hundreds of openings and strategies floating around in her head. It was almost as if those had always been there, dominating her headspace, crowding anything else out of her mind.

In contrast, Clara was basically a baby. Unformed. Innocent.

"If you only ever react to other people, you give up all of your power." In chess, and in life. "You have to set the agenda for the game; otherwise, your opponent will walk all over you."

Clara's smile was wry. "I bet that never happens to you."

Except it had with Jaime.

Scarlett had to learn how to be the woman he thought she was, the reckless one who crashed through other people's lives without a second thought. A few more days of licking her wounds and she'd get there.

"Not anymore," Scarlett lied. "Okay, let's learn a few basic openings and defenses."

Clara didn't need them to play this part. Scarlett could probably just teach her how to touch the pieces. How to scrunch up her face while thinking between moves. How long to pause.

But Clara needed to learn some things, if only so she would stop reminding Scarlett of a baby doe wandering through a forest thick with hunters. No one ought to be that vulnerable, in chess or in life.

Scarlett reset the board and gestured for Clara and her to switch places. "I'm going to teach you how to respond to white using the Sicilian. It's all about countermoves and playing with aggression."

"I love it already."

Hearing this, Scarlett could tell she was going to love working with Clara—which had to be enough to make facing Jaime's cold disdain worth it.

Chapter 17

Jaime usually loved the first production meeting. The crew, loud and jovial and energetic, who could build and fix anything; the artist types who decorated the set and made the costumes and otherwise ensured everyone look good; and the actors who became fearless when the camera was on.

It was Halloween and the opening day of baseball and a long-anticipated party, but a thousand times better because they were making *television*. Jaime still couldn't believe that despite everything, he got to do this. But today, he was in a desperately foul mood, and not even the prospect of filming could make him feel better.

Jaime could put a time and a date on his bad mood: the moment Scarlett told him that she'd decided all by herself to call the police on his dad.

It was almost funny how the two worst moments of his life existed in precise moments of time. Everything had seemed perfect, and then an instant later, everything had been awful.

The person responsible for both moments swanned into the room. Scarlett had traded yesterday's pink sheath that had hugged her generous curves like a lover for a navy blue suit-dress. This outfit would've been conservative but for how low the neckline dropped. A teardrop turquoise pendant dangled between her perfect cleavage, and Jaime had never been so jealous of a piece of stone before.

She was still the prettiest woman he'd ever seen.

Jaime swallowed—or he tried to. His mouth had gone dry.

Across the large conference table, Scarlett made eye contact with him. Her eye shadow was smoky, her eyeliner winged nearly into her hairline, and her lips were painted an almost girlish shade of pink. He knew that every touch had been perfectly planned, and beyond bringing him to his knees, he couldn't begin to speculate about what she wanted to happen here.

Checkmate, he wanted to tell her, because he'd already lost. Whatever game they'd been playing, the way he felt had to mean she'd conquered him.

But when her coy smile fell and her gaze darted away from him, he wondered if she was taking any pleasure in it. Or if it was the kind of Pyrrhic victory where everyone was a loser.

Next to Jaime, Nate cleared his throat.

"Yeah?"

"Stop staring at her, or everyone will figure it out."

Nate thought he knew what had played out between Scarlett and Jaime, but since the guy wasn't a Shakespeare fan, he couldn't begin to imagine the kind of betrayal that had been involved.

"*You* haven't even figured it out," he said.

"I know enough, old man." Nate patted Jaime on the arm.

"I'm six months older than you are."

"And you wear them so badly. But seriously, no one likes it when Mommy and Daddy are fighting."

"She's not the production's mommy."

"Isn't she?"

Clara Hess had come in and thrown herself into Scarlett's arms. Then she'd proceeded to drag Scarlett around and introduce her to everyone—and really, Jaime ought to be doing that, but he was too tongue tied and hurt to manage it.

"Maybe," he finally said to Nate after watching the fifth person in a row light up like the Empire State Building when Scarlett greeted them. She was going to be the center of gravity on this production, that was for sure.

"Okay, everyone," he called out, more gruffly than he'd intended to. "Let's settle down."

Scarlett looked at him over her shoulder, and he almost staggered backward. There were so many different emotions there, he couldn't have untangled them if he'd spent all day on it.

Someday, maybe, he'd be able to have a rational conversation with her, and she'd tell him all about those feelings, where they'd come from and what they meant and how he could learn to live with them.

"You've got to cut that out," Nate muttered.

"Shut up."

"I'm just saying—"

Jaime took his seat before Nate could go on making sense. He had a job to do.

When the room quieted, he said, "I hope everyone is adjusting to Canada. Sheryl is the best source of restaurant recs on the crew, FYI." An appreciative chuckle went up. "But beyond telling you where to get the best bannock in town, our main goal today is for everyone to meet, ask any questions, and then review the rehearsal and production schedule."

Jaime pointedly did not look at Scarlett as he opened this meeting. He was going to have to ignore her as much as possible. She was only a coproducer. How hard could it be?

He felt her raised hand before he saw it. Her request for his attention radiated heat like an open oven door. The side of his face burned.

Everyone's eyes darted to her and then to Jaime, willing him to see her wordless demand for his attention. Someone eventually pointed.

At last, Jaime turned toward her. "Yes, Ms. Arbuthnot?"

He was acutely aware that those were the first words he'd uttered to her face in nine months. The familiar mixture of longing and pain walloped him.

"Can I say something?" she asked, sweetly submissive.

She'd said plenty, hadn't she? But it had been eighteen years too late.

"Sure," he gritted out. Denying her would seem rude to the group—and Jaime really didn't want to seem rude.

His entire plan had been to act like the consummate professional until he didn't have to act anymore. Until he managed to bottle up everything she made him feel and cast it into the sea and never, ever think about it again.

But he was struggling to keep it together and endangering everything.

Scarlett let her gaze sweep over the crowd. Everyone ringing the table was gazing at her as if she were a solar eclipse, something rare and cosmic and powerful.

His gut throbbed at how accurate that was.

"I wanted to say how grateful I am for all of you. This book is really personal, and it means everything to me that you want to help tell this story." Then Scarlett looked right at Jaime as she said, "I trust you with this, with me, and I know you're going to do a wonderful job."

Did she mean it, or was she yanking his chain? In the two months they wrote together, she hadn't said anything remotely like this to him—and there were days when he would've really liked to hear it.

What the fuck was she up to?

She held his eyes with hers, and with a deliberate slowness, she raised her brows to prompt him. Then she waited—waited to see how he would respond to what she'd said. In front of everyone.

Dammit.

Scarlett was putting him on the spot, with the entire cast and crew as an audience. Nate was entirely right: Jaime had to be careful here, or everyone on the set of *Queen's Kiss* was going to guess that he and Scarlett had a complicated past. A past featuring the kind of explosive sexual duplicity soap operas only aspired to.

It was a bummer that in real life, unlike in tournament chess, you couldn't take twenty minutes to ponder your next move. Jaime needed to game all this out, but he didn't have the time. And unlike Scarlett, he wasn't any good at masterminding every situation.

"Thanks," he said carefully. *Thank you* was solid in every situation, right? "It's quite a story. That's why I wanted to adapt it. You tell it exactly like it is, and that kind of extreme honesty is . . . powerful."

Jaime hadn't torn his gaze from Scarlett's, but he didn't need to look at Nate to know that the guy was slack-jawed and blinking *SOS* at him in Morse code.

Then Scarlett said, "Not everyone wants the truth."

In the most sincere way, up until the moment she'd told him what had actually happened with his dad's arrest, Jaime thought he had. Whatever else he felt about her confession, the shame he felt about his own inadequacy was part of it.

Jaime knew he ought to be a better person. One who could hear what she'd said and not feel angry and betrayed that she'd made the decision to go public all by herself. But he wasn't a better person.

No, just like his father, it turned out that Jaime was a piece of crap.

But none of that had any place in this moment and in this room. "Especially not PAWN," he joked, trying to keep this about her book.

"Among others," she replied, forcing the issue back to them.

Jaime had spent so many months just trying to put one foot in front of the other, to think only about the details because then he didn't have to think about the big picture. When he'd wondered how he and Scarlett might interact on set, he'd immediately shoved the thought away.

I'll be the perfect showrunner: that had been his plan. Of course Scarlett was going to make it hard for him to do that.

Jaime sighed and glanced around the room. Everyone was aghast, because he wasn't showing proper deference to their inspiration, to their queen.

"You inspire us all," he made himself say—and it wasn't even a lie.

In his case, she inspired him to want to crack his forehead open on the table.

"The story we're going to make based on your experiences . . . it's going to be amazing. And I appreciate that you're letting me—letting all of us—tell it." Someday, when he stopped feeling like a stubbed toe, that was going to be true. At least, he had to act as if it was.

"It's my pleasure," Scarlett cooed, and he suspected that, at the very least, she was enjoying the hell out of this moment.

When Jaime sat, Nate muttered under his breath, "Nice recovery, boss."

But it hadn't been.

After stumbling through the rest of the meeting, Jaime flagged Scarlett down. "Do you have a minute?" They had to figure this thing out. He couldn't function like this; he'd never get through the shoot.

"I'm meeting with Clara," Scarlett said, "but for you, I have all the time in the world." Then she fluttered her eyelashes at him.

If Jaime hadn't known it was an act, he would've fallen to his knees. As it was, he flinched.

Scarlett saw him do it, and he would've sworn she bit the inside of her cheek so as not to laugh. "Should we go to your office, or—"

"No, here is fine." If he put a door between them and everyone else, there was no way he'd be able to keep his head on straight. Any conversation they were going to have needed to be in public. That was going to be the key to him holding it together for the next few months.

Jaime waited until Nate shooed a few stragglers out, and then he slid a hand into his pocket. Too bad his attempt at acting relaxed felt artificial as fuck.

Staring at the carpet near her shoes, he asked, "How do you want to play this?"

"Shouldn't it be 'How do you want to play this, Ms. Arbuthnot?'"

Jaime scrubbed a hand over his face. *"Scarlett."* Her name was sweet and bitter in his mouth, like high-percentage-cacao chocolate. It was much too much to eat, but so concentrated it made everything else taste fake.

"I think we're playing it all right," she said.

"You're playing it all right—better than all right." She always did. "But I'm drowning here."

"Then you should learn how to swim." Of course she would make it sound that easy.

"We have to work together for *months*, and we both want the show to be good." Whatever she might think, he was committed to this production. For the sake of his career and his reputation, he needed *Queen's Kiss* to be amazing. There simply was no other choice. "And we have to clear the air because . . . I'm still feeling a little blindsided."

The word was so mild compared to his feelings, he almost laughed. But Jaime wasn't sure if he'd so much as giggled in the months since she'd left him standing in his doorway, feeling as if a bomb had detonated in his lower intestines.

For once, Scarlett didn't appear to be amused. Her response was utterly serious. "I get that, and I apologize for the shock of it."

"But not for the rest." He matched her tone, making it a statement and not a question.

"If I did, I'd be lying."

Jaime never should've talked to her about honesty and truth and all the rest of that bullshit—because it very much felt like bullshit to him now.

If it would help matters for him to admit that he was being a hypocrite, he would've done it, but he didn't think either he or Scarlett would feel better if he did. He knew it was stupid, but he felt the way he felt. It was his *feelings* that were the problem, and he couldn't talk himself out of them, because he was being irrational.

"I don't want to rehash the past," he said.

"What a reversal."

"Jesus, Scarlett, cut me some slack." He pinched the bridge of his nose. "Sorry, that was—too harsh. All I need to know is how I can be in the same room as you and not want to . . ." He trailed off.

Jaime honestly didn't know what exactly he was asking for. He'd considered quitting the production, but it would torch his career. And besides, despite everything, he still loved the project. He just needed—

"Not want to what?" Scarlett prompted.

Kiss you. Loathe myself. "Everything. Anything. How can you be in a room with me and not . . . not *feel*?"

Because at the end of the day, that was the problem: Scarlett destroyed Jaime's ability to be calm and poised. One saucy look or smart-mouthed comment from her, and his insides began to riot and storm—except he had a television show to make. He didn't have the emotional bandwidth to manage the mess she set off inside him and do that too. He could be a first-rate showrunner and director, or he could long for this woman. That was the choice.

"Oh, Jaime." Scarlett strolled over to the door. When she was almost in the hallway, she stopped. One of her hands rested lightly on the frame, and he could see her nails were painted the same pale shade of blue as forget-me-nots.

The anger was still there in his chest, fresh as the day she'd told him the story. The frustration that her independent tendencies meant they were badly suited.

But in the middle of those swirling winds, in the eye of the hurricane, was something softer. Hungrier. He still loved her, still wanted her. Even now, after she'd mowed him down twice. That part would never go away.

Scarlett watched him over her shoulder. She took in and released a long, long breath before giving her head a sad shake. "Who said I wasn't feeling anything?"

Chapter 18

"I'm going to hang this pawn, aren't I?" the spark asked Scarlett, with the kind of grimace that said he already knew the answer. Knew it and hated it.

"Telling you would be cheating." It would also mean telling him that the writing had been on the wall from his third move on. He was an expert at lighting—maybe he ought to stick to that.

The guy examined the chess board, unblinking, for a few long minutes. Then he buried his face in his hands. "I'm totally screwed."

"Yup."

"Damn." He pushed his king over in the universal sign for resignation.

"Hey, you made it longer that time." Scarlett offered him a hand, and he shook it vigorously.

"I thought I was decent, but you're on another level."

That was kind of the point. But Scarlett only offered a demure smile, one that felt unfamiliar on her mouth. "I've got to find Clara, but let's play again soon."

"We'll see if my ego can take it."

Every day, Scarlett found herself sitting across a board from the show's hairdressers and makeup people, the caterers who brought in the food, and the grips who moved things around. Seemingly everyone on the set of *Queen's Kiss* was learning to play, and they all wanted to challenge Scarlett.

Everyone except for Jaime freaking Croft, who couldn't stand to look at her.

Good riddance. Scarlett had wanted to sneer. But it wasn't good, and she and Jaime weren't rid of each other. Honestly, they would probably never be either of those things.

Bad togetherness was more like it.

As they'd marched through the rehearsal period, Scarlett had tried to give Jaime a wide berth. He'd asked for space (sort of). Except she'd confessed what she'd done almost a year ago now—how much more of a break from her did he need?

Whatever. She couldn't make him get over it. Maybe it wasn't one of those things where getting over it was even an option.

Nate tried to fill the gap between Jaime and Scarlett, making sure she got to all the meetings she was expected to attend and she understood the production. But mostly, Scarlett handled her slapped-face feelings the way she always did: by playing a lot of chess.

Being on set was great. Everyone had a job at which they were amazing, and they all worked together to produce magic. Chess itself was solitary, so it was somewhat flabbergasting that making a television show about chess took an army.

Scarlett had never been part of an army before, and it was kind of awesome.

Yeah, she couldn't believe it either.

She knocked on Clara's dressing room door.

"Come in." The actress was contemplating the game they'd suspended yesterday. Every day, they squeezed in several quick games in between Clara's fittings and rehearsals.

"You ready to pick up where we left off?" Scarlett asked.

"Yup." Clara reached for a bishop.

"Not that one." With everyone else, Scarlett just played, but with Clara, she *instructed.*

Clara, her pointer finger still resting on the top of her piece, glanced up. "Why not?"

"What would that do to your king?"

A few seconds clicked by, and then Clara saw it. When they'd started, this would've taken a good five minutes. She was getting better. "He'd be unprotected."

"Indeed."

"Well, now what the fuck am I going to do?" But there was amusement in Clara's voice, not disappointment.

It was exactly what Scarlett would've been thinking in the same situation.

"Take as long as you need. I'm not in a hurry."

Jaime would probably say more time between plays gave Scarlett more time to scheme—or at least that was what she imagined he would've said if he'd been speaking to her.

Except while she waited for her opponents to figure things out, Scarlett had more time to contemplate her last conversation with Jaime. She'd meant to bait him mostly because she couldn't take another moment of the silent treatment from him without screaming. But instead, his reaction had made her question everything.

Scarlett had correctly taken the measure of things back at his cabin: she was the bull, and he was the china shop. Telling him about the call she'd made to the police had been a massive mistake. She ought to have taken that story to the grave and left Jaime alone. It would've been so much better for both of them. Only she could be so selfish as to have spit it out to him because she'd deluded herself into thinking they could be together again.

"What do you think about?" Clara asked, her eyes still glued to the board, searching for the best move. "During a tournament?"

"The game."

That was mostly true. At least it was true when Scarlett was focused. She definitely hadn't been focused in Stavanger. She'd played decently, if uninterestingly, and won the tournament. Her performance should secure another invite to Candidates—at least if PAWN didn't screw her over again. She'd know either way in a week.

"Not, like, your clothes?" Clara asked.

"That's for before the tournament." Scarlett wasn't going to deny caring about her appearance. Sue her. "What do you think about when you're acting?"

"Honestly, during most of my best performances, my mind was blank. I wasn't acting. I was *being*."

"Ah, that sounds—lovely." It did, actually. Scarlett didn't know if she'd experienced a single moment when she hadn't been gaming out every choice, weighing every option.

Nope, that wasn't quite true. The times, few that they'd been, when she'd managed to turn down the constant churn in her brain and be fully, totally present, had been moments with Jaime because he had simply consumed all of her.

Sometimes literally.

"Chess isn't like that for me. Not even blitz." Scarlett relied on reflex in speed games, but it wasn't blissful or natural. No, playing blitz made her feel like a finely honed knife.

"Does all that thinking get exhausting?"

"I didn't really have the chance to *not* do it. And I guess stopping, at this point . . . it would feel scary. Here's the thing." Scarlett paused, searching for the words she needed with Clara. "Always thinking through fifty scenarios before choosing one . . . can be tiring. But I don't regret it because it was the only way to get out of where I was. I've never been able to just drift on the breeze and assume things would be okay. Being calculating was the only way to give myself choices. Now that I have them, it would be disrespectful, maybe, to stop being deliberate. It's not that I'm conventional or safe." Scarlett was clearly neither of those things. "But since I managed to get some power, I have to use it. I want to use it."

"I would think taking action wouldn't be hard for you."

"And I would think you could figure out what move to make here." Scarlett said that lightly enough that it wasn't a rebuke, not really, and Clara knew it.

"Fair," Clara said with a snort. After a moment of hesitation, she moved a knight into the gap that Scarlett had purposefully left open, wanting to see if the actress would notice it.

"Very good." Scarlett advanced a bishop.

"Damn it, those always come out of nowhere."

Not really—but Scarlett wasn't going to say it, not to Clara.

"If you're all about deliberate action, carefully using your power and all that, does that mean that I'm a drifter?" Clara threw this out like a joke, and Scarlett couldn't tell if the actress was just talking or if she was really asking.

"You're a product of where you grew up, you know? The same as I am. I wouldn't wish my hardscrabble childhood on anyone. But sometimes when I look at people who grew up safe, who always knew where their next meal was coming from, I suspect they can't understand my choices."

This amused Clara. "And vice versa?"

"Yup. So no, you're not a drifter, Clara, and I do envy you."

Scarlett certainly envied that if she had been a little more like Clara, she might have held on to Jaime, back when they'd been kids, possibly—and now, certainly. She wanted to find Jaime and point out she could be restrained. She didn't *always* choose to plunge the knife in. But the problem was that with Jaime, she hadn't always schemed. And look where that spontaneity had gotten her.

It was impossible to convey that she'd let go *because* she loved him. She'd been more real and less premeditated with Jaime than with anyone else, because she cared about him.

But admitting that made her feel as cruel as he thought she was.

If Scarlett hadn't felt as if she *needed* to act, she might not have called the cops on Dr. Croft. If she had been less certain of herself, she might have let Jaime in more. Or if she had trusted that he could know what had happened and still love her, she might have told him the truth earlier.

But the unfortunate reality was that Scarlett hadn't been anyone but herself. And so she'd done what she'd done, without regrets.

Without *real* regrets.

"But?" Clara prompted, because the girl was as bright as a new penny.

"I worry about you," Scarlett admitted. "Not in terms of your acting—you're gonna be great on the show. But I worry you're that cinnamon roll who's too sweet for this world. Babe, you work in *Hollywood*. You need to learn chess if only for backbone-strengthening purposes."

"It isn't always a kind world to the meek," Clara agreed.

"It isn't always a kind world for anyone." At the end of the day, that was what Scarlett had been born knowing.

She would always hate that what she had done had taught Jaime this lesson in the most brutal way possible, and as a result, he wasn't going to be able to forgive her.

"They're crap lessons to absorb, Clara, but you always have to be looking over your shoulder. You can't assume that the people around you have your best interests at heart. And sometimes, you have to strike first to keep yourself safe."

"Like this?" And with a flick of her wrist, Clara took one of Scarlett's bishops: a vulnerability Scarlett hadn't even seen because she'd been too wrapped up in mourning Jaime.

Scarlett could only laugh. "Exactly."

Clara looked up from the board with a crooked, proud smile. "I see what you're saying, but being on defense constantly and assuming that everyone's about to attack you all the time—doesn't that get lonely?"

You have no idea, Scarlett wanted to say, but the vehemence with which the words jumped up in her stomach surprised her.

Scarlett had spent a lot of life operating as a free agent. Her dad was gone, her mom was more of a friend than a parent, and her relationships had always felt transitory. Deep roots, people who had your back—those were ideas for the movies, not for Scarlett's life.

But all of that was darker than the lessons Scarlett wanted to teach Clara. And at some level, the mess that she'd made of things with Jaime: it had made Scarlett doubt herself.

She knew how she'd come to see herself as an army of one, poised against the rest of the world. But she didn't like it.

"Nah," Scarlett said, moving to protect her king from the attack Clara was mounting. "I can't be lonely when there's more chess to play."

Except both Scarlett and Clara knew the words were a bluff.

Chapter 19

Jaime *liked* filming. The technicalities and careful planning that went into every scene. The decisions about the camera's movement and the editing. The giddy way you had to change your approach to a sequence on the fly or as someone's performance developed.

But on this set, Jaime was the conductor on a runaway train, holding on for dear life while they flew, brakeless, down a hill. The stakes, much like their budget, were so high here. If Jaime got *Queen's Kiss* wrong, he'd be branded a one-hit wonder.

He could've used someone to confide in about his worries, but Nate would've blithely told him everything was fine. Honestly, the only person who could possibly understand was Scarlett. Almost every match she played had these kinds of stakes, and she managed it with unnatural coolness.

But if Jaime looked at her for more than ten seconds combined, he plunged back into the moment when she'd told him what she'd done. His feelings were as fresh as wet paint—one of those splatter pieces by Jackson Pollock, maybe. Just an explosion of anger and confusion.

Things reached a fever pitch on the day he walked onto the set, trying to think about the pages they had to shoot today, and was immediately confronted by Scarlett chatting with Nate and two other people he'd never seen before. As he approached, the woman next to Scarlett aimed a look at Jaime that would've frozen running water.

Great. Today was off to an *amazing* start.

"Jaime! Perfect timing," Nate called.

Jaime might actually stab his codirector before this shoot was over, and not only because the guy was nursing some ridiculous notion about how Jaime must still be wildly in love with Scarlett. No, a murder might help with promo. Maybe people would like the show more if they thought Jaime had lost it while filming. There was still a lot of currency in the misunderstood-genius piggy bank.

"Looks like it," Jaime deadpanned. "Who do we have here?"

Scarlett's smile was beatific: oh boy. That always happened right before a thunderstorm. "Martina and Kit. They wanted to swing by and catch a few days of filming."

Jaime knew exactly who Martina and Kit were: two of the best chess players in the world and Scarlett's allies in challenging PAWN. They were collecting prodigies here.

"We had to make sure you aren't butchering Scarlett's story," Martina—the one with the Bond-villain glare—said faux sweetly.

Clearly, Scarlett had told them everything, and they loathed Jaime's guts. They could join the club. These days, he mostly loathed his own guts too.

"Trying not to," Jaime replied, which was the honest-to-God truth. As mad . . . annoyed . . . betrayed . . . hurt as he was about what Scarlett had done, he wanted to get the show right. For himself, sure, but also for Scarlett. He didn't know what exactly he wanted for her these days, but he didn't wish her ill.

"Are you?" Kit said, obviously amused by Jaime's awkwardness.

Jaime shrugged. "The show being good is in everyone's interests."

"Of course it is," Scarlett interjected smoothly. Other than her words in front of the entire cast and crew at the first production meeting, this was just about the only vote of confidence she'd cast for Jaime since they'd started filming. "And while they're here, they're going to play a few games with Clara—and anyone else who's up for it. They're both grand masters." She addressed that last part to Nate.

"I can tell they're grand." Nate was watching Kit with far more than friendly interest, and Jaime wanted to smack the guy with his script. They were making television; it wasn't the best time to lust over someone.

Jaime shot a quick look at Scarlett, and his body made its typical response. As complicated as his feelings were about her, she still turned his libido over as if it were a car engine and she had the only key.

So he kept his warnings to himself. People in glass houses should hoard their stones, or whatever the line was.

"Great," Jaime said, sounding hollow even to himself. "I have to check in with the DP, but it's good to meet you both."

Martina, though, wasn't having it. "The director of photography? Oh, interesting. Can I come see the camera? I'm *fascinated* by filmmaking."

Sure she was.

But Jaime wasn't going to be an asshole—or at least he wasn't going to be any *more* of an asshole. So he said, "Of course."

As they walked away, Nate asked Kit why white always went first in chess, and Jaime could practically hear their eyes roll in response. At least Jaime wasn't the only one sticking his foot in his mouth this morning.

"We're using a Sony Venice camera," Jaime began to explain to Martina. He could at least keep up appearances here. "It gives a real filmic look with great depth of field, and—"

"I don't care," Martina interrupted. "I wanted to get you alone."

Of course. "Uh-huh."

Martina swung around to look him dead in the eye. "You need to leave Scarlett alone."

"I swear to God, I've been trying to." Jaime was barely speaking to Scarlett. He certainly wasn't trying to make her feel bad or mess with her or anything. "We're just working together until the shoot is over."

As confusing as all this was—and it was—Jaime and Scarlett had an expiration date. Three months of filming to go, plus whatever promo

Videon asked them to do, but then they truly would never see each other again. This was nearly their last dance. After it was over, Jaime was going to avoid any and all mention of chess as if it were botulism. His next project was going to be about football or fighter pilots—whatever the absolute opposite of this was.

The prospect was strangely antiseptic, though. He disliked how seeing Scarlett made him feel, but it was hard to deny that next to her, everything else was flat and colorless. She was an IMAX movie—brash and hypersaturated—and everyone and everything else was a washed-out home movie from the seventies.

Life without Scarlett would feel like *less*. It would be less.

But if she didn't think there was anything wrong with the fact that she'd made a major decision about Jaime's family without so much as giving him a heads-up, Scarlett wasn't someone he could build a life with. End of story.

Martina snorted, disbelieving. "You had better, mister. She has been a *mess* these last few months. I've never seen her so much as rattled before. Then you come back into her life, and everything went to hell."

Jaime almost laughed. "Scarlett never gets rattled."

"Bullshit. She just hides it better than most people. But whatever happened when she was in Virginia, she can't seem to hide it anymore, and that's your fault. She held it together in Norway, but she's going to Candidates again and she'll need to be more focused there. Stop screwing around with her feelings."

Jaime . . . screwing around . . . with *Scarlett's* feelings?

"What?" he demanded, because the word was so loud in his head that he had to put it out into the world.

"Stop hurting her."

Jaime's eyes darted around, as if something on set could make what Martina was saying more clear. This was the strangest conversation Jaime had had all day, and he'd spent thirty minutes earlier discussing which shade of light-blue shirt would be better on camera.

Martina thought Jaime was at fault for Scarlett's turmoil. Was utterly convinced he was.

But he hadn't known Scarlett was *in* turmoil.

Scarlett clearly hadn't told her friends what had gone down in Virginia. A few weeks ago, he would've assumed the omission was because Scarlett was protecting herself by not sharing a story that painted her in an unflattering light. But looking into Martina's accusing face, Jaime wondered if Scarlett might have done it to protect *him* by keeping the lid on his family's dirty laundry.

Scarlett had said as much, but he'd dismissed the possibility out of hand. If she were telling the truth, though, it would knock everything off kilter.

Suddenly, Jaime was looking at the world through a Dutch angle shot. What else might he be wrong about?

Jaime almost argued with Martina. He almost explained. But he still couldn't quite believe Martina's admonition was real. The only thing keeping him upright was the conviction that if anyone were rattled, it should've been *him*.

"Did she put you up to this, to get me to stop glaring at her or something?" He couldn't imagine Scarlett not choosing to fight her own battles, but maybe she let her friends in more than she ever had Jaime.

Martina clearly thought this idea was absurd. "Don't be stupid. She has no idea I'm talking to you. But I mean it: I have my eye on you, Jaime Croft, and I am vicious when provoked."

At least Jaime could rest easy knowing Scarlett wasn't as alone as she sometimes liked to pretend she was. He'd be able to chill out in the future, because she had people around her who would at least try to protect her. She'd done everything in her power to keep him on the outside, and now he was done trying to scale her castle walls. Martina and Kit could be on guard.

"I believe it," he told Martina. "But I'm not—I'm not hurting her. Not on purpose. I'm just trying to get through this shoot. No one has more riding on this than I do."

"Except her."

"Except her," Jaime conceded. Because at least for the moment, he and Scarlett were still linked together by the show.

◆ ◆ ◆

The rest of Martina and Kit's visit to the set of *Queen's Kiss* was thankfully threat-free, but Jaime couldn't shake the effect his conversation with Martina had on him.

What was the likelihood that Jaime had been wrong? Not only wrong, but *unfair* in how he'd responded to Scarlett's confession?

Naw, his gut protested. But once the petulant denial faded, worry took its place.

Jaime could admit he had been selfish in how he'd processed the news, focused only on himself. But maybe there was another angle here, one equally important and totally different: Scarlett's.

He just couldn't shake the fear that, in this situation, he hadn't acted like the man he tried so hard to be.

So when Jaime collapsed in his hotel room late one afternoon, he called Evelyn. His little sister was aggravatingly grounded and good at seeing every side of something. It came with being an artist or something.

"I have a hypothetical to run by you," he said when she answered.

"Listening."

Which probably meant she was painting and he only had approximately ten percent of her attention, but that was fine. Ten percent of Ev's attention offered more insight than one hundred percent from a regular person. His baby sister was the best.

"What if someone close to you told you they were responsible for Dad's arrest?" There was no point sugarcoating it.

Over the phone, Evelyn drew a sharp breath.

It sounded like vindication. "You'd be incandescently pissed, right? And you'd feel betrayed they made the decision without consulting you, yes?" Because if so, Jaime was on solid ground, and he could squash the doubts Martina had sowed.

Evelyn exhaled, because of course she would want to know who exactly he meant by *someone*.

"No," Evelyn said carefully after a long pause. "I would feel . . . I mean, I would feel a lot of things. But I wouldn't be pissed."

Jaime almost gawked at his phone. "Why not?"

"This is Scarlett, right? And it's not hypothetical?"

"Yes." Jaime's response covered both things, and it gave him the space to digest the fact that Evelyn had achieved a higher state of zen than he had. "But I'm not quite ready to move on to that yet. How are you not mad about this?"

She really ought to be, and not simply because it would make him feel better. No, Jaime's position made emotional and logical sense, and Evelyn ought to admit that.

"You said the details didn't matter," Evelyn countered.

"That was before I knew them!" It turned out that the real details—not the fake ones he'd once been consumed with before he'd shoved them away forever—were pertinent and aggravating. They justified his response.

Didn't they?

"I don't see how this changes anything," Evelyn said. "Dad did it, someone caught him, and he's paying for his choices. What else matters?"

"It matters because the someone is my—*was* my—" He had no idea how to finish that sentence.

Jaime knew how it had felt sometimes, when he and Scarlett had been kids and when she'd stayed at his cabin, as if she were his *everything*. But Jaime couldn't say it, not even in the past tense. It would make him feel too exposed. Too needy.

"It matters." Jaime might not be sure about anything else, but he knew that. "It matters that Scarlett did it. And it matters that she didn't tell me."

Okay, Jaime might have oversimplified things, and he might have been melodramatic in responding. But he didn't know if he could get past those two things, and he didn't think that made him a shitty person.

"Except she did tell you, obviously."

"*Decades* later."

"Hmm. When?"

When Scarlett had returned to New York, Jaime had put more distance between himself and his family. It had been all too easy to come up with excuses for skipping family dinners or cutting their phone calls short. He hadn't wanted to answer their questions, and he'd known that if he was around them too much, he would end up blurting out what he'd learned.

He got absorbed when he was about to film—everyone knew that. If it also helped him deflect their attention and hide in plain sight, well, then those were just upsides.

"Nine months ago," he admitted.

"Nine months!" Evelyn yelped. "Okay, you gotta move on, big brother. You have to forgive Scarlett, and you have to forgive Dad, and you have to forgive yourself. That's what you're really mad about, by the way: Scarlett saw this, and you didn't."

"I'm calling Mom." Jaime hated how juvenile he sounded. Next, he was going to tell his sister to stay out of his room and to stop touching his LEGOs. "She'll have my back."

"You can call her," Evelyn said, "but deep down, you know I'm right."

Deep down . . . Jaime didn't know what the hell was true anymore. But having said that he was going to phone his mother, he did. She deserved to know the truth too.

"Hi, dear," she answered. "How's filming going? Are things rolling?"

His mother's ideas about moviemaking mostly came from *Singin' in the Rain*, but there were worse sources, he supposed.

"The first few days were good." They'd made their pages, at any rate. "I wanted to ask you something. Do you have any theories about how the police got wind of what Dad was up to?"

In the weeks following Dad's arrest, Jaime had declared that subject to be off limits. For so long, he'd had so little energy. He'd had to save it for the things he could control. He must have learned to manage his life better if he thought he had room for this now.

But his mother brought him up short when she said, "No, not really."

"Why not?" Jaime was genuinely curious.

"Because so many people knew. Honestly, it's shocking it didn't come out sooner."

He'd wondered the same thing, but his own version had been more like *Why didn't* we *know sooner?*

"But if you could know the details," he pressed, "would you want to?"

"No. It wouldn't change a thing."

His mom sounded so *confident*, it only fueled Jaime's doubts.

But then his mother's follow-up question proved the apple didn't fall far from the tree, where Evelyn was concerned: "Did something set you off?"

Right, his mom had seen more than he'd intended her to.

He had long ago discovered that his grief and shame were, at best, buried in a shallow grave. Sometimes he could go months with things locked down tight, and then Jaime would glimpse someone on the street who looked like his father, or flip through Videon and see Dad's favorite Tom Clancy movie, and it would all come back. Scarlett's admission had sent Jaime into the longest and most acute wave of grief he'd ridden since those early days, though.

"Why am I the only one who's curious about this?" he asked, partially because he did wonder and partially to buy himself some time.

"I'd guess because you know who it is—and they're someone who means a lot more to you than they do to me."

Busted. "Yeah, so eighteen years ago, Scarlett figured it out, and she called the police tip line. That's why Dad got caught."

The pause that followed was endless. Jaime cycled through all the feelings he expected to experience, but they were blunted a bit. Maybe not quite as intense as he would've expected them to be.

Now that he'd shared this information, he could process it abstractly and not bodily. The nausea in his gut was more like a dull ache. It was like a broken ankle that had almost healed but still twinged now and again to remind you of the injury. Uncomfortable, but not enough to make you sick.

His mother, though, was still in the initial throes of hearing it. Maybe she was going to hurl.

"No commentary?" he asked. "You've never liked her. I would think you'd be baying for her blood."

"I don't dislike Scarlett." His mother sounded far away, and he was certain she was going through her own cycle of emotions—but he wasn't going to push if she didn't want to share them.

He wasn't going to leave that ripe lie uncommented on, though. "Sure."

"I do worry she's too independent for you."

Jaime was tempted to lift the phone from his ear to glare at it. Maybe he ought to have done this on a video call. "I *love* that she's independent," he protested.

"But not that she made this call without you."

That was a pretty sassy line from his mother. She generally went for passive aggression versus actual aggression. She was right about this, though. "Yeah, I wish she would've told me. Asked me what to do about it."

Making decisions together was the baseline for being together. Jaime hadn't realized how strongly he felt about that until Scarlett hadn't given it to him.

"What would you have said?" Mom asked.

"I don't know." Jaime could pretend he would've believed Scarlett's story instantly and would've supported her calling it in. But being honest enough with himself to admit he might *not* have responded well didn't ease the sting of her unilateral decision. "It feels reasonable to want your partner to make these kinds of decisions with you. Wouldn't you have been pissed at Dad if he'd kept something like this from you?"

"He did keep something like this from me," his mother said drolly.

Oh. Right. And in comparison, Dad's betrayal was far worse.

"You were pretty pissed," he reminded her.

When the initial shock had melted, his mother had been even more volcanically angry than Jaime had been. But she'd kept her rage inside, focusing it on scrubbing baseboards and seething. If Jaime had tried to be cold and reserved and icy to Scarlett, Mom had just rumbled at the world. But somewhere along the way, she'd clearly released her grip on her fury.

When she sighed now, it was motherly and concerned. "There are some key differences, though. You and Scarlett weren't married, and you were kids."

"Youth isn't a defense." Not a good one, anyhow.

"But it's relevant." She paused, and Jaime could feel the conversation shift. Whatever was coming next, he wasn't going to like it. "As is personality. Part of why you're so upset Scarlett made this decision without you is that you loved to be *needed*, Jaime. Even before Dad went to jail, you liked to take care of people. To manage things. I never meant for you to take over so much when he was convicted, but you seemed to enjoy doing it, and you were so good at it. As long as you were also going to school and you eventually left the nest, well, I thought, *Where's the harm?* But that was wrong of me, and I'm sorry. I should've made you give me the reins a long time ago."

What was Mom going on about? Jaime didn't want to talk about himself. This was about what Scarlett had done. "No, that's not—this isn't about me."

"It's very much about your desire to take care of everyone."

Which included Scarlett, Jaime supposed. He'd wanted to take care of her, and he'd wanted her to recruit him to be on her team, the way she'd clearly allowed Kit and Martina to be. He respected her independent streak, but it was also the thing that kept her from letting him in—which he was holding against her.

Even if Evelyn and Mom were right here, and Jaime wasn't ready to admit that they were, he couldn't see how to resolve *that* conundrum.

"Wasn't wanting to take care of you and Ev after Dad's arrest a good thing? We're a family. That's what family does." Jaime didn't regret stepping up to help Mom manage things, not remotely.

"You were still a child," she said gently. "It wasn't your job to right the ship. And I'm sorry you missed out on a lot because you were helping me."

"You missed out on a lot too." His mother should've had a normal life, a normal marriage. Instead, she'd had to face the prospect of life alone, with two grieving and confused kids and the scorn of an entire community to deal with.

"I didn't say what happened was fair," his mother said. "I'm only talking about what I should've done."

Well, that was a mouthful.

Jaime rubbed his forehead. A headache was brewing in there. He'd called Mom wanting to have his frustrations validated, and instead, she'd ripped the rug out from under him. Mothers, man.

Stepping up after Dad's arrest had changed Jaime's life. Given him a sense of purpose. Helped him become the person he was today, the director and the man. Jaime couldn't feel bad about that, even if it had meant he'd missed out on other things.

"Maybe we all made the best choices we could have, given the circumstances," Jaime said, finally.

"Maybe we did," his mother agreed. "And I would include Scarlett in that."

Jaime . . . had no idea what to say in response. The conversations he'd had today with Martina, Evelyn, and his mother had mixed him up utterly. He wanted—so many things. To cry. To scream. To be certain again.

Most of all, he realized, he wanted to believe what his mom was saying, because if Scarlett had done the best she could, then they could be . . . well, he didn't know if they could be together, but at least the possibility could reenter the universe.

"The woman I saw in Musgrove last year, the one you were writing with," Mom pressed on, "she wasn't the same girl I knew eighteen years ago. Just like you're not the same boy. You're not going to punish her or yourself for the choices those other people made, are you?"

"I have no idea."

Jaime honestly felt as if he didn't know *anything* anymore.

Chapter 20

Scarlett was fixing to snatch a king off the chess board and lob it right into Jaime Croft's forehead. She'd aim between those dark-brown eyes of his, right where the skin wrinkled when he was glowering at her, and let it fly. It'd make a satisfying thunk as it nailed him. Maybe he'd holler. All she wanted was one good angry *Scarlett!* and she could die a happy woman.

Because these days, where she was concerned, Jaime flitted between his stern professional routine, the one where he tried to ignore her or be glacial cold, and something more disconcerting, where he'd glare at her as if he were trying to figure her out. As if he could survey the crevices of her soul or perform an MRI on her moral fiber with his eyeballs.

Scarlett didn't want to be known, thank you very much. She wanted to remain mysterious. Was it too late to become a hermit?

Yeah, probably. They were on the set of her biopic, after all.

The thing was, the man was an absolute machine on set. Twelve-hour days were nothing to Jaime. He'd do three more takes just to ensure someone's fingers were pressed into the tabletop enough during a close-up.

Scarlett cared about details—her entire life was mostly concerned with what happened inside two-inch squares—but Jaime was on another level. He was pedantic and competent . . . and that made him more than a little bit hot.

Except that when he stalked around being imperious and controlling and sexy, he kept either giving Scarlett the cold shoulder or scrutinizing her, seemingly unsure of what he wanted from her.

She didn't like it. Not one bit.

Take now. They were finishing the opening and closing sequence of episode three, when Emily won her first international tournament in Tokyo—the very tournament Scarlett had left Musgrove and Jaime for—and he was vacillating.

"Don't you think she needs to be triumphant?" Jaime asked Clara, regarding Emily's reaction to her win.

Despite all Scarlett's best efforts, the actress's spine was still composed primarily of Jell-O. "Maybe."

But lack of confidence might be contagious, because Jaime's own spine seemed to be quavering. Shouldn't they have a clearer direction here?

The way Scarlett saw it, Emily was glad she'd won, sure, but she was feeling a zillion other things too: exhaustion, relief, anxiety about the future. And that was without taking into account her recent breakup. Scarlett had broken up with Jaime and likely condemned his dad before she'd left town, but those things hadn't made it into her book.

Except if Jaime wanted the scene to feel *true*, well then, this moment hadn't felt jubilant when Scarlett had lived it.

"If Emily is just elated, it'd be too simple," Scarlett said.

"Would it?" Jaime demanded—and it very much felt as if he were asking about something besides the script.

His eyes were probing her again, and Scarlett fought an impulse to fidget with her hair.

"*Yes*," she said, hoping that it was the right answer for whatever Jaime was truly asking.

Jaime wasn't convinced. "Can't it be simple? She did what she needed to, and she got everything she worked for."

He addressed that to Clara, but he was talking to Scarlett.

Oh, this befuddled dingleberry. Jaime clearly hadn't understood what she'd tried to tell him nine months ago. He still didn't appreciate why she'd acted the way she had. He couldn't make a television show about her feelings—sorry, *Emily's* feelings—if he didn't grasp them.

Scarlett had spent weeks tiptoeing around his feelings because when he'd told her he was drowning, she knew he'd meant it. But she was done with the kid gloves. Scarlett wasn't going to let this go.

"But she didn't get everything. I just don't think it's as easy as her winning and hooray." Victory wasn't all this had been about for her. "Winning has always felt complicated to me. It's a vindication in some ways, but at this tournament, Emily also realized how messed up the system is. She's getting the Elo rating she wanted and some money, but it's only on PAWN's terms, and she knows how unfair those are to a lot of other people. The last shot of the episode needs to convey all of that."

Jaime watched Scarlett intensely. His gaze was . . . assessing, like a scientist contemplating a sample under a microscope. Scarlett would've rocked back on her heels if she hadn't spent years learning how to hide her feelings from her opponents.

"But isn't the impact bigger if we have her high here and then low later on?"

Jaime was asking about *Scarlett*, how she had felt after she'd left him. About what she'd really wanted. Because he still didn't get it.

"No, it isn't," she said. "I was there, and it wasn't all high."

Part of why it hadn't been was because Scarlett had been distracted about *Jaime*, about what she'd done before she'd left Musgrove. It was imperative for him to understand that, even if she wasn't going to lay all that out for him while they had an audience.

Jaime and Scarlett were so focused on each other, they both startled when Clara asked, "Can we maybe try one take Scarlett's way?"

Right: filming now, personal conversations later.

Scarlett turned toward the actress and grinned. If Clara's interjection hadn't been so darn tentative, she would've cheered too. All the time they'd been playing chess, Scarlett hadn't simply been teaching Clara strategy and confidence so she could perform the moves to get to the Queen's Kiss believably. She'd been teaching her so she could stand up for herself.

A good thirty seconds ticked by while they waited for Jaime's response. Scarlett hoped he wasn't going to disagree with his lead actress and his cowriter. She doubted she'd won him over—either at the script level or the level of their private war—but he was too polite, too professional, too respectful to pitch a fit.

Probably.

At last he nodded. "Right. We'll give it a try. Play the emotional beat more mixed."

Scarlett winked at Clara, who beamed.

The nonactors moved out of the shot, and there was a flurry of activity involving the lights and the camera and all that jazz.

"Camera set," the AD called.

And with that, they were filming.

Unlike in the rehearsal, when they got to the key moment, Clara let fifty things flash across her eyes. Regret, anxiety, pride, hunger, and exhaustion were all there, along with more stuff Scarlett had experienced but couldn't name. Fancy emotions you needed to have a graduate degree to describe. It was a gut punch, reliving that moment through Clara's performance, and it made Scarlett's own eyes heavy and watery.

Clara had a face like a movie screen. She could put any old feeling up there—or even an entire kaleidoscope of them, like she'd just done—and every beat of it read to the audience. Holy crap, she was amazing.

"Cut!" Jaime yelled.

His attention was glued to the monitor, and he was chewing on his bottom lip. Scarlett could *feel* the moment when he wanted to look at her, because he'd seen the truth in Clara's acting. He'd taken a baby step toward understanding Scarlett's stew of emotions in Tokyo. That didn't mean he got why she'd called the police tip line—Scarlett didn't want to get carried away—but something had clicked here.

This hadn't been a gambit, honest. Scarlett hadn't pushed a sacrificial poisoned rook toward Jaime, hoping that he'd snatch it and fall into a trap. But in the other game they were playing on set, the one entirely between Jaime and Scarlett, the personal one that was about the past and the future, she might just have won a point.

"It was—good," he finally said. "I want to do one more, but Clara, deliver the line a little softer this time."

"Okay."

They did it again, and this take, Clara was even better.

"That's the one," Jaime said. "That's a full lid for today. Thanks, everyone."

As the crew began to pack things in for the night, Scarlett crossed over to him. "Do you see it now, why it had to be messier?" *Why it was messier for me?*

"Sure."

Jaime sounded so tired, Scarlett knew that she ought to leave him alone. But part of why he was tired was because he refused to trust her or to listen to her side of things.

"You could've given my way a spin earlier," she said.

"Sure. I could've," he agreed.

"That's why you want me to be here, right?" she pushed on. "To help with these moments. To make sure that things are reading right. That they're good."

That was what she thought she was doing here, anyhow.

Jaime finished packing up his bag. "I don't know" was all he said as he latched it.

Didn't know why she was there, or didn't know what her role was? Scarlett set a hand on her cocked hip. "Isn't that a loaded statement?"

He just shrugged.

"Jaime, we need to talk about this." Because whatever he was struggling with, it wasn't only about today's scene.

"Later. Tomorrow, maybe."

She knew he wanted to get some space from her in order to fashion a new mask for himself, one that covered all his wounds, but Scarlett wasn't going to let him do it. They needed to have a conversation while his breakthrough was still fresh and they might be able to come to a new level of understanding.

"No, we need to talk about it *now*."

Jaime ignored that. He handed his headset to a PA and started off down the hall. He had an office somewhere in the bowels of the soundstage, but Scarlett had never seen it. Whatever meetings they had were in one of the conference rooms.

Scarlett was wearing two-inch heels and not as practiced as he was at navigating the dark, narrow hallway. Plus, it took her a few seconds to get off her own gear. But after a brief and aggravating delay, she was after him.

When Jaime had said the cast and crew were done for the day, it seemed as if everyone else had vaporized. Seriously, a few minutes ago, fifty people had been in the building, but now, Scarlett and Jaime might as well have been the last humans left on earth.

The winding maze of the studio was vacant, and Scarlett's heels echoed down the hall until she arrived at Jaime's office door. He stood just inside, his back to her and his hands thrust into his hair. Every cell of his body was clearly humming, his taut posture overwhelmed.

"We need to talk," she said.

Jaime didn't turn toward her. "Please. I can't do this right now with you."

She ought to walk away. No, Scarlett ought to *run* away. It was very clear they were on the brink of something here, and if she had a single ounce of self-preservation in her body, Scarlett would scram.

She hadn't gotten where she was by playing it safe, though. She might be an adrenaline junkie underneath her chess-playing exterior.

So she took another step into his office. The rug was probably left over from the Louis B. Mayer era. Scarlett's heels sunk into it as if it were a soggy lawn.

"If we wait, you'll get yourself all nice and composed. You'll add up the columns and balance the checkbook." He'd find those two-cent bank errors, she was certain, and report them, even if they were in his favor.

"So? What's wrong with that?" he said, still safe in the cocoon of his arms.

"Life doesn't work like that, Jaime. It isn't neat. You must have seen that out there. It was better when you let Clara embrace the mess." It was better when Jaime had realized Scarlett hadn't had simple motives for what she'd done to him and his family, and she hadn't felt simple things about it.

"I know." His tone was so agonized that, for a moment, Scarlett almost retreated.

She hated causing him pain, but they had to cauterize this wound. If she ran away now, they would have to reopen it to get the job done.

"Talking about this is the way we balance our emotional checkbook."

"Yeah, I know that too. But right now, I have *a job to do*. If we get into this, I'll lose it." Jaime finally twisted around. His eyes clashed with hers—and whoa. His gaze was dark and intense.

He might've wanted Clara to play that scene with a single emotion, but there were more things in his face than had been in the actress's. If Jaime could summon all of this—this angry, sexy, lust-filled mix—on command, he would've had a good career ahead of him as an actor or a model. A million romance novel covers would've been calling his name.

But Scarlett suspected that the blame for his current emotional hurricane rested firmly on her own shoulders. "Talk to me, Jaime."

"You make me doubt myself," he finally said.

If Scarlett were as smart as she was sometimes accused of being, she would walk away now. But after months of careful exchanges from him, of polite distance and cool words, she wanted every ounce of his pain. The current flowing between them right now was real, and she was tired of anything that wasn't real.

"Because I give you explanations for the past that don't match those bedtime stories you tell yourself?"

"Something like that."

"You're the one who told me that the truth matters," she said mockingly.

"That was before I knew what it was."

"So now you're all about soothing lies?"

"Maybe."

"Coward."

"Probably," he agreed.

Scarlett wanted to spit. "You are strong enough to deal with this."

He shook his head as if he didn't believe her. "When I look at you, I don't know what I want."

That was a much worse lie than any she'd ever told him. Than any lie she'd ever told anyone. The air in the room was heavy with what they both needed.

"I do. You want this." Scarlett took two steps and pressed her lips to his.

It was a slap of a kiss, one that was going to bruise them both, but was all the sweeter for it.

Scarlett spent hours contemplating the moves she was going to make on the chess board. Trying to see and weigh every possibility and to imagine how her opponent would respond to each one.

Here, she hadn't hesitated. Hadn't even really decided to do it until she was already doing it. An instinct as much as a kiss.

Shit. Shit shit shit—

But before she could even finish the thought and plan an escape, Jaime was kissing her back. Kissing her back with such ferocity and urgency it was as if he were trying to compress an entire love affair's worth of kisses into one urgent encounter.

His tongue swept into her mouth and tangled with hers, while his pelvis forced her backward. Seconds later, Scarlett's back slammed against the wall of his office, right next to the door.

One of his hands left her waist for a second. He slammed the door shut, and then he was groping her again. There wasn't another word for how he was touching her. His hold had the right amount of force, but his fingers digging into her hip, that was entirely the wrong place. She moaned anyhow, in encouragement, anticipation.

This—this was what they'd been missing.

Jaime's hand shifted and squeezed her ass, tugging her up and into him. Yup, that was the spot.

He freed a hand from Scarlett again to fumble with the lock on the door, which gave Scarlett a second to fuss with her skirt. She ought to be able to take it off somehow, right? She'd put it on this morning.

But with Jaime moaning into her mouth, she'd be damned if she could remember how it worked. So she just yanked the thing up around her waist. Then she was hooking her calf around him, pulling him into the center of her.

He managed to engage the lock just as his hips ground against hers. She was about ten seconds away from exploding here.

With the door secured, Jaime rubbed the skin of her upper thighs in a way that was almost an end in itself. Or maybe that was just the hungry noises he was making, as if the fact that he hadn't touched her there in the better part of a year was a crime.

His fingers were pushing past the gusset of her panties and over her lips. Scarlett was already so wet she would've been mortified, except for how Jaime was humming in approval.

He swept her lips apart with his thumb. He lifted his mouth from hers while he skimmed over her clit so lightly she wanted to cry.

"Have you done this . . . since?" he whispered.

Had she slept with someone else since that week they'd spent screwing each other's brains out in Virginia? That was what he meant.

Time stopped. His hands on her stopped. Everything stopped.

"No," she whispered back.

That earned her a firm push against her clit that had her panting. Scarlett lifted and rotated her hips. Not enough. It wasn't nearly enough.

"Have—have you?" she got out.

She tried to tell herself it wouldn't matter, but she worried, if he said yes, it would very much matter.

"No." His response was as swift and unyielding as how he was stroking her now.

"Jaime."

His fingers thrust into her then. Just straight in and up and *God.* He was fucking her with his fingers, his rhythm fast and her body slick.

"I want," she panted. "I want you."

She didn't want to think. Couldn't think, really. Every time they'd done this, there had been good reasons not to. But in the end, not doing it hadn't made anything hurt less. So they might as well do it.

If she'd been able to say words, that would've been what she would've said.

But apparently, he didn't need to be convinced. His fingers were gone, and Jaime was pulling her down. Office-floor sex wasn't exactly something Scarlett had on a bingo card or anything, but she couldn't have cared less. All that mattered was this.

They were both fumbling with his zipper. Then Jaime was pulling her panties off—ah, that was how that worked—and then his cock was out and her knees were falling apart and he was positioning himself.

Sweet Lord, they were seconds away from this.

"Is this okay?" he asked.

Because Jaime didn't have a condom, and they were barely talking to each other, and things between them were still as emotionally raw as a fresh amputation.

Those last two, they weren't okay. But sex wasn't going to make them worse, Scarlett knew that. And as they'd talked about back in Virginia, she was on the pill and she got tested regularly, as did Jaime. So there was no problem where the first item was concerned either.

Scarlett absolutely knew that if she said no, he would return to sanity. If she so much as hesitated, Jaime wouldn't push it any further. But she wanted this. He wanted this. And things were already a mess.

Which was why she said, "God, yes."

"Thank Christ."

And then Jaime was there, pushing into her, and her hands were clenching on him, and her hips were rising to meet him, and his name was on her lips. Whatever came next, Scarlett wasn't going to regret this. Because while it was probably a mistake, it was also vital, necessary, in a hundred ways she couldn't name but couldn't deny. The second Jaime rocked into her, some little fissure in her heart closed up.

It was the fastest, roughest, crudest sex she'd ever had. Jaime had never held back less with her than he did on the floor of his office. The way he moved over her, in her, made her feel as if every other time they'd ever been together had been censored.

And it turned out she loved being with him without the guardrails. Loved his lack of finesse. Loved the way he was pistoning into her. Loved the blunt way his fingers moved over where they were joined. Because even now, he still wanted things to be good for her.

Then Scarlett was coming, and she was begging him not to stop, and his knuckles were pressing right where she needed them, and he was promising her that he wouldn't ever stop. It was the kind of lie you blurted out during sex and worried about at three in the morning, when things were over and your head was cooler.

Except Scarlett was going to worry that he *didn't* mean it. Because the things she was saying to him, about how nobody made her feel this way and how good he was and how much she needed him, every one of those statements was absolutely true.

When the last contraction of her orgasm had passed, Jaime pulled out from Scarlett's body. He wrapped his fingers around her wrist, and he pushed his cock, still hard and wet, into her palm. Then he drove himself into her hand and into the softness of her lower belly until, with a grunt, he came across her skin.

It was the smuttiest, hottest thing she had ever seen. Bar none.

"Fuck," she whispered, marveling at the evidence of his orgasm. Her core clenched, hard, at the sight. If they hadn't just finished, she would've wanted to—

Jaime raised himself onto his forearms. He flipped his body and collapsed on his back next to Scarlett. His breaths were coming in great, whooshing gasps. In the quiet of his office, their breathing was like a twister, and their spent bodies were the wreckage left behind.

"You okay?" he managed after a few moments.

Because after that, all he could think about was whether *she* was all right.

"Terrific," she deadpanned.

But for all that Scarlett was going to have rug burn on her back, and they were going to need to talk about what they'd done and to figure out how not to disrupt whatever equilibrium they'd established, she was legitimately terrific.

"I'm sorry for—"

"If you finish that apology, I will smother you. Feel free to fuck me on the floor of your office anytime."

"Noted."

And she could only hope he knew she meant it.

Chapter 21

At thirty-four, Jaime was too old for this shit. He had a mortgage, for crying out loud—he ought to be stable and staid. He ought to spend his weekends pressure washing his deck and not breaking into a sweat when he accidentally caught Scarlett's eye.

But no, every time he made that mistake, his cheeks flamed and his bloodstream ignited. He kept missing what people were saying to him in meetings because he was too busy reliving what had happened with Scarlett on the floor of his office.

It was mortifying. He hadn't been this fluttery when he'd been an actual teenager. He needed to grow up, but that meant asking Scarlett what the heck their encounter had meant. Had it been an inevitable release for two people who had too much tension built up in their bodies, the sexual equivalent of shocking yourself on a door handle after rubbing your feet on the carpet? Or was it more serious than that?

It would also probably necessitate clearing the air about what had gone down on set, but Jaime wasn't ready to do that either. Scarlett had been totally right to call him out. His job as the director was to know what he wanted and to listen—and he'd failed at both because he'd started to doubt whether he'd been right to be mad at Scarlett.

He still felt as if he were in free fall, no more confident about which way was up than he had been when he and Scarlett had ended up sweaty and panting together. He was a *mess.*

If the sex had been about releasing tension, it hadn't worked. No, if anything, it felt as if they'd actually ratcheted things up. And as for it being serious . . . well, Jaime knew that things with Scarlett and him couldn't ever be anything except momentous. It was how they rolled.

In order to get through the shoot, Jaime had to keep putting one foot in front of the other and not get distracted. Except this was very distracting.

So one week after it boiled over, Jaime decided to go clear the air. He wanted to talk about it with Scarlett in person, because he wasn't a goddamn coward, but he also would prefer it if no one else from the production saw him knock on her hotel room door.

And that was why, as he tried to slip from the stairwell onto her floor, he cursed under his breath when he saw Nate.

Nate turned toward the noise and clocked Jaime immediately. "Hey! I thought you had plans tonight."

"I do." He had to prove he was an adult by having a somewhat mortifying conversation with his ex. Those were plans.

"With?" Nate prompted.

Scarlett, the woman I can't seem to get over. See, we stupidly had sex on the floor of my office last week, but I can't manage to have a real conversation with her. The entire thing has me pacing the floor and talking to myself—and I'm starting to think I've cracked.

Yeah, no.

"I was going to see if Scarlett was free to talk about tomorrow's scene, and then I was going to turn in early."

That was perfect. He really ought to ask Scarlett about the stuff they were filming tomorrow, to consult her and involve her more because she was a valued member of the production team. He'd give up a little of the precious control she thought he was unwilling to part with as a cover for this conversation . . . just as soon as they established that the sex had been a not-to-be-repeated error.

"I mean, jeez," Nate said, in a faux whiny voice. "I know I'm not as pretty as she is, but you passed up a sure-thing dinner with me for a maybe conversation with her?"

"Them's the breaks," Jaime said.

"Fair enough. I think she's in that one." Nate indicated the door that a glance at the production binder had already confirmed to be hers.

Jaime hesitated for a minute.

This was a bad idea. It was such a bad idea.

If Jaime had been alone, this was where he would've realized that and run away. But Nate was standing there, looking at him. Waiting for him to rap on the door. And so Jaime was stuck.

"You gonna knock, or are you just waiting for her to intuit that you're there?" Nate asked.

"Knock. Definitely." Feeling as if he didn't know how to work his body, Jaime lifted a fist and tapped on Scarlett's door.

Maybe she would save him by being out, or in the shower, or ignoring interruptions, or—

"Who is it?" Scarlett called.

Dammit. He had the worst luck. The absolute worst luck.

"Jaime." His voice came out high and strained. "I want to talk about filming tomorrow." He flashed a smile at Nate, who was watching him suspiciously.

Nate had probably put together seventy-five percent of what had happened. If Jaime could redo things, he definitely would've picked a less perceptive collaborator.

Scarlett pulled the door open. She'd ditched the fancy outfit she'd worn on set in favor of a wine-colored tank top and black leggings. She'd washed her makeup off, and her skin was endearingly bare and shiny.

Jaime swallowed. Whenever they came face to face, his insides went marshy. Maybe those green eyes of hers brought the tide in. It swept up the prickly emotions, making them bob around in the mix of things she made him feel.

"Tomorrow's scene?" Scarlett's eyes darted over Jaime's shoulder toward Nate. "Is it a group convo?"

"Nope, I'm leaving." Nate patted Jaime's back far, *far* harder than he needed to. "Have a good night, you two. Don't do anything I wouldn't do!" He shouted that last bit back at them from halfway down the hall.

"What wouldn't he do?" Scarlett asked, stepping back so Jaime could enter her room. "Because I don't know him that well."

"Where Kit is concerned, I don't think there's anything Nate wouldn't do."

"He ought to be careful, there. Kit leaves a trail of broken hearts wherever they—nope. Let's not do that. We shouldn't start matchmaking our friends."

Because that was what a couple would do, and no one would confuse Jaime and Scarlett for a couple.

What were you, when you had an intense shared history but you had broken up twice now? What was left behind when a relationship crumbled? Who were you, even?

Jaime wished his other exes all the best. He could think about the good times and the bad times with them and feel *neutral.* But with Scarlett, there was never any neutrality, never any distance. Everything still hit as fresh as the day it had happened. All the lust. All the jokes. All the intensity. But also the rejection and the betrayal and the truth. His eyes snagged on her, and that encyclopedia of emotions went through him.

Standing here, a few feet from Scarlett, with amusement making her eyes sparkle, Jaime felt as if his chest had been cleaved open. She'd always put her independence first, and he'd always crave genuine emotional intimacy. They weren't suited for each other. But he would never stop wanting her to be the one for him. Not ever.

Jaime had meant to come here and clear the air. To put a stop to things.

What an idiot he'd been.

He'd actually convinced himself that what happened in his office had been a onetime thing, that he didn't want to repeat it, and here he was, almost panting for her again.

"I mean, Kit hates blind dates. They're much more of a make-eyes-at-someone-across-a-crowded-room type," Scarlett was saying. "And Nate strikes me as—"

"Stop talking."

Then Jaime's mouth was on Scarlett's, and they crashed into the wall. Her hands were in his hair, and her tongue was in his mouth, and everything was perfect.

That was better. That was what he'd wanted.

When Jaime was kissing Scarlett, when he was touching her soft skin, when she was pulling his clothing off and making impatient, hungry noises, the kind that said he couldn't get inside her fast enough, everything was perfect.

You couldn't clear *perfect* from the air. You couldn't get the taste of it off your tongue.

Why would you even want to try?

Jaime didn't have to feel that messy stew of frustration and anger and confusion when they were wrapped up in each other like this. With her body under his hands, things between them reduced to their elemental components. Everything became a matter of taking and giving. His pleasure, her pleasure. His fingers, her sighs. His moans, her mouth.

Moral questions and ethical quandaries and the issue of their compatibility didn't figure here. Not when they were stumbling toward her bed, shirts dropping to the floor along the way.

Scarlett pulled back from him and set her hand in the center of his chest, right over where she'd ripped his heart out. The thought set off a dull ache, which proved the thought was a lie. It only felt as if she'd taken it. Sadly, the organ was still there. Still beating. And still hurting.

With a coy smile, she shoved, and he sat on the bed with a grunt.

"Dreamed about this," she whispered, rolling to the floor between his spread knees. With a few efficient movements, she'd freed his cock and set about doing the kinds of things with her mouth and her teeth and her tongue that made it hard to think about anything else. "If you hadn't come to see me . . ." She trailed off, but it was a sentence she didn't need to finish.

What did it mean before, and what does it mean now? he wanted to demand. But wasn't the way he felt when she pulled down his zipper a better answer than anything she might have said?

The look she shot him was meant to be seductive—and it was plenty successful. Scarlett could do whatever she wanted to and with Jaime. He was hers.

But her expression was a little too coy for him to fully buy that she felt in charge here. Underneath things, Jaime hoped Scarlett was every bit as uncertain as he was. She had to be every bit as swept away by their attraction as he was—and just as unable to control it.

"You don't have to," he said.

"I want to."

Jaime knew she did. But he also suspected it was easier to have him like this, where she was directing the action and he was at her mercy, than it would've been if the situation had been reversed.

Still, when she put her mouth on him, it felt as if they were both taking the easy way out. That it was easier for them both when he was begging, when he was gasping her name, when he was the one saying please.

Please please please. The words fell from his mouth like sheets of rain from a stormy sky. But Jaime knew he wasn't only begging for Scarlett not to stop. He was asking for her to love him, to forgive him, to let him in, to make any decision *with* him next time—that and a hundred other things he wasn't yet ready to voice.

Pleasure was the thing it was easiest to ask for, but it wasn't one-tenth of what he needed from her.

Which was probably why he was soon threading his hands in her hair, pulling her up and into his lap. It wasn't enough for him to find release; he needed to give it too.

"I need to taste you." Then he set about stripping her and laying her out.

Scarlett, sprawled over the bed, her hair loose around her shoulders, her eyes bright with arousal—she was the most beautiful thing he'd ever seen.

"Baby." He should keep the tenderness out of his voice, but he couldn't. It had been too long. Entirely too long.

"You said you needed to taste me?"

"I do."

He kissed her breasts, her stomach, down and down her skin until he was buried in the core of her. The dance of his tongue and her hips and his hands and her cries—goddamn. Scarlett gave herself over to pleasure so completely. She let him lead her wherever he wanted, but she was really the one leading, wasn't she?

It was her gasps, her moans, that he was chasing. The moment when all her muscles drew tight, when she was shaking and sobbing his name, he knew this wasn't all in his head. Knew it wasn't one sided.

Then he was next to her on the bed, and their hands were tangling together on his cock. His own release was almost an afterthought, albeit one that had him begging, pushing against her thigh, their eyes locked, her lips flushed. Jaime clenched the fist of his free hand on the comforter so hard it was a miracle the fabric didn't rip.

When he finally came, she made a soft noise of surprise, as if she'd wanted the moment to last forever.

He got it. If only they could stay suspended in that spiral forever, things would be . . . easy.

Scarlett half sat up and tapped around on the nightstand. She came back with a tissue, and with painful gentleness, she cleaned up his stomach.

"There you go," she whispered, and it felt like the truest thing anyone had ever said.

Jaime had come here wanting to know what was true—and he'd gotten it.

He loved her. This hadn't been an itch to scratch or a onetime blast from the past. No, Jaime would never get enough of Scarlett, not ever, and no one else would ever be right for him.

The only outstanding questions were whether they could grow enough to be together. Could she be *with* someone, and could he live with her wariness?

"Did you really want to talk about the scene?"

"No."

"So do you want to talk about this?" She gestured at their nakedness. She'd asked the question so softly she might have been talking to herself.

But just the same, he'd heard her.

Did they need to talk about it? Sure.

But did Jaime want to talk about it? Hell no.

Not until he knew how to ask for what he wanted.

"No." Jaime got to his feet. He found his clothes, and despite the fact that his digits and limbs weren't working yet, that so much of him only wanted to slip back into her bed and wrap himself around Scarlett's soft body, he made himself dress.

When he was done, he set one fist on the bed and leaned over her.

Scarlett's expression was sober. Alert. She knew exactly what he was doing and exactly why he was doing it.

He couldn't resist her. He absolutely could not. But he wasn't going to let himself get swept away. He couldn't afford to. Not until she let him in.

"I don't want to talk about anything."

Which would've been more convincing if he hadn't dropped a soft kiss on her forehead before bolting from her room.

Chapter 22

Scarlett couldn't remember learning the rules of chess. They had always been there, as surely as she'd always known that if she dropped a glass, it'd hit the floor. She and Jaime might be having an affair, but there hadn't been a moment with a burning bush and stone tablets on top of a mountain. They'd never negotiated what was allowed, but Scarlett had figured out this affair's commandments all the same.

They weren't going to have a meal together in a restaurant, but sharing room service was fine. They could enjoy every sex act known to humanity together, but they didn't fall asleep in the same bed. Any talk about deeper feelings was forbidden, but when they were naked, neither of them managed to hide how overwhelmed they were.

Wasn't a whispered *Fuck, baby* in the throes tantamount to a declaration of love? Scarlett was too worried to ask. The rules of the game didn't account for feelings, you see, and acknowledging them might wreck things.

Even still, a week into it, she was already gnawing through the bit . . . which was hilariously two-faced. Scarlett had spent months in Jaime's cabin trying not to talk about anything that mattered. Then, she would've emptied her bank account if it had meant she could have sex and jokes with him without any discussion about their hearts, pasts, or traumas.

Hypocrisy, thy name is Scarlett.

She'd briefly had everything with Jaime, and it turned out she liked everything a hell of a lot. She wanted to be seen by him in all her flaws and imperfections and dirty underwear—literal and otherwise. She wanted everyone on set to know that she was the reason he was smiling more and that he was the reason she had started blushing—actually blushing.

She wanted all of it, an entire real-ass relationship, with him.

I'm finally ready, she wanted to scream.

Except she hadn't so much as whispered it, because if she did, Jaime might take back the tiny morsel of their lives they were sharing. Sometimes, Scarlett would walk past him in a hallway at the studio, and he would catch and hold her attention. And just like that, she would know to expect his knock.

But the hard crumb he offered wasn't satisfying . . . or it wasn't wholly satisfying. They could have it all if she could just find the right way to say it.

Or she could keep being a coward. Like tonight, when they'd finished, and Scarlett had flipped on the TV. *Indiana Jones and the Last Crusade*: bingo. Jaime couldn't resist Indy. According to him, the series had two entries: film one and film three, and absolutely nothing else.

Trying not to smile smugly, she waved at the TV. "That's the most beautiful speedboat in movie history." The water taxi in question was all gleaming burled wood and chrome, and wow, they just didn't make things like they used to. "Probably *in history*."

"I can think of motorboats I like better." Jaime heaved himself up onto his shoulder and pried down the sheet Scarlett had draped over her chest. He gave a lasciviously appreciative sigh as he took in her cleavage.

Which was kind of silly. The man had spent *plenty* of time appreciating it earlier.

"You're so crass." He wasn't really, but Scarlett knew he thought she had the best figure in history.

Jaime pressed a kiss to her shoulder and flopped back down onto his back. "Doesn't your motorboat crush get chewed up in a second here?"

"No, that's the bad guys' boat."

He scoffed in pretend scorn. "They're the Grail protectors. The Nazis are the bad guys."

"Shh." She pressed her hand over Jaime's mouth. His lips against her skin immediately had her pulse clicking up a notch or two. "I'm having a moment with this boat."

When the scene had finished and an ad for sports betting came on, she took her hand back.

"I thought you got seasick," he immediately said, which was promising.

That at least acknowledged they knew each other outside the context of these four walls. *You know me so well. We should really be together forever, huh?*

But wanting to keep things light, not wanting to upset the applecart, she said instead, "That's why it's a fantasy."

"I can't believe Harrison Ford is right there and you're salivating over a boat."

As if she could see Harrison Ford—or anyone—with Jaime in the room. "Varnished wood does it for me. What can I say?"

She wanted Jaime to make a joke about wood. She wanted him to roll her underneath him and show her which wood *really* did it for her. She wanted him to stay all night.

Most of all, she wanted this inane conversation to melt into something real. Something like *So are you over my confession yet? And are we together now or what?*

All the words Scarlett wanted to say crowded out the air in the room until it was almost hard to breathe. But the fact that Jaime was even in her bed at all . . . for the moment, it was enough. Because at the end of the day, Scarlett worried she would pop this bubble if she so much as blew on it. And much like all bubbles, it was too pretty to risk.

So instead of jeopardizing what they had over a dose of truth or rehashing the past, she launched into a tirade about how hats could make a movie scene funny and hoped that was enough to show Jaime that they were more than just friends with benefits. That she was finally ready for everything he'd ever offered her. Way more than ready.

Production meetings absolutely—and Scarlett was pretty sure this was a technical assessment—sucked. They stood out because most of what Scarlett did on the set of *Queen's Kiss* was pure pleasure. She relished getting to know the crew, whose passion for making movies and shooting the breeze and trying to beat her at chess was infectious.

Her coaching sessions with Clara had also become much more than instruction about endgame strategy. Those hours had become an endless conversation about the character they were creating together, with digressions about acting and life and fashion. Those exchanges didn't feel like work; they were a chance for Scarlett to pretend she'd finally gotten the little sister she'd always wanted.

And she enjoyed watching Jaime film. The focused way he attacked the tedious work of setting up a shot, and the patience with which he would capture this moment and then that one so he could eventually sandwich them together, like layers of cake, into a glorious whole. That was fun . . . and it was hot.

But before they could do those good parts, they had to have meetings. So many freaking meetings. Why had she wanted a producer credit again?

To annoy Jaime.

Yeah, it hadn't been worth it.

Across from her, a location supervisor was currently updating the key crew and the main producers for the travel schedule after they left Canada. They were filming all the interior stuff and the set stuff here in Vancouver, but then they had a whirlwind, round-the-world two weeks of location and exterior shooting. Videon certainly hadn't skimped. They would be hitting Tokyo, Paris, Casablanca, Dortmund, and Wijk aan Zee, before wrapping up filming in Las Vegas.

Scarlett had warned them that telling her life story was never going to be cheap, but she didn't think they would actually cough up the necessary cash to do this right. How delightful it was, just once, to learn she'd been wrong.

"We're still going back and forth about the final match in Vegas," Gloria, the producer, explained. "The space that we booked doesn't have a view of the Strip, but Scarlett said—"

"Asked," Scarlett interrupted Gloria. "I *asked*."

Scarlett didn't mind so much when Jaime teased her about being a diva because he said it with affection. Even now, when they weren't allowing themselves to converse in public, Jaime couldn't help but inject some flirtation into their exchanges. That warmth was basically the ghost of romantic relationships past, and it wouldn't stop haunting them.

Someone ought to call the Ghostbusters.

But yeah, while she'd take the diva thing from Jaime, when other people on set implied she was difficult, Scarlett wouldn't put up with it. This was *her* book after all, and she was a producer for the show. It was reasonable for her to have some input. Why else would she even be here?

"I asked if it made sense to go film in some generic hotel ballroom when we could film in some place that actually feels like Vegas," Scarlett finished. "Such as the STRAT."

One of the PAs ringing the room oohed. Because it was clearly an amazing idea. The scene was going to be great either way, but it was going to be extra great with the Strip glittering out every window.

"What's the cost difference?" Jaime asked.

Gloria sighed. "Fifty thousand."

"Do we have it in the budget?"

"Yes, but the actual tournament was at Bally's."

Gloria had loathed Scarlett from the start, and Scarlett had never been able to figure out why. Everyone else on set seemed to like her fine. Even Jaime, whose feelings about her were understandably complicated, was far more cordial to Scarlett than Gloria was. Maybe Gloria was a closet PAWN fan.

But whatever was going on here, Scarlett wasn't going to let them make the show worse for stupid reasons. And up to this point, they hadn't let reality constrain them.

"Sure, but in actuality, I look like this"—she gestured at her own face—"and Clara Hess looks like a movie star."

Nate started to laugh, but he converted this to a cough when Gloria glared at him. Seriously, that woman was humorless.

But Jaime wasn't going to be cowed. "If Scarlett says it should be the STRAT, then that's the way it'll be, everyone."

Gloria started to argue with him, and Jaime just gave her a look, the kind of look that he was always trying to quiet Scarlett with. But with Gloria, it worked. She swallowed her complaint and hid behind her laptop.

Jaime said to a PA, "Get the STRAT booked. It'll be quite the finale. Is there anything else?"

During the pause that followed, Nate was clearly trying not to laugh and Scarlett was trying not to fluff her hair. Jaime had just slayed a dragon for her. Wasn't that basically an official declaration that they were together? She'd expect him to change his lock screen to a pic of them kissing at any moment.

She was so pathetically thirsty for the man, even the stray thought that he might made her heart double tap.

"Great," he told everyone in the conference room. "I'll see you in the morning."

This meeting was coming after a long day, and normally, Scarlett would be dragging. But tonight, she snatched her stuff up and bounded after Jaime into the hallway. "Do you have a second?"

"Only just. I have to get back to my office for a Zoom call with Videon. Sorry about that." A few months ago, he would have said it curtly, but now, she knew he was sorry to have to rush her.

Scarlett wanted to beam like a loon, but she kept the corners of her mouth pinned in a more neutral expression. There was hope here. There was. But she had to play it carefully. She couldn't barrel into things without a plan. Some of the worst mistakes she'd ever made on a chess board had come from overconfidence.

Play the long game.

Speaking quickly, Scarlett said, "No worries, this won't take long. I just wanted to say thank you for having my back. With Gloria."

Jaime's brows came together. "Of course. You're the expert—it's your biopic. And your instincts, they're good. Everything you've gone to the mattress over, you've been right about."

She couldn't keep the smile in then. She couldn't. It would've leaked out like light through a keyhole. He saw her as part of the team here, not his obnoxious ex who'd gamed her way onto the set. Which, well, she *was*.

"You really think that?" she asked throatily.

"I wouldn't say it if I didn't."

How many things had they said to each other over the years that, it turned out, they hadn't meant? And how many things weren't they saying to each other now that they really ought to?

"I just didn't know you felt that way about me," she said, lightly but not jokingly.

Jaime's eyes shifted away from Scarlett and went unfocused. The subtext in this conversation was like smog: so thick it made her tear ducts go into overdrive.

Scarlett needed to get more comfortable with the surface level and not keep pushing them beyond it to the deeper place where they got in trouble. Not before they were ready to go there.

Eventually, Jaime's attention snapped back to her. He shrugged, as if he wasn't certain about what he was going to say next. But then he said, "Well, now you do."

It was so little. But it contained everything.

Chapter 23

When Jaime answered his phone—which he'd scrambled to find after dashing from the bathroom postshower—Ev asked neutrally, "Hey, are you done for the day?"

After everything that had gone down with Dad, he answered the phone when it was Evelyn. Always. And this, whatever it was, was the reason for that. All it took was the one question for Jaime to know that the shit had hit the fan. Something was not right, really not right, with his family.

Jaime wrapped the towel more firmly around his hips. It didn't do much to stop him from dripping onto the hotel carpeting, though.

"Yup." He matched Ev's tone, as if this conversation was about their joint gift for their mom's birthday or some other normal, happy stuff. The kind of stuff they might get to care about if their lives had been totally different. "We wrapped almost an hour ago."

Jaime was exhausted, probably because he'd spent too many nights lately burning the midnight oil—among other things—with Scarlett. And that was after endless long days in which he had to make a million decisions and manage this unwieldy production.

His body had spent months in constant high-alert mode, and whatever Ev was calling about only pushed him further. Adrenaline was bitter on the back of his tongue, and his muscles had tensed. The last two decades had involved a lot of fight or flight, and Jaime had often been stuck in the worst position: watch.

"Great!" Evelyn said, in a faux chipper tone, the one that communicated *We're going to get through this, the way we've gotten through everything.* "So . . . I don't want to freak you out or anything, but FCI Petersburg is locked down."

Prison lockdowns were all too common. At minimum, it meant no one went in, and all other perks, like education services, stopped. At their most restrictive, lockdowns meant inmates were limited to their cells for more than twenty-two hours a day. The guards could instigate them for any reason, from something as small as a fight to something as major as a riot. Sometimes, Jaime would've sworn they did it based simply on vibes.

"Is Dad okay?"

"Bobby"—their attorney—"says so. But there was a stabbing in another wing."

"Yikes." Still caught up in his relief that his dad was physically unharmed, Jaime couldn't manage to be more eloquent than that. Stumbled-tongued understatement was going to have to do.

"Yeah." Evelyn gave a deep sigh, the first moment of the conversation that felt real. The mixture of release and anxiety and exhaustion in it mirrored everything in Jaime's gut. "Anyhow, Mom and I can't get over there, obviously, and it's been making some waves around here. I didn't want you to hear the news somehow and worry. You have enough going on."

"I appreciate it."

Jaime scrubbed a hand over his face. Filming was almost done for *Queen's Kiss*, but the last few weeks of any shoot—they were a lot. Nate could step in if Jaime needed to get away, but it wouldn't be the same. Nate was technically proficient, but he would say it himself: he wasn't much of an improviser.

So many of the moments in Jaime's previous projects that felt magical, the ones that critics had praised and of which Jaime was most proud, hadn't been planned. They'd arisen in the moment or had been accidental. If Jaime had to run off to deal with a crisis, it wouldn't be good for *Queen's Kiss*, that was for sure.

"Is filming going well?" Ev asked.

He had no idea. "There comes a point when all you can do is finish and sort it out in postproduction."

"That sounds kinda demoralizing."

"Making TV is often not very good for morale," he agreed.

"Well, I better let you go," Evelyn said. "I just didn't want you panicking for no reason."

"If you figure out the one weird trick to stop me from worrying, you'll have to let me in on the secret."

"Dad is okay, Jaime."

But that was wishful thinking, just one step up from an office motivational poster.

The larger point, the point neither Jaime nor Ev could ever forget, was that prison—where Dad would likely spend the rest of his life—wasn't a safe place to be. He was okay *this* time, but what about next time? Because, rest assured, there would be a next time. There would be another fight, there would be an outbreak of some illness, or there would be a cruel guard. And few people who didn't have family or friends inside would care, because they bought into that great, intoxicating myth: if you ended up in prison, you probably deserved it.

Dad *did* deserve to face consequences for his mistakes, but he was also a human being, as was every other incarcerated person. Both things could be true at the same time.

But Jaime was too tired to say all of it to Evelyn, and besides, she knew it.

"Have a good night, Ev." Jaime knew his sister would hear the undercurrent in those words. *We have no way to make sure he's safe. Not now, and not ever.*

"Love you," she said.

"Love you too."

Jaime hung up and dressed before he collapsed at the room's desk. He checked the website of the *Musgrove Messenger*, the local paper at home, and read a story about the lockdown. The blasé tone made him want to squeeze his phone into fragments of metal and plastic, and he shoved it away before he did.

Until Ev's call, he'd been feeling okay. He was almost entirely certain that the production was fine. It was some kind of miracle given how Jaime had almost messed up the first few weeks, what with being unable to have a conversation with Scarlett and all. But now that they were sleeping together, he could look at her again without wanting to gouge his eyes or his heart out. Better yet, he could listen to her. He could argue with her.

It was a good thing, too, because Scarlett was great at dealing with the cast and at offering suggestions for the production. Jaime had spent more than a year adapting her book and getting ready to put her story on screen. And now, filming said story, he knew that she got the big stuff right. If Jaime didn't like every one of her tactics, fine, but she was usually right about strategy. She chose to fight the right wars, even if she sometimes waged them sloppily. On set, certainly, and maybe also in her personal life . . .

Jaime shook off the thought. Now wasn't the time for that. He'd pick up the revelation again later—say, when he wasn't thinking about whether his dad was okay and when he wasn't exhausted from working ninety twelve-hour days in a row. He'd try to schedule five minutes to think about it during that gap between postproduction and the marketing push for the show, six months or so from now. His feelings remained a mess. A Superfund site that, like all environmental disasters, was better ignored than acknowledged. So he just didn't acknowledge them.

But the nonfeeling stuff was good. The scripts Scarlett and Jaime had written were great, the episodes taut and carefully constructed. Clara was giving an incredible performance as Emily, nuanced and intuitive, powerful but vulnerable. And the crew was working together like a well-trained army. If Jaime needed *Queen's Kiss* to be amazing in order to prove that he wasn't a one-hit wonder, then the show they were making ought to do that.

Jaime ran a hand over his still-wet hair. The air-conditioning vent was blowing right onto him, and he was chilled. Jaime didn't move away from it. He just let the air numb him until the ache in his chest wasn't so acute. The worries about his dad, they would never go away; the confusion he felt about Scarlett . . . that was probably a permanent condition too.

When he dropped the veil of fiction and let himself see what they were making as an honest examination of her life, he was in awe of Scarlett. Her discipline. Her accomplishments. Her ruthlessness.

His goose was cooked, that was for sure.

Jaime got to his feet and paced a bit, as much as he could in a hotel room. Videon wasn't skimping on the production, but sexy chess dramas didn't get sexy-dragon-fantasy dollars, and so it wasn't a massive room.

Maybe he could hit the hotel gym and work out some of the anxiety zipping around his body, but he'd just showered. Besides, he'd been on his feet for the better part of ten hours: a workout was the last thing he needed. Maybe he could call Nate and see if he wanted to grab a beer.

Or maybe he could be honest with himself and admit that the only thing he wanted to do right now was see Scarlett.

That was more or less always true these days. But the twist was that, right now, he didn't want to see her for carnal reasons. No, at the moment, he wasn't interested in sex at all. If he could just clap his eyes on Scarlett, he knew it would be like pressing Tare on a scale. He'd be zeroed, and he'd never needed that more.

So he grabbed his phone and his room key, and he headed down there.

When he arrived at her door, he knocked more loudly than he usually did, probably because this wasn't a booty call. Jaime didn't feel vaguely sleazy and embarrassed about this visit, mostly just needy and raw.

The door bumped gently into the frame as she checked the peephole. When Scarlett swung the door open a moment later, she was smiling coyly. "I didn't know you were coming."

Jaime, bumbling Casanova that he was, tended to stop just short of shoving a note into her hand on set to arrange a hookup. *Can I come over for sex? Circle Y or N.*

He was so smooth. It was such a miracle that she'd ever seen anything in him.

"Tonight, I didn't come for . . . that."

Because she knew him nearly as well as he knew Evelyn, Scarlett's expression immediately sobered. "Okay. Why are you here?"

"I thought we could hang out."

For a second, after he'd asked to come inside and *not* have sex and instead to use their mouths for purely communicative purposes, Scarlett appeared to be vaguely stunned, which made sense. Jaime had been pretty clear that he wanted ninety-nine things from her and talking wasn't one of them.

A year ago, he'd known exactly what he'd wanted from Scarlett: the future, every bit of it—the future they hadn't quite been able to grab back when they were kids. It was as if they had been buying it on layaway all these years and they were almost ready to bring it home, to possess it fully.

But then the truth had crackled between them, as red hot and destructive as a wildfire. And now, Jaime couldn't untangle what made sense from his lust and his anxiety and his exhaustion. Those things were braided together, and he wasn't certain if or how he could separate them again.

After the news about the stabbing, though, it didn't matter. Jaime's bruised heart and ego were still there, but they were incidental. He felt better when he was with her. It wasn't any harder or more complicated than that.

"Of course we can." Scarlett gestured, and he trailed her into her room. It was the twin of his: chic in that generic way boutique hotels tend to be, but impersonal, small.

Jaime took the chair at the desk, and Scarlett curled up on the small couch by the window. She'd obviously been reading when he showed up, though she didn't pick up the book she'd abandoned when he'd appeared. Instead, she pulled her knees to her chest and rested her hands on them.

She had such pretty hands.

"What's wrong?" she asked.

"Why does something have to be wrong?"

"It doesn't have to be, but it is."

For a split second, Jaime considered pleading that he was simply tired or stressed. But instead, he blurted out the truth. "There was a stabbing at FCI Petersburg. Dad's okay, but the place is in lockdown, and it was . . . a reminder."

Scarlett's mouth twisted in concern. "That's awful. Does stuff like that happen often?"

"Yes." He said it flatly.

"And you . . . blame me?"

"No! I didn't come here to yell at you." Jaime honestly hadn't. Whatever impulse he'd had to yell at her had long since scabbed over. He was embarrassed that he'd ever felt it. "It isn't your fault. I came because I feel better when I'm with you."

Jaime didn't *only* feel better, and what he wanted from her wasn't as simple as *better*. Scarlett was a jumbo box of 120 Crayolas. You didn't reach for it when you wanted something straightforward like red. That was what your backup box of eight basic colors was for. You grabbed the big box when you wanted Atomic Tangerine and Jazzberry Jam.

Scarlett was gazing at him steadily, and just as if this were a chess match, her expression wasn't giving a thing away. But he recognized what she was thinking all the same: she was trying to decide what move to make next, and then seeing all his possible responses to that move rippling out from hers in fractal patterns.

He didn't have the energy for her machinations, not tonight. So what he said was, "Can we watch a game, order some food, and just be?"

Jaime had no idea what Scarlett might say to that. Some part of him didn't know what he even wanted her to say, because in many ways, it was a more intimate request than what he normally asked from her.

Can you be with me in my pain and, by your simple presence, comfort me?

Jaime had kissed every inch of Scarlett's skin, had had her in every way that he knew how, and had been had in turn. But his request left him feeling exposed beyond all that. Beyond anything.

Which was the reason he found himself exhaling when she said, "Yes."

Chapter 24

Scarlett and Nate were on set, watching Jaime do a run through with Clara and the DP before the camera started to roll. Since the sequence in question didn't require Scarlett or Nate to weigh in, they were placing bets on how many takes Jaime was going to do of Emily's critical monologue.

"You'd be stupid not to take the over on five," Nate said. "So by all means, take the under."

Scarlett snorted. "Your best friend is a wee bit meticulous."

"No, he's a massive glob meticulous." Nate's expression went serious. "But that's why we love him."

It wasn't a question. It was very much a question.

"Yes it is," Scarlett said solemnly.

Nate twisted his mouth into a sly grin, as if to say *I knew it.*

But before Scarlett could think of a smart, evasive comeback, Jaime's phone, which was sitting on the chair in between them, rang.

"That might be Larry Gomez. We've been expecting him to check in," Nate said.

Gomez was the main point of contact between Videon and Jaime and Nate's production company. Jaime had been very clear with everyone that they should kiss Gomez's butt as much as possible.

Scarlett reached for Jaime's phone, intending to hand it to Nate to answer. Except the caller ID read *Musgrove Messenger.*

This could be about Jaime's dad.

Without even really deciding to, Scarlett pressed the green Talk button. "Hello?"

"Is Jaime Croft there?" a man asked.

"He's busy. Can I take a message?" *And please feel free to be as detailed as possible.*

"Oh, sure. This is Daniel Douglas."

"From the Musgrove High class of 2008?" She vaguely remembered someone with that name from her chemistry class.

"The very same."

"This is Scarlett Arbuthnot."

"Oh, hiya, Scarlett. I heard that Jaime was adapting your book."

"He is. What do you need him for?"

"I was calling to see if he wanted to weigh in on the lockdown at FCI Petersburg, to talk about how the families are handling it."

Scarlett suspected that in the wake of *The Devouring Sun*, this kind of request must be common, but she also knew that Jaime didn't need to deal with this right now. Filming was wearing him down. He was the first person on set every morning, and the last to leave every night. The sheer number of plates he was spinning in the air and the list of decisions he had to make every day—it was a lot.

She had watched in alarm as the bags under Jaime's eyes had swollen and gone purple. He was losing weight too. His muscles stood out in stark relief on his back and abs. If there was anything Scarlett could do to help Jaime, of course she was up for it.

"Is everything okay with Dr. Croft?" she asked Daniel.

"As far as I know. But I figured Jaime and the Crofts might have some things to say about it."

Scarlett blew out a long breath. She was intimately familiar with how ruthless the press could be when they wanted a story. Daniel's questions wouldn't be about the facts of what had happened, which the Crofts didn't know anyhow. No, what he was after was sensationalism. He wanted them to share their fears and worries and tears so that he could print them for their neighbors to tsk over.

Daniel quickly added, "And I'd love to chat with you, too, about *Queen's Kiss*. You'd make a great profile subject. There's a lot of local interest."

Scarlett might not have believed him before going back to town, but she'd exchanged several emails with folks from Emery's book club. She knew Daniel was telling the truth: at least some people in Musgrove would lap up a profile of her.

Her best play here was to use that to redirect Daniel away from Jaime, Evelyn, and Mrs. Croft.

"I'd love that," she gushed. "And we could catch up too. Let me get your number." She typed it into the Notes app on her own phone. "I'll call you back in a bit," she assured Daniel.

After hanging up, she tossed Jaime's phone back onto his chair.

"Clearly that wasn't Larry. Anything I should know about?" Nate asked.

"Nope. I'll handle it." It was the very least she could do.

A few minutes later, Jaime came over and collapsed into his chair. He was rubbing circles into both temples, and his eyes were pressed closed. He still looked good—it was impossible for the man to look bad—but he was pale and clearly worn out.

"Headache?" she asked gently.

"A bit." He was totally lying. His head was clearly throbbing.

If it wouldn't make him dig in and deny that anything was wrong, she would've tried to get him to go back to the hotel and let Nate or Walter take over for the rest of the day.

"I'll get you some water and aspirin," she said instead, knowing that was as much assistance as he would accept from her. But she would definitely keep the *Musgrove Messenger* thing off his plate. Diverting the press was one of the things she did best.

A few hours later, she slipped away and phoned Daniel back. "Look, the Crofts have been through enough, don't you think? If you promise not to bug them again, I can offer you something pretty juicy."

"I'm listening."

And just like that, Scarlett had Daniel.

The press were so easy, when it came down to it. All you had to do was to remember your interests were not the same as theirs and to never say anything that didn't serve *you*.

When Scarlett had left Musgrove and gotten famous, she'd taken control of her image. Or at least she had learned how to use what people already assumed about her for her own ends. The press were going to write about her, no matter how she felt about it. She was just too much of a novelty, and she'd been too successful for them to ignore her. As she told Clara: in life, you could play offense or you could play defense—and no one with any power would choose defense.

The chess world didn't seem to understand that attention was currency, but Scarlett did. And thanks to her, chess had a younger, sexier vibe. Honestly, PAWN ought to worship the ground Scarlett walked on, but she'd been entirely too much of a mosquito bite on their butt for that.

The point was, she was going to have no trouble giving Daniel Douglas plenty of things to write about that weren't the Crofts.

"Get your tape recorder and a pile of napkins ready, Daniel, because I'm about to spill a whole pot of tea about one of the biggest scandals in chess. Your exclusive interview with me is going to get picked up *everywhere*."

"You're willing to go on the record about the Kratos Staniades story?" the reporter asked, proving that he got outside of Musgrove every now and again.

The scandal in question had been at least as big as anything Scarlett herself had gotten mixed up in. Staniades had been publicly accused of cheating, and the tournament organizers had brought in a machine to detect silicon electronics in case he'd secreted anything on his person that might be able to receive messages.

Yeah, that was right: they thought Staniades had been hiding a device of some kind where the sun did not shine.

"Honey, I'm going to tell you the tale of how I tried to convince the tournament staff that we should all play naked as a precaution." And every word of it would be true too.

Jaime ought to like that.

He ought to like all of it.

◆ ◆ ◆

Unlike Christmas morning—which never seemed to arrive, no matter how hard she had wished for it as a kid—the final days of filming for *Queen's Kiss* came before Scarlett was ready for them. Which was to say before she knew where she stood with Jaime.

Back during those first weeks on set, when he'd been as jumpy as a cat and twice as cantankerous, she'd wanted nothing more than to go home. Now, not only had filming gone well, but Scarlett and Jaime had spent months having incredible sex. The night when he'd shown up wanting to eat and watch basketball together and nothing else, she'd known she as good as had him.

He was so close to crumbling and letting her all the way back in, Scarlett could almost taste it. She needed, like, one more week, tops.

But since an extension wasn't in the cards, Scarlett was watching him direct Clara for the final time in what was normally one of the restaurants in the STRAT in Vegas. There were a few more days of filming, but this was going to be Scarlett's final day on set. It was a great way to go out.

The production had transformed the restaurant into a chess tournament, while out the panoramic windows, one of the world's most famous skylines flickered and gleamed. Scarlett would've sworn it was a dollhouse village decked out with a million twinkle lights, if she didn't know better.

"That take sucked." Clara didn't sound as distraught about it as she would've early on in filming. Instead, she offered this assessment with a kind of wry, matter-of-fact humor that reminded Scarlett of how she rated her own poor performances after brutal matches.

"Let's reframe that with a growth mindset," Jaime said as he watched the playback on the monitor.

"It sucked, and maybe in the next one, I'll find a new way to suck," Clara said cheerfully.

"That's not quite what I meant," Jaime replied.

"Super helpful, *Dad*," Scarlett put in.

But actually, it was. Jaime never let the cast or crew beat themselves up; his focus was always on what they could do differently to evolve and get closer to the goal. It was like *Jurassic Park*, but with fewer raptors.

Clara reached out and played absently with one of the rooks on the board, a move Scarlett had seen her do a hundred times in the last few months. She was nervous, uncertain.

It fit with what they were filming. The show was going to end with one of Scarlett's wins in the Candidates Tournament four years ago. Everyone in the room had been rooting for her to lose. It had been wall-to-wall haters in the audience, which had made it one of the hardest games of Scarlett's life.

She'd never felt as alone, had never wanted to have an ally or a friendly face in the room, more than she had in that moment. But at the same time, she'd known that if she didn't play well, it would've been all too easy for PAWN to dismiss other players who didn't fit the traditional mold. The stakes had been so high.

Even now, Scarlett was ashamed of finishing sixth out of eight in that tournament, and she was doubly determined that the upcoming Candidates Tournament would have a different ending.

Clara threw Scarlett a look. "I don't know how you got through this one."

"I did what I needed to do to protect my own headspace."

Scarlett had asked for the tournament organizers to clear the room and to remove the cameras from the table. Even just knowing the people who'd paid to watch from home didn't have access to a close-up so tight they could've practically counted her eyelashes had helped. There was still an overhead shot of the board and a wide shot of both players sitting across from each other, so the "fans" at home still would've been trashing her in the comments, sure. But Scarlett didn't have to let them into her personal space.

A dozen editorials in chess magazines and blogs had called her a diva and said she'd initiated the delay as a mind game against Ilya Morozov. But the truth was Scarlett had just needed to draw a boundary, and it hadn't mattered if anyone else could understand or not.

"Weren't you worried about what they were going to say?" Clara asked. "I would've been." Clara still cared what strangers said about her online, because she was still young.

"No," Scarlett said. "I didn't."

Jaime crouched down next to Clara. "Here's the thing about Emily . . ." He was good at reframing this so that it wasn't about Scarlett, but about the character. "She always does what she needs to do. Every action, no matter whether the bozos at PAWN might call it selfish, makes sense when you look at it from the inside. She's not likable in that Emma Stone, girl-next-door way. She's so much more interesting than that, and she has more integrity than that."

Scarlett almost ruined the moment by guffawing. Jaime thought Scarlett had *integrity*? That was funnier than a clown slipping on a banana peel—but okay, most things were. You could never trust a clown.

Then, as what Jaime had said actually penetrated into Scarlett's brain, everything went fuzzy. In her chest, Scarlett's heartbeat started to trot along faster. If he thought she had integrity, that meant he might be open to other things, like accepting certain choices she'd made with all that integrity.

Breathing faster, Scarlett leaned closer to listen to what else he was saying.

"So much of what we call ethics is actually about being polite. Will this make a social situation more or less uncomfortable? Not will this hurt someone or exploit them, but will it be *awkward.* Emily is more honest than other people because she just doesn't care about that, and it makes her . . . free. When you're on the other side, when you are more comfortable with the way things are, you'll go along with whatever PAWN says and the way they run things. Emily is threatening because she wants to take the man apart. Honestly, some people will look at her, at your performance, and say *Does she have to be so abrasive?* But what they really mean is *I don't mind how things are.* Emily would never accept that. It's why she's so brave."

He addressed that last bit not to Clara but directly to Scarlett. He looked right at her, speared her with those dark-chocolate eyes of his, and he called her brave.

Scarlett's heart was in her throat, or at least her pulse was. As loud and insistent as a timpani, booming away in the back of an orchestra and flattening everything else.

Jaime got it. He got her.

In the end, he'd finally grasped what she had been trying to tell him. He'd finally understood who she was.

He must get it now—that everything she'd done, the mistakes the same as the triumphs, she'd done for good reasons. She'd wanted to build a better world, a more just one. A world in which someone like her didn't have to be extraordinary in order to crawl out of the dumpster. A world where ordinary was enough to get dignity.

She'd stepped on some toes to do it, and she'd stubbed her own pinkie toe a time or ten. But her motives had been good.

If Jaime knew that, if he could say it out loud, then he understood it. He understood *her.*

For the rest of the afternoon, Scarlett had trouble keeping her head out of the clouds as she watched Clara nail the scene.

"That's good, everyone," Jaime said, his eyes still attached to the monitor, rewatching the last take. "We can pack it in for the day."

Scarlett removed her headset and gave an exaggerated yawn. She couldn't wait to get back to her hotel room . . . and then into Jaime's hotel room.

"I saw this," Nate said to Scarlett, passing her his phone. "I can't believe that you finally broke your silence on the Staniades thing."

Scarlett beamed as she read. A quick skim of the piece confirmed that Daniel Douglas hadn't run anything on the Crofts, but he'd also only used half the quotes she'd given him. She might be losing her touch.

"What's this?" Jaime asked as he walked over to them.

"An interview I did with Daniel Douglas from the *Musgrove Messenger* about the show."

Nate was wrinkling his nose at Scarlett. "Is this interview *really* about the show?"

"Hey, I said lots of good things about *Queen's Kiss*."

"They didn't make it into the piece. The link's on the chess subreddit, by the way."

"It's made it to Reddit?" she asked.

"It's everywhere."

Jaime had taken Nate's phone from Scarlett and began scrolling rapidly. She could tell when he hit the money section—the part about the salacious details of the allegations against Staniades.

"Jesus, Scarlett, kids read this paper."

"Um, print media is dead, so I seriously doubt that. But it's not my fault there's no polite way to imply *vibrating butt plug*. You have to say it."

With an annoyed shake of his head, Jaime handed Nate his phone.

"Hey." Scarlett stepped closer to Jaime, putting her body in between him and Nate. Under her breath, she said, "I talked to Daniel in order to protect your family. He called you to ask about the prison lockdown, and so I offered him this story instead."

Lots of reporters had asked Scarlett about this over the years. It was a good thing she'd kept it in her back pocket. She'd been happy to exchange it for the Crofts' privacy.

Jaime's eyes flared. "And you didn't think to come to me?"

"Why?" she asked, confused. "You were overworked, and I could take care of it—"

"You could make yourself the story, you mean. It's gone viral."

"No kidding." Going viral was what Scarlett *did.* Here, at least, she'd gone viral for a good reason.

"Whatever," Jaime said as he began to stalk off. "I need to talk to Walter about tomorrow."

"You know you love me," Scarlett shouted at Jaime's retreating back as he crossed the set to talk to an assistant director. Having admitted as much to Nate a few weeks ago, it seemed funny not to say it to Jaime. Scarlett could only hope he wouldn't stay miffed at her for too long. She had other plans for them tonight.

It took Scarlett a long time to say goodbye to the cast and crew. Clara hung back, waiting until Scarlett had talked to everyone else.

When Scarlett crossed over to her, the actress was trying very hard to smile. But even she wasn't talented enough to manage it.

"I am still in denial that you aren't going to kick my ass at chess every day anymore," Clara said, wrapping her arms around Scarlett.

The hug that Scarlett gave her back was painfully genuine. Scarlett couldn't remember feeling a part of, well, anything before. One of the many things Jaime had given her when he'd adapted her book was a sense of belonging. The set of *Queen's Kiss* had been . . . if not a family, then certainly a team.

"We can still play on CheckMate.com," she said, pulling back.

"We can?"

"Of course. And we can text about nonchess and show stuff." For starters, Clara had stronger and more informed opinions about Korean skin care products than anyone else Scarlett knew. "Also, I live in New York, where I assume you work sometimes."

"My agent thinks I should do Broadway." Clara went a little green. "The thought of a live audience makes me want to puke."

Clearly, Scarlett hadn't managed to fix the girl's ego deficiency. "I bet you'd be amazing. You were a better me than I am."

"You are a freaking exemplary you," Clara said, aghast. "It was an honor to even try."

"I promise that you haven't seen the last of me," Scarlett said, because that was less cheesy than the truth: the real honor had been Clara becoming Scarlett's friend.

You could've knocked her over with a feather, but Scarlett had become fond of *everyone*—well, maybe not Gloria—on set, and she hadn't figured out how she was going to fill the hole the wrapped production was going to leave in her life.

If Jaime decided to forgive her, that would go a long way.

Chapter 25

Hours later, after Scarlett had eaten and showered, she still felt downhearted. In the past, she'd shrugged off goodbyes more easily than a duck did the rain. This one was going to sting, though.

Old Scarlett would've chided herself about how silly she was being. But New Scarlett went in search of Jaime. He wouldn't think she was being silly, and he'd make her feel better.

For reasons she didn't quite understand, their affair had been conducted exclusively in her hotel rooms. Maybe it was chivalry, but Jaime seemed to want to give her the opportunity to deny him access to *her* space, to make sure that she was in control.

As she knocked on his door, the racing of her heart was giddy, just on the fun edge of manic. Like a fairground ride you just *know* is going a little faster than it should be.

When Jaime answered, he didn't seem surprised to find her on his threshold, but he also didn't seem excited. He ushered her inside, but after she had shut the door, he kept them both in the little hallway that led to the bedroom.

"I don't think I'm up for it tonight," he said carefully.

"Amazingly, I'm only here to talk."

"Go ahead."

Here went nothing. "Right, well, I think we should be together. For real. I want to move to Musgrove." She wouldn't even hate it, though she would one hundred percent have all their groceries delivered. That bit was nonnegotiable. No one wanted to be judged in the pickle aisle.

As for the rest of it, the town had grown on her during the months she'd spent there, and it wasn't only Jaime. She found that she'd liked air that smelled like pines instead of moldering city. She really liked the farm-fresh vegetables and the sourdough bread. She enjoyed seeing Evelyn and reconnecting with her old friends, and she had even learned to like the quiet—though not the threat of giant owls carrying her off at any moment.

No, Scarlett knew she could be happy living in Musgrove, and it wasn't just the promise of amazing sex with Jaime that made her think so. She could thrive there, and because it was the twenty-first century, she could get out a few times a year when she needed a big city and a bagel. It would be the best of both worlds . . . if Jaime would agree to it.

When Scarlett made her proposal, however, a strange thing happened. Nothing.

She'd said to him that she wanted to be with him, that she would rearrange her life in order to be with him, that she was going to give him the thing he had always wanted from her for what felt like most of her life—making their relationship real. And his response was . . . neutrality.

Not excitement.

Not relief.

Not delight.

His eyes and his mouth betrayed not a single thing.

All the air vacated Scarlett's lungs. If she'd missed the bottom step and wiped out, she wouldn't have lost her breath so completely.

She'd expected something here. She had no idea what to do with nothing.

At last, he asked, "Why?"

That was reasonable. On some level, Scarlett had assumed she could say *I'd like to be together* and all the old arguments would still apply. It made sense that he wanted her to remind him what those old arguments were.

But since her brain was still oxygen deprived, she bungled it and went too literal. "Because Musgrove is where you live, and—"

"No, why do you want us to be together?"

Jaime would force her to actually use her words and say exactly what she wanted as if she were a grown-up, wouldn't he? The bastard.

The frustrating, sexy, aggravating bastard.

"Because we love each other, you dingbat!"

There, now Scarlett sounded extremely petulant. She'd shouted it at him like a teenager arguing with their parents about whether she could leave the house in a miniskirt—or at least the parents in movies, because Alma had never cared what Scarlett left the house in.

Jaime absorbed Scarlett's shouted declaration of her feelings without so much as blinking. It was like making an argument to a pillar of granite—and it was beginning to freak her out.

Where was the soft, foolish boy Scarlett had fallen for the first time, the one who didn't know he needed to keep his emotions guarded because sharing them gave people too much power over you? Had she destroyed him for good?

Scarlett shook her head in disbelief and watched the hair around her face stir. It was good to see at least some things in the universe still behaved the way they were supposed to.

Okay, so she'd blundered, but she could still turn this around.

Jaime looked tired and surprised. He wasn't making this easy for her because she hadn't made the last year easy for him. Or any year, really. That didn't mean she couldn't do this. She would do this. She would nail this pitch, and then they could both have what they wanted.

Softer, more genuinely, she said, "Because we're never going to find anyone else who we want to be with as much as we want to be with each other. Who suits us as well as we suit each other. We are it for each other, and I'm tired of pretending that isn't true."

The admission made Scarlett want to crawl out of her body and find another home for her soul, much like a molting crab searching a beach for a larger shell. But she pushed her shoulders back and met

Jaime's eyes. For him to see, hopefully, that she meant every word. That it had taken her too long to admit it, but that she'd gotten there in the end.

Being with Jaime was what she wanted—and crucially, obnoxiously, what she knew he wanted. How difficult could it be to admit that? To decide to do *that*? They had found each other, and they had fallen in love, and she had told him the truth. Those were the hard parts.

All they had to do was get over the teensy-tiny speed bump where she had sent his father to jail, and the rest would be like rolling down a hill. If they could let go, gravity would take care of it.

The bald truth of what Scarlett had just said, the vulnerability of it, sat between them for several bloated seconds.

Maybe—maybe—the line of Jaime's brows was beginning to soften, but then the shields went back up as he looked away from her. "I'm exhausted."

That was certainly better than a flat no.

"I can imagine. You're going to take some time off, right? Before you start postproduction?" Maybe Scarlett could convince him to go someplace sunny and tropical with her. The kind of place where unlimited fruity drinks appeared in your cabana, and all you had to do was nap and stare at the ocean. She could use a break before she had to start preparing for the Candidates Tournament.

"We could go somewhere," she said. "I spent a week in Mayakoba once. You'd love it. And look, we're both beat because the shoot was long, but also because stuff with us has been so unsettled. We've been fighting the inevitable. I guess I thought I couldn't let anyone in because I needed to be independent and blah, blah, blah. But I'm going to stop doing that. No more walls, Jaime—that's what I'm saying. I'm going all the way in with you. I love you."

She'd never said those three words to him with her clothing on. It had been like a secret he'd dragged out of her, using orgasms like truth serum. She'd never been certain if the circumstances in which she'd blurted it out had made it more or less true. But obviously the only way he was going to believe her was if she gave him the entire truth. Every corny, warty detail of it.

"I do too."

"You do what too?" she demanded. Because it was very unfair that she was standing here in all her mortifying feelings and he hadn't reciprocated.

"I love you."

Scarlett would've melted if he hadn't spat the words out as though they tasted bitter in his mouth.

He buried his hands in his hair and tugged at it. "And I want you. It's not like this with anyone else. It won't ever be. But I just don't know—take today."

"Today?" Scarlett had no idea what had happened today.

"The *Musgrove Messenger* profile."

"What about it? Like I said, I was trying to help you out, so I gave the reporter something in order to change the story."

"To one about you."

None of this made sense. Why wasn't Jaime listening to her? "If that's what it took."

"*You* confuse attention and affection."

"And *you* can't recognize when someone is trying to help you."

"Without asking me about it?" he snapped.

No good deed went unpunished, clearly. "That's the problem, that I didn't *consult* you?"

"That's a big part of it, yes. I can't—I don't want to feel alone inside my relationship, and you're so independent, I worry that I would be."

It was if they'd slid through the looking glass, and everything was now upside down. Scarlett felt sick. Not like *being sick*, but the way that sick itself must feel: achy and guilty. Sick couldn't possibly feel good about infecting you, and Scarlett didn't feel good about the way she'd infected this relationship. The way she'd ruined it.

"Would you bring me inside?" Jaime asked, the question clearly an ultimatum.

"I would try to." That was the very best Scarlett could do.

When Scarlett had thought Jaime was mad at her, she'd been able to deal with it because rage was something, and deep down, she'd been confident in her ability to take *something*, even something bad, and turn it around. That was why she was good at chess: she didn't give up. Even when you blundered in your opening game, if you kept at it, a strategy would open up. Never say die, and all that.

But he wasn't mad. Not anymore.

Instead, and worse, Jaime didn't know if Scarlett could give him what he wanted from her. And Scarlett couldn't tell him he was wrong, because she didn't know if she could give it to him either.

But Scarlett couldn't say that. She absolutely could not say that. So she asked, "What have we been doing the last few months?"

Because she had been there. She had lived every caress, every orgasm. Whatever he might pretend now, those moments had mattered a lot to them both. They had showed that whether she let him in or not, they were good together.

Jaime scrubbed a hand over his face. The lines around his mouth suddenly seemed canyon deep. "We were . . . blowing off steam together," he said. "But that's not enough, not to build a life on. I want a partner. I *deserve* that."

He did. He honestly did.

Scarlett suddenly felt as old and desiccated as Jaime looked.

"Okey dokey." *Okey dokey?* What the fuck was wrong with her?

This conversation, that was what. None of this was going the way she'd thought it was going to. She'd been prepared for Jaime to be unable to forgive her. But she hadn't been prepared for him to want more than she could give.

"I'm going to go," she said. When she opened the door, though, and stepped through it, she found herself calling back to him. "Jaime?"

He took a half step into the hallway. The overhead light was harsh, unflattering. It cast a dark shadow from his brow ridge down and over his face, hiding his eyes from her.

So she couldn't see his expression as she lobbed a bomb at him. "Who's running now?"

Literally no one was. To the extent that one of them was leaving, it was Scarlett. But she'd showed up and asked for a future, and Jaime was the one pushing her away. In demanding something she might not be capable of giving, he was running away from them—just like he'd accused her of doing.

A minute ticked by. In any other world, Jaime would've tackled her. In frustration, in annoyance, in arousal: the line would've provoked a zillion different responses from him, depending on when and how she'd said it.

But now, they really might be done with each other. Because Jaime just released a sigh that seemed to come from the soles of his feet before he stepped back into his hotel room and closed Scarlett out.

Maybe for good this time.

PART III

THE ENDGAME

Chapter 26

Six Months Later

"Here you go, Mr. Croft," the driver said as he parked in front of a Manhattan TV studio.

Hear Her was the top-rated morning talk show with women, making it a necessary stop on any publicity tour. But Jaime was dreading it, and for once, it wasn't because he was going to have to face Lana Larkin—the show's resident fashion expert and a legendary gossip—and her prying questions about his personal life.

No, the problem was going to be sitting next to Scarlett. Breathing the same air as her, at least until she incinerated him.

"Thanks." Jaime dragged himself out of the car.

No cheering crowds waited to greet him. They'd probably cleared out after seeing Scarlett half an hour ago, but they would no doubt return for her exit after the show. Jaime had timed things so that he was going to walk in with only seconds to spare before he needed to be in the makeup chair. If he was lucky, he'd only see Scarlett on the set, where he could keep his professional mask in place and not have to think about the fact that, this time, he'd been the one who had ended things.

In the days after Dad's arrest, Jaime had discovered he could push through bad days, because they'd all been bad days for a while. If he had waited until he had felt like doing something, he never would've gotten up off the floor. For days, weeks, lying on the floor had been all he'd wanted to do.

But much like a tightrope walker, he'd learned to concentrate on the destination and put one foot in front of the other: *Don't look down, don't get distracted, and it'll be over in no time.* He got through things the way someone else might cross wire strung between two skyscrapers.

Maybe someone healthier, someone like Evelyn, would've said he was disassociating. But Jaime preferred to think that being a professional meant working even when he didn't feel like it.

All those lessons served him well while he edited *Queen's Kiss*. These days, he'd managed to forget that Emily was a stand-in for Scarlett. The show had become fully fictional to him, the television cocoon in which he'd wrapped himself so he didn't have to think about anything that might cause him pain.

Which ruled out pretty much everything.

A PA met Jaime just inside the door. "You're a little late."

"I'm sorry." Jaime *was* sorry that he was messing up this kid's morning, but not that he was doing what he needed to do to avoid chitchatting with his ex. That was going to utterly wreck his cocoon, and he still needed the thing until *Queen's Kiss* debuted on Videon to acclaim and Jaime could finally leave this entire cursed project in his rearview mirror.

According to his watch, that would happen a few months from now, or whenever Videon scheduled the damn thing. They were going to premiere a rough cut of the first episode at the Brooklyn Film Festival tomorrow—it coincided with the opening game of the Candidates Tournament, and that had proved too big a publicity opportunity for Videon to pass up—but the streamer had stayed silent on when the entire series would drop. They were probably waiting to see if Scarlett made the open-division world championship game. That would be a cross-promo opportunity too big to ignore.

Jaime arrived on set, all made up and wired, with only seconds to spare. As he took the seat next to Scarlett's, she was laughing operatically at something one of the hosts had said. And she looked . . . well, as usual, Scarlett was just beyond beautiful. Her black dress lovingly hugged every one of her curves, her mouth was painted crimson, and her skin glowed under the stage lights. If Jaime hadn't locked up what was left of his heart behind three sets of bank-vault doors, it would've broken right then and there.

"Mr. Croft," she whispered to him without so much as glancing in his direction.

"Ms. Arbuthnot," he whispered back, staring into the reflection of the stage lights on the middle of the table. It was probably too late to feign shingles. He ought to have sent Nate to handle these promo events. This was going to be a disaster.

Unaware of the metric ton of sexual tension and resentment Jaime and Scarlett were emitting just by sitting next to each other, Grace Choi said to Jaime, "You're cutting it a little close."

She had no idea.

"Traffic," he apologized.

"And we're on in five, four . . ." The producer signaled the last three counts on his fingers and then pointed to Denise Strong, who handled the lead-ins for the segments.

"Welcome back, everyone. I'm here today with two folks who are returning to *Hear Her*: writer, director, and showrunner Jaime Croft, whose critically acclaimed docudrama *The Devouring Sun* was nominated for several Emmys a few years ago, and the chess grand master Scarlett Arbuthnot, who wrote the bestselling memoir *Queen's Kiss* and who'll be competing in the open division at the Candidates Tournament, the first step in making the world championship, in a few days. Jaime has just finished filming an adaptation of Scarlett's memoir for Videon, and a rough cut of the first episode is going to kick off the Brooklyn Film Festival tomorrow. It's great to see you both again."

"How kind of you to have us." Scarlett sounded like she was doing an Eliza Doolittle impression, after her transformation at the hands of Henry Higgins.

Jaime almost snorted. No one else would know she was mocking Jaime, saying *he* was the pedantic asshole in this scenario.

Luckily, Grace launched right into things. "We've all read *Queen's Kiss*, I think."

"I haven't," Rylee Lagrange put in, unhelpfully. Rylee was the daughter of a pop star, had herself been a pop star, and was raising her kids to be pop stars. Her primary function on the show seemed to be creating drama and keeping the US sequins market humming.

Grace didn't roll her eyes at her colleague, which Jaime thought showed amazing restraint. "Well, the rest of us loved it. It's funny and feminist. I mean, I don't even play chess, and I couldn't put it down. But before we talk with Scarlett, I'm curious about how you ended up adapting it, Jaime. It strikes me an unusual follow-up for you because it's so different from your previous work in genre and tone. What made you want to do this project?"

The PR people had, of course, unearthed that Jaime and Scarlett had graduated in the same high school class, and so there wasn't any way for Jaime *not* to share that nugget of information. It was probably in Grace's notes, because she was the most serious journalist on the *Hear Her* panel. "Well, if someone from your hometown became the celebrity bad girl of the chess world and wrote a massively successful memoir about it, you'd read it too. And once I'd inhaled it, I couldn't get it out of my head. The whole thing was so cinematic. I couldn't stand the idea of someone else making it, so I . . . made my pitch, and Scarlett got on board."

If they could just talk about the cinema of it, Jaime would be fine here. He didn't want to think about whether he would take back the choice to show up in her lobby and beg her to let him do it. He'd told her that he wouldn't regret the second act of their love story, and even now, he wasn't certain if what he felt—the mix of loss, pain, and nausea—could be boiled down to that word.

Regret was too simple. Too pat.

Scarlett had said she wanted to have a future with him, and he'd turned her down cold because he worried she would never let him in. As a result, he was sad and alone, rather than being uncertain and with her.

Back in Vegas, he'd felt as if he had to say no. He'd kept himself so busy with work that he hadn't had time to mourn the choice. But here, sitting next to Scarlett and without anything to do but autopsy the past, doubt flooded him.

It probably hadn't been the right decision.

Across the table, Grace was determined to stay the course with this line of questioning. Her White House reporter instincts were engaged, and she knew there was a story here. "You and Scarlett were friends in high school?"

"Great friends." Scarlett slanted a look over her shoulder at Jaime, and he wasn't prepared for the wallop of emotion that followed. He was so susceptible to her.

"I moved to town junior year," she went on, "and Jaime just made me feel so welcome."

"Do I smell a teenage romance?" Lana Larkin asked, nearly panting. Jaime had seen the woman get excited about precisely three things: tacky gowns on awards show red carpets, the sex scenes from *Waverley*, and the amorousness she sensed between Jaime and Scarlett.

If Grace Choi could be relentless in pursuing an actual news story, she had nothing on Lana Larkin's nose for sensation.

"Oh, I don't know about that," Scarlett replied, in a tone that suggested she very much did know but wasn't going to say anything else about it. The kind of thing that sounded as if she'd told you something, when in reality, she'd told you nothing. She deployed it with the press a lot. "But the short version is that I never would've let anyone else adapt my book except for Jaime."

For better or for worse, Jaime had done so, and they'd come crashing back into each other's orbits. At the moment, he felt much like the asteroid that had taken out the dinosaurs. He'd asked Scarlett for too much, and he'd destroyed himself in the process.

Everyone around the shiny table was looking at him expectantly. They wanted him to weigh in on Scarlett's version of things.

"Yup," he said.

The members of the *Hear Her* panel all blinked. Apparently, that wasn't enough to satisfy them.

"Scarlett and I were . . . real good friends. And in *Queen's Kiss*, she told one heck of a story. I disagree with you a little, Grace, because there are parts of what Scarlett wrote that resonate with my previous work. I think we both feel protective of the people in Musgrove and places like it. One of the many, many things about Scarlett's career that I find impressive is how her success demonstrates you don't have to be born with a silver spoon in your mouth to make something of yourself. That even if you're born poor or if your dad's in prison, you can still become a chess grand master or get nominated for an Emmy, you know?"

"I agree, Jaime," Denise put in. She was the grande dame of *Hear Her*, an actress of so much talent and gravitas, she'd become a certified living legend before joining the talk show. "But with all that shared history—and everyone who's read *Queen's Kiss* knows about your temper, Scarlett—there wasn't any conflict on set?"

Ha. In the end, it had been *his* temper that had been the problem, but he wasn't going to offer *that* juicy detail for public consumption. "We both cared a lot about getting the show right. We want it to be accurate to Scarlett's experience, but also a good ride for viewers. Whatever little speed bumps we may have hit along the way, Scarlett handled them like a total pro."

Jaime . . . less so.

"Whatever Jaime says, I'm sure," Scarlett said, and all the hosts just whooped.

She sure was good at playing the press. Even if Jaime had loathed the stunt she'd pulled with the *Musgrove Messenger*, it had worked. She was as good with it as she was at everything else.

Everything except letting him in. And if that was her only flaw, surely it didn't matter in the grand scheme of things.

"When it all drops on Videon, we'll have you back," Denise said, "and you can tell us about all the dirty laundry."

Scarlett only smiled serenely. "No, honestly, it was amazing to watch this kid I sat in English class with manage a film set. He's great with the talent; he's amazing behind a camera. I loved watching Jaime do the thing he always wanted to do."

"And tell your story?"

"And tell my story," Scarlett echoed.

When Jaime had been working on *The Devouring Sun*, he'd realized how sacred that act was and why storytellers had been priests in ancient times. In giving him her book, Scarlett had trusted Jaime with so much. He could only hope that he'd managed to do it justice, even while he'd acted like such a dirtbag.

"And that story will continue in a few days as the first stage of the world chess championship gets underway," Grace said. "Tell us about it."

Scarlett nodded. "Well, the Candidates is held every other year—"

"And there was some controversy when you didn't make the last one."

"Yes. Chess rankings are . . . well, *Byzantine* is a mighty fancy word, but I think it's the right one. The first time I went to Candidates, I was only the second woman to get an invite. Ever."

Grace shuffled the papers that rested in front of her. "We reached out to PAWN, and they insist that there isn't gender discrimination in the sport. Their spokesman told me that it's a math question. If more women were ranked in the top ten, then more women would be competing for the open-division world championship: that's their claim. They maintain that the protected class is the best way to grow the women's game."

"Oh, I'm familiar with how they defend their system. And I would love for more women and nonbinary folks to get into chess. But if chess doesn't feel inviting or safe to them—and if they see that there isn't diversity at the top, it probably doesn't—then there's not much reason to. Why devote yourself to a sport that doesn't want you and won't welcome you? That's why I wrote the book, and it's why I'm putting myself out there like this. Honestly, it's wild that I need to expose myself in ways a man never would, in order to promote my career or for the sake of other people in the sport."

Denise leaned forward. "Did writing the book or making the show expose things you would've rather kept private?"

Scarlett's knuckles tensed for a second. It was an almost imperceptible tell. If Jaime had been seated across from her rather than next to her, he wouldn't have seen it. She wasn't excited about answering this question. "Well . . ."

Jaime couldn't do much for Scarlett, but he could help here. "If I could weigh in, Grace. Fans of the book might be surprised that the show lightly fictionalizes things and makes some cuts and changes. But we did that to give Scarlett some cover. She shouldn't have to give people anything she doesn't want to give them." Because they, like himself, might not be worthy.

"That seems pretty chivalrous," Lana said, waggling her brows at him.

"I promise, it wasn't." No, Jaime hadn't even managed to be polite to Scarlett, in the end.

"But Jaime really does know how to listen to someone," Scarlett put in.

Except not how to handle how he might feel afterward, and right now, what Jaime felt was guilty.

Denise smoothly steered the conversation back to the fields at the Candidates Tournament, and Jaime was able to play backup to Scarlett for most of the rest of the segment as she talked about how she prepped for matches, her tips for kids who might want to take up chess, and how it had felt to watch someone else play her.

When it was done, Jaime followed Scarlett off the *Hear Her* set. When they'd returned their mics to someone on the production team, Jaime said quietly, "I hope that was okay." He was certain Videon would be pleased, but the only person whose response he cared about was Scarlett's.

"It was fine."

Fine was not really a Scarlett word. Someone else might use that to deflect or hide the truth, but if Scarlett was mad at you, she didn't bother stabbing you in the back; she drove the knife straight into your sternum.

"I just assumed that you wanted to make nice, not fight in front of Denise Strong," Jaime said. Arguing in front of her seemed like a rude thing to do—the woman had won an Oscar. It'd be akin to throwing a hissy fit at his mother's dining room table.

"Sure, whatever. But Jaime?" Scarlett waited until he was looking her in the eye to finish her thought. "I'm done fighting with you, in public or in private."

Why did Scarlett refusing to holler at him feel like the saddest thing he'd ever heard?

Chapter 27

"If Svensson draws white and he plays the Scotch Game—and Martina is wrong about him going Ruy Lopez. It'll totally be the Scotch Game—how will you counter?" Kit demanded.

This was how they'd spent more or less every minute of every day since Scarlett had gotten back to New York from filming *Queen's Kiss*: analyzing games, playing against each other, and walking around the city speculating about endgames and countermoves.

Most people (a.k.a. Alma) thought that chess was a "sport" for nerds who sometimes sprained their wrists playing blitz chess too vigorously and managed to twist their ankles sitting at the chess board.

Yeah, Scarlett had heard all the jokes. But the truth was chess was grueling, physically and mentally. Sure, people outside the sport probably thought it was horse hockey to compare it to tennis or swimming, but Scarlett knew better.

High-level chess matches had more minutes of gameplay than football or basketball, and there wasn't an instant in one when Scarlett wasn't thinking *hard*. Afterward, she felt like a depleted battery, and unlike her phone, Scarlett couldn't plug in and recover in an evening. It could take her days to recuperate after a single difficult round; a tournament could knock her out for months.

Norway Chess had been difficult enough, but Candidates was going to be on another level. In a literal way, Scarlett had to build up her endurance if she was going to survive and get to the actual world championship—and that had been her goal since she'd read about it as a kid. She couldn't go shirking from practice now.

So her life had turned into the training montage from *Rocky* but with fewer cow carcasses and no triumphant posturing in front of a museum. Kit had even gotten a navy blue knit cap, and they treated Scarlett and Martina to a pretty-on-point Burgess Meredith impression when things were getting dicey.

But the jokes about how she should eat lightning and crap checkmates aside, Scarlett couldn't ask for two better trainers and seconds than Kit and Martina. Honest to gosh, Scarlett had never been so grateful in her life for anyone as she was for these friends. When she'd been younger and stupider, Scarlett had tried to do this on her own—and it had been nearly impossible.

Given that Alma wasn't exactly mother of the year material and that Scarlett was in touch with precisely no one else she shared DNA with, given how often she'd moved and how terrible she was at keeping up with old friends, and given that most other top chess players hated her for one reason or another, Scarlett had sometimes imagined she was alone in life.

But the last six months had proved what ripe garbage that was. Scarlett needed support, desperately. You might play chess one on one, but you didn't play it *alone*. At least not if you were going to be any good at it.

Something had shifted in the last two years: writing with Jaime, teaching Clara to play chess, watching the crew film *Queen's Kiss*, and preparing for Candidates with Martina and Kit. It had melted the chip off her shoulder, the one that had had her asserting that, whatever she'd done, she'd done it entirely by herself.

Scarlett might be polarizing, but she wasn't a maverick—and she didn't want to be. Scarlett could be scrappy and capable and still get help from other people. From her friends.

It might have been better to have realized that earlier. Say, eighteen years earlier, when she'd made a unilateral decision about what to do about Dr. Croft. Or six months earlier, when she'd tried to shield Jaime from nasty stories in the local paper—but nope, that was the third rail. It was the subject she'd made off limits inside her own head. Nothing good came from spending any more time contemplating that particular boondoggle.

Besides, she had other stuff to deal with. Like how to handle the Scotch Game when she was playing black.

"Well, Kasparov would want me to regain the upper hand in the middle of the board," Scarlett answered Kit. They'd spent a lot of time studying Garry Kasparov the last few months; Scarlett had made *WWGKD* beaded bracelets, and they were all wearing them now.

"How?" Kit pressed.

"I take the d4 pawn."

"Then?"

"Well, I have to be careful with my king. I don't want to lose the ability to castle."

"And how are you going to *not* do that?"

See, this was the point of friends: Scarlett would've chewed the face off anyone else who'd spent ten hours with her day after day, especially when she'd returned from the set of *Queen's Kiss* almost feral with heartbreak.

The necessity of it aside, prepping for Candidates had been a tunnel out of the darkness. Scarlett hadn't been able to sink into depression: she had ten thousand moves and game diagrams to memorize. She knew her first-round opponent would be Alik Svensson, and he was the favorite to win the tournament and face the reigning world champion. That round would be followed by thirteen more. Altogether, she would play seven opponents multiple times, over a punishing two-and-half-week schedule. She had to crawl inside their minds and understand what made them tick. What did they do when they were confident? What did they fall back on when they were afraid?

Chess was almost like getting to know a lover. It felt that intimate and, at times, that brutal.

And these days, Scarlett was an expert on the brutality of love.

When she'd gotten back to New York, Kit and Martina had managed to ask precisely the right amount of questions, both about Scarlett's recent breakup but also about her soon-to-be chess opponents. And they showed exactly the right amount of rage on her behalf on both scores.

"So I set up the two-knight variation of the Italian Game," Scarlett concluded her response to Kit. "But Svensson probably counters with the Max Lange Attack."

"Very good," Kit said. "And then—"

"How do we counter Jaime Croft when he goes on TV and continues to make it sound as if he's *your* white knight?" Martina had watched *Hear Her* this morning, and she was currently plotting a different kind of game, a much more bloodthirsty one. If Jaime weren't careful, he was going to find himself getting maimed by a grand master.

Scarlett had had to tell her friends *something*. She'd kept most of it to herself—what had happened was honestly too sordid and embarrassing to admit to it all out loud—but she'd stuck to the original ending: Scarlett had shot her shot, and Jaime had said no. On that basis alone, Martina thought he deserved to pay.

If Martina had known the entire story, she would already have exacted retribution, and it would have been far messier than whatever Scarlett was going to do to Svensson on a chess board.

"Jaime wasn't trying to make himself look good," Scarlett said wryly. "He was trying to give me some cover." If anything, he'd let Scarlett do most of the talking on *Hear Her*, acting as if he were her arm candy. Though he'd seemed too jumpy and guilty to truly pull it off.

"After that asshole turned you down—"

"Which was his call to make. I mean, I called the police about his dad, and then in his eyes, I went rogue with a reporter." Scarlett had told them that part of the story too. It was possible that getting through it had involved a lot of ice cream, Kahlúa, and tears.

Interestingly, Scarlett had felt better afterward. Maybe she should have started spilling her guts to Kit and Martina years ago. Maybe that was actually—breaking news here, someone ought to call Dionne Warwick—what friends were for.

"Look, that was the right thing to do," Kit assured her. "He's entitled to get miffed because—"

"He's an ungrateful louse!" Martina said.

"—you didn't talk to him first, but punishing you is overkill."

If Jaime was punishing anyone, it was himself. He wasn't nearly as good as Scarlett at keeping those things stuffed down. Emotions ended up written all over his body. If he wasn't careful, the man would ruin that pretty face of his with scowl and stress lines.

"He's on his own journey, y'all, and he's been very clear that he doesn't want me on it with him. So I wish him the best." Somewhere inside her, Scarlett could probably find a good wish for Jaime. She wished petty things for him too—that his pillow would always be lumpy and his avocados eternally bruised—but honestly, being Jaime Croft seemed exhausting. He needed to cut himself, and everyone around him, some slack. Or else he was going to snap like a rubber band.

It wasn't his fault his dad had been a prick. He didn't have to atone for that, and he couldn't. He couldn't raise his sister; he could only be her brother. He ought to be there for his mother, but he didn't need to manage her life. He didn't have to reimagine television and create new genres. He could just make stuff people liked. It wasn't his job to reinvigorate Musgrove, Virginia. Or fix how people perceived Appalachia. Or whatever else he might say in interviews. Why had he signed himself up for all those jobs?

As for his love life, well, he was crap at handling that too. Scarlett knew, absolutely knew, he loved her. But if he wasn't sure whether she could give him what he needed, and if he thought her most chivalrous acts were selfish, then that was that.

It was what had given her a postage stamp of peace, in the end.

Scarlett was a flawed person, but she knew what she could do and what she couldn't do. And at this point, she couldn't take on Jaime's issues and she couldn't reassure him any more than she already had.

She stopped at a DON'T WALK sign and glanced up the street. They were walking along Broadway near city hall, down a canyon of granite and concrete and glass that echoed with the memories of a hundred ticker tape parades. She'd never get one, but it was fun to pretend. To roll around in the accumulated glory.

"I'm amazing," Scarlett told Martina and Kit. "I'm a total boss at chess, and my memoir is getting a movie version. I pulled myself up by my darn bootstraps, and then I made a big stink about how unfair the entire system is. Oh, and I'm super hot."

"*Super* hot," Martina echoed, patting her shoulder.

"If Jaime doesn't want me, well, whoop-de-do. I'll find someone else."

Scarlett believed everything else she had said, but that last part was a total bluff. If Jaime didn't want her, she would be fine, but there would be a rip in the fabric of her life that nothing and no one could stitch back together.

Scarlett didn't want to be a person who believed in fate or karma, but they seemed to believe in her. Specifically, they seemed to believe that she got one and only one big love in her life: Jaime Croft. She'd faced impossible decisions where that love was concerned, and she'd played her position the best she could. But in the game she and Jaime had been locked in since they were kids, the one where her heart was on the line, she'd hung her queen.

There was nothing she could do to salvage things, so she was resigning. It sucked, it totally sucked, but that was what happened sometimes. It was better to know when you were beaten than to keep up hope.

The light turned, and Scarlett, Martina, and Kit started down Broadway again.

"So if we're done with Svensson and his Scotch Game, what about Kaushal Bhatia? He loves rook endgames," Scarlett said.

Martina tsked. "You cannot lose your bishop early against him."

"Easier said than done." Which was true about pretty much everything.

Scarlett had blown things with Jaime. She wasn't going to make the same mistake with her chess career.

A few hours later, Scarlett had grabbed a quick nap and poured herself into a gown. While she'd told herself things were over with Jaime, she'd strategically picked every item of clothing for this promo push in order to maximize his pain and suffering. He had always liked her cleavage, and she had no qualms at all about reminding him of what he was missing.

Hey, she'd never claimed to be a nice person or anything.

When Scarlett emerged from her car onto the red carpet for the Brooklyn Film Festival, Clara was already dutifully posing for the cameras. Emphasis on the *dutiful* part. The girl did not seem to enjoy the fame portion of her job—which was a bummer, since *Queen's Kiss* was going to make her really famous.

Clara and Scarlett had stayed in close touch over the last six months: playing chess online, exchanging memes, and snickering about celebrity gossip. They'd even coordinated so they were both wearing burgundy tonight. But in contrast to Scarlett's deep-V gown, Clara's bateau-necked retro number was positively demure. Scarlett looked as if she'd escaped from Vegas, and Clara was ready for a tea party.

"Who's the movie star here?" Scarlett demanded, hugging the actress while the photographers went wild.

The thing about being in public since she was a teen was that Scarlett could almost predict which candid was going to dominate tomorrow's coverage. This was going to be the shot.

"You are." Clara clutched Scarlett's hand. "I'm so glad you're here."

Scarlett leaned close to whisper in her ear. "Just remember that they're here to see *you*."

Clara looked amused at the prospect, but at least that brought out a genuine smile on her face.

After they posed for a few more shots, they stopped and schmoozed with several reporters. That part at least seemed to center Clara, and she was almost her normal chatty self by the time they got to the head of the red carpet.

There, Jack Davis, one of the most influential reviewers and entertainment writers in the business, was interviewing Jaime.

Tuxes were . . . they were so unfair. They were basically a uniform, right? What could be more mass produced or standard issue? But upon seeing Jaime in an extremely well fitted, extremely flattering tux, Scarlett's heart started going like a hound chasing a possum.

He won't let himself want you. He's not going to change his mind about that, she reminded herself.

But when he looked like *that*. When he glanced over at her and, for three seconds straight, stared into her eyes. When, at last, his gaze slid down her body and got stuck on her cleavage.

Well, it was very hard to talk herself out of being a dingbat where Jaime Croft was concerned.

It was a good thing that after tonight, she wasn't going to have to see him again for months. And once *Queen's Kiss* debuted on Videon, she wasn't going to have to see him at all.

The thought left her inexpressibly glum.

"And here's Scarlett now."

Unnecessary as that observation was, Scarlett appreciated how Jaime's voice cracked when he made it.

"Scarlett Arbuthnot." Jack Davis shook her hand firmly. Now *there* was another finely aged man. But sadly, he was wearing a wedding ring.

It was a double bummer because, in the wake of Jaime, Scarlett had had trouble even noticing other men. It wasn't as if she'd had any free time, what with all her preparations for Candidates, but she'd like to be able to look.

"It's great to meet you," he said.

"Likewise," Scarlett said. "And this is Clara Hess."

"I've heard great things about your performance, Clara. I can't wait to see it."

"You a chess fan?" Scarlett was curious if reporters who didn't know squat about the game would be able to follow the show. Because if they couldn't, she and Jaime would've failed at their jobs.

"Oh yes. And I've always wanted to ask you—how did you decide which way to move your king in that match with Petrov?"

Scarlett had no difficulty knowing exactly which match and exactly what move Jack meant. She should've been steamrolled by Petrov—he was a former runner-up for the world championship, and she'd been a nobody. But that hadn't been what had happened.

"Well, I knew I'd lose if I went left, so I went to d7 instead, hoping to eke out the draw." When she had, commentators had called the result "amazing," because she'd blundered early.

Scarlett had never truly adjusted to the reality that sometimes you won by not losing in chess. Maybe that was why her mother would never consider it a real sport.

"Mind blowing," Jack said. "Your play is—ballsy." That sounded like the ultimate compliment from him.

Jaime's attention was flicking back and forth between Scarlett and Jack, and he seemed *deeply* annoyed. Wasn't having reporters drool over her a good thing? Wouldn't that ensure the show got good coverage?

Besides, Scarlett had had so many men fawn over her for similar plays over the years that she knew Jack didn't really mean anything by it. He wasn't hitting on her.

Still, Jaime did not like it. Jaime didn't want Scarlett, but he apparently didn't want anyone else to want Scarlett either.

It was sexy and aggravating in equal measures. But the thing was, it didn't have to be like this, did it? It was only Jaime's own stupidity that had made it so.

Despite the wedding ring on Jack's finger, and without any intention of doing anything other than pissing off Jaime, Scarlett set her hand lightly on the reporter's forearm and leaned in close. "You have *no* idea."

She loaded that up with enough heat and innuendo that Clara blushed and looked away. Jack just blinked at her, several times in quick succession: she'd stunned him into silence. Scarlett didn't even have to look at Jaime to feel the blast of displeasure from him.

Served him right.

Scarlett dropped her hand from Jack's arm and straightened. She'd learned how to do that, to fold up the flirtation and slip it into her pocket the same way someone else might with a tissue. But she didn't need it any longer; she'd made her point. When she spoke again, the suggestion of *more* was completely gone from her tone. "You find me afterward, and we'll dissect more of my matches."

Jack, who'd returned to himself from wherever her smolder had sent him, cleared his throat. "Will do."

"You ready to go in?" Scarlett asked Clara. She was still determinedly *not* looking at Jaime, but she could feel his displeasure as clearly as she could feel the plush carpet cushioning her shoes. Where he was concerned, she was an unerring mood ring.

"Yup," Clara chirped.

Then Scarlett took off into the movie theater, trusting Clara was behind her and Jaime was glaring at her retreating back.

She hoped he was enjoying the view.

When Clara and Scarlett were inside and an usher was showing them to their box, the actress again slipped her hand into Scarlett's. "So I gotta ask, what was that about out there, with Jaime and the reporter?"

Scarlett should've known Clara would ask. The girl was too perceptive, and Scarlett had spent several months training her to notice things.

She arranged her skirt around herself as she sat. "How much time do you have?"

Chapter 28

The reviews for the first episode of *Queen's Kiss* were stellar, and Jaime couldn't care less. Well, he was relieved. Appreciative. If the show wasn't any good, it would've destroyed whatever reasons he'd had for making it. He'd look like a one-hit wonder, and he'd probably never get to produce another television show. Or at least that was what he felt would happen.

Sure, sure, sure, from that perspective, the write-up in the *Times* bearing the headline Croft Delivers a Potent 'Kiss' in Brooklyn allowed him to take a deep breath. But Jaime didn't feel good about it, and he didn't have to call his therapist to work out why: Scarlett Arbuthnot and the fact that he'd torched any hope of ever being with her again.

It had happened because he was a proud, emotional asshole who couldn't come to terms with the past. The *irony*.

Whatever he'd achieved professionally had been because Jaime was supposedly "unflinching" in his self-examination. But it turned out, when the rubber met the road, he was actually full of shit.

Here Jaime was, sitting on a Manhattan patio, eating breakfast the day after *Queen's Kiss*'s successful premiere, with the city in full bloom mode all around him. He ought to be on top of the fucking world, but instead, he felt like a slug. Lower than a slug, actually. Jaime was the slime that slugs left behind, smeared down the side of your pots after they ravaged your basil.

Across the table from Jaime, Nate was cooing over his plate full of pancakes. He obviously didn't feel like slug slime. "Nowhere else does brunch like New York. Other cities try—oh, they try—but they fail." Nate held up his fork, loaded with a bite of pancake slathered in pecan honey butter. "Tell me this doesn't look like the best breakfast food in history."

"I have completely fucked up."

Nate regarded Jaime's own plate with pity. "You're right, those waffles look sad in comparison."

"No, you jackass. I mean with *Scarlett*." Jaime would've thought that was completely obvious.

She'd stood in his hotel room in Vegas, and she'd said she loved him and wanted to be with him in Musgrove. It was everything he had ever wanted from her for eighteen years, and he'd thrown it in the trash. Seeing her again had brought it all back. The gift of what she'd offered him, and his stupidity at turning it down.

He'd spent yesterday in a daze. The last few months, really. He knew why he'd made every choice that had led to this place, but he hated it so much. The past was, it turned out, past. Goddamn it, Jaime was turning into a cliché, but that didn't mean it was untrue.

The only way he was going to cross the gaping canyon Scarlett's confession had carved in the previously smooth plain of his life was to realize the crap that had happened couldn't be changed and that life without her sucked. Even if Scarlett's inclination was to go things alone, it would still be better for Jaime to accept being her backup than to not have her at all.

It was both as easy and as hard as that.

When Jaime looked at the situation dispassionately, when he imagined it was a letter sent to an advice columnist and had nothing to do with his own life, he could see that eighteen years ago, both he and Scarlett had played their positions in the best way they knew how. Scarlett had uncovered something he'd been too stupid and privileged to see, and she'd responded better than anyone else would've. Full stop.

And by giving the *Musgrove Messenger* that silly story, Scarlett had thought she was helping his family. She *had* been helping. Only she could deploy vibrating butt plugs as a diversion and end up getting wall-to-wall international coverage—though admittedly, the bar for that was pretty low in the chess world.

So what if she hadn't consulted with him first? That didn't mean she wouldn't next time. That was what he would've told anyone else if this thing had happened to them.

All Jaime had to do was say that to himself in a way that actually penetrated his thick skull. Watching Clara up on that screen last night, perfectly playing a miracle of a character who brimmed with contradictions and life and cleverness, all while sitting next to the very real Scarlett and seething because she'd done some pro forma flirting with Jack Davis, Jaime had realized that this infuriating, brilliant, and, yes, deeply moral woman was the only one for him.

Nothing else mattered.

If Nate had regarded Jaime with pity when he'd thought the subject at hand was pancakes, it was nothing compared to how thick his condescension was when he knew they were talking about Jaime's heart. "Yeah, Kit and I were talking about that last night."

Nate and Kit had been texting since Scarlett's friends had visited the set of *Queen's Kiss*, and they'd left the premiere together looking very cozy.

Well, at least someone hadn't shot themselves in the foot where their heart was concerned. That meant there was still some hope in the world.

"Your pillow talk was about how much I suck?" Jaime clarified.

"Pretty much. You and Scarlett need an intervention or something. Can you be sent to the romance principal's office, and if so, am I empowered to send you there?" Nate seemed pleased by the prospect. "Wait, can I *be* the romance principal?"

"Did Kit tell you that Scarlett sent my dad to jail?"

Nate was Jaime's friend. He ought to be, at least a little bit, on Jaime's side. While Jaime was willing to concede that his reaction to the news had been extreme, it had been decently motivated. Several operas hinged on smaller acts of disloyalty.

"But is that what Scarlett did, though?" Nate popped the pancake into his mouth and chewed in a way that clearly communicated they both knew the answer to that question.

"It *feels* like it," Jaime said, trying to sound reasonable and not petulant.

He failed. Utterly failed.

"Well, if it feels that way, then it must be true," Nate deadpanned.

Contextualizing his emotions and recognizing them for what they were, rather than letting them control him, was something Jaime had learned to do in therapy, and he wielded that knowledge in his writing and on set. In those other situations—situations in which he managed to act like an adult and not an embodied paper cut—he'd lectured everyone who would listen about it.

Tease out what's real from how you feel about it, he'd say, smug in the knowledge he'd broken out of that trap.

Jaime didn't know if it made him feel more or less like slug slime to know this was the one case in which he couldn't be rational. Also to know that he was a hypocritical prig.

More. Definitely.

"It's frustrating when you deploy my own lines against me," he told Nate.

"I can imagine. I avoid getting slapped with the hypocrisy thing by never saying profound things."

"Smart."

Nate beamed. "Hey, you're the one who's asking for my advice here. I can't be *too* dense."

It would probably be more accurate to characterize this as Jaime having a revelation in front of Nate, but whatever. Those were details. He wasn't going to fight with his coproducer about semantics. Jaime needed to stop fighting with everyone for every reason. It only made him feel like a bigger horse's ass.

Jaime had spent more than a year marinating in pain, but what he really wanted was for his dad to have woken up one day and turned himself in. Except that hadn't happened. Jaime would always hate that it hadn't, but he couldn't will it into being.

It was right and fitting that Dad had faced consequences for what he'd done. Scarlett had made an impossible decision, and she'd done it out of genuine concern for people in Musgrove. He shouldn't punish Scarlett for making that call, and he shouldn't punish himself for not seeing what his father had been up to either.

Jaime knew all that. But when Scarlett had told him what she'd done, he'd regressed into some damn-fool place where lashing out made sense. It had been stupid and cruel, and he was done doing it.

He was going to stop acting like a jerk, *and* he was going to make it up to Scarlett. Whether she forgave him or spat in his eye was totally up to her—and he wouldn't blame her if it was the second one. He'd earned it.

"She didn't talk to me about it," he said.

"That is frustrating," Nate agreed.

"Scarlett . . . she's been a team of one for a long time. But I have been too." It wasn't as if he'd treated Mom and Evelyn as equals in their family unit. He'd very much cast himself as the coach and manager. "We'd both need to work on that, I guess."

He wanted to believe what Scarlett had said to him, that she would involve him in big decisions in the future. But he was so miserable without her that it didn't matter. If she made another unilateral decision, he'd live with it, because being with her was infinitely better than being without her.

"If she agrees to take you back."

That was a big *if.* "How do I convince her that I've realized I was a massive tool and that I'm sorry?"

"Sorry isn't going to cut it." Nate took another bite of pancake. "You know the Candidates Tournament starts soon?"

He pulled his phone out of his pocket, opened an app, and passed it across the table to Jaime. It was a schedule of Scarlett's matches, starting with one a few hours from now, in Jersey City.

"This is bananas. How is Scarlett going to survive?" She had a major match most days for the next two and a half weeks.

"She's been training, like, fourteen hours a day for six months."

And all the while, she probably hadn't been taking care of herself decently. Jaime had been working long hours getting the show edited and put together, but Scarlett's work ethic put his to shame. When she was absorbed in memorizing every single opening played at the Zurich Candidates in 1953, she wouldn't have spared a thought for whether she was getting enough sleep.

"Did Kit say how Scarlett's been?" Jaime asked.

Scarlett had looked stunning, both at *Hear Her* and at the premiere. But Scarlett could put on a mask when she wanted, and she usually did. Her gorgeous gowns and her careful smiles didn't tell him a thing about how she was feeling.

"Kit said you should probably avoid Martina Vega."

"Will do."

"And they said . . . Scarlett will get through it."

If *it* was her feelings for Jaime and her pain about his rejection, Jaime didn't want her to get through it. Scarlett was larger than life. She ought to fly over it, blast through it, vaporize it, reverse the flow of its particles, or something else magical and transformative and science-fiction-y.

When Jaime had been at his lowest, he'd thought she'd betrayed him. But now, he knew he had actually betrayed her. Maybe it wasn't possible to heal that kind of breach. He had to try, though.

Even if she didn't want anything to do with him, he needed to apologize. Not with the objective of getting her back—okay, not *only* with the objective of getting her back—but because he'd messed up.

And when you messed up, you showed contrition. That belief was at the core of who Jaime was.

"Can you check in with Kit, see if it would mess Scarlett up if I went?" he asked Nate. Jaime didn't want to make Scarlett's big day about him, and he definitely didn't want to throw her off her game. But when the person you loved competed at one of the biggest chess tournaments in the world, you showed up.

That was as key to a relationship as scratching each other's hard-to-reach itches and bitching about the latest bad Supreme Court decision.

"Can you even buy tickets to this thing?" Jaime asked.

"Sure, but they're sold out."

"They're sold *out*?"

"Chess is really popular, man."

"I'm aware of that." That was why Jaime had made a soon-to-be-massive-hit television show about it. "I wonder if people resell them on StubHub."

"Or you could just ask your best friend in the entire world, who happens to be dating the second of one of the players."

"You have tickets?" This day just kept getting stranger and stranger.

"Yup. Scarlett gets an allotment, but her mom isn't coming, and she doesn't have any other family. So she gave them all to Kit and Martina."

Other than her friends, Scarlett was alone in the world—and Jaime had responded to that by cutting her off from him. Jeez, he'd been a self-absorbed snot. She really might not ever forgive him.

Nate took his phone back from Jaime and gave it a waggle. "What's the magic word?"

"Please," Jaime said cautiously.

"And?" Nate prompted.

"You're an excellent AD and coproducer?"

"And?"

"I have no idea what you're looking for here."

Nate dropped his phone to the table with a thud. "That you'll never act like a big man-baby where Scarlett Arbuthnot is concerned again. I love you, Jaime, but you've been a total ass to her. If I help you get her back, I have to know you won't do it again."

"Oh." That was . . . reasonable, and it showed more kindness toward Scarlett than Jaime had recently. "I *have* been a total ass, and if she'll let me, I'll tell her that every single day for forever. Believe me, I've been paying for this one big time. I won't risk doing it again."

He meant every word of it.

"There we have it." Nate had picked his phone up and was already typing out a text. "You can call me Cupid. He was the god of love, right?"

"I will not be calling you Cupid."

"And you're the lovesick swain. Oh, after I text Kit, I'm getting us T-shirts. It'll be great."

"Arg." But Jaime said it without any animosity.

He was done with anger and bitterness of any kind. All that mattered was apologizing to Scarlett and hoping against hope that she could forgive him.

Chapter 29

In three moves, Scarlett was going to win this match. Her opponent, Alik Svensson, knew it. Scarlett knew it. Most of the people watching knew it. But because he'd played fast in the midgame, Svensson had time to burn on the clock.

He was taking it, which was his right.

It just turned out that winning was hers.

Svensson had a better Elo rating than Scarlett, and he was playing white. In other words, he'd come into this match with every advantage. But just like she'd done so many times in her life, Scarlett had refused to do what her circumstance would suggest she should do and what everyone wanted her to do: lose. She'd stolen this match fair and square, but since he'd never seen it coming, Svensson was taking it badly.

Really badly.

With a grunt, he thrust his hands into his floppy blond hair. It stood straight out between his fingers in tufts, making him resemble a doll that had stuck a finger into an electrical socket. His brown eyes were riveted to the chess board, searching for a move, any move, that could delay his inevitable loss.

But there wasn't one.

Scarlett had lulled him into a sense of confidence by sacrificing several power pieces, and he had probably thought her play was simply chaotic. He certainly would've clocked that she wasn't playing any known strategy or pattern.

The problem for Svensson was that he had snatched up what he thought she hadn't meant to give away without asking himself *why* she seemed to be playing so sloppily. And in being greedy and inattentive, he'd stumbled right into the trap she'd set.

Two moves ago, the iron jaws had closed around his ankle. The harder he struggled, the worse it became.

It was beautiful.

As her opponent tried to come to terms with the mistakes he'd made—*good luck with that, buddy*—Scarlett relaxed in her own chair and glanced around the room. She hadn't allowed herself to do that earlier; she'd been absolutely focused for hours. She was going to need a big meal and an even bigger nap when this was over. After all, she had to do it again tomorrow.

The wall to her left boasted a dark backdrop decorated with white-and-gold logos. Chess had gotten big enough that it had product placement, as if this were NASCAR or figure skating, and how weird was *that*?

Honestly, Scarlett found it a little tacky, especially the fifty plugs for CheckMate.com. Did anyone need to be reminded of the website where they were probably watching the matches? It was like how your purse kept advertising the name of the designer to you after you'd bought it. Such nonsense.

Four identical tables stood in front of the backdrop, each with their own identical chess boards and timers. Lipstick cameras stood at the corners of the board to get a close-up shot of both players. A spiky, black metal stand held another camera high above them, capturing the bird's-eye view of Svensson's mistakes.

Little placards with everyone's name and Elo rating hung off one side of each table. There were a few crouching reporters and photographers on the playing floor itself, and most of their lenses were trained on her. Everyone wanted to watch Scarlett Arbuthnot, the bad girl of chess, go in for the kill.

Up in the balcony, looking down on the action, was a small crowd of spectators. Scarlett locked eyes with an older white man wearing an honest-to-gosh ascot. She quirked a brow at him, as if to say *I sure had Alik's number, didn't I? He didn't even see it coming.*

The guy swallowed and looked away.

While shocking stuffy dudes was always fun, the thing was, the folks out there watching her destroy Alik Svensson wanted the iconic Scarlett, not the human one. Icons didn't get much of a life, did they? They didn't eat or drink or use the bathroom. They certainly didn't fall in love or get their hearts broken.

None of the spectators were there for Scarlett herself. She'd asked Martina and Kit to stay in the VIP room and watch on the monitor because she didn't want to risk being distracted by them. And beyond those two, Scarlett didn't have any other close friends.

Clara had a photoshoot today and couldn't come. Emery had sent a good-luck text. Alma had said she was going to watch the match from Albuquerque, or wherever she and Sean were hanging out at the moment. But if her mother was actually glued to the feed on CheckMate.com, Scarlett would eat one of her pawns smothered in gravy.

There was Jaime . . . but, well, who knew where the heck he was.

That morning, when they'd been killing time, Kit had mentioned the reviews for *Queen's Kiss* were good, and Scarlett was pleased for him and for herself. The better the reviews, the better the ratings, she assumed. And the more people who watched it, the more likely PAWN might be to make some changes.

For the possibility of that, the small chance that something might shift and the game might become more inclusive, Scarlett had paid what felt like everything. She never would've believed it at sixteen, but your bank account could be flush and your name could be famous and you could still feel poor.

Right now, Scarlett might as well have been in a spaceship on her way to Mars, for how alone she felt. A cold universe stood between her and anyone who knew or cared about her as a person.

Across from Scarlett, Svensson sighed loudly. It was the sigh of a man who couldn't believe he'd been taken in. That he, like so many before him, had played like a rube and could now join Team "Scarlett Arbuthnot Exasperates Me."

They ought to get membership cards. She could press a lipstick kiss to every one.

Scarlett settled down farther in her chair, feeling more than a little bit like a cat who had a mouse pinned by the tail.

A few more seconds ticked by, then Svensson pressed the heels of his hands to his eyes.

Okay, this was getting sad. If it went on much longer, Scarlett might actually start to feel bad. If the shoe were on the other foot, Svensson wouldn't have had so much as a wiggle of sympathy for her. But wasn't it always that way? Scarlett got stuck with the reputation for being thoughtless, but inside, she was a hurricane of thought and emotion.

A hurricane who was going to win her first match of this Candidates Tournament.

Scarlett glanced down the length of the room. She knew she was the odd one out in lots of ways. Of the eight people playing chess here, she was the only one wearing a dress. She was the only one in a bright color (yellow). She was the only one who didn't have a suit jacket hanging from her chair.

Outwardly, she didn't fit. But she was about to crush the favorite to win the tournament.

Alik Svensson dropped one hand to his lap, and with his other, he reached for his remaining bishop. For a poignant second, his fingers hovered above the piece. He could make this play, and then she would put him in checkmate. Or he could recognize the inevitable and resign.

How beaten did he feel—that was the question.

Svensson flicked his eyes up to Scarlett and opened his mouth. They weren't supposed to talk beyond offering a draw or resignation. That was actually, literally against the rules.

He pressed his lips together with a rueful twist, and it communicated more than any words could. Svensson couldn't believe how stupid he felt, and he knew it was over.

Svensson held his palm up and gestured to the board. To the hopeless mess that he'd created there. "I resign."

A small flurry erupted in the room as people craned to look and camera shutters clicked and shocked whispers zinged around.

Scarlett experienced one blazing, golden second of joy. She'd wanted to win in round one so much, to make the point that she should've been here last time, that she *deserved* to be here now, and that she was going to make the most of this opportunity. But she shooed the joy under the bed as if it were a dust bunny. She had so much further to go. She couldn't lose focus now.

"Good game," Svensson said as he shook her hand.

Scarlett wanted to say *I know*, because she had played well. That was just a fact.

But she went with the more traditional "You too." It was kinder, and honestly, she could afford to be nice after trouncing her opponent.

Svensson scoffed. They both knew that she'd lied. This match was going to haunt him for the rest of his life. Some of them were like that. Scarlett had a list of her own, times when she'd misread the signs or had gotten the chances she needed but hadn't capitalized on them. Those were much harder to live with than the ones where you'd never gotten a look in.

That was why things hurt with Jaime, why they would always hurt. Because in all the chaos, there had been a one-in-a-million chance of them being together. It had been in their grasp, until it had shattered.

She'd done it, or Jaime had, or maybe it didn't matter. The point was, it was over.

One of Scarlett's knees cracked as she stood up, and she tried to stretch discreetly. The endgame of that match had gone on for an eternity.

Svensson and Scarlett signed their score sheets and left for the VIP space, trailed by security. They were supposed to shake hands with the folks who'd paid for insider access and do a press conference, but all Scarlett wanted was to hug her friends, inhale a steak, and crawl into bed.

Thank God they were close to New York and she could sleep in her own space. The sterility of a hotel room would've snuffed something out in her.

When Scarlett stepped through the door into the VIP room to a smattering of applause, Martina enveloped her first.

Her hug was fierce. "Congratulations."

"When he played his rook to b4," Kit said, wrapping around both of them, "I knew you had it."

"I never underestimate anyone's capacity to underestimate me," Scarlett said, which was just good advice for life.

She wasn't going to be able to rely on that for the rest of Candidates, though. Everyone else was going to have her number. But for today, it had been enough.

"Listen." Martina stepped back. "I have to tell you . . . Jaime's here."

"He's *what*?" Scarlett hadn't meant to shout that, but Jaime's appearance was so stunning, so unexpected, she almost couldn't process it.

What on earth was he doing here? And why on earth was he doing it?

Yup, she had nothing. It was possible the game had burned something out in her brain.

"I know," Kit said. "He came with Nate, and he wants to apologize for—everything, I think."

Scarlett had to stop herself from launching into a host of follow-up questions: what exactly constituted *everything*? Could she get an itemized list? What was he taking responsibility for, and what was he going to do about it? Did he think saying he was sorry was enough to—

Nope, she needed to pose those to Jaime and not to Kit. At least, if Scarlett was open to hearing what Jaime wanted to say.

Which she very much was.

Suddenly, Scarlett had her second wind. The exhaustion she'd been feeling had gone on vacation, maybe for forever. She could've played the rest of her matches right now, one right after the other, if the man she loved would be waiting for her at the end of it.

Because whatever he'd done, she still loved him.

"We told him that you've had an epically long day and you might not have the emotional capacity for this," Kit said, rubbing Scarlett's shoulder.

"I'd be happy to march over there and tell him to leave." From how Martina said it, it was clear this was what she wanted to do. "And I wouldn't have agreed to even mention it to you if I didn't think he'd listen to a no. He will drop this—if you want him to."

Scarlett ought to have some self-respect. She ought to refuse to listen to him. Or she ought to make him do some first-class groveling, the kind that came with roses and champagne and Jaime crawling over hot coals or something.

But they'd ended up in this stupid situation because he hadn't been willing to forgive her. Why would she want to make the same mistake? She should wait and find a brand-new mistake to make instead. She trusted Jaime and herself where that was concerned.

"Well, get his butt over here."

"You want to sit with it for a minute?" Kit asked.

"I've had plenty of time to sit with it." Life without him sucked peach pits. Scarlett didn't want to do it any longer, not if she didn't have to.

"Okay," Kit said. "Let me find him."

"I know you think this is a blunder," Scarlett said to Martina as she watched Kit disappear into the crowd.

"Not necessarily." *Yes necessarily,* based on her tone, but Martina gave Scarlett too much credit to say that, even if she still clearly had some private doubts. "But I don't think he deserves you."

"Who could?"

They laughed and hugged again, and Scarlett felt . . . almost peaceful. She was still hungry and her shoes were starting to pinch, but the anticipation in her stomach now was hopeful, not anxious. Whatever happened with the tournament, this could be good.

A minute later, Jaime wove through the crowd, his eyes scanning for her, with Kit and Nate trailing him.

The thing about wearing goldenrod in a sea of navy and black was that you tended to stand out. And Scarlett could see the exact moment when Jaime found her. She could appreciate how his eyes closed for a second and he shook his head.

That dress is even brighter in person than on the monitor. That was what his body language was saying. And also, she hoped, *You look amazing.*

When he opened his eyes, she gave a little shrug, as if to say *Yes, of course. Yes, at last.*

Six more steps, and then he stopped in front of her. Scarlett squeezed Martina's hand, and their friends melted away, leaving Scarlett and Jaime alone. Or as alone as it was possible to be in a crowd.

Jaime was smiling down at her, and Scarlett was smiling up at him, and it was so close to being perfect.

"Hey," Scarlett finally said, because while she might be a brilliant chess player, she wasn't exactly operating at full capacity here. He was going to have to take the lead for this particular conversation.

"Hey, yourself. Congratulations on the win."

"Thank you."

"Kit and Martina tried to explain it to me, but, well—"

"You don't know crap about chess?"

"I know you won. You seemed to demolish that guy."

"He'll live." And regardless, she definitely didn't want to sit here and talk about Alik Svensson, the poor sap.

"Look, I'm sorry to show up here like this."

"I'm not sorry," Scarlett said, hoping he would know she meant it differently—so differently—than the last time she'd said that to him.

"Good. I just . . . I realized there were things I needed to say to you, and I couldn't wait to say them. But I want to be clear: I don't want to steal your thunder, and I definitely don't want to throw off your game. I know that you have to play again tomorrow. So if you want to wait and talk when you're done, I would understand."

"And if I don't want to talk at all?" Scarlett *did*, but she was curious how Jaime would answer that.

"Then I'd leave you alone. You don't owe me shit, Scarlett. I've used up more chances than you should've given me, that's for sure."

"How nice of you to see that now." But this was the problem, wasn't it? She could be snide, or she could find out what he was doing here. "But no, please, talk. My brain is shot, but I can listen."

His face went serious as he looked her dead in the eye and said, "You were right."

Mother of pearl, those were the sexiest words on earth, right there.

"About?" she prompted.

"You were right to call the cops on Dad. When you told me, it made me feel . . . like you didn't trust me. And it made me feel guilty that I hadn't seen it. I'll always wish I had, maybe because I dream that if I'd known, I could've convinced him to stop. Isn't that stupid? I'm so full of it, Scarlett. You're the real deal, and I feel like a poseur."

"You aren't a poseur." It was all Scarlett could get herself to say. The rest of what he'd said was still working its way around the circuits in her brain, and given how sluggish she felt, it was going to take a while for her to make sense of everything.

But her tear ducts were already feeling full and hot, and if he kept this up, she was going to shed tears.

Lots of stupid, happy tears.

"I think I am," Jaime said ruefully. "And I think that's fine. After Dad went to prison, I grew up real fast. I wanted to make up for what he'd done, and I had to stop myself and my family from spiraling. But I began to believe my own story."

Scarlett reached out and set a hand on Jaime's forearm. His skin was warm and his muscles firm. For the first time, he felt *certain* to her touch. Whether that radiated from him, or from her or from both of them, she couldn't say. But she was grateful for it.

"It's a good story."

"Not if it keeps me from being with you. The truth of what happened and why felt . . . threatening, I guess. And it's taken me way too long—way, way too long—to realize that you did it to protect me. You were right: if I really could've held Dad responsible, it would've messed me up, more than I got messed up. I didn't even thank you for planting that story to protect my family."

"You didn't need to."

"I do, though. You know what else is really crap? All this time, I never checked in with you. I was so focused on me, I never asked how *you* were doing and what I could do to help you heal from the immensity of what you were dealing with."

The tears were coming fast now, pouring down Scarlett's face in rivulets and gathering together on her chin. Her dress was going to get soaked if he kept this up.

Jaime gently turned them, putting his back between her and the room, to give her some privacy. He curled one of his hands around her nape. "You're everything that I want to be, Scarlett Arbuthnot. But ten times prettier."

"Only ten?" she asked, which would've been coy if her voice hadn't broken as she said it. Scarlett could fake a lot of things, but not that eruption of emotion.

This was too much. And it was exactly the right amount.

"Infinity," he said, and at that, she fell forward onto his chest.

She would make her own confession at some point, after she'd eaten, after she'd fallen asleep smooshed against Jaime's side.

And not to brag, but whatever speech she made would be amazing. He'd be dazzled.

But for now, this was enough.

"I understand why you didn't tell me. I know why you feel like you have to fight all of your battles alone. And if you keep making decisions on your own, I'd be okay with that because I trust you and your brilliant mind."

Scarlett appreciated Jaime recognizing her brilliance, but she knew that things had changed. *Everything* had changed. "Hmm. What if this feral cat kind of liked it when you domesticated her?"

Her meaning hit Jaime slowly. His eyes lit first, then his mouth curled up in a smile, and finally the lines of his body softened. He'd been trying so hard to convince her—to convince both of them—that he would've been satisfied to be with her no matter what. What he really wanted, though, was to be with her as an equal. As a unit. Luckily that was what she was offering.

"Well then," he said, sounding very, very satisfied indeed, "I'd do my best to take care of her every day from here on out."

Which was exactly what Scarlett wanted too. "I'm tired of fighting on my own, Jaime. I couldn't have prepared for this tournament without Kit and Martina, and I know now that if I stopped playing after this that they would still be my friends. Our bond is *real*, you know?"

"I do."

"And it's not only them. It's also Evelyn, and Alma, and Clara, and maybe the people in Emery's book club. And it's you. Most of all, it's you. I am not alone in some spaceship flying through the void. I want to let you *all* in more. And if you can be patient with me, I think I can learn how to do that." She'd learned much harder things, that was for sure.

Maybe there was a book of communication openings she could memorize.

"Even if you don't, being together would be enough."

"Are you sure?" Scarlett didn't mean to sound so vulnerable, but, well, she didn't want him to change his mind again.

Jaime seemed to understand. He pressed his mouth to her temple in gentle reassurance. "You know how bad it's been without you?"

That was like asking if she knew water was wet. "I have some idea, yes."

He chuckled so softly that she felt it more than she heard it. "The last few days, I started playing chess on the CheckMate.com app. It made me feel closer to you."

She laid her cheek on his shoulder so she could look him in the eye. He wasn't kidding. "You're playing chess?"

He shrugged and resettled his arms more tightly around her. "I wouldn't call what I do *playing*, but yes. I keep getting my ass kicked."

She had ten thousand questions about how he played and what openings he liked and what his rating was. But they had time for those. That was the amazing part: now that Jaime had come to his senses, they had all the time in the world.

So with the promise of that time, Scarlett was able to let him take more of her weight, to let the questions simmer, and to simply say, "It's your fault you weren't actually close to me, you dingus."

With all seriousness, Jaime replied, "I don't deserve this, Scarlett, I realize that I don't. But you were right: we love each other. I know who you are, and I adore every bit of you. I'm not going to get in a snit again because you outsmart everyone else in the room."

"What will you do the next time we have a fight?"

"Remind myself that you're always right."

"Damn straight."

Then Scarlett popped up on her toes and planted her mouth on Jaime's. This was one victory she was going to savor.

Epilogue

Two Years Later

"Test. Test, test, test, *teeeeeeeeeeest.*"

Every time Jaime set up the camera and asked Scarlett to say something while he checked the sound levels, this was what she went with. She'd switched it when he pointed out that *Testing, one, two, three, testing* was generic.

He had to hand it to her, she could hold that *eeeh* sound for an incredibly long time.

"Got it. We're good to go." Jaime looked through the camera lens. Scarlett was sitting on a rock framed by pine trees, with a stunning Appalachian vista spread out behind her.

And just like always, it was his wife's beauty that took his breath away.

It was a good thing he'd gotten his head out of his ass and she'd forgiven him, because otherwise, Jaime didn't know what he would've done with himself.

Scarlett was looking at him straight on, a slightly smug smile on her lips, as if she knew he was admiring her and thinking he was the luckiest man on earth. Which she probably did. He said it to her often enough.

"You can start now," he said after a ridiculously long pause. The kind of pause that was going to be mortifying to explain to the editor later on.

Well, you see, I was checking out Scarlett, but his editor should be used to it by now. Everyone else who interacted with them had already commented on it.

"What do you want me to talk about again?" Scarlett asked teasingly. "I clean forgot we were filming there."

"The camp's mission."

"Right." Her attention shifted from him down into the valley. There was a slight breeze that made her hair wave against her cheek. She was flushed from the walk over here and probably from what they'd been up to before they'd gone on that walk.

One thing was certainly true: life with Scarlett Arbuthnot was never boring.

After a second, she turned her attention back to the camera. "It's the camp I wish I'd had. It's free, and we provide high-level chess coaching, the kind that most kids can't get in their high schools."

They were able to make it free because Scarlett was *incredible* at raising money. CEOs were putty in her hands. Within weeks of having the idea, she'd established a foundation and filled the coffers. Jaime had been able to provide some Hollywood contacts with a major assist from Clara Hess, who was becoming an A-lister. Scarlett and she were planning a splashy fundraiser in LA next year.

When Jaime and Scarlett worked together, they made quite a team.

"What I didn't expect from that first group last year was how many of them would tell us that the benefit was *social,*" Scarlett told the camera. "So many of the players who came feel like weirdos because they don't know anyone else in person who plays as well as they do. Or they don't know anyone who plays who looks like them."

She meant the camp prioritized admitting girls, trans and nonbinary players, nonwhite kids, and low-income kids. All the folks who didn't fit the stereotype of the chess genius.

"We were able to provide support and a lot of great in-person play. But we were also able to give them a community, to help them feel less alone."

"So it's going to be bigger and better this year?"

"Well, of course it is, Jaime. I don't do small or mediocre."

No, she did not. Even when things didn't go her way, she still managed to fall short fabulously.

In the end, Scarlett hadn't made the open-division world championship game. She'd been painfully close. One more win for her or one more loss from the eventual winner at Candidates, and she would have been able to play for it.

If it had been Jaime, he would have tortured himself, scrutinized every mistake and become fixated on the past. And there had been a few weeks of game analysis, for sure. Everyone—Kit, Martina, and Nate—had come home to Virginia with Scarlett and him. Nate and Jaime had worked all day on *Queen's Kiss* in his office, while Kit, Martina, and Scarlett had taken over the den.

But one night at dinner, Scarlett had looked up from her plate and said, "Okay, it's done."

As far as Jaime could tell, that had been it for her. She'd examined all her games, whined about them, sobbed about them, and then closed the book on her second Candidates Tournament. She had the most endless capacity to look toward the future, and he was in awe of it. He was in awe of her.

Scarlett was already gearing up to make another run at it, convinced this cycle was going to be hers. But she was also beginning to think about what her life was going to look like once she was done with competitive chess.

That was part of why she'd started the foundation: her legacy could still be impressive, even if she never managed to win the open-division world championship. She was so much more than any title could be.

"What else is your foundation up to?" Jaime knew, of course, but he needed her to explain it on camera for the documentary he was making.

"We have hardship grants for individuals who can't afford to travel for tournaments, and grants that school chess teams can apply for, to support supplies, coaching, and travel. And then there's our prison chess program."

That one, she'd surprised him with.

As soon as she'd moved in with Jaime, she'd started visiting Dad with him. She was amazing at making conversation with Dad, at letting the strangeness of the setting flow over her without comment, and at treating everyone with grace and humor and kindness.

Jaime had been making that pilgrimage for eighteen years, but from the first time, Scarlett had been able to be so chill and normal about it. It made Jaime feel foolish and stuffy and unnatural.

"How many facilities are you in now?"

"Eighty-five."

Jaime had to clear his throat against the emotion rising there before going on. "And the early results?"

"Really promising. So, you know me—I see that, and I want even more. To raise more money, hire more instructors, and to get in more places. There are just so many benefits for the folks in our programs: the strategy, the concentration, the socialization—those are all transferable skills. Plus, it's fun. Who doesn't love chess?"

Who indeed?

Queen's Kiss had been a massive hit for Videon, and it had done everything for Jaime's career that he could've wanted. More awards, and more publicity, sure, but more importantly, Videon had given him a bunch of money to find up-and-coming documentary filmmakers and support their work before giving them a massive distribution platform. And he and Nate were working on the script for their first feature film, a completely fictional story about teens coming of age in 1970s Appalachia against the backdrop of a coal-workers' strike.

But all of that felt small against the things that had shifted in his personal life.

Scarlett and Mom—they got on surprisingly well, in the end. They were both strategic thinkers, and they both had carefully developed public personas. People thought they knew who the women were and judged them harshly, and from that shared experience, his wife and his mother had forged a bond.

Of course, Evelyn couldn't be more delighted to have Scarlett in the family, and it had expanded, too, to include Alma and Kit and Nate and Martina. Scarlett had joined Emery's book club, and she was the honorary coach of the Musgrove High Chess Club. At this point, even Scarlett was having trouble pretending she was all alone in the world now, when it was so clear she wasn't.

As for Jaime . . . for so long, he'd been running, pretending that if he just kept moving, he could undo what had happened. He could take care of his mom, and he could raise his sister, and he could get everything he'd wanted before his dad had been arrested. Then later he could become the critically acclaimed filmmaker, and he could build the house, and he could keep himself relatively sane through it all.

Look, Mom, no hands, or some shit.

When he'd walked into Scarlett's lobby that day to ask for the rights to her book, all that frantic need to take care of everyone had come crashing down. He'd smacked into some hard and implacable truths, but also into the limits of what he could get done on his own. And maybe the loneliness of the hamster wheel he'd built for himself.

Snagging every one of your goals could feel damn lonely if you didn't have someone by your side who made you laugh at yourself. Who would sit by you in a prison visiting room or at the Emmys. Who wanted, even more fiercely than you did, to make the world a better place.

Scarlett centered Jaime. She was his magnetic north, the location to which he would always point, no matter where else his attention might be pulled.

With her, the past didn't seem so scary, and the future was bright as the noon sun pouring down on her nose, turning her hair to flame and pinkening her cheeks.

Thank Christ she'd taken him back. Forgiveness was the most precious substance on earth, Jaime was fairly sure, and Scarlett's supply of it was endless.

She was opening up, too, bit by bit. From the start, Scarlett had shared her worries about quitting competitive chess with him.

"So what should I do?" she'd asked.

In that moment, Jaime had to admit he couldn't really help with the situation in which she found herself. As much as he wanted to, he couldn't solve this conundrum for her. But the fact that she'd talked to him about it was all he wanted. At the end of the day, he wanted nothing more than to be a valued member of her team.

"Well, hell, Jaime, why didn't you say that in the first place?" she'd retorted.

And just like that, it had become easy. His past worries seemed so silly, now that he could see how they were, and would be, together.

Here and now, Scarlett repeated her question into the camera. "Who doesn't love chess?"

"No one," he answered. "But that's because you're an incredible teacher." Jaime was only half teasing. Scarlett had raised the popularity of the sport and made it sexy and glamorous in ways PAWN still couldn't seem to adjust to.

And she'd basically done it all in her spare time.

She was a wonder.

Scarlett's eyes caught the light and flashed at him. "I'm incredible at *lots* of things."

Jaime would never forget it again.

Acknowledgments

The idea for *Bold Moves* arrived while I was watching my kid compete at a local chess tournament. I didn't know how to play—a detail!—but much like a mystery and Benoit Blanc, chess compelled me.

In short order and with the enthusiastic assistance of my child, I learned the basics and started downing biographies of grand masters and live streaming the Candidates Tournament. (Seriously, it's pure human drama. You *must* watch the next one.) I'm grateful for folks who've written about the game in an accessible way, including Yasser Seirawan, Michael Weintraub, Bruce Pandolfini, Frank Brady, and David Bronstein. I'm particularly indebted to interviews with and books and essays by female players such as Jennifer Shahade, Irina Krush, and, of course, Judit Polgár. Scarlett is entirely a fictional creation, as is PAWN, but I wanted to fit them inside the contours of real international chess.

In terms of researching how opioids affected Appalachia, Beth Macy's *Dopesick*, Barry Meier's *Pain Killer*, Eve Marson's *Dr. Feelgood*, and Elaine McMillion-Sheldon's *Heroin(e)* were invaluable to me.

And Ashley C. Ford's *Somebody's Daughter* is a brilliant memoir about understanding your identity when you have an incarcerated parent.

As I penned my exceedingly long, exceedingly angsty second-chance romance, a dream team supported me every step of the way: Genevieve Turner read approximately a zillion drafts of this book, cracked several plot and character nuts, and never once stopped returning my emails; Olivia Dade met me on FaceTime almost daily for months to write and gave me detailed feedback that improved every dimension of this book; and Jan W. read all the chess scenes and helped me avoid several major mistakes. I adore you all.

My agent, Sarah Elizabeth Younger, much like Scarlett's agent, is faster on email than anyone else on earth and is always kind, hilarious, and insightful. I would not still be trying to become a real author without her. My editor Lauren Plude's peerless belief in me and my stories means everything. Who else would cheer when I declared that my next project would be *sexy chess*, and who else would go to bat for me as completely as she does?

Kristi Yanta didn't flinch when I dumped this project into her lap. You cannot imagine how hard we worked to edit this book and how much stronger it is because of Kristi's brilliant notes. She is never satisfied with *good enough*, and I am so thankful for it. And the production team at Montlake, notably Nicole, Jenna, Angela, and Katherine, is quite simply the best. From the masterful (and kind) copyediting to the beautiful covers you've put on my books and to your smart and enthusiastic marketing, it is a gift to make books with you.

Finally, my family helped massively with this one. My husband and kid played many games of chess with me and only teased me some of the time—and always with good humor—as I struggled to wrap my head around castling and en passant captures. You are the best, and I love you very much.

About the Author

Emma Barry is a novelist, college lecturer, and former political staffer. She lives with her high school sweetheart and a menagerie of pets and children in Virginia, where she occasionally finds time to read and write. You can visit Barry on her website at www.authoremmabarry.com.